TEMPEST
TOSSED

TEMPEST TOSSED

a novel by
JOSI S. KILPACK

BONNEVILLE BOOKS ™

Springville, Utah

ISBN: 1-55517-751-4
e.1

Published by Bonneville Books
Imprint of Cedar Fort Inc.
www.cedarfort.com

Distributed by:

Cover design by Nicole Cunningham
Cover design © 2003 by Lyle Mortimer

Printed in the United States of America
10 9 8 7 6 5 4 3 2 1

Printed on acid-free paper

Library of Congress Cataloging-in-Publication Data

Kilpack, Josi S.
  Tempest Tossed / by Josi S. Kilpack.
      p. cm.
  ISBN 1-55517-751-4 (pbk. : acid-free paper)
  1. Medication abuse--Fiction. 2. Women--Fiction. I. Title.
PS3561.I412T46 2004
813'.6--dc22
                                    2003027058

To Mike

July 9, 1980
March 3, 1995

"Not everyone gets a second chance . . . at least in this life.
You are missed."

ACKNOWLEDGMENTS

Once again I could never have done this without loads and loads of help. My husband Lee is the backbone of all I do and I wish to tell him again how much I appreciate all he does for me. I couldn't be the person, mother or writer I've become without your loving support and friendship. You have always brought out the best in me. Hugs and kisses to my kids for their ongoing enthusiasm and patience with me. Seeing the light in their eyes when I tell them of my latest success renews my marvel that I am here at all.

Next, I would like to thank the talented staff at Cedar Fort Inc. for their continued faith in me and all the time and effort they put into all they do. I appreciate their commitment to provide books that appeal to all readers and their courage to address things many LDS publishers resist.

Thanks to my readers of the initial manuscript, Tristi Pinkston (author of *Nothing To Regret*, Granite 2002) and Mickel Woodland—this was not an easy book for me to write and your enthusiasm and support kept me going when the revisions never seemed to end. Thank you to all the members of LDStorywriters for your continued support and education in all my writing endeavors—I marvel at all I've learned through your endless advice and talents.

To Lloyd Call and Nida Lloyd, words are not enough. Thank you for sharing your stories with me and so many others through the pages of this book—your details made all the difference and your strength is empowering to all of us.

Thank you to my family and friends who cheer me on and to the readers that make the words worth writing.

Last but not least, thanks to my Father in Heaven for all of the above and so much more.

PROLOGUE

February 3, 5:42 p.m.

Janet wrapped her arms around her knees, pulled them to her chest and dropped her forehead, wishing she had the strength to cry. She wanted to somehow release all of this; but she'd been empty for too long, and the tears, what few there were, had all been spent. She turned her head and looked out the window. There was still patchy gray snow on the ground, but it hadn't snowed in weeks. The sun was just beginning to set in the clear winter sky, silhouetting the barren trees against the horizon and illuminating the dark room with an orange glow. At another time she would have found some beauty in the scene, but tonight it only seemed to reflect the dead coldness of winter, a very real representation of what she'd created in her own life—what she'd allowed her life to become. Across the room the glass on Josh's portrait reflected the evening light, but she refused to look at the smiling face of her son, a picture taken during happier times. It hurt too much to be reminded of what once was, and what could still be if she hadn't ruined everything.

The truth she'd come to accept over the last several hours was that after doing everything she could to leave her past behind her, to become more than she was raised to be, she had turned out just like her mother; a bitter, mean drug addict. The escape the drugs brought her had been apparent throughout her life, only in different forms. Depending on the phase of life, she had lost herself in school, marriage and work until that just hadn't been enough. Then she had turned to Xanax, Oxycontin and any other tablet form of oblivion or motivation she could find. The need to hide from emotion, from pain and loss had made all these obsessions necessary. In hindsight, it seemed silly that she actually believed she could run forever. Of course the day would come when the deep recesses of her soul would be unable to hold anything more. But she'd never dwelled on that, or what it would be like when she was finally forced to feel. How or what she felt had always been in her control, but it wasn't anymore. All her work, all her perfect plans had been destroyed.

She looked at the kitchen table on the other side of the room, at the multicolored pills perfectly arranged in six straight lines and wondered why she didn't feel any hesitation—she dared herself to raise some kind of protest. There was a time when a voice within her would tell her that she had a reason for living, that things would get better; but even it had given up on her. It had been months since she'd felt the Spirit, and several weeks since she'd felt any evidence it had ever been a part of her life. She reviewed the events of the last several months and wondered again how it had happened. It was as if she had become a different person, but she knew she alone had made the decisions that had brought her to this point. She'd driven the Spirit from her life, then her husband and child followed. And there was nothing she could do to make things right.

Slowly, she straightened her legs and stood up, ignoring the moving boxes scattered around the house as she walked to the table. After Tally had taken Josh last week, she'd thrown herself into the task of packing, hoping that by showing Tally the changes she was willing to make he would give her another chance to be the wife he had thought her to be in the beginning. But wanting Tally and Josh hadn't been enough to override her need for oblivion. She'd realized that she couldn't survive without the pills, but she couldn't survive without Tally either, and all the feelings she'd been hiding began to rise up. Tally and Josh were the best things she'd ever had in her life, and they were gone. She couldn't live without them but she was unable to make the changes necessary to have them back.

She filled a glass with water before pulling out a kitchen chair and sitting down at the table. Her eyes were drawn to the row of envelopes lined up on the opposite side of the table and she could only stare, seeking again some kind of restraint within herself. Silence. Inside each envelope was a letter she had written, her own impotent attempt at explanation. Josh's letter was the longest, almost three pages full of good memories and encouragement of what he should and shouldn't do with his own life. She hoped someday, when he was old enough to understand, he'd read it and know that she loved him very much. The letter she'd written to Tally was much shorter. She'd thought of a hundred things to say, but finally, in a few short sentences she told him to go on with his life. They had only been married for six months; he had his whole life ahead of him. He wasn't Josh's natural father, but Tally had been more of a parent to her son in six months than she had ever been. After their last few encounters Janet had little doubt that Tally would feel great relief at not having to fight with her anymore. Included with his letter was the official paperwork making him Josh's legal parent—it was likely the best thing she'd ever done for either one of them.

Next to Tally's Letter was left a brief note for Kim and Allen, thanking them for their support and friendship. She knew they would be shocked and disappointed, but then they'd put her name in the temple, pray for her son and go on with their lives, secretly relieved that Allen's ex-wife was no longer an issue between them. She was glad they were happy together, glad that after her marriage to Allen he could find someone who filled his life as well as Kim did; Janet certainly hadn't. It was now abundantly clear that she had used Allen just as she later used Craig, Josh's father, and then Tally. She didn't know how to be married; she didn't know how to be much of anything to anyone. And she was tired of being the stumbling block, the hard thing people had to deal with. She just wanted peace for everyone—including herself.

She picked up the first pill and with a practiced motion placed the pill in her mouth, took a sip of water and swallowed. *It will all be over soon*, she told herself as she picked up the second tablet. In her mind she was simply cleaning up the mess she'd made. Now that she couldn't control her feelings, she could no longer stand to disappoint the people she loved. Watching them hurt, understanding what she'd done, and knowing she was the cause of that pain was more than she could take.

CHAPTER ONE

June 19—Eight Months Earlier

Janet's alarm went off at 5:30 a.m. filling the room with an overly cheerful advertisement enticing listeners to book their next vacation online. Her big blue eyes fluttered open and she took a deep breath as she stared at the ceiling that was just beginning to reflect the light of early dawn. Every cell in her body screamed at her to stay in bed. However, she couldn't afford the luxury and turned off the alarm as she sat up and took a deep breath. During the night she'd been overcome with the anxiety and fear that was becoming increasingly familiar. The panic had caused her to search out her pills to ward off the attack. The medication left her groggy, but she knew from experience that the best way to recover was to act as if it hadn't happened at all. So instead of giving in to the inviting lethargy, she attacked her morning regime with fervor she didn't feel.

When the panic had finally claimed her in the early hours of morning her chest was tight and she could hardly draw a breath. She'd dumped the bottle of pills on the empty side of the bed in her haste, and it took nearly a minute to collect them now. However, she made sure to find all of them; they were like diamonds to her. Based on how many she was taking lately, it was time to get a refill; in fact, before she went out of town today if possible. The thought of having an attack without the meds to stop it was petrifying.

After her half hour 'Tae Bo' exercise video she took her daily vitamins: two No-Doz tablets, a multi-vitamin and an extra Vitamin C. Some days she added a Percocet or a Loritab, but she didn't have any aches or pains today so she skipped it—she didn't need the extra mental muddle they would create. Then she undressed and stepped into the shower.

By the time she turned off the water she finally felt awake enough to face the day. She brushed out her long dark hair and pinned it into a perfect French twist. As she applied the most basic of cosmetics to her sculpted features she ran through her day's schedule in her mind. Daycare, pharmacy, the office, and then the airport to catch a plane to Chicago. Then she would go to the hotel, change her clothes and go to a dinner meeting with the sales agent of a new clothing line Dillard's might be interested in trying out. If she liked the new designs and approved of the wholesale price, they would sign contracts until late that night. It was a full day, a long day, but that's how she liked it.

After she laid a black pantsuit and a white silk shirt across the bed, she placed the matching shoes on the floor and added jewelry; diamond studs and a matching diamond pendant hung on an almost invisible silver chain. She wouldn't get dressed until just before she left for the office. She knew from experience that her two-year-old son could make short work of her office attire, therefore getting dressed was the last part of her morning routine. Moving to the open suitcase on the dresser top, she inventoried the articles again, smiling when she was sure she'd remembered everything. She zipped it closed and tightened the belt of her red satin robe around her slim waist as she smoothed the fabric over her hips.

Breast implants a few years back had given her a figure that turned men's heads, although that hadn't been her motivation—at least not her main one anyway. At the time she was married to a man who encouraged a bigger bustline, and still believing she was in love with him, she conceded. It was a rather silly thing to do, but she sensed he was unhappy in the marriage and if a D-cup would help their relationship she was willing to do it. It didn't work quite as she'd hoped however, and he'd left only six months later. Giving birth to her son not long after that had given shape to her hips and the result was almost too perfect. She'd always gotten a lot of attention from the opposite sex, and the added curves only increased it. However, these days she was a career woman first, and a mother last; there was no room for anything more and she'd become very good at ignoring the looks she seemed to draw wherever she went. Whenever a man showed too much interest, she was quick to douse it one way or another. Yet, when she dared be truly honest with herself she admitted that she liked the power her face and figure gave her. In this business, looks were a definite bonus.

Josh was already awake. She could hear him talking to himself in garbled toddler talk when she reached his door. He'd started sleeping in a 'big boy bed,' complete with side rails of course, just a few weeks ago when he turned two, but he hadn't yet realized he could get out of it by himself. He would talk and play as if he were still confined to his crib until Janet came in and got him. As soon as she began opening the door he went quiet and pulled the blanket over his head. She cleared her throat in preparation for their game.

"Where's Josh?" she asked in feigned surprise. He giggled beneath his blankets and pulled them up higher, although still not high enough to hide his dark curls completely.

"Jo-osh," she called as she kicked a toy truck and opened a drawer of his dresser, making as much noise as possible in order to increase his excitement level—he loved this. His entire body wiggled under the blankets and she had to pinch her lips together in order to keep from laughing. "Are you in here?" she called as she opened another drawer. "Hmm, not there either." She sat on the edge of the bed, her knees propped up and hanging over the side rail so that her feet couldn't touch the floor. He wriggled away from her until he was penned in by the wall. "I swear I put him to bed last night," she continued, glancing toward the top of the blanket to see if he was peeking yet; he wasn't. "Maybe I left him in the car."

He giggled some more.

"Well," she said in surrender. "I guess I'll just lay down and wait for him." She laid back and, as expected, encountered something solid. "Wait a minute . . . Josh, is that you?"

He began to laugh and she pulled the blankets off. "You were hiding from me!" she announced, as if they hadn't done this every morning since he'd gotten his new bed. "Now you're in big trouble," she said and immediately began to tickle him. He squirmed and wiggled delightfully until she stopped after several seconds. She waited for him to stop moving before tapping his nose, signaling play time was over. "How about Cheerios for breakfast?"

"Ee-o's," Josh announced, reaching his arms toward her. She lifted him quickly and as soon as his feet hit the floor he bolted from the room, his blue pajamas a blur of color. She followed him out after making his bed, straightening the room and grabbing his clothes from the dresser where she'd set them out the night before. Her mind had already moved beyond the silliness of the game and began tightening up her day's schedule. There was never much time for her to be playful or lighthearted, and that wasn't where she felt most comfortable anyway.

She decided to stop at the pharmacy after dropping Josh off at daycare in order to get a refill for the prescription. She'd been taking Xanax, an anti-anxiety drug, since shortly after Josh's birth when the stress of being a mother and an executive had become too much. The panic attacks were just that; a state of absolute fear and terror, so much so that she could hardly breathe. When they hit it was as if every stressor in her life took on physical properties and they all conspired together to make her completely powerless against them. It had been frightening, overwhelming and more than once she felt sure she would die. But after a trip to the ER one night when the panic had completely overpowered her, she'd learned that there were medications to help ease the symptoms.

She'd met with her doctor the next day and they decided that the attacks were likely attributed to the incredible changes Josh had brought into her life. Between the stress of a new baby, the hormones following his birth and a job that was more demanding than ever, it seemed perfectly understandable that she would need a little intervention. In time, as she grew accustomed to raising a child on her own, the panic attacks would probably go away on their own. However, rather than going away, the frequency of the attacks had steadily increased over the last two years. Since her mother's death just four months ago they had been worse than ever and her current doctor had recommended she see a psychiatrist, after explaining that often, the key to stopping the attacks was psychological, not pharmaceutical. Deep down she believed him; she'd felt inundated with all the sad memories of her childhood since her mother's unexpected death, and it had caused her to reflect not only on her past but also on her future. She hated thinking about either, but couldn't seem to escape it any longer.

Her mother had been alone when she died, leaving behind fractured relationships with two daughters who didn't even speak to each other. There had been no need to have a funeral—no one would be coming. It had forced Janet to examine her own life, her own legacy. She hated being alone, and although she'd convinced herself that Josh was enough, she wasn't sure she believed it anymore. The introspection was unwanted and she had no desire to discuss those things with a stranger; therefore she decided against seeing a therapist. She told herself over and over again that the memories were best forgotten and the worries of her future would likely fade as well. Xanax was her way of avoiding all of it. The pills made it possible for her to keep up with her life and she felt sure that in time her need for them would go away. All that really mattered was that she accomplish all she needed to get done; who cared if she took a few pills now and then?

Her current doctor was the fifth one she'd seen about the problem. She didn't like that she'd had to move on so many times, but inevitably each doctor would want to 'discuss' her need of the medication in more detail. Once or twice she'd tried to talk to her doctor about it, but it was almost physically impossible for her to do. The words wouldn't come, and each attempt had brought on such severe anxiety that she'd had to stop trying all together. Losing control was the most humiliating thing she'd ever experienced, and although she knew there were reasons why she was having these problems, she knew she wasn't ready to face them. It was easier to find a new doctor than to convince the old one that the pills weren't as big a deal as they seemed to think they were. After changing doctors so many times she knew just what to say, and how to say it; what to include and what to leave out in order to make it a very simple visit that resulted in a new prescription. This new doctor had been more understanding than the others. The first four began to question her need of the medicines after just a few months but Dr. Lennon was older than the others, semi-retired and much more accommodating. Unlike the young doctors that received arduous prescription training in medical school and had licensing reviews to worry about, Dr. Lennon had practiced medicine for forty years and such things didn't concern him much so long as his patients were happy.

Even after her mother's death, when he encouraged her to see a psychiatrist, he hadn't brought it up again. She'd been getting a new bottle of pills every few weeks for eight months and he even gave her automatic refills on all her prescriptions so that she rarely had to make an office visit to get the prescription renewed. Thank goodness he was so easy to deal with; she really didn't have time to play the games the other doctors had started.

"Good morning," she said as she approached the pharmacist's counter. Josh had been safely dropped at daycare and she had exactly 15 minutes before she was due at the office. Perfect. She pulled the orange plastic bottle from her purse and put it on the counter. "I need to get my prescription refilled, please."

"It'll just take a moment," the pharmacist said with as smile as she stepped toward the computer while reading the information on the label.

Janet was just turning away, making a mental list of other items she could shop for while she waited, when the pharmacist called her name. She turned to look at the other woman expectantly.

"I'm sorry," the pharmacist said with a sincere smile as she placed the pill bottle back on the countertop and pushed it toward Janet. "There are no refills on this."

"Oh, I should have told you," Janet said as she stepped back to the counter with a smile. "I'll be paying 100 percent, you don't need to bother with the insurance." Her insurance only paid for refills when 80 percent of the previous prescription had been used and since it was prescribed for 'occasional use' the computer would automatically deny the prescription based on how soon she'd come back for a refill. She'd lost track of when she could use her insurance a long time ago and never bothered anymore. It was easier, and faster, to just pay for all of them herself.

"It's not the insurance," the pharmacist replied. "It says 'no refills' on the bottle."

The pharmacist pointed to the label. At the bottom it clearly read 'No Refills'.

Janet read it three times, then she looked up. "He's always given me refills in the past," she explained. She'd run out of refills on her last prescription just a couple weeks ago, and when she'd gone in for an appointment he'd given her this new one. She had assumed this new prescription would be like the others, but she realized now that she hadn't bothered to check the label.

The pharmacist was silent, as if wanting to respond but unsure what to say. Finally she just apologized again. "I'm sorry, it says no refills. You'll have to go to your doctor, then come back and I'll be happy to fill your new prescription."

Janet grabbed the bottle and spun away, angrier than she should have been and not bothering to be polite any longer. As she walked out of the store she called the doctor's office on her cell phone, nodding her thanks to the man who held the door open for her and ignoring his lingering stare as she walked swiftly to her car. After pushing several buttons on her phone to navigate the different menus on the automated answering service, she ended up with the doctor's voice mail. She left a brief message and hung up. *Don't people have any idea how busy I am?* she thought to herself as she threw the phone onto the passenger seat and started the car.

By the time she got to work, she had succeeded in pushing the morning's aggravation from her mind. As soon as she entered her office building she went downstairs to the break area and bought herself two Diet Cokes—one for breakfast and one for lunch. She went upstairs and poured the canned caffeine into her personal insulated mug that her secretary washed for her at the end of every work day. She absolutely despised it when her drinks got warm. Then she began sifting through the pile of phone messages on her desk. Yesterday had been her salon day, and so she'd left at three to have her hair, nails and feet done, but the phone apparently hadn't taken much of a break. It would take her a couple hours to catch up, but she was perfectly centered now, ready to focus on the day.

After several minutes there was a knock at the door. Janet recognized the soft, almost hesitant knock as the one her secretary, Cathy, always used. Cathy had been hired several months ago, and when Janet first met her she'd been convinced Cathy wouldn't last the week. Cathy was a petite, yet stocky, brunette with a head of tight curls and big brown eyes that reminded Janet of a baby bird. She was soft-spoken and . . . mousy, for lack of a better word. At first glance Janet had been sure that this job would send Cathy over the edge; she just didn't seem to have it in her to meet the demands. But Janet had soon been pleasantly surprised. Although seemingly overwhelmed much of the time, Cathy managed to stay on top of everything. She was dependable and hard working. Long hours now and then didn't upset her and she kept her personal life to herself. Cathy's most attractive quality, however, was the awe in which she seemed to regard Janet. All of those details made Cathy the best secretary Janet had ever had.

When Cathy entered the room, Janet looked up expectantly and smiled politely.

"Is there anything else I need to do before you leave?"

Janet shook her head. "Did the nanny ad get placed?" She'd asked Cathy to research and choose an agency through which to hire a nanny. The online ad was supposed to start running today.

Cathy nodded. "I checked it this morning; it looked great."

"Good," Janet said as she continued to go through the piles of paper on her desk. Now and then a page or two would be tossed into the garbage, but too many of them simply got moved to a new stack. "If you get any responses that sound interesting, schedule phone interviews for Saturday—I plan to spend the day here."

Cathy nodded. "Anything else?"

"If Dr. Lennon's office calls, forward the call to me immediately."

Cathy nodded and shut the door behind her as she stepped back out. Three hours later Janet placed all the papers and itineraries she would need for the trip into her large black day planner, or her "brain" as she called it to herself, and zipped it up. She slid her cell phone in the side pocket of the planner and turned off her computer. As she scanned the desk one last time, her phone rang. Cathy announced over the speaker that it was Dr. Lennon's nurse. Janet picked it up immediately, glad they had called before she left.

Less than a minute later she hung up, feeling an odd mixture of relief and discomfort. Although the nurse wasn't happy about it, she eventually agreed to call in a refill of just ten pills. Janet knew how to make people see things her way, but she sensed she had gone too far on this one. The nurse had valid concerns, and yet Janet had rationalized every one of them. *But I have to have those pills*, she argued with herself. With the increased frequency and intensity of the panic attacks she didn't dare leave town without an adequate supply. Just imagining the possibility of running out of pills caused her heart to race and she took a deep breath. The prescription was waiting for her. She didn't need to get upset about it now. She'd won. She would go in to see the doctor as soon as she got back. With that decided, she pushed the guilt away and signed a few papers on her desk. She could pick up the prescription on her way to the airport but it meant she had to move even faster.

As Janet hurried to her car in the parking garage she mentally reviewed all the information associated with this trip. She would be gone two nights and three days. The first night would be in Chicago and the second would be in Boston. She had checked her packing twice and was certain she'd forgotten nothing. Kim would pick up Josh from daycare this afternoon and keep him until Janet picked him up Friday night. Thank goodness for Kim and Allen, she thought to herself as she used the keyless entry on her key chain to automatically unlock the door to her silver Mercedes AMG.

The first time she asked for Kim and Allen's help with Josh for an overnight trip it had been awkward—Allen was her first ex-husband and *not* Josh's father. Kim, his new wife, surely didn't like having her husband's ex-wife around. But Allen had been helping Janet here and there since Josh's birth, and luckily Kim supported his assistance. Each time she'd asked them to watch Josh since then had been a little more comfortable, and they seemed sincere when they offered their continued help. Josh had changed her whole life and without Kim and Allen she knew she'd have lost her mind a long time ago. Still, she was looking forward to the prospect of getting a nanny; it would make life so much easier to have the same caregiver all the time, especially for Josh. She hated that he was constantly shifted. Finding some security for him would be a gratifying investment.

Tally Blaire parked his dark green King-cab pickup truck in long-term parking, removed his single carry-on bag and slung it over his shoulder. He was a few steps away from the truck when he remembered that he'd forgotten his planner. He'd only had it for a couple of weeks and still hadn't gotten into the habit of keeping it with him. For a moment he considered leaving it behind, but it had all the proofs he wanted to check for his last photo shoot. He hadn't had many opportunities to use his hobby for anyone outside his immediate family until now and was excited to go over the proof sheet and see how the pictures had turned out. Then he could decide which shots to get printed. The planner also had his meds, and he would need them after the flight.

He unlocked the passenger door and removed the black leather planner, making sure to zip it up so that none of the loose papers he continually stuffed inside would fall out. He'd already determined he'd be better off getting a purse, since that was basically what he used his planner for anyway, but of course, his manhood wouldn't allow such a feminine display and so he held the planner by the convenient handle and began making his way to the nearest shuttle pick-up point.

Once he caught the shuttle, he pulled his paper tickets out of his back pocket and reviewed the information again, just to be sure he remembered everything. United flight 1298 was scheduled to leave at 1:33; he glanced at his watch to confirm he was at least two hours early. The flight had a layover in Atlanta before continuing on to Baltimore. He'd then take a cab to the hotel where he'd meet up with Jason, his cousin and business partner, who was flying in from Oklahoma. In the morning, they'd head to the factory where they'd spend the next three long days repairing machinery, stopping only to sleep so that they could get the job done by Friday night. His return flight would leave Baltimore at 8:20 a.m. Saturday and he'd be home by 2 p.m., in time to prepare his lesson for Elder's Quorum and get a good night's sleep.

His doctor didn't like these trips, and Tally knew he'd spend the next week nursing his sore knee to pay for it, but what else was he supposed to do? At least this way he only had to work in spurts since they only scheduled a few jobs a month. Besides, his body seemed to be adjusting to his exertions better than ever and since buying a portion of Jason's business he felt a renewed commitment to his own future. Knowing that he wasn't going to live the rest of his life on disability was a very liberating thing. He'd already accepted that the aches and pains would be a part of his life forever and he hardly noticed them anymore. He intended to make the best of what life he had left and this job was a big part of that—even if he wasn't quite sure how to move on with the rest yet.

Janet stepped off the Park n' Jet shuttle as soon as it came to a stop at the curb. While she was gone her car would be cleaned and have the oil changed—she loved efficiency. Handing the driver a ten dollar tip, she descended the steps. She'd kept her carry-on and her planner on her lap, so she had nothing to pick up from the racks against the side of the shuttle. Because of her Sky miles membership through Delta airlines, she could upgrade to first class for fifty dollars; she didn't even hesitate and immediately moved to the front of the line. At the ticket counter, she handed over her electronic ticket confirmation, the credit card she'd used to purchase the ticket over the Internet and her picture ID before glancing at her watch again. The flight would start boarding in fifteen minutes. She berated herself for being so late. With the heightened airport security the days of showing up an hour early were all in the past, but she still managed to push the limits nearly every time. In her pocket, however, was a tiny orange bottle with ten pills— having them was worth being a few minutes late.

The agent handed her the ticket and Janet took it quickly, smiled and hurried toward the metal detectors. There was a line and the blue-clad security guards seemed to be moving in slow motion. She clenched her teeth and suppressed an audible groan as she took her place at the end of the shortest line. She did not have time for this!

Tally had waited in line for twenty minutes, but he smiled politely as he took his ticket from the United ticket agent and headed toward the security screening just as his cell phone rang. He fished it out of his pocket and read the caller ID before pushing the 'talk' button.

"Are you there already?" he asked.

Jason went on to confirm that he had just arrived. He was planning to check in at the factory and do the initial inspection of the machinery before going to the hotel. The tools Tally had shipped by ground carrier a few days earlier hadn't arrived yet. "I'm sure they'll be here this afternoon, and since I'll be at the factory anyway it's no big deal that they're a little late."

"They assured me they would be there this morning at the latest," Tally said, more concerned about the delay than Jason was. "If they mess it up again we're going to have to find another option." Because of the inevitable rough handling at the airports, they packed and shipped their tools separately. It was usually a better option in every way, but now and then the arrival got delayed, leaving them stuck at a job site without the precision tools they needed to do the job. Tally sincerely hoped that wouldn't be the case this time. Tally's Uncle Tom, Jason's father, had been instrumental in the design of a specific type of punch press used to cut sheet metal. When the machine he'd helped design became popular with metal fabrication companies, Tom began his own business of contract repair. Thirty years later the presses were employed by factories all over the world to cut specific patterns for numerous commodities such as appliances, fixtures, cars—anything that used sheet metal. Five years ago, Tom retired and Jason, who had worked for his father for nearly a decade, had taken over. Because of the precision required in making the repairs there was almost no competition and the profit margin was generous. However, the tools couldn't be replaced easily and getting them to and from job sites was a source of continual annoyance.

"For now there's nothing more we can do, I'm sure the tools will get here before you do," Jason said with his usual optimism. "Everything else okay on your end?"

"Just peachy," Tally said sarcastically as he took his place in the back of the line at security. He was glad Jason wasn't too concerned. "I'm about to go through security though, so I better go."

"Okay," Jason said. "I'll see you tonight."

"Okay, bye."

Janet listened distractedly to the phone call going on somewhere behind her. *Just peachy*, she repeated to herself. How long had it been since she'd heard that expression?

As she approached the big metal doorway, the plump security guard instructed her to empty her pockets and place all articles on the conveyor belt. She placed all the loose articles in a small plastic tub before placing her carry-on and planner on the conveyor belt. She hurried through the metal detector, anxious to get to her gate, when the alarm sounded. She let out a frustrated breath as all her hurrying came to an abrupt halt.

"Please move over to the row of chairs and remove your shoes," another security guard instructed in a lazy tone.

Janet knew that arguing would do no good, but she looked toward the conveyer; her things were just coming through but she knew they wouldn't allow her to touch them until she'd gone through the extra security. "Can you put my bag and planner to the side?" she asked another guard, an older gentleman who smiled and nodded as he headed toward her things.

The security guard placed the items on a small countertop next to another row of chairs. Janet smiled her thanks, sat down and pulled up her pant leg in order to unzip her knee-high, black leather boot.

Tally was placing his loose articles in the box when he happened to look up and catch a glimpse of the dark haired beauty removing her boot. It was a simple thing, and there were several other people removing their shoes, but the way she moved caught his attention and he couldn't look away. She had long slim fingers and, as she removed her boot, she revealed a shapely calf and narrow foot covered with a black stocking. Beyond those things that caught his attention, by leaning over as she was, the neck of her blouse had fallen open, showing more than she likely meant to. He wasn't the only one watching her, he quickly noticed, as he looked around and saw several other sets of male eyes as intently focused as his own had been. *Men are such pigs*, he said to himself as he forced himself not to watch the woman any longer. She's just taking off her shoes, for Heaven's sake, and he felt guilty for looking as long as he already had. He knew better than that.

When it was his turn he placed his bags, planner and shoes on the conveyor belt. He knew the alarm would sound when he walked through and already having his shoes off would make the extra security go a little quicker. He was a pro at the extra security.

He walked through the metal detector, noted the alarm, and continued on to the row of chairs without hesitating, nodding his understanding to the guard instructing him to take a seat. He sat a few chairs away from the dark haired woman, but she didn't make eye contact and he didn't try to get her attention. Instead, he took in her appearance with short, unobtrusive glances. She was tall and slender, but with all the right curves in all the right places. Her black hair was pulled up into some kind of uppity do that women seemed to create by pure magic. She had no bangs to frame her heart shaped face, but her sculpted cheekbones and refined features needed no fanfare. She looked a little like Demi Moore, except that her complexion was fair and her eyes were blue, framed with thick dark lashes. He felt his mouth go dry just looking at her and forced himself to look away again. She was likely the most beautiful woman he'd ever seen up close and he shook his head. Women like her just made things harder for men like him since they spurred impossible expectations. She should stay on the magazine covers where she belonged!

They were both told to stand at the same time and Tally didn't look at her again as he stood in his appointed area and spread his arms and legs wide. "It's some pins in my leg," he said as soon as the guard began waving the detection wand around his body.

The guard nodded and continued the screening as if he didn't care what it was, he just wanted to get this over with. "Would you lift your pant leg?" he asked when the wand squealed near Tally's knee.

Tally complied and lifted his pant leg far enough to expose the jagged twisted scars that covered most of his lower leg and knee. Where there was once a kneecap, the area was now nearly flat, criss-crossed with pink scars and staple marks that would make any horror movie make-up artist proud, although this wasn't latex. The guard flinched and couldn't help but stare for a few seconds longer than he should. "You should see the other guy," Tally said with dry humor.

The guard smiled uncomfortably and indicated that Tally could lower his pant leg, which Tally did quickly. He'd come to terms with the changes in his body, but he wondered if he would ever get used to the look on other peoples' faces.

"You're free to go," the guard informed him, seemingly embarrassed and unwilling to meet Tally's eye again. "I believe your things are over there." Tally walked to the counter the man had indicated and removed his shoes from the pile, leaving his other things with the other peoples' belongings that were mingled among his own. Then he sat down and put his shoes back on. The black haired woman walked past him, her boots already on. She gathered her things and hurried toward the escalator. For just an instant he was disappointed that he wouldn't have a chance to speak to her, but then he shook his head. He wasn't the kind of guy that introduced himself to strange women, especially not strange women as beautiful as she was.

Once his shoes were on, he picked up his planner and carry-on and headed for the escalators. When he reached the top, he looked around one last time but she'd already disappeared. *Just as well*, he said to himself as he headed for the nearest gift shop and pulled his wallet out of his back pocket. He'd buy a book and get comfortable, since he was plenty early for his flight. With any luck he'd finish the book about the same time he landed in Baltimore tonight.

Janet's hurrying paid off after all and she was able to take her seat before the coach passengers boarded. She sat down with a grateful sigh and immediately opened her complimentary bottled water. Then she took the bottle of pills out of her pocket, removed one, and swallowed it in order to insure she would be able to relax. Just knowing that the familiar calming sensation was soon on its way relaxed her and she let out a long deep breath she felt she'd been holding for hours. She considered opening her planner and reviewing her schedule, but decided against it. Right now she just wanted to unwind; the calm before the storm. By eight o'clock tomorrow morning she'd be running like a chicken with its head cut off, meeting with designers and line representatives. She loved the frenzy of it, the high energy, but right now she was still jittery from the fear of missing this flight and so she determined to leave the work for later. She'd have plenty of time to review the information when she arrived at the hotel.

When traveling, Janet always kept a roll of ten dollar bills in her pocket. They served to pay cabdrivers and tip valets without having to hunt. The cab dropped her off at the hotel around eight o'clock, Chicago time, and she handed him several tens to pay the fare. She was staying at the Drake Hotel, and admired the foyer as she made her way to the front desk. Janet was a woman who appreciated the best of everything—and the Drake was definitely one of the best.

"Janet Stewart," she announced to the front desk clerk. The middle-aged blonde smiled and tapped away at the keyboard.

"Everything is in order," the clerk said. "We'll need a credit card number so that we can charge services directly to the room."

Janet nodded and began unzipping her planner in order to retrieve the company credit card that would cover her expenses. No sooner had she finished the zipper than numerous papers seemingly burst out of the binder, falling all over the floor and countertop. "Oh my . . . ," Janet gasped, wondering how it was that a simple plane ride and cab drive would unsettle her planner so much.

She quickly bent down and began retrieving the papers, embarrassed at such a public display of her apparent disorganization. As she gathered the papers, however, her hands slowed and then her mouth opened. "These aren't my things," she whispered as she stood and opened the planner fully. The desk clerk watched as Janet began flipping pages back and forth, finally stopping on the identification page on the front. "Talmage Blaire," she read out loud.

"Excuse me?" the desk clerk asked, seemingly confused at what was happening.

Janet looked up at her and wondered what to say, her mind was running a mile a minute although she worried that the additional pill she'd taken just before landing was slowing her thoughts. "Uh, can I bring down the card later?" she asked, covering up the situation as she closed the planner, stuffing the unbound pages back inside as she did so. "I think I packed it."

"That's fine," the desk clerk said, "but there will be a lock on your phone until we have the card."

Janet smiled politely and turned away. Immediately her face fell and she hurried to her room. She dropped her bags upon entering and picked up the phone to find no dial tone. Only then did she remember that she couldn't use the phone until the hotel had her card number on file. She slammed the phone down and left the room. A few minutes later, armed with a pocket full of quarters, she picked up the handset of the lobby pay phone and dropped a few quarters into the slot.

CHAPTER TWO

Tally's row had just been called and he stood behind 30 or more people waiting his turn to show his ID and ticket before he'd be allowed to board the plane. His knee was already throbbing a bit and he was dreading the next part of his trip. He used his pain medication as seldom as possible but decided he definitely needed one today. He'd dig it out of his planner once he was seated. He heard a cellular phone ring close by and it reminded him that he'd be instructed to turn off his own phone once the plane was ready to take off. He searched his mind to see if there were any other calls that needed to be made. The phone stopped ringing without being answered but immediately it began ringing again. *Just answer the stupid thing*, he thought to himself and out of habit checked his own phone to be sure it was in his pocket. While he had it in his hand he decided to turn it off now, rather than wait. The ringing of the other stopped, but again, it began to ring almost immediately. It had to be close, perhaps right behind him—he wondered why they didn't just turn off the ringer if they didn't want to answer it. It stopped ringing after 5 rings, and then immediately started ringing again. He rolled his eyes.

The woman behind him in line tapped him on the shoulder. "Sir, I think your phone is ringing."

Tally pulled his own phone from his pocket to show her that it wasn't his. Then she looked at the planner he held in his hand and pointed. He looked at the planner too and realized that in fact there was a phone there, and it *was* ringing. Smiling with embarrassment and apology, he tried to look as if he knew what he was doing as he quickly opened the Velcro phone case attached to the side and stepped out of line. This was obviously not his planner, but he didn't have much time to dwell on it.

"Hello?" he said cautiously, not sure why he'd chosen to answer it at all.

"Who is this?" the female voice on the other end demanded.

He looked back at the planner to reassure himself it wasn't his, but it was silly—it definitely wasn't his. "Who's this?" he said back, only now wondering where his own planner was. He stopped when he was about 10 feet out of line and scowled at the fact that he'd lost his place.

"I'm the owner of the phone you're talking on," she spat back.

"Hey, calm down," he said with just a touch of frustration, his irritation peaked by hers.

"Calm down!" she echoed. "You stole my planner and you're telling me to calm down!"

"Stole," Tally countered. "I didn't steal anything. Now if you can stop shrieking maybe we can get this whole thing figured out."

He heard her take a deep breath and hoped it was one of calming, not gathering steam to blast him with again. "Talmage Blaire?" she asked after another moment.

"You've got my planner?" he asked—obviously she did, how else would she know his name.

"Yes," she said simply, apparently not interested in being angry anymore.

Tally's own irritation was softened by her forced calmness and his tone of voice mellowed. "What a mess," he offered as the full reality seemed to make itself apparent. "How did the switch happen?"

"I don't know. But my planner has my phone and all the other information necessary for my trip. Where are you?"

"I'm in Atlanta just about to board a flight to Baltimore. Where are you?" The next section of rows was called to board the plane.

"Chicago," she said with audible deflation. Her anger was gone now; he was glad she'd worked through it so quickly. "But without that planner I may as well go home."

They were both silent for several seconds as if waiting for the other person to come up with a solution. "I can Fed Ex it when I get to the hotel," Tally offered.

She sighed. "I guess that's the best option, but..." her voice trailed off. "You're not going to steal my credit cards, are you?"

"Are you going to shred my photo proofs?" She knew his name, so undoubtedly she'd seen inside the planner. They both seemed to realize they had no choice but to trust each other, and he was glad they both seemed to understand that.

"No," she said, her voice lighter. "When do you land in Baltimore?"

"About 8:30 Eastern time," he answered.

"I have a dinner meeting I've got to go to right now," she said after a thoughtful pause. "I'll call you when I get back to the hotel—I'll need some information before you send it off, if that's okay."

"That's fine," Tally said. "I'll be waiting for the call."

The final boarding call was announced and he hurried to say goodbye before walking quickly to the boarding gate. The attendant checked Tally's ID and ran his ticket through the machine before nodding that he could enter. He hurried down the corridor and forgot the little precautions he needed to take in simple things like walking. He was hardly conscious of the slight adjustments he normally made; the zing that now shot down his leg reminded him that being quick was never a good thing. He paused and winced slightly before continuing on, his limp more pronounced and his knee hurting more and more by the minute. As he took his seat, wincing as he bent his leg, he remembered the pain pills were in his own planner. *Great*, he thought to himself as he leaned his head against the seat and tried to ignore the discomfort he knew would only get worse. *This is just what I need.*

When the plane landed in Baltimore he found he could barely stand long enough to let the other passengers on his row get out. As soon as they were through, he sat back down and tried massaging his knee in hopes of loosening it up a little. He didn't typically go on jobs that required more than one flight, but he'd made an exception in this case and was deeply regretting it. His knee only acted up like this when it was forced to remain bent for too long a period of time and twisting it as he had didn't help a bit.

After all the other passengers had exited the plane he forced himself to stand and, using the seats as his support, hobbled toward the front of the plane.

"Sir, are you all right?" the flight attendant asked when he reached the door.

Tally wanted so badly to say that he was fine, but he sincerely doubted he would be able to walk once he didn't have the seat backs to hold him up; his knee was burning. He hated giving in to the pain, but he hated the thought of falling on his face even more. "Do you have a set of crutches I can use?" he asked.

The flight attendant shook her head and pointed to the walkway connecting the plane to the airport. "Just a wheelchair," she said apologetically as she indicated the folding wheelchair a few feet away. "But I can push you."

Tally forced a smile he didn't feel. "Thanks, but I can do it myself." She nodded and retrieved the chair. He sat down heavily and adjusted the footboard. When he'd transitioned from wheelchair to crutches almost three years ago he'd sworn he'd never use another chair as long as he lived. He hated going back on that oath even a little bit, but a strict weight training program had kept his upper body strong and capable for moments just like this. The flight attendant handed him his bag and he thanked her as he began wheeling himself up the ramp. Once in the main airport he ignored the looks he got and simply rolled along, swallowing his pride. He stopped at a store and bought some Advil; it was better than nothing. Then he wheeled himself out to catch a cab. He wondered when the planner woman would call him back, and realized he didn't know her name.

During the flight he'd tried to figure out when the switch had been made, but he hadn't come up with anything concrete. It could have been at security, or while he was waiting for his plane or even when he'd stopped to buy his book; any time he'd put his planner down, she could have done the same. He'd entertained the thought of her being that black-haired woman, but then he'd berated himself. Enough about her!

The whole time he'd thought about it, he knew that everything he wanted to know was in that planner; but he'd forced himself not to pry, it wouldn't be polite.

A cab pulled up and he managed to get inside without assistance, handing the wheelchair off to an airport employee who had been hovering nearby. In the cab he was able to straighten his leg out along the seat. That alone gave him enough relief that by the time he reached the hotel he was able to limp to the room he and Jason were sharing.

Jason was laying on one of the beds with his hands behind his head and his ankles crossed as he watched TV. He glanced at Tally briefly when the door opened, then his gaze returned to the screen.

"You look horrible, Tal," he said off handedly.

Tally smiled sarcastically. "Thanks." Was a little sympathy too much to ask?

Jason looked at him again, longer this time, and sat up, apparently realizing there was a reason for the deep furrow in Tally's brow. "You okay?"

Tally nodded as he sat on the other bed and lifted his leg, straightening it out again, wincing as he did so. "Those flights are murder and I tweaked my knee."

"That's what narcotics are for," Jason said, watching Tally with concern. "Can I get you anything?"

"A hammer," Tally said, clenching his jaw as he laid back on the bed, "so I can beat myself unconscious."

Jason was tall and lanky, with arms that seemed to reach his knees and a neck that looked twice as long as a normal man's. He had big blue eyes and couldn't grow a beard if his life depended on it. Both features made him look much younger than he was. Right now, looking at Tally with a lost expression, he looked about fifteen.

Tally smiled. "I'm kidding," he assured his cousin. "It's not that bad, I just need to keep it up for awhile. Could you grab me some pillows and . . . get my heating pad out of my suitcase; some heat will probably help."

"Sure."

Once his leg was elevated and the heating pad covered his knee, Tally told Jason about the planner mix-up and that his pain pills were in Chicago.

"And you didn't look in her planner?"

"Of course not," Tally said, placing his hand on his chest with dramatic flare. "I am a gentleman."

Jason snorted and stood up, looking around the room. He spotted the planner by the door where Tally had dropped it when he'd entered and smiled mischievously. His eyes were sparkling.

"Jason," Tally said in a warning voice.

"Ta-lly," Jason countered sarcastically as he plopped on the other bed and unzipped the planner. "I've never professed to be a gentleman." He opened it without looking at Tally again and started scanning it with his eyes. After several seconds a slow smile spread across his face. "I think you've hit the jackpot, cuz."

Tally said nothing, but his curiosity was growing.

Jason pulled something out of the planner and handed it over. "She's a hottie."

Tally took the item hesitantly and then his eyes went wide. In his hand he held the owner's drivers license, and it was *her*!! All hesitation disappeared.

"I bet she spends two hours a week just keeping this thing organized," Jason said a few minutes later. "She must work for Franklin Covey."

"Dillard's," Tally said. "Here's a pay stub." He handed the paper to Jason.

"I'd kill for my wife to have a job like this, I'd never have to work again."

Tally snorted. Jason had five kids, two of which were twins, and a wife who was constantly at her wits end with every one of them. Tally knew that working out of town every week or so was something Jason looked forward to. "If Leslie worked, you'd have to take care of the kids."

Jason stopped and looked at Tally with exaggerated fear. "Good point!" He smiled and went back to the planner.

"So who's Josh, do you think?" Tally asked. There were appointments for Josh scattered here and there throughout the planner.

"Oh, oh, oh," Jason said excitedly as he held up another treasure and handed it to Tally. It was a black and white photo, with Janet laying on her side, her head propped up with one hand as her long dark hair fell over her shoulder. A toddler with dark black curls sat in front of her, his hands frozen in mid-clap and his mouth open as if he were laughing at something. Janet was looking at the little boy, an indulgent smile on her face. As tally studied the picture, the photographer in him sighed at simply the content; it was a breathtaking photograph. He'd love to have something like that in his own portfolio. He turned it over in his hand. In bubbly writing it read, 'Josh 2 yrs old'.

Suddenly, Jason leaned forward and handed over another piece of paper. It was an announcement for the Salt Lake 26th ward Enrichment night that month. "She's a member too," Jason said with satisfaction. "You don't think she's married, do you?"

Tally shook his head. "She doesn't have a ring, and her official title is Ms—that usually means unmarried, doesn't it?"

Jason nodded. "On her info page it doesn't list a spouse, I think she must be single." Another second or two passed and Jason's already big eyes went even bigger and his head sprung up. He stared at Tally for several seconds before he spoke. "You should take this to her!"

"What?" Tally said incredulously, looking at Jason as if he'd just grown two heads. "She's in Chicago."

Jason smiled, put the planner to the side and leaned forward with his elbows on his knees. "I'm serious, Tal, take this to her."

Tally was shaking his head before Jason even finished the sentence. "That's crazy."

"I've got a good feeling about her," Jason continued, rubbing his hands together as if to keep them warm. "I don't think this is an accident! I mean you're single, she's single, and she's gorgeous. I think she's—"

The cell phone rang and both men looked at each other. Tally held out his hand and although Jason hesitated for a moment, he finally undid the pouch and handed Tally the phone. Tally nodded his thanks, pushed the 'talk' button and put the phone to his ear.

"Talmage Blaire?" she asked after he said hello.

"Call me Tally," he said.

"O-Okay," she continued. "Did you come up with any other ideas?"

"I think the only thing we can do is overnight it," he said, ignoring Jason's dramatic head shaking as he paced back and forth at the end of the bed.

She was silent for several seconds. "Yeah, I didn't come up with anything better either, but I leave tomorrow evening for Boston."

"I can send it to Boston instead."

Janet let out a breath. "That's probably the best idea, that way I'll be sure to get it. Thank goodness I kept my passport with me."

"I'll take it to the front desk right now and get it all arranged so it goes out in the morning, and . . . I'm sorry about all this." Jason rolled his eyes dramatically and shook his head as he crossed his arms and tried to stare Tally down. Tally made a point of not looking at him.

"It's my fault; I should be more careful," Janet offered. "If you've got a pen I'll give you the information you'll need to send it and I'll need to know yours too. And then I need some more information for my day tomorrow."

After a few minutes of finding all the information she needed, they said goodbye and he hung up the phone. Jason was waiting, his eyes showing that he was not giving up. "You have to take it to her."

"No, I don't," Tally said with slow calculated words to ensure that Jason didn't misunderstand. "But I do need to take it to the front desk."

"Tally," Jason said in a lecture tone that Tally had never heard from him before. "How many women have you gone out with since the accident? And I'm not counting Tabitha."

Tally's jaw hardened. Tabitha had been his girlfriend for nearly three years before the accident. A year or so later he heard that she'd gotten married to some professional rock climber. It had been one devastating blow after another; he still wasn't sure which had been harder to get over, losing so much of his physical abilities, or losing the one person he'd thought would never give up on him. Since then, it was hard enough just meeting women, let alone going out with anyone. But he had been dating, a little; however, it was incredibly awkward and intimidating to do so and he hadn't gone on any second dates even though some of the women had seemed interested. There was many a battle he had yet to fight inside himself and gaining the confidence to let someone else into his heart was a big one he hadn't conquered yet. "I don't want to talk about this," Tally said evenly, not wanting to betray how painful it was for him to talk about this subject. It was one thing to dwell on it himself; it was a whole new animal to say it out loud.

"I know you don't," Jason continued. "But it doesn't go away just because you don't want to think about it. Look how well you're doing! You've got a beautiful home, a great job and your health is improving all the time; you hardly even limp anymore. You need to stop counting yourself out and take any opportunity that comes your way to—"

"This is not an opportunity!" Tally interrupted with irritation. "It was a mistake and we came up with a solution; it's done."

"Tally, I just—"

"If you're so dead set on this, you take it to her; tell her all about your poor crippled cousin. If I went it would be just as effective."

Jason was silent, but Tally could see he was just gathering his thoughts. Tally wished Jason understood what it was like to know that the woman he married would likely end up as his nurse before too many years had passed. It was an issue Tally was still trying to accept but it was slow in coming. He did believe that there was a woman out there; he just wasn't sure how to go about finding her and was willing to wait until he was ready—whenever that would be. Jason suddenly looked at Tally again, the look on his face determined. "If you do this, I'll sell you Thunder's colt."

The room went completely silent and Tally blinked. Thunder was Jason's quarter horse mare, and one of the most beautiful horses Tally had ever seen. It was Jason's dad, Tally's uncle Tom, who had gotten Tally interested in riding when he was just a boy. Tally had been a passionate horseman ever since, even competing in rodeos through high school and college. He'd been quite good, and after the accident he had used his love of horses as a main source of motivation. Jason had purchased Thunder while Tally was still in rehab and Tally had been green with envy. Eight months ago, Thunder had given birth to her second foal, a butter-colored colt that showed incredible promise for show and for breeding. Tally had asked to buy the colt right away; Jason had refused without hesitation. That Jason would even offer the colt showed how serious he was and Tally was instantly much more intrigued with the idea.

"You feel that strongly about it?"

"Yeah," Jason said with a nod and shrug, the insecurity of the offer he'd just made already showing up on his face.

Two hours later Tally was standing at airport security showing his scarred knee again. It was almost eleven o'clock, Eastern time; he couldn't believe he was doing this.

"Could you ring Janet Stewart's room for me please," Tally asked when he reached the concierge desk. It was after 1:00 a.m. and the lobby was nearly empty save for a few people wandering in and out of the bar.

"What is this regarding, sir?"

Tally lifted the planner up so the desk clerk could see it. "We accidentally swapped planners at the airport earlier. I'm here to trade back."

She continued to regard him with suspicion so he placed it on the counter and opened the planner to show her Janet's information in the front. "If you ring her room, she'll confirm all of this." He didn't add that Janet didn't know he was bringing it in person, he could only hope she'd handle it with decorum.

The clerk nodded hesitantly and picked up the phone. She turned away from Tally so he couldn't hear the conversation and he shook his head at his own actions. This was likely the dumbest thing he'd ever done. What did Jason really expect was going to happen?

The desk clerk held the phone out to him. "She'd like to talk to you."

He gave her a polite smile, took the phone and then took a deep breath. This was so awkward. Janet probably thought he was a stalker. "Hello?" he said, hoping he sounded confident, because he sure didn't feel confident.

"Tally?" she asked.

"Yeah," he answered. "I know you probably think I'm crazy, but," he searched for a reason he was here other than his cousin 'had a feeling,' "I was worried about the situation and . . . I couldn't sleep anyway."

She was silent and he imagined her hanging up and calling the police. "You flew from Baltimore to bring me my planner?"

Tally's confidence, shaken as it was already, was weakening by the second so he offered her an olive branch. "I'll just leave it at the front desk and you can pick it up in the morning, okay. Sorry I woke you."

"No, wait," she said quickly, then she paused again. "I need a few minutes, but can you wait for me in the lobby?"

"Um, sure."

"Okay, I'll meet you there."

It was the longest five minutes of Tally's life. He sat on an ornate gold fabric sofa and tried to straighten out his knee without being too obvious. The short respite he'd had in Baltimore hadn't been enough and his knee was throbbing like it hadn't in a long time. The desk clerk watched his every move and he felt sure she was itching to push the panic button if he gave the slightest cause for worry.

When he heard the elevator doors open, he turned and watched Janet step out. She scanned the lobby until she met his eyes and they both smiled. She was wrapped in a thick white robe, probably the hotel's, and black silk pajama bottoms showed beneath the hem. Her hair was down, falling to almost the middle of her back but he'd bet money she'd brushed it before coming down; it was sleek and shining. She was more beautiful than he remembered and he hoped he'd be able to make intelligent conversation. She walked to the front desk and he watched her talk to the clerk for a few seconds before the clerk bent down and handed Janet his planner. Apparently she'd wasted no time in getting it ready to be sent off. He liked that she was on top of things.

Opposite the couch he sat on was another one just like it and she sat down, her knees together and his planner in her lap. She smiled nervously and met his eyes for the first time. She had such beautiful eyes, and he believed he could truly drown in them if he stared too long.

"I still can't believe you did this," she said softly, smiling again.

This was it! This was the moment when Tally would find out if being in the presence of such a beautiful woman would turn him into a blubbering idiot. He opened his mouth and prayed for intelligible words to come out. "What's another three hours in the air?" he said nonchalantly, and in that instant he felt all the anxiety melt away and the confidence he remembered from his days in high school and college, when talking to beautiful girls was second nature, began to restore itself. "Besides, I realized I needed my planner more than I thought I would." He leaned forward and reached her planner toward her. She did the same and in a matter of seconds the whole situation had been undone. They each placed their own planner in their laps and sat there in silence.

After another few awkward moments, Janet cleared her throat. "You're a very good photographer," she said. "Not that I was snooping or anything," she added quickly. "I opened it at the front desk and everything kind of . . . well . . ."

"Exploded?"

She laughed. "Yeah, that's a good word. I put it all back though."

As if to make sure nothing was missing he opened his planner, handling it carefully so it wouldn't 'explode' again. To his surprise it was all neat and organized . . . like hers. He quickly zipped it up and handed it toward her. "This isn't mine," he said with feigned sincerity.

She laughed again. "I'm kind of an organizing freak; I couldn't help it. I hope you don't mind."

"Mind?" he said, pulling the planner back and opening it again to inspect her work. "I'd say that alone is worth a flight to Chicago, but I suppose now you know all my secrets."

Her smile this time was a little uncomfortable, and he took that as confirmation that she knew more than he wanted her to. "I'm sure I don't know all of them. Only that you're a very good photographer, you travel a lot and fix some kind of machinery in metal fabricating companies . . . and that you're probably in a lot of pain right now."

Tally managed a polite smile although he felt very uncomfortable as he flipped pages until he found where she'd put his medical information. Over a year ago he'd typed up a letter of explanation in case

something should ever happen to him. It had been more of a thera-
peutic practice at the time, a kind of written acceptance of the truth,
but it embarrassed him that she'd read it and he wasn't sure what to say
now. Along with the written explanation was a photo copy of an x-ray
showing the metal rods and pins that held what was left of his leg
bones together. On the film they looked like a jumble of dark spots
against varied shades of gray with little order to them. In truth he
knew that it was a medical miracle that he didn't have a complete knee
replacement. It would come; the doctors had all assured him that their
handiwork wouldn't last more than a decade, but for now the pins and
rods kept him from feeling quite so geriatric.

"I'm sorry," she said. "I shouldn't have—"

"It's okay," he said quickly, looking up at her with a forgiving smile
and pushing his embarrassment away. He didn't want his discomfort to
ruin this moment. Perhaps it was because they weren't on an official
date, but he felt a certain level of comfort and calmness so rare to him
it was difficult to define.

"No, I—"

"Really," he said with firmness this time. "I looked through yours
too."

"You did?" she said with surprise. Then she smiled as she realized
how ridiculous she sounded. Her tone turned sarcastic and she lifted
her chin, "How rude!"

Tally laughed as he continued to flip through the pages in his
planner. For several seconds they were quiet, then he looked up at her.
She looked uncomfortable, not as much as she had when she first sat
down, but like she was still trying to figure him out and he decided
that the comfort he was feeling only went one way. He didn't like the
awkwardness he began to feel and decided to get it over with now,
before she did. "I better go," he said, but as he tried to stand his knee
refused to straighten; he'd almost forgotten about how badly it hurt
during their conversation but the burning throb beat its way back into
his consciousness. He avoided her eyes as he tried to make another
attempt, but he could feel her watching him. He wanted to scream;
he'd done so well and now he looked like a fool, unable to stand on

his own two feet by himself. So much for feeling at ease with this woman. Without meeting her eyes, he scooted to the end of the couch, hoping that by using the arm he'd get the leverage he needed. If he could just get up, he knew his leg would pop straight, then he could hobble out with a trace of pride left.

Janet suddenly stood and he looked up as she walked toward him, feeling like a child. She sat down beside him and took his planner from his lap. He didn't bother protesting but he eyed her with suspicion as she opened the planner and flipped to the zip pouch that held his prescription bottles. "I'm going to get you some water," she explained as she opened the lid and indicated for him to put his hand out.

"No," Tally quickly said, hating to have her act as his nurse. "I can get it," he added as he attempted to stand again. She put a hand on his good knee and looked at him. The expression on her face wasn't pity or embarrassment, she wasn't searching for words to explain her actions, she just smiled a smile of understanding and nodded.

"Put out your hand," she said as she withdrew her hand and opened the bottle. He considered protesting yet almost without thinking about it he put his hand out as she'd instructed him to do. She shook one pill into his hand and put the lid back on before returning the bottle to the planner. Then she stood and disappeared around the corner.

As soon as she was gone he began massaging his knee furiously, hoping to loosen it up so he'd be able to stand when she returned, but then his hands slowed as he remembered the look on her face. There was something in that look that set her apart from the other women he'd spent time with and his curiosity to find out what that was stopped his self-therapy completely. Maybe he didn't want to stand just yet. If he couldn't stand, he couldn't leave and despite his own embarrassment, she didn't seem to be bothered too much and that intrigued him. By the time she returned with a bottle of water, he'd swallowed his pride, accepted that he couldn't hide his shortcoming, tried to make himself as physically comfortable as possible and made a deal with himself not to give up so easily.

Tally thanked her and swallowed the pill while she returned to her seat across from him. "What time's your flight back to Baltimore?" she asked. Her manner was relaxed, easy, and he felt himself following her example as he watched her closely and wondered why she didn't tell him to leave.

"Not til' six," he said.

She smiled and he smiled back as he felt a silent confirmation of something he couldn't put into words. It was like an agreement of some kind, a goal to learn everything he could about this woman before he had to leave. Strangely enough he felt pretty sure she was thinking the same thing. Something inside of him clicked, like a key turning in a lock and all his discomfort seemed to drain away. The way in which their eyes met was something he'd never experienced and something in his mind told him this would be a defining moment in his life.

With all that in mind, he decided to step up the process a little by being a lot more daring than he normally would; heck, he'd flown across several states to return her planner, she was sitting across from him looking as curious about the silent messages being communicated as he was. Surely he had nothing to lose now.

"Where's Josh?"

Her eyebrows went up and she paused for a few seconds, before seemingly understanding where he'd gotten the information. In the next instant she relaxed again and laid back against the couch, placing her hands in her lap. "Oh, he's with Kim and Allen," she said as if it was totally normal for him to ask. "How was your appointment with Dr..."

"Reaves?"

She nodded as if it had been on the tip of her tongue. "Reaves," she repeated with a snap of her tapered fingers. "Was it on Tuesday?"

Tally smiled and nodded and searched his memory for more of her personal details. "And Enrichment Night? How'd it go?"

"I didn't make it," she said with a shake of her head. "I had to work late."

"Right," Tally said with a nod. "Are you going to get your visiting teaching done this month?"

"Probably not, but I didn't see any appointments in your planner for your home teaching either."

"That's because I'm not an organizing freak," Tally teased.

"You can say that again." They both laughed before Janet spoke again. "What are the photo proof pages for?"

Tally shrugged. "I'm kind of a photographer I guess. I'd someday like to do it professionally, but for now I just do favors. Those shots are of my neighbors; their oldest daughter's getting ready to go away for college and they wanted one last family picture."

"They're quite good," Janet said. "I've worked with a lot of photographers for ad layouts and things like that. You've got a good eye."

"It's fun," Tally said humbly. "And it's good to have a hobby."

"So tell me what happened," she said, glancing at his knee as if she'd finally worked up the nerve to ask.

It was still stiff and sore but feeling better; unfortunately the medication made his thoughts fuzzy, so he was sure to think before he spoke. "I was hit by a truck."

"Ouch," she said after waiting for him to expound. "You don't like to talk about it?"

"People don't like to hear about it much," he said.

"Oh," she said with a nod, as if she understood everything now. She leaned forward and put out her hand. "Well, I'm not 'people,' I'm Janet Stewart. I don't believe we've ever been formally introduced."

Tally laughed and shook her hand quickly before they both pulled back, the simple contact was much more intimate to him than it should have been. "You really want to hear this?"

"It's two o'clock in the morning," she said with a shrug. "What else is there to do?"

Tally liked her more with every word she spoke, and decided to take things even further. He usually preferred to let people, women especially, think he was perfectly normal for as long as possible. Somehow making this exception seemed like a very good idea. "I served a mission in Los Angeles and one day, just a few months before I was due to come home, my comp and I were riding our bikes to an appointment. We rounded this corner just as a delivery truck ran a red light. The truck smashed into a car, overcorrected to avoid another car and ended up hitting us instead."

"Both of you?" she asked with wide, sympathetic eyes.

Tally nodded. "My comp broke some ribs and suffered a mild concussion, but I was crushed between the truck and a cement retaining wall. It was one of those instances of being in the horribly wrong place at precisely the wrong moment."

"Oh, my gosh," she breathed. "That must have been terrible."

"I don't know, I was unconscious," he said with a shrug, although just remembering everything made him relive the incredible emotions of the whole period of time. "I was in a coma for almost two weeks because of a head injury, but when I woke up it was horrible. My knee had been crushed, but they'd managed to put it back together pretty well, minus the cartilage and knee cap; several pins hold it together, but I guess you saw the pictures of that already." She nodded and he continued. "My other leg was also broken in two places, as was my right collarbone and shoulder. I had a skull fracture, lacerated liver and punctured lung."

Janet just stared.

"But enough about me," he said flippantly, not enjoying the spotlight. "Let's hear a little about you."

"I was in labor for eight hours," she said lamely. "Doesn't quite measure up."

"Well, since I don't plan to give birth, and I doubt you plan to get crushed by a delivery truck; why don't we call it even?"

She smiled and placed her hands between her knees as she leaned forward. "Why don't I buy you breakfast," she said. "It's the least I can do."

"It's two o'clock in the morning."

"Room service delivers 24 hours a day."

Tally didn't respond for several seconds as a sensation closely akin to being covered from head to toe with warm butter descended upon him. "I believe room service implies that you're in a room."

She shrugged, her light blue eyes sparkling. "If you try anything I'll kick your knee out, deal?" She stood up and cocked her head to the side as she waited for his reply. The pose was endearing and made her look angelic in her thick white robe.

He laughed, but his mouth was dry. "And if you try anything?"

"You'll just have to take your chances," she said with a smile that made his good knee go weak.

Hours later, long after their early morning breakfast had been removed to the hall, Tally asked to see her planner for a minute.

She looked at him queerly but handed it across the small table by the window in her room where they had enjoyed their early meal. "What are you doing?" she asked after several seconds, standing up in hopes of getting a peek.

"Changing all the area codes in your address book."

She laughed and shook her head as she sat back down.

"You'll figure it out soon enough," he said as he finished, zipped up the binder and handed it back. He glanced at the digital clock on the nightstand and made a face, "I have to get going."

She'd taken off her robe to reveal modest, but very flattering black satin pajamas that seemed to cling to every curve as if they simply couldn't help it. Looking at her now, she was even more beautiful than she'd been the first time he'd seen her at the airport. She was relaxed, and soft. He liked it much better.

"According to your info sheet, I'm almost ten years older than you," Janet said, changing the subject completely.

Tally wondered what thought had prompted her to make the calculation and why she'd chosen to bring it up now. But he decided to pursue it. "If it makes you feel better, I might be 26, but I feel about 50 or 60 when it gets cold outside, and sometimes life makes people grow up before their time."

She regarded him for several seconds as if trying to decide whether or not to continue the line of discussion. "I wish—" she started to say, then stopped, as if hesitant to finish.

"You wish what?" Tally prodded, raising an eyebrow.

"I wish . . . you were staying in Chicago."

Tally smiled and felt sure his face was glowing. He hadn't slept in almost thirty hours, yet he felt as if he could fly if he wanted to. They'd talked and laughed all morning long. She was smart, with a quick wit and an easy smile. There was no tension, no need for him to feel the necessity to hide or gloss over his limitations. All morning long he'd been wondering if this was really happening. The whole situation seemed unreal, and even as he watched her now it was hard to believe he was here. The weirdest part, however, was that the vibes he got back from her seemed to be a perfect reflection of his own feelings. They were on the same level, playing the same game and he gloried in it.

"Me too," he said sincerely. "Hopefully, I'll hear from you when you get back to Salt Lake." He stood with minimal awkwardness and she stood too. "I'm sorry you didn't get any sleep. Your day's going to be longer than ever."

"Like I told you," she answered, "I don't sleep very well anyway."

They stood there awkwardly for a moment and Tally realized he was only an inch or so taller than she was. If he ever saw her again he'd be sure to request that she never wear heels. "I guess I'll see you around."

She smiled and put out her hand, "I guess so."

He took her proffered hand, but didn't shake it; instead he just held it for a moment, enjoying the sensation of actually touching her while he rubbed his thumb across the back of her hand. There was nothing left to say so he smiled again and let go before turning and heading for the door. As he stepped across the threshold he looked back at her once more and waved before shutting the door behind him and heading toward the elevator.

Tally stepped into a cab a few minutes later and smiled to himself as the cab pulled away from the curb. He'd been told that after being freed from the truck and put in the ambulance, his heart had stopped beating and they thought he was dead. That was almost four years ago; he'd never felt so alive as he did right now. *Janet Stewart*, he said in his mind, *is going to change my life. I can feel it.*

As soon as Tally left, Janet opened the planner, flipping through the book page by page until she found what he'd written. On her daily planning page for Saturday he'd written 'Dinner at Koyo with Tally 6:00, 2300 East 3300 South Salt Lake.' Then she flipped to the address book and looked under Blaire. Sure enough, his phone number and address were written; in pen she noticed. With a smile she looked out the window and took a deep breath. It had been a very long time since she'd let down her guard with anyone, especially a man. For a moment she wondered what was different about Tally, but she already knew the answer, or part of it anyway. He treated her like a person, not a trophy, and he made her laugh. She couldn't remember the last time anyone had made her laugh like he did. He wasn't the best looking man she'd ever met; he had a stocky build and a round face, but he had soft brown eyes and a warm smile that was very inviting. A little thrill ran down her spine as she considered what his presence in her life right now could mean. She couldn't be sure, but she knew it was a good thing.

The clock caught her eye and she realized she had just over an hour to get ready before her first appointment. She hurried to the bathroom and turned on the shower before twisting up her hair and putting on the shower cap. Then she retrieved a bottle of pills from her bag. A few capsules would make up for the sleep she'd missed. She swallowed them dry and returned to the bathroom with a little more spring in her step than she'd had of late. Tally seemed to be good medicine.

CHAPTER THREE

Tally sat at the table and tapped his chopsticks nervously. After leaving Chicago he'd gone back to Baltimore, managing to sleep on the plane. The tools had arrived that morning and despite how tired he was, he and Jason managed to finish the job on time. Janet had left him a message on his cell phone Friday that she'd be at Koyo for their date. He'd kicked himself for not answering the 'unknown number' once he realized it had been her—he'd have loved to hear her voice again. As they'd worked, Jason tried to change his mind about selling the colt, but Tally wouldn't let him out of it. Rotating his wrist enough to check the time on his watch, Tally felt the knot in his stomach tighten. It was 6:12 Saturday night. He didn't know what he'd do if she didn't come.

He'd no more said it to himself when her head popped around the corner. He couldn't help sitting up a little straighter.

"I'm so sorry," she said as she came into full view. Her further apologies were halted as she looked around the restaurant. They were almost at eye level, but Tally was seated inside the little Japanese room, called a Tatami, while she stood on the restaurant floor a few feet below. Within the Tatami was a recessed table that gave the illusion of the guests being seated on the floor. There was also a sliding bamboo door that ensured a private dinner. Janet finished her initial inspection and met his eyes once more. "What a great place!"

Tally wished he could jump up and help her in, but as he'd known it would be, his knee was sore from the weekend of working and he was in no condition to be 'spry.' "You can put your shoes next to mine and the waitress will be here in a few minutes to take our order."

She smiled, and using the paper-paned Shoji door for balance, removed her black pumps and placed them next to Tally's loafers. She was dressed similar to how she'd been at the airport the first time he saw her. Black slacks and a white short-sleeved rayon blouse. Her hair was pulled up in a bun, with only a few perfect tendrils left down to frame her face. At her throat hung a pendant of some kind of black stone, with earrings to match. He'd never known a woman who, when dressed professionally, still looked so incredibly attractive.

Within a few moments she was seated across the table from him, smiling prettily while his heart raced. "I'm glad you made it," he finally said after too long of a pause.

"I'm so sorry I'm late," she said again as she undid the fan-folded napkin and placed it in her lap. "I've been at the office all day finishing up expense reports and last minute fall fashion orders. I guess I lost track of time."

"Saturday at the office, yuck," Tally said, surprised that after the out-of-town trip she'd still be required to put in office time.

"Unfortunately, I've spent more Saturdays at the office than away from it lately. Luckily, there's a girl in the ward who watches Josh at the house. Sshe's great and Josh loves her so it works out pretty well. But I hired a nanny today."

"A nanny," Tally repeated. He'd never known anyone who had their own nanny.

"It will be so much better for Josh," she continued, oblivious to his surprise. "That's another reason I had to go in today—to do phone interviews. I talked with several candidates and decided on a girl named Kelly. She lives in California, but she's 22 years old, Mormon, and she's been working with a family for almost three years."

"Why isn't she staying with them?" Tally asked. He could see the benefit of having a live-in babysitter but wondered at how casual she was about it.

"The father got transferred to London; she didn't want to go with them. But she seems really good, and after watching three kids, Josh will be a breeze."

Tally nodded. "When does she start?"

"In about two weeks, I'm very excited." Just then she noticed his foot propped up on the 'floor' a few inches away from where she was sitting and looked up at him with a questioning look.

"Do you mind?" he asked, pulling it back. "I don't—"

"No, no," she quickly interjected as she placed a hand on his ankle and pulled it back up. "That's fine if it feels better." She allowed her hand to linger on his ankle and he felt sure his heart rate increased at her touch.

"It helps if I can keep it straight," he said with a grateful smile.

"Well then, do it," she said easily.

He smiled again at the same time their waitress came to take their order. "Do you need a minute?" Tally asked, since Janet hadn't had a chance to look at the menu yet.

"Do you mind ordering for me?" she asked after looking up and down the menu one last time.

"Are you sure?"

"Yeah, I trust you." She winked and whereas his pulse had been increasing since her arrival he thought his heart might stop beating altogether now. There was just something about the way she looked at him that put his whole body on alert. He order the Nachi, or teriyaki chicken. Included in the meals came a dish of shrimp and vegetable tempura, a Japanese soup called Miso, rice, and salad with a spicy peanut dressing. Janet took one bite of the salad and looked up at him with surprise. "This is so good," she said once she swallowed.

"You like it?" Tally asked.

"I love it!" she said as she took another bite. "I've driven past here a million times, I thought 'Koyo' was some kind of Japanese company, not a restaurant. How'd you find this place?"

"My brother Chris served his mission in Japan. After moving here he made a point to eat at every Japanese restaurant in the area; this is his favorite. He brought me when I moved here and I've been a big fan ever since."

"I can see why," she said. "I can't believe I've never heard of it. Do they sell this dressing?"

Tally laughed. "In fact they do, so long as they have enough; I already ordered a pint for myself."

Janet laughed and met his eyes, seemingly reading his thoughts. "Creepy," she said.

He just nodded and went back to his food as Jason's voice echoed in his mind: 'I just have a feeling about her.' When they finished their salads he showed her how to drink the soup from the small bowl; she loved it too.

"What if I told you that my brother once made me promise only to marry a woman who liked this stuff, so that we could all go here together?"

She met his eye again and then she raised her eyebrow as she smiled. Tally had goose bumps. The air in their little Tatami was getting very warm and Tally could feel himself blushing at his own forwardness. As they continued to hold one another's gaze he could feel the mood shift into something very intimate. He'd never felt anything like this with a woman, not even Tabitha. He couldn't help but wonder if perhaps it wasn't nearly as rare for her.

"Are you involved in a relationship, Janet?" he suddenly asked, deciding that it was time to get to the heart of their connection. He'd already blurted out the whole marriage thing, he may as well keep going.

She shook her head, "Are you?"

"No," he answered. "How is it that you aren't? I have to guess that it isn't for lack of male interest."

Janet expression was instantly guarded. "You think I'm lying to you?"

Tally raised his eyebrows, surprised by the cutting tone of her voice; he hadn't expected such a quick change in her attitude. "No, it's just that . . ." he wasn't sure how to explain it. He licked his lips nervously. "I'm sure I'm not the first to tell you this, but you're easily the most beautiful woman I've ever met. It's hard to believe you don't have a hundred men begging for your time."

Her expression remained hard for a moment, and he wondered why. But then it softened. "Tally," she said quietly, leaning forward despite the fact that they had plenty of privacy. Her face had softened considerably, and he was surprised again at how quickly her mood had changed. "I have no room for anything in my life other than my work and my son right now. I swore off men after Josh was born, and I've done a very good job at keeping that promise to myself. I'm still not sure why I've fallen back on that decision, except that . . . there's something . . ." she looked away as if struggling for words. Tally could only watch her intently, hoping that the words she found would finally voice his own inexplicable feelings. She met his eye once more before continuing, "there's something about you that makes you an exception."

The screen slid back as the waitress set their dinners in front of them. When she shut the door again, their eyes met. "Maybe we should go back to the beginning," Tally said, "and just learn about each other."

"That," Janet agreed, pointing her chopsticks at him, "sounds like a great idea."

For the rest of the meal they kept the topics of their conversation very basic, almost frivolous. In the hotel room they'd talked about current events and things like that. This time they got a little more personal, but not too much so. Tally told her about his house in Willard, forty miles north of Salt Lake, and the horses he kept there. She listened intently, seeming to enjoy the picture he painted of his life in the country. They also talked about his work, and then her work, her home, her family, what little there was. It was the only time in their conversation that she seemed to close off and he wondered about it. She told him her only sister lived in Arizona, her parents divorced when she was young—they were both dead now. But it stopped there, and he could tell she was uncomfortable so he didn't press the subject. Her family background was completely opposite of Tally's, and he could feel just a hint of envy as he told her about his parents, still living in Oklahoma, and his three younger siblings: one brother, Chris who lived in Bountiful, and two sisters, Camilla and Emma. Camilla lived in Oklahoma with her husband and two kids. Since Emma's marriage two weeks ago, he was the only single sibling left.

Before they knew it, the waitress was informing them that their table was needed for another reservation. They apologized profusely, having lost complete track of the time, and Tally left a generous tip to compensate. As they exited the restaurant and stepped into the hot summer night, Tally hoped she wasn't going to hurry home. They turned to each other at the same time, then smiled simultaneously.

"I really need to get home to Josh," Janet said regretfully. "I've been working all day and it's almost his bed time."

Tally's heart sank and he looked at his shoes in hopes to hide his disappointment while he thought of what to say.

"Would you like to come?"

His head and his heart lifted. "Are you sure?"

Janet smiled brightly. "Of course."

So Tally followed her home. She lived in a gated community in the Mill Creek area of Salt Lake, only a few blocks from Koyo, in fact. The community seemed plopped in the middle of an average neighborhood and, in his mind, didn't quite fit. She entered the security code and he followed her through the gates, around a corner and into the driveway of a large white stucco home. It fit her perfectly—clean, formal and elegant.

"Mama-mama-mama-mama." A little black-haired fireball ran from the other room, nearly crashing into Janet's legs as soon as the door shut behind them.

She laughed and picked him up with a grunt before turning to face Tally. "Tally, this is my son Josh—Josh, this is Tally."

Josh became instantly shy and with his fingers in his mouth shrank against his mother, watching Tally closely.

"Hey there, buddy," Tally said with a smile. He tried to tickle Josh's chin, but Josh pulled back even more and regarded him much the same way Tally regarded his dentist.

"Don't worry about it," Janet laughed. "In a few minutes he'll be crawling all over you."

They both looked up just as a tall skinny teenage girl turned the corner to enter the room. She must have heard them enter, since she had her purse slung over her shoulder and looked ready to leave. Janet introduced the girl as Shanna, and Shanna smiled nervously while shifting her weight from one tightly jean clad leg to the other. There were several inches of bronzed belly showing between her low-slung jeans and skin tight pink tank top that showed the lines of a black bra being worn underneath. Tally wondered when it was that young Mormon girls started wearing their underwear in public. They'd never done that when he was in school, but then again he'd attended a private Catholic school; it probably wasn't the best comparison. He wondered if her mother knew she was dressed that way or if she had a sweatshirt stuffed in her purse that she'd put on just before going inside her house.

"Oh, I left my wallet in the car," Janet said with a sigh, she took a step toward Tally. "Will you take him for a minute while I walk Shanna out?"

"Uh, sure," Tally said as Janet leaned into him and successfully transferred Josh to his arms. Josh leaned way back in Tally's arms, so he could still watch him, but he didn't cry and for that Tally was grateful. Tally smiled and pulled his keys from his pocket with one hand while shifting Josh to one side. He jingled the keys and Josh grabbed them, instantly sticking them in his mouth. Tally cringed, unsure if that was a health hazard or not. A moment later Josh slapped Tally's cheek, Tally just smiled and hoped it wasn't personal. Then Josh reached up one hand and grabbed Tally's nose hard and Tally said the only thing that came to mind.

"Honk."

Josh froze and watched him carefully as he slowly did it again.

"Honk," Tally said again, only this time he added a little more effect to his voice.

A slow smile spread over Josh's face and he did it again.

"Honk."

And again.

"Honk."

And again.

"Honk."

Janet's laughter got his attention and they both turned to look at her. "Guess he warmed up to you."

"Ahh, kids love me," Tally said with a shrug. Then he turned to Josh. "Don't ya?"

Josh answered by honking Tally's nose again.

Half an hour, and 37 honks later, Janet shut the door to Josh's room. Tally had heard Janet sternly telling him it was time for bed over and over again as he fought her, and Tally felt the tension. It couldn't be easy working the way she did and still being Mom when she got home. Luckily, the whimpering stopped soon after the door was shut. When she came down the stairs, Tally was sitting in the living room, flipping pages in a coffee table book about Picasso, pretending he hadn't overheard the struggle and wondering if he should stay now that they were un-chaperoned.

Janet perched on the arm of the couch a few feet from where Tally sat and his eyes traveled slowly up her body until they met her eyes and his stomach was instantly on fire again. He couldn't get over how beautiful she was and wished there was a way he could tell her without sounding like a thousand other men that had likely told her the same thing.

"I know I've made this one heck of an evening," she said. "But I still have to prepare my lesson for tomorrow."

Another unanswered question disappeared from his very long list. Not only was she a member of the church, she was apparently actively involved in her ward. Another point for Janet! "What do you teach?" Tally asked.

"Eleven-year-old girls," she said. "I team teach with two other women so I only have to do a lesson every three weeks, which is a good thing since I'm not much of a teacher."

"What's the topic?"

Janet hesitated, shook her head in embarrassment and smiled slightly. "Setting a goal for temple marriage."

Tally's eyebrows shot up and he broke into a wide grin. "Really." He turned his attention back to the book and flipped another page. "What do you know about it?" he asked with feigned flippancy.

"Too much and too little," she said with a sigh as she began tracing the damask pattern of the back of the sofa with her finger. He turned to look at her once more and her eyes suddenly leapt up to meet his. "I've been married and divorced twice."

Tally felt himself pause. "Twice?"

She watched him intently as she continued. "In the temple the first time, lasted ten years, out of the temple the second time, lasted less than a year."

"And Josh?"

"Is from husband number two."

Tally nodded and offered a polite smile as he tried to digest the information. He turned back to the Picasso book.

"Have I scared you yet?" she asked after a few seconds, her voice was soft and a little sad.

Tally looked up and told the truth. "A little."

"That's probably healthy."

They sat in silence for several seconds. "Have you been married?" she finally asked.

Tally shook his head.

That seemed to deflate her a little, as if she'd hoped he had one shipwreck in his past. "Oh," she said with a nervous smile. She looked away and they went silent again.

"But I was engaged once."

"Really? What happened?"

He tried not to smile at the hint of relief he heard in her voice. "I got hit by a truck." It was the same answer he'd given her in the hotel lobby to explain the injury to his knee, and he felt sure she'd understand the implication.

"I'm sorry."

"So was I."

"What happened?" Janet asked as she slid off the arm of the couch and turned to face him, pulling her knees to her chest and resting her back against the arm of the couch. Before putting Josh to bed she'd changed into some black cotton pants and a matching black T-shirt; she'd also redone her hair into a different twisty bun thing with a pen stuck through it. He wondered if the pen was there to hold the hair in place or to keep her from losing it. Regardless, he liked the easy going look; it was . . . cute, for lack of a better word, and it made her look young and innocent somehow.

"She just couldn't handle it."

"Just like that," Janet challenged his flippancy. "So you shrugged your shoulders, said 'that's life' and carried on."

Tally managed a chuckle, although he knew she could tell he took this very seriously. Now it was his turn to trace the damask pattern on the sofa and avoid her eyes. "My folks put us in Catholic school because the public schools in our area weren't very good and so I didn't date much. The only other Mormon kids I knew were at church and after a few dates with both the girls my age I decided I ought to put more time in my studies so that I could get a scholarship and go to another ward in another town."

Janet chuckled. "That bad, huh?"

"One of the girls insisted we pray about every fifteen minutes for one reason or the other, and the other girl tried to talk me into stealing a six pack of beer. So, I waited to date until college and it got better. The studying paid off and I got a four-year scholarship to the University of Oklahoma, in Norman; about 40 minutes from home. The scholarship had to be taken in full though, it isn't like some of the scholarships you can leave for a mission and come back to, so I decided to get my schooling done and then serve a mission.

"I met Tabitha my junior year. We both loved horses and hiking. I was majoring in civil engineering and she was majoring in accounting. Within a few months we knew that we were going to get married. But I still felt strongly about serving a mission, which would put our marriage off for four years. I'd never really liked school, and so we eventually decided that I would forgo the last year and a half of my scholarship and put in my mission papers instead, to speed things up a bit. Tabitha was going to finish her degree and I talked to my cousin, Jason, about working for him when I got back—it seemed like everything was going to work out just perfectly. Through my whole mission she wrote almost every week and I never doubted she'd stick it out. If it weren't for the accident I think things would have been just fine." He paused and had to shake himself out of the gloomy recollections for a moment before he could finish. He wished he could stop right there, hating to relive it.

"She came out to see me after I came out of the coma, but she stayed as far away from my bed as she could get. I couldn't talk very much, I was still so sedated, but I could tell she was scared out of her mind. She went home a few days later without so much as touching me. She wrote to me for a month or so and then she came out again to see me. That's when reality hit like a brick wall. The doctors were saying it would be a year before I had any hope of walking more than ten steps without help. They weren't sure if I'd ever have full use of my right arm, and that it would be at least 18 months before I'd live outside of a rehab center. She stayed for three or four days. I think she was really trying to find a place for herself in my new life, but it was a little too much for a twenty-year old girl who loved to camp and hike and water-ski.

"She went back home early and called my mom crying a few days later. She said she just couldn't do it. My mom didn't tell me for almost a month. I hadn't had any letters for weeks by then and I kept asking about her. My mom finally broke down and told me what had happened. For awhile I was devastated, I'd hadn't even considered that it wouldn't work out between us. But once I accepted it, I took the whole experience as one more motivation to get better. She wrote me a few times but I never even read the letters, just threw them in the trash. I learned to use the heartache as fuel and it worked."

"But it had to have hurt," Janet sympathized.

"Like hell until I learned how to channel that pain," Tally confirmed. He looked up at her again and felt the comfort of her smile. "But I'm sure you know all about that kind of heartbreak."

"Yes and no," Janet said with a little shrug of her shoulders. "The truth is that I married two men who wanted me to be what I couldn't and I never really loved either one of them the way I should have."

Tally turned to face her and propped his elbow up on the back of the couch. "What do you mean?"

"When Allen, my first husband, and I got married, we were both chomping at the bit to be real grown-ups. Allen was starting medical school and I was just about to graduate with my degree in fashion. We got married and took off like rockets, but in different directions. We didn't spend a lot of time together for the first five or six years; we were so busy with our own schedules and careers. And then, when Allen's schooling started to wind down, he decided he was ready for a family. I wasn't." She shrugged as if to say there was nothing she could do about it. "I was up to my eyebrows in the industry and I wasn't ready to throw away the last seven years of my life to fulfill a dream that had always been more his than mine. Then—"

"What do you mean more his than yours?" Tally interjected. He wasn't going to let an important conversation like this pass him by without getting all the answers.

Janet hesitated, but after looking at Tally again, continued. "I'm not a nurturing type of person," she admitted with just a touch of disappointment in herself. "I always figured that, as a girl, I'd grow into it and one day want kids and the whole motherhood dream of the minivan and homemade cookies, but I never really did. By the time Allen was ready, I decided I liked the life I was living, not the one he wanted me to live with him."

Tally wasn't sure what he thought about that. Part of him was very put off by what seemed to be a very shallow and selfish position, but another part of him admired her honesty and respected the strength she had to say it. He knew women who probably felt the way she did but lived the life they were 'supposed' to live anyway, and he agreed that it would be pretty frustrating. However, the life she didn't want was something he himself wanted more than anything.

"We tried to find a middle ground, but I think we'd both given up a long time before it got to that point. But he's a really good guy. He moved back to Salt Lake after the divorce and remarried a couple years ago. He and his wife help out with Josh when I'm out of town."

"Kim and Allen?" Tally asked, remembering that she'd said they were watching Josh when she'd gone to Chicago.

"Yeah," Janet said with a little laugh that communicated that she knew full well how weird that sounded. "He has a little girl of his own now and he's a great father; Josh loves him and it's good for Josh to have a man he can spend time with." Tally felt a little jealous, but wasn't sure why exactly.

"And the second husband?"

"Craig," Janet said in a way that just saying his name should explain everything. "I'm still trying to figure that one out myself." She smiled and shook her head. "To understand Craig you have to realize where I was in my life when I met him."

"Okay," Tally prodded. He clenched the sides of the couch tightly, as if bracing himself. "I'm ready."

She slapped his arm playfully and rolled her eyes. "After Allen left, I was still living in our house and attending our ward. There was a lot of attitude from the members about our decision to break up. Most LDS women would give their left arm for a man like Allen; he's smart and funny, involved in the Church and makes a good living. I was always different from the women in my ward and there was a lot of pressure at that time for women not to work, to stay home and raise babies instead. But that never worked for me and then Allen and I got a divorce which just seemed to affirm to them what a wicked woman I really was. I'd never gotten very close to anyone there anyway and after a few tense weeks I stopped going to church all together. I was going through a divorce; it wasn't my best moment and feeling the judgments of all those people; many of whom were still good friends with Allen, was more than I could handle. But I knew that I needed the church in my life, so after I sold the house and moved to a new ward, I started going again. I met Craig on one of my first weeks back. He was a chef and worked almost as many hours as I did. He hadn't been active in years and when we started dating we realized we both wanted the same thing in life; space and independence. We decided to do it together; but then I got pregnant and when I told him, he didn't even think twice about leaving me and Josh to our own devices."

It was Tally's turn to say "ouch."

"Breaking up wasn't that bad, he wasn't good for me and I don't know that I ever really loved him enough to be married to him," she admitted. "And he had only been playing around with the idea of coming back to church. He didn't live the church standards, not that I was perfect either, but there was a lot of friction. It was best that it ended and I'm lucky he has no part of Josh's life. He wouldn't have been a very good father. I reverted to my maiden name, Stewart, after the divorce to fully rid me of the man."

"But you were left with what you didn't want."

"Oh wait," she said, putting her hands up to emphasize her point.

"I love Josh more than I ever imagined was possible. I would never change having him in my life, I didn't mean to imply that at all—Josh is . . . amazing. Being a mother has changed me for the better and I'm so glad he's here. I can't imagine life without him."

"I only meant that you had the career and the family and couldn't give up either one."

"I guess that's a good way to put it," she said with a nod, her defensiveness gone. "I transferred to Salt Lake just before he was born, and now here we are, two years later; still pluggin' along. He was a good baby and is a sweet little boy. I'm very lucky."

"When did you go back to church?"

"About a year ago," she said. "I believe in the church wholeheartedly—I always have, whether I'm active or not. But I struggle with the culture and the judgmental nature of so many of the 'saints.' I've never really fit in. Those of us women who don't bake or keep a running list of our food storage are always on the outside of things. It's been that way in every ward I've ever belonged to. Being a single working mom, I feel constantly bombarded with criticism and sometimes that's all I need to talk me out of being involved. I like to work and I think I'm a better mother because I enjoy my success, but I've met very few people who can understand that."

Now Tally was even more confused. Again, he liked her strength and the power of her feelings, but he couldn't help but wonder if they weren't skewed a little bit. Then again, wasn't she telling him how tired she was of being judged? He didn't like to think of himself as one of the people she felt were against her.

"I think I know what you mean," he said after a short silence. She raised her eyebrows and he could feel her suspicion. "When I moved to Willard about ten months ago I was called almost immediately as second counselor in the Young Men's presidency. I loved it. After about six months the bishopric was changed and I was called in to meet with the new bishop, a doctor I'd met only briefly. It was just a casual visit and since he was a doctor we discussed my accident and my injuries. He asked if I had a hard time keeping up with the young men and if I felt okay about going on the summer camps. I assured him that it wasn't a problem and didn't think much about it. Two weeks later I was shocked to be released. In the exit interview I asked him why he'd chosen to release me and he said that he just felt I could better serve in another way. Then he launched into the reasons why I should be going to the singles ward. I think it's because he's convinced I have limitations I don't have and that ticks me off—it was a major blow to be released from a calling I liked so much after only a few months. He's been bishop now for about four months, and I don't doubt that he's a good man, but I think his decision was pretty insensitive and I'm still working up to trusting the guy."

Janet nodded. "That would be hard," she commiserated.

"I guess it's one of those tests of faith," Tally said with a shrug. "I know I need to sustain and support him, believe that his decision was for the best, but it's sure hard to do. In that way I understand what you mean about it being hard to deal with the judgments of others."

"Although you didn't go inactive because of it; I did."

"But you came back," Tally said. "And you do believe in the Church, right? You're not living some secret life when no one's looking?"

Janet laughed and slapped his arm again. "No, Tally," she said with a sarcastic smile. "I'm not a wicked woman of Babylon; but I am aggressive and independent. Josh is my little darling and he continually teaches me more and more about myself. He'll always come first for me, but my life doesn't revolve around him and I don't think it should. I think a lot of women want to be home with their babies all day, every day, and more power to them, but I'm just not one of them."

"Hey, you don't have to defend yourself to me," Tally said waving his hands as if in surrender.

She smiled and he knew that his support was important to her. They held each other's eyes for several moments and the intimacy from the restaurant seemed to descend on them again. He couldn't help but allow his eyes to travel the length of her body once more and he could feel her watching him as he did so. She was so close to him and when he met her eye again he felt his insides quiver. She smiled and cocked her head slightly, not at all embarrassed by the brazen way he was

watching her. To him it seemed to be an invitation and he simultaneously wondered if he should leave or if he should kiss her . . . and then
Josh started to cry. The moment was ruined and Janet groaned loudly
as she stood up and headed for the stairs.

"I'll be back in a minute," she said, and Tally could hear the frustration in her voice.

Josh's crying got louder, as did Janet's attempts to quiet him. After
a few minutes Janet returned downstairs. Josh's cries echoed behind
her. "I'm sorry, Tally," she said. "I think it might be best if we cut the
evening short. Josh is getting a molar in and it's just a little frazzling
right now. I'm sorry it wasn't much of an evening."

"It's been a wonderful evening," Tally said. He took a few steps
toward her and looked at her for a moment before acting on an
impulse he'd been ignoring for much of the night. He reached out and
slowly removed the pen stuck in her hair. Her hair cascaded from her
head like a shampoo commercial and his stomach flipped despite the
crescendo of toddler shrieks in the background. She was so beautiful.
She continued to look at him with those big blue eyes and he questioned, not for the first time, if all this was really happening. The longer
he was with her, the more he could feel himself twisting around her
finger. He finally smiled. She just continued to look at him and so he
spoke once more; almost afraid of what might happen if he dared kiss
her or stay much longer. There was an electricity between them that
he found exciting and yet a little scary too. "Can I call you some—"

"Yes," she interrupted, meeting his eye again and smiling widely.
"Any time."

Monday morning found Janet back at the office and up to her
earlobes in work; the usual. The phone rang and she immediately
answered it.

"Janet Stewart," she said quickly as she continued going though
the stack of orders she needed to approve by noon.

"Janet, it's Suzanne from Dr. Lennon's office; he asked that I call
and make an appointment with you about your medications."

Janet put down the order she was reviewing and straightened in her chair—she'd been waiting for this call ever since leaving a message this morning that she needed another prescription. "Yeah," Janet said slowly as her train of thought switched to a new track. "Well, I've got an incredibly busy week ahead of me and absolutely can't squeeze in an appointment. Is there anyway you could call me in one last refill, and I'll make an appointment for next week?"

"Well, that's kind of the problem," Suzanne said. "He needs to discuss how much you're taking before okaying another refill."

Janet was quiet for several seconds before launching into another plea for the pills. She talked and talked and talked, until Suzanne cut her off and said with force that she absolutely would not get any more pills until she met with the doctor. Janet took a deep breath. "I'll have to check my schedule," she said with forced calmness. "I'll call you back."

She hung up the phone just as Cathy tapped on her door. "Come in," Janet called briskly as she turned her attention back to her paperwork and tried to hide her irritation. She knew she'd never go back to Dr. Lennon.

"I'm ready to go run those errands. Is there anything else you need me to do?"

Janet shook her head and went back to her paperwork, but in the back of her mind she could feel the panic building.

Cathy watched her for a moment. "Is everything okay?" she finally asked.

Janet let out a long breath. "The doctor won't refill my prescription so you can scratch that errand off the list."

"The Xanax?" Cathy asked. It was often her job to pick up the prescriptions, she was well aware of what Janet took.

Janet nodded and began rubbing her temples with both hands. She had two pills left, two—and then they would be gone. How was she supposed to function without them? She was already searching her mind for ideas on what to do—she was coming up completely empty.

"Uh, I could probably find you some."

Janet's hands froze and she slowly looked up. "What?"

Cathy shifted uncomfortably from one tiny foot to the other. "My boyfriend used to work at a pharmacy and he still has some friends there, he helped me get some painkillers a while back when my insurance hadn't kicked in—I could ask if he could manage a few pills."

Janet felt instant doubt bursting in her mind but she quickly squashed it. She had to have those pills—she had to, and there was no way she could find a new doctor by tomorrow. She spoke before she'd finished justifying her decision. "Why don't you ask him about it," she said in a calm tone, as if it didn't matter either way.

"Sure," Cathy said, shrugging as if to show that she didn't think it was any big deal either. "Anything else you need?"

Janet shook her head and went back to work as if they had been discussing something totally benign like the weather or a missing report. Her heart was pounding in her chest, though, and a little voice in her mind was telling her she was crossing another line—but she was getting better and better at ignoring that little voice and she was desperate to ignore it right now. It came down to the fact that she *had* to have those pills.

A couple of hours later Cathy placed an innocent looking white paper bag on Janet's desk. After Cathy left, Janet opened the bag and found a regular prescription bottle. It had no label, only an X written on the lid and the little orange tablets were exactly like the two she had left. She let out a deep breath and smiled as the panic that had been slowly building began to ebb. She was safe for a little longer. With the pill was also a hand written receipt for $300. She wasn't that concerned with the price—she'd been paying full price for the prescriptions for a long time—but she knew that this was not a legal prescription. She had no right to it, yet again she asked herself how she could not take it. Lately, she'd begun taking a pill before the attack ever set in; it made sense to pre-medicate if she felt the stress and anxiety creeping up on her. But she knew she was taking too many too often. At the same time, there was so much going on and she needed these pills to ensure she could meet the demands being put on her.

She wrote Cathy a check for $300 and told herself that once the promotion she was working toward was secured, she would really look at the issue of why the pills were becoming so important. But right now she needed to focus, and those pills helped her do that. She put her purse back into the desk drawer and pushed the entire incident from her mind.

That night, at eight thirty, her phone rang. She looked at the caller ID, smiled and picked up the phone. Josh was asleep and the stack of work she'd brought home was easily left on the desk in her study as she put the cordless phone to her ear and flopped onto the couch.

"Well, hello," she said.

"Hello," Tally answered back in that deep voice she liked so much. Even just talking to him on the phone relaxed her and she smiled to herself as he continued. "How did your lesson go?"

It was almost ten before she hung up, a smile still on her lips. She stretched her arms out over her head and tilted her head to the side. *What are you doing?* she asked herself as she stared at the ceiling, but rather than answer she jumped up and went back to her study to catch up on all the work she'd brought home. Time flew when Tally was involved, but she couldn't afford to fall behind. Next month her regional manager was moving to the New York office, which meant that if Janet could keep up this pace, she'd likely get the management position. It was her dream, what she'd worked toward for over a decade; she wasn't about to let it pass her by.

CHAPTER FOUR

Over the next two weeks Tally and Janet spoke on the phone several times. Tally had flown to San Francisco for a job during that time and Janet had traveled to New York, but they managed to keep in touch. When they did make contact, they would talk for at least an hour about everything from Josh, to the frustrations of Janet's workday, to whether or not Tally's knee was bothering him. On the two week anniversary of their first official date, they met in person again; this time, however, it was at Tally's house in Willard, in the morning, with Josh in tow.

Tally gave them a tour of the house. It was a red brick rambler with a three car garage. Half of the 4,000 square feet of living space was in the basement and completely empty except for some tools, a spare bed and a few boxes that hadn't been unpacked yet. Everything he needed was on the main level; the master bedroom, complete with full bathroom and a walk-in closet, a large kitchen, living room, home office and additional bedroom and bathroom.

Outside was a large barn with three horse stalls and ample storage room for the equipment required to tend to and harvest the alfalfa growing on the back three acres of his land. Tally tended and baled the hay himself throughout the summer. The house was hidden from the road by a small but thickly wooded area that, when combined with the three acre alfalfa field behind the house, completed the feeling of privacy, if not a little isolation. The alfalfa was ready for its second cutting of the season and little purple flowers had sprung up on the tips. White alfalfa moths further added to the charm by fluttering across the field, adding contrast to the green and purple canvas. It was absolutely breathtaking.

Josh stayed in his mother's arms for the first part of the tour, but became mesmerized when Tally showed them the two horses he housed in the barn. He immediately wiggled out of Janet's arms and

Tally helped Josh feed the mare, Ginger, a carrot. Janet was surprised that Josh wasn't afraid—she was, a little. But Josh was entranced and eventually Tally sat him on the horse and walked him around the outside corral. After getting his fill of horses, Josh went to chase moths in the field, the alfalfa reaching well past his waist. Tally took the opportunity to break out his photography equipment and take some shots. Janet couldn't wait to see how they turned out. After lunch Janet put Josh down for a nap in the portable crib she'd brought with her and set up in the spare bedroom on the main floor.

When Josh finally calmed down enough to sleep, Janet found Tally looking up at Willard Peak, the highpoint of a rocky mountain range which rose majestically from the valley floor just half a mile or so behind his home. His back was toward her as he rested his elbows on the chest high fence that separated the alfalfa field from the backyard. As she walked toward him she admired his muscular back and arms. She knew that his injuries made it difficult for him to do a lot of the things he'd once loved, like basketball and hiking, but she was impressed at the discipline he used to ensure he stayed healthy and fit. She knew that for him, keeping in shape was a necessity, but she appreciated the way it made him look too, and felt a little tremble at having noticed at all.

"It's beautiful here," Janet whispered as she approached, not wanting to interrupt his mood. It was early July, but an unusual batch of cool weather had blessed Northern Utah for the last few days, bringing the temperature down to the low 90's. Therefore it was barely tolerable to spend just a little time outside. Judging from the bronze color of Tally's arms and face, he seemed to spend a great deal of time out here no matter how hot it was.

He turned his head to look at her and smiled. "I love it," he said in a reverent tone.

She joined him at the fence and followed his gaze to where the rocky face of Willard Peak cut into the blue summer sky. A jet had left a billowing trail above them that looked like chalk as it faded to the west. "How did you ever find this place?" she asked as her eyes returned to the field of green before them. There was just enough breeze to keep the alfalfa waving lazily in the hot summer sun and she took a deep breath. She hadn't expected to find it so refreshing to get away from the city but she felt more relaxed and comfortable than she had in a very long time.

Tally was silent for a minute before he spoke, like he usually was when discussing anything personal—although she wasn't sure why asking how he found this place was personal, still it seemed to be somehow. "I got a settlement from the accident just over a year ago. I'd been living with my parents since getting out of rehab and I was ready to get out on my own."

"And Willard, Utah just popped into your head?"

Tally smiled and looked at her sideways. "I moved to my brother's place in Bountiful, and spent the next three months driving all over the place, looking for the perfect place to, hopefully, spend the rest of my life. I knew I wanted a place to raise horses, and I've always wanted a little farm of my own, but I needed something that wasn't too far from the airport since I had already purchased a percentage of Jason's company. I hadn't planned on going north but when this house was listed I saw it on the Internet and decided to give it a look. I hadn't expected to get something so . . . big and luxurious, but I fell in love the first time I saw it—it was everything I wanted and then some."

"It's beautiful," she said for probably the hundredth time. "I didn't know you were a partner in the company."

Tally nodded. "I only own about 25 percent, but it's something and even if it gets to the point where I can't do the work myself, it will bring in a little bit of money for a long time—Jason and I figured out all the details. I'm lucky to have something so accommodating, but I do have to work for it. Jason's great, but he's as intent on making sure it's fair to him as I am that it's fair to me. It really worked out perfectly."

"So the settlement paid for the house and the business investment?"

"Yeah," Tally said. "Well, sort of." He cast another look at her and she realized that she might be coming across badly. The last thing she wanted to do was give the impression that she was some kind of gold digger, although it made her feel better knowing he didn't need to be looking for money himself.

"I'm sorry, I'm being nosy."

"No," Tally said quickly. "It's okay. I was paid in a lump sum that allowed me to pay Jason for the percentage and put a good down payment on the house, I got a mortgage to cover the rest. The remainder of the settlement will be paid over the next ten years. The trucking company is also responsible for paying my health insurance for the rest of my life, and that helps."

"So why did you move to Utah? You could have gone anywhere."

"I didn't want to be dependent on my parents and I knew if I stayed too close, my mom would be hovering for the rest of my life."

Janet smiled and ignored the pang of jealousy she felt. Was a hovering mother such a bad thing? But she understood what he meant. "My brother Chris had been living in Bountiful for a few years and liked Utah a lot and . . ." he cast a quick glance in her direction. "I knew my chances of getting married to a Mormon girl were a lot better here than they were in Oklahoma."

Janet felt a little tremor in her spine and turned to look at him. He avoided her eyes and she smiled at his embarrassment. The more time she spent with Tally, the more she wondered how it was that he hadn't already been 'discovered.' Part of her felt anxious about the possibilities of losing him somehow, as if she'd found this buried treasure and knew it would be gone if she didn't take it now. Without consciously admitting it, a few more plays in her game plan began to settle in place. Janet knew how to get what she wanted, and she didn't want to manipulate or force anything; but then she wondered if she could help it. "Then why haven't you tried to kiss me?" she said when he finally looked at her again.

Tally was startled, obviously not expecting that. She moved a few inches closer to him, so that their arms touched, but she just continued to look out across the fields as if what she'd said was completely casual. The silence stretched for a few moments and then Tally leaned toward her. She felt sure he was going to kiss her now and felt her belly get hot but he stopped just an inch or two from her face and when he spoke, his breath tickled her ear and sent warm shivers down her spine.

"When I'm ready to kiss you, I won't just try," he said in a low voice. She turned to look at him, ready to try herself, but he was already stepping away from her. "Want to help me feed the horses?" he asked innocently.

Janet furrowed her brow; why could she never anticipate his reactions? She liked the challenge he presented her, and nodded. He took her hand and they walked to the barn. She enjoyed the feeling of his big strong fingers wrapped around her own and was glad he didn't let go. The large garage door of the barn was open and she had to squint her eyes to adjust to the darkness as they entered. She'd taken no more than two steps inside when suddenly he pulled on her hand and brought her nearly crashing into his chest. He let go of her hand and wrapped his arm around her waist, pulling her to him. She barely had time to register what he was doing before his lips touched hers. Time seemed to stop and a hush settled around them as he kissed her lightly, allowing his lips to linger gently against her own for a few seconds before pulling back as if he were going to release her. She quickly put one hand behind his head and the other around his shoulders and pulled him back, only this kiss was far from the sweet and soft one he'd initiated. His grip on her tightened and she clasped her hands around his neck as the stuffy barn grew even hotter. The kiss lasted for several minutes until Janet leaned into him a bit too much and caused him to lose his balance. She instinctively pulled him upright so that he could get his balance once again, but the kiss had been interrupted and they both stared at each other for several moments. Then Tally smiled, his flushed face giving him a boyish quality that made Janet smile too.

"That...was nice," he said quietly and Janet couldn't help but laugh at the simplicity of the statement. The discomfort of being with someone so new, so unknown had completely disappeared and she felt as comfortable with him as she ever had with anyone in her life. There was something . . . safe and . . . familiar about him, as if she'd known him all her life. She shook her head in confusion at her own thoughts and with a soft smile Tally opened his arms, inviting her. For a moment she hesitated; it was ironic that after sharing something so passionate, the tenderness of his embrace should seem invasive, but somehow it did. Until she looked into his eyes. They seemed to communicate something powerful, something she didn't want to lose by cowering to her reservations. She stepped forward and closed her eyes slowly as his muscular arms circled around her back. She laid her head on his shoulder as the last of her discomfort was snuffed out. Taking a deep breath she inhaled the scent of cologne, Obsession if she wasn't mistaken, and counted the rhythm of his heartbeat against her own chest. He held her tightly and the intimacy of it, the connection was deeper than it had been during the kiss. It seemed more than physical and in that moment, in Tally's arms, she knew she wanted him in her life. She wanted to be held this way at the end of every day. She wanted to be wanted by him. She didn't need someone to take care of her, but she was lonely and he made her feel so good, so safe. The thought scared her and reminded her of her failures in the marriage depart-ment, but with Tally it seemed so different—could it work?

She left Tally's house around 8 p.m. and by the time she got home the doubts had returned. How could she even consider getting married again? She'd screwed it up twice already! But it all came back to the way she felt when she was with Tally, like the something she felt she'd been missing all her life was suddenly made whole. But how would they make it work? She hated the complexity of it and wished that she was a normal person with a normal life that could meet a guy like Tally and fall in love without questioning her own motives, or what the future would hold. But she wasn't a normal person and she knew too well that love was never enough in and of itself. Love didn't make everything better and it didn't conquer all.

Even as a little girl, Janet's life had been crazy and complicated. Her mother, Colleen, lived life in a frenzied state, dragging her daughter through the frazzle with her. By the time Janet was eight years old, Colleen had already been married and divorced, lived with two different men and was engaged again. At that time, Janet had been responsible for most of the housework and cooking, as well as taking care of her little sister Theresa who was two. She hated every minute of it.

By some kind of miracle, the man her mother married, Travis, was a wonderful guy. Colleen had ended up in Salt Lake City by accident when Janet was seven, through one of the men she lived with, and she wasn't interested in the Mormon church. Travis, however, was a member and although he was inactive in the beginning, shortly after the marriage they began attending church as a family. Janet had loved church, and Travis was able to baptize her just before her ninth birthday. By then Colleen was no longer interested in religion, especially one that required its members to give up things like vodka tonics and Bloody Mary's. Shortly thereafter, Travis fell back into inactivity, but Janet remained faithful.

Besides the spiritual peace she drew from church, it also gave her the opportunity to gain perspective on what other families were like. The church was the first place that ever told her she was in control of her own life; that she could make her own future. It was through church that she realized other moms didn't sleep till noon, yell all the time, cry themselves to sleep more often than not, and require their young daughters to run the household. Janet's surprise at this discovery, however, slowly turned to bitterness. It wasn't fair that she'd been denied a childhood most kids took for granted, and she determined then and there that she would make sure her life was different from her mom's. Her future would not consist of dishes and diapers—she had little doubt that the continual aggravation of such things were what had driven Colleen to drink in the first place. She hated doing her mother's work for her, but she had no choice—when she refused, the punishment often kept her home from school until the bruises healed. But each beating made her that much more determined. She would likely have children. She'd accepted that and had looked forward to it so long as certain conditions could be met; she would have a career of her own, a housekeeper and with any luck, a nanny too. There was no way she would choose to spend her adulthood doing something she despised so much as a child. She felt robbed, but she felt confident that she could make up for it.

After the first year or so of their marriage, Travis transitioned into more of a caretaker to Colleen than a husband. Janet felt sorry for him; she knew how miserable it was to have to cater to her mother.

Eventually she came to believe that the only reason he'd stayed was for Janet and her little sister, Theresa. He even adopted both girls and Janet took his last name, Stewart, as her own. Every time Janet looked into his eyes she saw the sacrifices. Travis encouraged her to work hard in school and stay active in church, even though he didn't go himself. She set lofty goals and worked hard, every day, to make sure that she accomplished every one of them, but through it all, she was haunted by the fear that if she ever lost sight of those goals she would someday turn out like her mom.

When Janet was fifteen, Travis, the only person who seemed to understand her, was killed in a work-related accident at the construction site where he worked as an electrician. Janet was devastated. Travis had been the only safe person for her to talk to; in fact she had considered him her best friend for a long time since she'd never been very good at making friends her same age. His death reminded her that she had to take care of herself; there was no one there to do it for her anymore.

Beyond Janet's heartbreak, Travis's death had thrown her mother into a deep depression which took her drinking to a whole new level, and Janet was forced back into the roles of housekeeper and nurse. Seemingly out of nowhere, Colleen's drinking turned to drug use during Janet's junior year of high school, and Janet's determination to get away from everything became that much more important. Because of how hard she worked in school, Janet received a scholarship to Berkley and in the June following her high school graduation, she bought two bus tickets with money she stole from her mother's account. On the way to California, she dropped 12-year-old Theresa off at their Aunt Elva's house in Oregon, the only family they'd ever had. Colleen remained in Provo, living off of Travis's insurance money; Janet never looked back.

Now, at 35, Janet had attained nearly every goal she'd set for herself. She received her bachelor degree in fashion merchandising and climbed the corporate ladder at a steady pace. She had the lifestyle she'd dreamed of, and a commanding presence that caused people to take notice. She did not brag of her rags-to-riches story; she ignored her past and only focused on what to do next. A housekeeper cleaned three times a week and the nanny would be there in eight days. And yet here she was, trying to decide what to do about Tally and wondering why he was such a big presence in her life. She didn't want to marry again, she'd talked herself out of that option a long time ago; but she wanted Tally in an inexplicable way. In fact . . . she paused as a realization came to her, he reminded her of Travis; he made her feel safe, and loved, and needed. Feeling that way somehow silenced all the doubts, at least for the moment.

The intensity of her thoughts and memories brought on a throbbing headache and she went to the medicine cabinet for some Tylenol. She saw the bottle of Percocet and stared at it for several seconds. The root canal she'd had done several months ago had kept bothering her and the dentist seemed more than happy to continue filling the prescription so long as she had pain, but she'd been trying not to take them. With the increased need for the Xanax she had decided to taper off on the Percocets, but her head really hurt. For an instant she imagined flushing them down the toilet in order to remove the temptation completely, but she couldn't do that. She took a Tylenol and shut the cabinet. As she swallowed the pill she tried to remember when she'd last had trouble from the tooth; she couldn't remember. As she filled up the tub for a warm bath she waited for the Tylenol to kick in, but her eyes were continually drawn to the medicine cabinet. A Percocet would get rid of the headache, she told herself, but then she shook her head and stared at the water pouring out of the faucet. She needed to cut back, on everything, but her eyes went back to the cabinet. What if the headache didn't go away? What if it brought on a panic attack? It had happened that way before. In her mind she imagined just how bad the headache could get if she didn't take care of it. It could keep her up for hours, and she hadn't been sleeping well this week. Another night tossing and turning would make her incapable of dealing with Josh. It being Sunday tomorrow, she would need all the patience she could get. Finally, she gave in, convinced that she needed a good night's sleep.

After taking the Percocet she took a Xanax as well, just to make sure she could fall asleep. Relieved by the coming effects of her medications, she lowered herself into the warm bath water. While she soaked, she allowed herself to reflect on the day, the time spent with Tally, but especially that kiss. It was the kind of kiss that made her toes curl and she knew she'd kiss him again as soon as she got the chance. After fifteen minutes the bath seemed to have turned into her own little cocoon. She was warm and completely relaxed, living that kiss over and over as she floated through the calm and peaceful memory of Tally's arms around her. She'd sleep well tonight.

The next weekend gave her plenty of opportunity to enjoy Tally's company again. Janet arrived at Tally's house around noon, and was surprised to find him in the barn, saddling Ginger, the golden mare. The other horse, Tally's stallion Branson, was already saddled.

"Hey," she said with a heavy question in her voice as she entered the barn. Josh was already off in the field jumping off of the fresh cut bales of hay. When they'd planned the date, he hadn't mentioned any specific activity and she was hesitant to tell him that horseback riding was not her first choice—or second or third for that matter.

He turned to look at her. "Hello there," Tally said as he bent down to fasten a strap under the horse's belly. As soon as he finished, he walked over and kissed her softly on the lips. When he pulled back she smiled, enjoying the tingle and then quickly pulled him back for another one. This one was longer, deeper, until he finally pulled away, a smile still on his lips. "I thought we could go for a little ride," he said as he moved away with a wink that told her that he shared her desire but was trying to be a good boy.

Janet decided to follow his lead, this time, looked back at the horse and took a deep breath. "I've never ridden a horse," she admitted.

Tally was already back to work getting the horse ready to go. "I used to give lessons in high school; I'm a pretty good teacher, if I do say so myself."

"What about Josh?"

"If you're comfortable with it," Tally began, "I talked to my neighbor, my home teacher. He said they'd be happy to watch Josh for a couple hours. Or, he can ride with me."

Janet took a breath; he'd obviously thought this all out. She didn't think she'd be able to talk her way out of the excursion. So, she might as well make the best of it. Besides, maybe it would give her another chance to have him alone. She felt like a teenager the way she ached to be close to him, but it was exciting to want something so badly and so she refused to dwell on it. She smiled widely and nodded. "I think I'll need your undivided attention."

Tally smiled too and nodded. "Nothing against Josh, but I was hoping you'd say that."

For the next three hours Tally gently instructed her on the basic handling of the horse. She listened intently and committed each instruction to memory. This might not have been her first choice on how to spend her day, but she intended to conquer the activity. They spent the first hour walking circles in the field, then she trotted behind him as he led her through the back gate of his property, across the highway and up through the cemetery on the east side of the road. They followed a narrow dirt trail and after a while Janet found the whole experience quite relaxing. Once she knew how to guide the horse, she pulled up alongside of Tally.

"This is nice," she commented, looking around at the rocky slopes of Willard Peak as they slowly walked along the base of the mountain. If she looked to her left she could see the sunlight reflecting off of Willard Bay, a reservoir located at the north end of the Great Salt Lake. It was like living in a painting.

"I love it up here," he said, moving up and down easily as the horses moved forward. "It's almost like a spiritual experience for me."

Janet smiled and looked around. She was enjoying herself, but she knew she didn't enjoy it quite the same way he did. For one thing it was incredibly hot, her clothes were drenched with sweat, and if not for the felt cowboy hat Tally had given her, she knew she'd have passed out from heat stroke hours ago. He didn't seem too affected by the heat though, and it spurred her competitive side. She would not give in to sheer physical discomfort. "Where are we headed?" she asked a few yards later.

Tally smiled. "To my favorite place."

"And where's that?"

"A little cove another mile or so up this trail. I found it last spring and I love it."

"Then I'm sure I will too," she said with a smile.

She figured they rode for nearly another hour, veering off the main road at some point to head into a thicket of trees that seemed to end at the side of the mountain. To her surprise the path they were on twisted to the left and brought them around the side of the mountain and into a beautiful, if not small, valley. Janet just looked around in awe. She'd never been much of a nature lover, but she could get used to this. Tally continued along the trail for nearly a quarter of a mile, taking so many other trails and paths she wondered how he had ever found this in the first place. Finally they turned one last corner and Janet's breath caught in her throat.

Before them stretched an area of perhaps a full acre. A small stream ran through the middle and on each side was soft green grass. If she didn't know better she'd have thought it was mowed once a week. Tally moved forward, got down from his horse and let Branson wander to the thicker grass before coming to help her down.

"It's gorgeous," she breathed as he placed her on the ground, keeping his hands on her waist.

"I'm glad you think so," he said. Within a few minutes he'd laid a blanket on the ground and opened one of Branson's saddlebags to reveal a picnic lunch.

"You don't miss a thing, do you," Janet laughed as she sat cross-legged on the blanket.

"Not when it comes to you," he answered.

Lunch was quiet and then Tally laid back on the blanket, staring up at the aspens that shaded the little glen as they waved in the breeze. Janet laid down too, but with her head on his stomach and when he began running his fingers through her hair she knew that life just didn't get much better than this. For nearly half an hour they laid that way, listening to the horses, the birds, the gurgle of the creek, and then they packed up and headed back down the trail, both sad to have broken the moment together but both eagerly anticipating the future they were each mapping out in their minds.

"When can I see you again?" she asked late that evening after putting Josh in his car seat and sharing a long drawn-out kiss with her riding instructor.

"I'm leaving Monday for a job that will take most of this week," Tally said regretfully. "And then I'm shooting a wedding in St. George on Friday and Saturday."

Janet raised her eyebrows. "Really?"

"Yeah, apparently those neighbors I took those pictures for a few weeks ago have a niece that's getting married. They showed her folks the shots I took and they asked if I'd be willing to go down."

"Wow," Janet said with a smile. "That's quite a compliment."

"They probably can't afford a real photographer, but I'm pretty excited—Chris and Lacey are going to come down with their kids, we're making a weekend out of it . . . you don't want to come with me, do you?"

Janet frowned. "I wish I could," she said as she tucked a lock of hair behind her ear. "I've got some appointments on Saturday; besides, this will be Kelly's first week."

"The nanny?" Tally asked for clarification.

"Yep, the nanny," Janet confirmed. "But the next weekend should work."

"Maybe I'll come to you this time," Tally said as he reached up and tapped her nose. "You've been a good sport about coming all the way up here."

She didn't mind at all. Every day she spent here felt like a week-long vacation, although she could already feel the beginnings of very sore muscles in her legs. She'd be miserable in the morning. "Two weeks then?" she asked with a slight tilt to her head and wondering how she would ever wait that long.

"It's a date," he said and she smiled as he leaned in to kiss her goodnight—again.

CHAPTER FIVE

July 24th

Three-and-a-half weeks after leaving Willard for the second time, Janet entered her condo—actually a house in the condo complex. She often called it a condo just because the complex did all her yard maintenance, but she had nearly a quarter-acre lot and plenty of privacy so it wasn't like an actual condo at all. It was after eight p.m. and on the counter was a note from Kelly—she had taken Josh to the park. Janet smiled; Kelly had been a Godsend and Janet was convinced that getting a nanny was the best decision she'd ever made. Each Sunday they mapped out a schedule for Kelly the following week. Anything over 60 hours a week, Janet had to pay extra for, but she didn't mind and Kelly didn't either. Kelly was great with Josh. She had family in Salt Lake and some friends in Provo so she didn't stay home much when she was 'off the clock.'

In the kitchen, Janet put the teapot on the stove and got everything ready to make a cup of herbal tea while she waited for Josh and Kelly to return. She was exhausted and wondered what time Tally would be home. She wasn't sure she'd be able to stay up too late tonight, but she longed to talk to him. She'd been going out of town so much, and had so much work to do when she was in town, that they hadn't followed through on the date they set. Today was the twenty-fourth of July, a vacation day for Utah, since it was the anniversary of their statehood being awarded in 1847. Tally had invited her to his brother's house in Bountiful for a barbeque, but she had to call him that afternoon and bow out of it, much to her disappointment. She'd been out of town most of last week and was now completely immersed in catching up with the final details of the fall fashions that were already marching their way into every Dillard's store in the state. Back-to-school shopping was just revving up and, as always, there were a hundred things that should have been done months ago just now appearing on her desk. During weeks like this she wished she were in charge of housewares, or jewelry; something that didn't change every season. But, as it was, she had work to do, and she was willing to miss a few barbecues if it increased her chances of getting the promotion.

As she poured the hot water over the herbal tea bag in her favorite mug, the front door opened and Kelly and Josh came in. Janet smiled and Kelly said she was meeting friends to go see the fireworks. Janet took over and Kelly left a little while later. After Josh went to bed Janet sat down at the computer to finish a report. It was nearly 11 o'clock when she heard Kelly come in. Expecting Kelly to be heading for her room for the night she was surprised when Kelly knocked on the frame of the study door. Janet looked up expectantly and was instantly concerned with the look on Kelly's face. She looked like she'd been crying. "What's the matter?" Janet asked.

Kelly was having a hard time controlling her emotion and held her cell phone in both hands like a bouquet of flowers. "I just got off the phone with my boyfriend," she said as the tears started to fall. When she spoke again her voice was a high-pitched squeak. "He wants to break up with me." She immediately started sobbing.

Kelly had met her boyfriend during her last nanny job in California and they talked on the phone every day. From Kelly's description, he sounded like a loser, a part-time student who had no job and lived with his parents even though he was nearly 24 years old. But Kelly was nuts about him and Janet knew she was having a hard time with the separation.

"Oh, I'm sorry," Janet said, standing and putting a hand on Kelly's shoulder. Kelly fell onto Janet's shoulder and just cried louder. Janet patted her back awkwardly; she really wasn't a cry-on-my-shoulder type. After what seemed like forever Kelly finally pulled back.

"I have to go back to California; he said we're just too far apart. If I want to keep him, I have to go back."

Whoa!! That was not what Janet wanted to hear. "Kelly," she said calmly, hoping the younger girl would follow her lead and get some control of herself. "We have a six-month contract and I'm sure that things will work out, you just need to—"

"It won't work out unless I go back," Kelly nearly squealed. "And I won't even make you pay me for last week, just please don't make me stay, Janet. He's the best thing that's ever happened to me; I can't let him go, I just can't."

Janet looked at her and let out a breath; she sincerely doubted that he was the best thing that had happened to her and was irritated by Kelly's fanciful thoughts. Ssome girls were so out of touch with reality. "Kelly, have you considered that it's extremely unfair of him to even ask you to do this? Maybe it means you two shouldn't be together at all."

Kelly just stared at her, horrified by the very thought and then her chin started quivering. "He loves me," she choked. "He loves me so much." She broke into sobs again, but she didn't fall on Janet this time, she just covered her face and bawled. Janet couldn't help rolling her eyes.

"The agency guaranteed your contract, Kelly. You made a commitment to them and to me," Janet said as calmly as possible. "You can't just walk away from it."

Kelly didn't even respond. She just kept crying as she turned and ran for her room, leaving Janet to stare after her. Janet stood there for nearly a minute and then let out a frustrated breath as she weighed her options. She could make Kelly stay; they did have a contract, but she'd have to put up with her pouting and if Kelly was determined to go, she'd find a way. Still, the whole thing was very silly to Janet and she shook her head as she walked to Kelly's door. When there was no response to her knock, Janet let herself in. Kelly already had her suitcase on the bed, still blubbering while she scurried back and forth gathering her things. Watching her, Janet knew there really wasn't much of a choice. She clenched her jaw and didn't bother keeping the irritation out of her voice. "Can you at least stay until the weekend, give me some time to make new arrangements?"

Kelly turned and nodded furiously. She picked up her cell phone and immediately started dialing a number. "I'll tell him right now," she said with a wide smile on her mascara-smeared and tear-streaked face—too bad the boyfriend couldn't see her now. Janet turned and left the room, disgusted with the whole thing. She sat down at the computer again and dropped her head in her hands. *Now what?* she thought. Things had been going so well.

As soon as she finished feeling sorry for herself, she called Tally. It was late and she knew he was asleep, but she needed to talk to someone and she knew he wouldn't mind. His voice betrayed that he had in fact been sleeping, but he said he'd been watching TV. They talked it over for nearly fifteen minutes and in the end he agreed that she ought to call the agency in the morning and see what they could do to fix the situation. Tally was sympathetic and his encouragement lifted her spirits, as usual. She was so grateful to have him as a sounding board. He was such a good listener.

First thing in the morning Janet called the agency and they agreed to list the ad again, at their expense, and to pay back a portion of Kelly's wages. Janet informed Cathy that they were going to be interviewing nannies again and Cathy said she would take care of everything. Saturday morning Janet called a cab to take Kelly to the airport. She drove away without waving and Janet clenched her jaw again. She hated silly-headed girls and she hated being the only care-taker at home again. She hoped Kelly's boyfriend dumped her anyway; it would serve her right.

That weekend Janet conducted almost a dozen interviews, but she didn't find a single applicant that interested her. She wasn't sure that her jaded perspective wasn't to blame for her inability to find a new nanny, but she didn't rule it out. The three weeks Kelly had been there had been heavenly, but she didn't want another 'temporary' nanny. Josh was back in daycare and Kim and Allen had agreed to watch him for the overnight trips. Cathy continued to set up phone interviews and Janet prayed she'd find someone soon—someone she could trust.

Tally was going to Oklahoma next week, to pick up Barrington, his new colt she'd helped him get. He invited her to go but they both knew it was impossible. The regional manager position was officially available and she was counting the days before getting the official word that all her hard work had paid off. But she wished he wasn't going—

she'd miss him.

A week after Kelly left, the day Tally was leaving town, Janet was at work trying to concentrate, but finding it impossible not to think about what the next week would be like. She would miss getting his e-mail messages during the day and hearing the phone ring each night—although she held out hope that he would find a way to make the calls and send the messages anyway. They had managed to meet for lunch on Monday, and it had boosted her spirits, but she'd found herself thinking of him more and more every day. He would only be gone a week, she kept telling herself, but it felt much longer. When Cathy gave a short knock on her door and entered before being invited, Janet looked up. Surprised at the lack of protocol, she was further surprised by the look on Cathy's face and thoughts of Tally finally left her mind.

"You won't believe what I just heard," Cathy said as she closed the door behind her.

Janet gave her full attention to her secretary. "What?"

"They're promoting Sheryl to the management position."

Janet froze for several seconds—did she hear that right? She repeated the words in her mind and then felt a fire start in her chest. "Where did you hear that?" she asked, her tone was heavy with suspicion. If this was just an office rumor she would let Cathy have it—this was not a subject to trifle with.

"Her secretary just told me," Cathy said quickly, her own anger easy to read and further convincing Janet that this was more than a rumor. Cathy would have been promoted too, her heart was as involved as Janet's. Cathy continued, "Sheryl had a dinner meeting with Jay and Paul last night, the entire corporate division ended up being there too, they offered her the position and asked for her acceptance in writing today. Her secretary typed it up first thing this morning."

Janet looked down at her desk, completely stunned as Cathy's words sunk in. That position was hers, they'd all been telling her she was shoo-in for months. The fire in her chest was now a raging inferno and she wasn't able to even speak to Cathy as she stormed out of her office. In the next instant she burst into Jay's office without knocking and stared him down until he finished his conversation on the phone and hung up. She could tell he knew exactly why she was here.

"I was just about to ask you to come down," he said with a stiff smile.

You coward! she thought as she continued to stare. Her hands were balled into tight fists as she tried to force herself to speak calmly. "I was told that position was mine," she spat out—apparently calmness was too grand an expectation.

"That's not exactly true," he said. "You knew it was between you and Sheryl the whole time."

"And you told me when I accepted the purchaser position and all the garbage that went with it that it was only a step toward a management position."

"But not necessarily this management position."

"That is such crap," she nearly screamed, spreading her arms wide. "You expressly mentioned this one."

"As a possibility," he countered with equal fierceness as he stood. "But when it came right down to it, Sheryl has the better qualifications for this position at this time."

"What does that mean?" Janet said between clenched teeth. Her eyes were wide and it was all she could do not to swear and spit at the man across the room. She couldn't ever remember being this angry in her life. "I'm the one living out of a suitcase half the time, placing orders, training store managers; she's not even involved in purchasing. How could she possibly have better qualifications?"

Jay folded his arms. "She just does."

Janet took a deep breath, gave him an evil look and stormed back to her office. She sat down heavily at her desk and stared straight ahead. How could this have happened? She'd done everything they asked her to do, traveled once a week for almost four months and put her future on hold for this position, and then they gave it to Sheryl! She was over Human Resources for heaven's sake and she laughed like a monkey! How could they give this job to her? It was impossible, it couldn't be happening. Janet dropped her head on her desk and tried to hold back the tears.

She'd wasted so much time, it made her sick to think of all the things she'd pushed aside for this job—and they'd given it to someone else.

The room felt like it was spinning and she tried to center herself, but to no avail—there was no calming these feelings inside. She quickly popped one, and then another Xanax and continued to review what had just happened as her physical panic began to drain away. But she still couldn't accept it. She felt betrayed and abandoned—utterly and completely drained. How could they do this to her? Everything she'd done was for nothing. How was she supposed to just accept that and move on?

When she passed Cathy ten minutes later, Cathy looked at her in surprise.

"I'm going home and I'm taking a week off," Janet said as she dropped a stack of papers on Cathy's desk. "Tell Jay I'll be back next Wednesday."

"But . . . uh . . . but . . . ," Cathy couldn't even talk, she was so surprised. Janet acted as if she didn't notice.

"Move all my appointments to next week and forward this after-noon's conference call to my cell phone." She was always behind anyway, so it wouldn't make that much of a difference and she just didn't care right now. She raised a hand to her head. It felt like it had been used as a trampoline.

"Are . . . are you okay?" Cathy asked with concern, watching Janet closely.

"No," Janet said evenly as she began sifting through the stack of papers, splitting it into the appropriate piles. "I've got another headache. But here are the things I need you to compile into folders for next week's training session, these are the fax reminders I've sent out for the fall orders and these are the forms Jay needed this after-noon." As she spoke she indicated each pile in turn, glaring hotly at the papers intended for Jay. She felt like burning them and wished she dared. Then she turned and headed for the elevator.

"Janet," Cathy called after her.

Janet turned toward her and raised her hand to try to catch the item sailing towards her. It hit her shoulder but she bent down and picked it up, noticing that her hands were shaking—she convinced herself it was due to her fury, not the pills she'd taken a few minutes before.

"Sorry," Cathy apologized before quickly adding, "They'll help with the headache." Janet looked at the bottle of pills in her hand. It had no label, but had the letter 'O' written in marker across the lid. Since the first prescription Cathy had managed to find her, and the pangs of conscience they had elicited, Janet had been able to justify the situation completely. She found a new doctor, but in order not to arouse his suspicions, supplemented his prescriptions with those Cathy got from her boyfriend. They didn't discuss it, not ever; Janet would just ask Cathy to pick her up some Xanax and give her a blank check. Thirty pills cost $300 and she didn't know how or where Cathy got them but she didn't care. She looked up and nodded her thanks as she put the pills in her purse. "I'll pay you for them next week," she said without bothering to ask what the pills were. She didn't care so long as they got rid of the headache. Cathy nodded.

Janet got into her car but she just sat there for several minutes, overwhelmed by what had happened. The search for a new nanny had come to nothing, the pills were becoming more and more important and she'd lost the dream that had kept her going for so long. It had been a very long time since she'd felt this small, this vulnerable, and she hated it. She didn't know how to handle disappointment; she wasn't used to not getting what she wanted. She felt betrayed by everything, by everyone and felt desperate for something good, something joyful. Only one person came to mind when she tried to think of what she had to smile about, and that was Tally. Tally cared. She longed for him in a new way, an almost frightening need for him. Surely his goodness could make the rest of the garbage pressing in on her seem lighter. Tally, she needed Tally.

Tally finished testing the lights on the horse trailer and only when he was sure everything was in order did he go inside to get his bag. Jason had continued to try and back out of selling Thunder's colt but Tally continued to stand his ground. Jason had promised and Tally couldn't wait to get the prized horse in his own pasture. After weeks of protest, Jason realized he had no choice but to comply, and now Tally was driving to Oklahoma and bringing Barrington to Willard.

When he was inside, the phone rang, he looked at the caller ID and lifted his eyebrows. "What are you doing at home?" he said when he picked up the phone. The silence he encountered on the other end of the line surprised him.

"They gave the position to Sheryl."

Tally's heart sank and he put his suitcase and planner back down. "I'm so sorry," he said with sympathy as he leaned back against the counter. "When?"

"Last night." She went on to tell him what had happened with the promotion.

"That's awful," Tally further commiserated when she finished.

"Are you still going to Oklahoma today?" she asked a moment later.

"I was just walking out the door."

"Do you still want some company?"

Tally paused and clutched the phone tighter. He stood up straight. "Are you serious?"

"I need to get away," she continued. "And I really want to see you."

"I'm going to be gone for a week," he reminded her.

"I know."

"Can you miss that much work?"

"No."

They both remained silent but she didn't add any other conditions. The idea of being alone with Janet for that long was almost frightening knowing the difficulty they had in keeping their hands to themselves, but he absolutely couldn't resist the opportunity. Finally, Tally spoke, "I'd love some company."

"Good," Janet said, her tone lighter. "I'll pick Josh up and pack us some bags, do you mind picking us up on your way through Salt Lake?"

"Not at all," Tally said with a laugh. "I'll see you in an hour."

Tally hung up the phone and punched both hands into the air. Not only was he going to see Janet, he was going to have her with him for a week! His whole body began to tingle and he hurried to the door. Their relationship had become more and more important to him every day, but his frustrations had increased due to the fact that they saw each other next to never. Now he had the whole week to bask in her presence! He felt badly that she hadn't gotten the position, but he had to admit it was a relief. Maybe now that she wasn't working so hard to prove herself, he'd have a chance to prove himself to her. And maybe he could convince her that some successes were better than others.

"Where are we?" Janet said with a yawn as she woke up from a nap the next afternoon. Josh was singing from the back seat and she turned in her seat to smile at him and tickle his toes, making him squeal with delight. Thank goodness he'd always been good in the car; in fact, he was often better in the car than he was out of it. She'd actually considered leaving him with Kim and Allen, not wanting to worry about him this week, but she was glad she'd decided to bring him along. Tally was entranced by her son and he was more than happy to help her with him. She'd never shared parenthood like this and it had given her several more reasons to love Tally.

"We've got about an hour until we pass through Topeka, Kansas. That was one heck of a nap," Tally commented, glancing at her briefly as she turned back around in her seat.

"I'm sorry," she said with sincerity. "This stuff Cathy gave me for my headaches sure does the trick, but it totally knocks me out—it'll take some getting used to." It was especially potent when she took it with a Xanax, but she didn't say that out loud. She hoped her head would clear though, she worried about saying something stupid when she was this muddled. Luckily she knew that Tally, of all people, understood. She'd seen him take something last night when his knee hurt and it made her feel even more comfortable around him. It was nice to know he wouldn't think she was some kind of freak if she told him about the meds she took, and there was the added plus that if she ever ran out of anything, he likely had something on hand.

"What's it called?" Tally asked.

"O–something," she said with a shrug of her shoulders. "It's exactly what I needed." She stretched her long arms above her head until they hit the roof of the truck, and then stretched them to the side, rubbing the back of Tally's neck for a moment before pulling her hand away. She loved how comfortable she was with him.

"Well," Tally said as he put on his right turn signal, checked his mirrors and changed lanes to pass a car. "We can either stop around eight at another hotel tonight, or drive on to my folk's house—but we won't get there until late. Which sounds better to you?"

"It's up to you," she said, repositioning herself as she looked at him. "How's your knee?"

"It's holding up," he said with a smile. "As long as we keep stopping every few hours so I can walk around, I'll be fine. But we've been driving all day long and if we need to stop for the night, we can. The trip home will be slower since we'll be pulling the trailer and Barrington won't be able to ride for so long at one time; but I wanted to get this first part over as quickly as possible."

"So do you want to go on to your folk's house then?"

He cast a look in her direction and shook his head. "Not really," he admitted.

She smiled and shook her head. "You're incorrigible."

"Why? Because I like the idea of snuggling with you in a motel room better than sleeping on the couch at my parent's house?"

Janet's cheeks colored. Last night they'd gotten side by side rooms at a Holiday Inn somewhere in Colorado. Janet had put Josh to bed while Tally put a heating pad on his knee. It wasn't until she realized that their separate rooms shared a common door that she realized how potentially inappropriate this arrangement was. But despite her internal warnings, she'd opened the door on her side and knocked. A few moments later Tally had unlocked his and they had stood there staring at one another. They decided to order a pay-per-view movie and watch it together, but after about ten minutes of not paying any attention to the movie due to the ardent attention they were paying one another Tally insisted on ground rules. They decided not to kiss anymore and hard as it was they were able to be true to their word, but they fell asleep in each other's arms. Janet had awoken first and just stared at him, amazed that after all that had happened the day before she could feel this happy. It was like Tally had blotted out everything else.

Tally had been the perfect balm for the events of the last week and she could truly say that she really didn't care about losing the position when she was sitting next to him. In fact she wondered if perhaps she was working so hard at a goal unworthy of her time and attention. She was beginning to wonder where things would be between Tally and herself if she had put even 10 percent of her energy into him instead. She felt completely at ease, as if she belonged with him.

"I think we better drive on to your parents'," she said, although her tone betrayed that she too would rather replay last night. Just thinking of how nice it had been made her all warm inside. But her reaction was all the more reason to err on the side of caution. "We'll be safer that way."

"You're probably right," Tally admitted just as Josh began to chant 'gwink, gwink, gwink.' They stopped for a 'gwink' at the next gas station and Tally called his parents from his cell phone. Janet changed Josh's diaper in the truck rather than risk going into the bathrooms that were far from clean. Tally had already told his parents that Josh and Janet were with him and they were even more excited about his visit because of it.

It was almost eleven o'clock when they pulled up to the two-story Victorian house. It was gray with green shutters and a porch swing. Janet thought it was a little old fashioned and small, but it was only for a few days. Tally's parents were waiting for them. Tally carried a sleeping Josh up the sidewalk while Janet followed him with the portable crib.

Tally's mother, Julie, was barely five feet tall with a stocky build and shoulder length chemically blonde hair. She was all smiles as she held the door open and let them in. Tally's dad was there too, a tall thin man with a gray fringe of hair and a full beard. Tally explained they needed to get Josh to bed and Janet said a quick hello as she followed him to the guest room, where she and Josh would sleep.

Tally watched her set up the crib and she tried not to notice his intense stare while at the same time she rejoiced in it and found herself moving slower, liking his eyes on her. "You are so beautiful," he whispered.

Janet turned to look at him, flipping her long hair over one shoulder as she did so. Josh was snuggled into his chest, his black curls barely brushing Tally's cheek. Janet's heart melted and she felt tears come to her eyes. For a moment they stood there, absorbing the moment, then she finished putting the crib together and helped Tally get Josh situated. When they both straightened up from covering him Tally reached an arm around her waist and pulled her to him. She pressed against him more than she should have, but she couldn't seem to help it.

"Janet," he whispered, kissing her lightly on the mouth.

"Hmmmm," she said as she snuggled in closer; hungry for more.

"I think I've fallen in love with you."

She went still and then she looked up at him; they'd never said those words to one another before. She reached up and touched his cheek, "I've been thinking the same thing."

They stared at each other in the dark for several minutes as they listened to Josh's breathing. Then she leaned into him and kissed him. He pulled her close and she responded immediately. Visions of what could lie ahead of them began dancing in her mind. He was a great kisser, tender and intense all at once. She wished they could stay this way forever, but finally he pulled back and touched her cheek softly. "My parents might explode if we wait too much longer."

Janet smiled and nodded as she turned to get one more moonlit glimpse of Josh. "Ah, in-laws," she mused, "you gotta love em." She turned toward the door, still holding his hand when he tugged her to stop. She turned and looked at him.

"In-laws?" he repeated, his eyebrows raised and a half-smile on his lips.

Janet paused and her cheeks colored. *Did I say that?* she wondered.

Tally took a step closer to her, "Maybe we should talk later." Janet nodded before kissing him once more and turning toward the door. Her heart was fluttering and she couldn't help but smile in anticipation.

"Later" ended up being after midnight. They had talked with Tally's parents for almost an hour over a plate of cookies and milk. He tried to read his parent's impressions of Janet, but found it hard to tell. She wasn't like most women, nothing like Chris's wife Lacey, and he was nervous about how they would accept those differences. They were, of course, very nice and cordial, but Janet seemed uncomfortable in their presence; he hoped his parents wouldn't misinterpret her nervousness. Finally, they all pleaded their fatigue and his parents went to bed, after his mother brought him pillows and blankets in order to make up the couch. Janet kissed him goodnight and headed off to the guest room while his parents looked on. As Tally tucked in the blankets he couldn't help but imagine Janet upstairs in that big double bed all alone; it was almost more than he could take.

About fifteen minutes after the house had gone silent Tally heard a soft footfall on the stairs and he smiled. A moment later he felt her approaching the couch in the darkness. He sat up, reached out for her and pulled her onto his lap. The kiss they shared was electrifying and when they stopped themselves Tally whispered, "I think we're steaming up the windows."

Janet laughed quietly and, still sitting on his lap with her arms around his neck, leaned forward so their foreheads touched. "So . . ." she said quietly, allowing her voice to trail off.

"So . . ." Tally repeated. They were silent for several seconds before he continued. "What's next for us?"

Janet let out a breath. "I think I'm ready to make some changes in my life."

"What kind of changes?" he prodded, afraid to say it first.

For several seconds Janet was quiet, and when she spoke her tone was reflective. "After Josh was born I decided never to marry again; it seemed obvious that it was an institution not meant for a woman like myself. But my thoughts have been changing. I'm tired of being alone, Tally; I want Josh to know what a family is really like."

"So what are you saying?" Tally asked, running his hand across her back.

"What would you think about getting married?"

She'd said the M-word! Out loud! He could hardly believe it. Tally smiled broadly and pulled back so that he could see her face. "If you're the bride, I'd have to admit I've entertained the idea." From their first meeting something had passed between them that made this totally reasonable. And then their first kiss, and all the others that had followed, had threatened to consume him. Perhaps it had been less than two months, but somehow it felt like he'd known her forever.

"It will be complicated," she continued, her voice still barely a whisper. "But I could talk to Jay when I get back; assuming I haven't been fired. I think I can eventually get a management position at the Ogden or Logan store, they're both only about twenty minutes from Willard, right?"

"Yeah," Tally said with excitement, glad she was willing to move. "But are you sure you can give up what you've worked so hard for with the regional office?"

"It was a huge blow not to get that position; I had no doubt I would get it. Now that I didn't, I feel differently. The promotion was the goal I was working toward, it made everything doable, but now it's gone. Not having that aspiration has weakened my motivation to center my life on this job, especially when they don't fulfill their commitments to me. I feel like I'm ready to move on."

Tally felt like bursting into song. "How long would it take to get the management position?"

"I don't know," she said, the frustration showing in her voice. "But I don't think it would take longer than a year."

"That sounds like forever."

Janet lifted her head and slid off of his lap, sitting beside him on the couch now. "Maybe it wouldn't take that long."

"I could move to Salt Lake," Tally said, trying to sound excited about the idea.

Janet was shaking her head before he finished. "That doesn't make sense," she said. "Living in that house is half the reason I want to marry you," she elbowed him playfully in the ribs. "And you've got the horses and the land. It would be much easier for me to go up there and I love the area—I think moving out of the city would make the change that much better, that much different. And I think you'd go crazy living in my little house."

He feared she was right but he couldn't imagine waiting a whole year. They were both silent, but an idea was forming in his mind. "What if we got married now," he finally said, his heart rate increasing at the mere possibility. "But we just resigned ourselves to living apart until the position came through? I know it would be hard, but the Church doesn't recommend long engagements you know."

She turned to look at him but she said nothing and he wished he could read her thoughts. He continued, "You could come up on the weekends and slowly start moving your stuff up to Willard—we could even put your place up for sale. Then when the store position came available, most of the work would be done."

"Wow," she finally whispered, laying her head against his shoulder. "I…I don't know what to say—you're willing to do that?"

"Are you kidding?" he said, trying hard to keep his voice down. She lifted her head and looked at him again. "I've spent the last four years of my life wondering what my future was going to be. In the last five minutes I feel like I'm being offered something I dared not dream of. I can make a few sacrifices." He could see her nod in the darkness.

"I could start going to your ward, get to know the area; in fact it might be good to have a transitioning period to get used to living together."

Tally's thoughts were moving a mile a minute. "And . . . what if Josh came up to Willard now? It would get him out of day care and you wouldn't have to keep looking for a nanny. I'd love to have him with me."

Janet's mouth opened. "Really?" she breathed. Tally nodded and saw her smile.

"He would love that," she whispered. "I'd sure miss him," she added, then she paused again. "But if I didn't have him with me during the week I could get a lot more done so that I wouldn't have any work to bring home on the weekends." Her voice got a little louder and she spoke faster; Tally liked the excitement in her tone. "When you're out of town I could keep him in day care and I bet Allen and Kim would still be willing to watch him when our road trips overlap. But . . . are you sure you want a toddler at your hip all day every day? It gets draining."

"If we go through with this I'm going to be the dad, right?" Tally said, feeling a rush of warmth at the thought. "I'd love it."

"Oh, my gosh," Janet said as if she suddenly realized something she hadn't considered before. She leaned over and grabbed Tally's shoulder. When she spoke, her voice was even faster. "Craig didn't sign paternity on Josh's birth certificate so that I couldn't go after him for child support."

"What does that mean exactly?"

"It means that if I were to marry, and that person wanted to adopt Josh, there are no paternal rights to fight."

Tally didn't think it could get better than this. "And if I adopt Josh, he can be sealed to both of us."

Her face fell and there was a long silence. Tally wondered what she was thinking. "Tally," she finally said, and her voice sounded deflated. He couldn't breathe. "If we didn't get married in the temple right now, if we waited to be sealed after the adoption was official, would it change how you feel about this?"

Tally wasn't sure how to answer; of course it would change how he felt. "Why wouldn't we get married in the temple now? Josh can be sealed to us as soon as it goes through. If we get married civilly, we have to wait a year."

"I know," she said. She let go of him and leaned back against the couch. He wished he dared turn the lights on so he could see her face but he didn't want to wake his parents, and his mother was a very light sleeper. "It's just that . . . I haven't had a recommend for several years and I'm not ready to go back yet."

Tally's heart, that had been slowly ascending to the sky, took a sharp nose dive, but he tried to keep his voice even when he spoke. "Why not?"

"I think I just need a little more time to get ready; maybe take some temple prep courses or something. I don't want to rush into it, even for something as important as this; or maybe especially not for something as important as this. I also have to cancel my sealing to Allen and that could take months."

She didn't want to rush into returning to the House of the Lord, but she was willing to rush into marriage? Tally wasn't sure what to think about that but he took several moments to gather his thoughts before he spoke. "I've always dreamed of a temple marriage, Janet, it almost doesn't seem worth it if we aren't going to do it right."

"Then I guess we should wait, until we're both ready; because right now I just—"

Suddenly the lights went on and they both raised a hand to shield their eyes from the searing light.

"What are you guys doing?"

"Mom," Tally said irritably as he recognized the voice. "Turn off the light, you're blinding us here."

The lights went off, and Tally and Janet came to their feet as Tally's mom repeated herself. "What are you doing? It's after one in the morning." The tone of her voice well explained that she wasn't happy.

"We were just talking," Tally said, glad that Janet had slid off of his lap before his mom had found them. *That* would have been embarrassing.

"Are you finished?" his mother asked.

Tally turned to Janet, but she was already moving toward the stairs. "I'm sorry Mrs. Blaire," she said as she passed by her, sounding like a teenager caught in the backseat. Again Tally's mom was silent, and he cringed inside. He'd had a hard time reading his parent's assessment, but from her coldness now he could tell that they weren't impressed with Janet. He was saddened by the realization and wondered what he could do about it—this whole encounter definitely wasn't helping.

His mother didn't speak until they heard the door to the guest room close upstairs. "Tally," she said in her motherly warning voice. "I would be a little more careful if I were you."

"I'm in the living room of my parent's house," Tally countered. "And we were just talking."

"I'd prefer you talk with the lights on when you're under my roof." She didn't say another word but he heard her go back to her room and wondered exactly what she was thinking. He waited several minutes before slowly going upstairs, glad to know that he still had every squeak of the floorboards memorized and praying his mother wouldn't come out to check on him. He turned the doorknob to the guest bedroom and slowly pushed it open. He could see Janet sitting up in the bed, with her back against the headboard, looking as if she were waiting for him.

"That was awkward," she whispered. "I don't think your mother likes me very much."

Tally crossed the room quietly and slid next to her on the bed. "Of course she likes you," he said as he found her hand and gave it a little squeeze. He decided to keep his own suspicions of his mother's feelings to himself.

"There are things you don't know about me," Janet continued, changing the subject. "Things you should know before we get carried away."

"O-kay," Tally said slowly. He didn't like the gravity in her voice.

"I've already told you about my divorce from Allen and how I stopped going to church. What I didn't tell you was that after Craig left I went into a tailspin—it felt like my life was spiraling out of control. I moved to Salt Lake just before Josh was born, hoping to find my direction again, but after Josh came along it got worse. I started having panic attacks; I was so overwhelmed by life and Josh—everything. In some ways I feel like I'm doing so much better. I've gotten used to my new roles and all the changes Josh brought into my life but the attacks haven't gone away and I still take medication . . . sometimes. My calling as a Sunday School teacher is the first calling I've had in many, many years. I still wear my temple garments, but I've only been paying my tithing for a few months. I'm working hard to get my footing; it hasn't been easy. I've never fit in at church and I still don't."

She'd told Tally much of this before, but he didn't interrupt, content to allow her to let it out. Janet continued, "The Mormon culture is uncomfortable to me and although I'm working out my issues and trying to overcome my own insecurity, I know I have a long way to go—a lot of things I need to make peace with. It's not that I don't want to go to the temple, Tally, it's that I can't—not yet."

He was both humbled and troubled by her sincerity. "Do you want to go?" Tally asked as he tried to work it all out in his mind.

"I do," she replied. "But I won't go until I'm ready. I wasn't raised like you, Tally, in a Mormon home with vigilant parents—my childhood was very different and my ideas and perceptions are different too."

"You've never told me much about your childhood; I'm not sure what you mean."

Janet took a deep breath and he knew by the tension in her voice that this was not easy for her to talk about. "My mom was an alcoholic all my life. The responsibility of running the house and taking care of my little sister fell to me more often than not because she just couldn't do it. When I was nine she married Travis," she paused and he wondered what she was thinking. "Travis was wonderful, he's the one that introduced me to the church. After he came into our lives I got my first taste of what a normal kid was supposed to do. He was such a good man." She paused reflectively for a few moments; Tally didn't interrupt. "He died when I was 15, and things went right back to the way they had been before, only worse. But I knew by then the kind of life I wanted and I've worked hard to live my life exactly opposite of the way my mother lived hers. I've never been close with my sister, who nearly worshiped my mother, and I left home as soon as I had the chance. I talked to my sister for the first time in years when my mother died a few months ago and I haven't talked to her since. She's never met Josh. We don't even send each other Christmas cards. It's not like your family at all."

Tally didn't know what to say. In just a few sentences she'd opened up to him in a way she never had before and he was touched both by her openness and the circumstances of her youth. "You're right," Tally said after a few more seconds. "We did grow up differently, but it doesn't change my feelings toward you." She said nothing, but he sensed she didn't quite believe him. "Look at you," Tally whispered. "Look at how much you've done in your life. You didn't turn out like your mother, you didn't let her life pull you down. It's amazing that you overcame so much, that you are who you are despite the excuses you had. Things are never easy, Janet, and neither of us are perfect. You have your issues, and I have mine."

"Oh yeah," Janet said with sarcasm. "You have a great family, a great job and a devout testimony of the gospel; horrible!"

Tally managed a chuckle and was surprised she hadn't taken his comment seriously. "The truth is, however, that I can't do most things normal guys can do. I can't ski, or play most sports. I'll never walk the streets of Paris or coach my kid's soccer team. Within the next ten years or so I'll have to get a knee replacement, and my medicine cabinet is full of Aspercreme and Ben-Gay. There are mornings when it takes me ten minutes just to get out of bed. My body is twice my age, and it'll give me problems for the rest of my life. So, if we're going to add up each other's deficiencies, maybe I'm the one that ought to be making sure you understand what you're getting into here."

Janet reached up and placed her palm on his cheek. "It doesn't even make me hesitate," she said. "It never has."

"And I feel the same way about your struggles; it doesn't take anything away from how I feel about you." He took her hand and lifted it to his lips where he kissed her palm before lowering it. "I thought when you said you needed to tell me some things, you were going to say you'd once been a man or something. That would have been a little harder to take."

"Only a little?"

He laughed quietly and he could hear her smile, if that were possible. She leaned her head against his chest and he stroked her hair softly. In that moment one thing he'd been missing fit into place. Despite his attraction to Janet, despite how much he enjoyed her company and admired her intelligence and success, not until now had he ever felt that she needed him. But she'd just shared some incredibly painful things with him and he wanted to be her hero, the one that made all the bad things in her past go away. He pulled her closer. "You don't need to worry about telling me things, Janet; I want to know everything about you."

"It really doesn't bother you?"

"That you're not perfect?" Tally replied. "It's a big relief, in fact if you've got any more problems, you might really make my day." He felt her smile again and his heart swelled.

"My biggest fear is that one day you'll look back on this moment and wish you hadn't ever met me."

Tally took her face in his hands so he could look at her. "I'm going to cherish this night for the rest of my life." He leaned down and kissed her softly, pulling back before it transitioned into anything else, which their kisses usually did. Before he spoke again he considered his options. He could say that they should wait until she was ready to go to the temple, but his heart recoiled and he felt the need to make sure that she understood just how much he wanted her in his life. He'd never wanted anything more than he wanted to marry this woman, right now, regardless of all the reasons not to. She wanted to change her life and he knew he could help her with that—it all made so much sense. "And now that I know all your dark secrets, I'd be the happiest man on earth if you'd agree to marry me."

Janet was silent and he could feel her hesitation. "What about the temple?"

"We can wait," Tally said. "So long as you request the cancellation of your sealing to Allen so that one year from our wedding day we'll be in the temple."

"I can promise you that," she said easily, a smile in her voice. "There's nothing I want more than that. But are you sure you want to—"

He silenced her with a kiss. When he pulled back she tried again. "I'm not the easiest per—"

He kissed her again, but when he pulled back this time he spoke before she could protest again. "I love you, Janet," he whispered. "I want to be with you. I'm not the easiest person to live with either, but I truly believe that we can work those things out."

"You really do love me, don't you," she said, her tone wistful as if she found it hard to believe.

Her insecurity made him feel all the more motivated to prove his love to her, accept her as she was and show her everything he saw when he looked into her eyes. "I really do," he confirmed.

"I would love to marry you, Tally," she said after a few more moments. He enfolded her in his arms and let out a long deep breath. This had to be heaven, holding Janet in his arms. It wasn't perfect, and there would be challenges; but she'd trusted him enough to tell him some difficult things, she needed him and they could fill the voids in one another's lives. In fact, based upon the way he felt right now, at this moment, it was hard to imagine that life could ever get better than this.

CHAPTER SIX

"Wait a minute," Tally's mother said the next morning as she sat across the kitchen table from him. Tally's father, Phillip, was already gone to work and Janet had taken Josh for a walk around the neighborhood. Her nerves were getting the better of her and she needed to work out some energy. Tally had taken the opportunity to inform his mother of their plans. She'd been strangely silent until he mentioned it wouldn't be a temple marriage until next year.

"What do you mean it won't be in the temple?" Julie suddenly asked. "You've always said you'd only marry in the temple."

"If we wait, and get sealed the following year, my adoption of Josh will be legal and final, then we can be all be sealed together."

"I don't see any reason why you and Janet can't be sealed now and have Josh sealed to you when the adoption is legal. It makes a lot more sense to do it that way."

"But it doesn't, Mom," he explained, wishing she were more receptive. He really didn't want to tell her everything he and Janet had discussed, especially after her not-so-warm-acceptance of what he'd already said. "We talked about it for a long time and it just makes sense for us to do it this way. Janet hasn't been to the temple for a whileand she doesn't want to rush into it." Saying it out loud brought his own reservations crashing back. But he reminded himself of the humble heartfelt prayer he'd offered after proposing last night and he couldn't forget the peace he'd felt. He knew what it felt like to get an answer to a prayer and he knew when he asked if marrying Janet was the right thing to do that the sweetness that followed was confirmation that they were doing the right thing. It didn't mean he wasn't still apprehensive or nervous, but he knew the Lord wanted him right where he was.

"I don't think it's right for you to settle for—"

"I'm not settling," Tally interrupted strongly. "I've fallen in love with a woman who completes my life, Mom." His voice softened as he spoke. "She is good, and kind and has a beautiful son that she's willing share with me. There was a long time when I thought I would never find this kind of happiness, and I hope that you'll look past the shortfalls long enough to see how truly happy I am. I'm disappointed that we won't be marrying in the temple, but we both intend to make absolutely sure that one year from our wedding day we are where we belong, sealing *our* son to both of us and making the proper covenants to him, as well as to each other." He paused but when she didn't speak, he continued, "I would really like your blessing."

Julie shook her head. "It doesn't feel right to me, Talmage," she said, using his full name. "She's been divorced twice, Tally, and she's ten years your senior. The two of you are from completely different worlds."

"No, we're not," Tally said defensively. "We've had different lives, and she's had a lot of struggles, but I've had my own problems too."

"But not a temple marriage?" Julie continued. She took a deep breath before continuing. "When Emma got married it was strange to see them make such empty promises to each other in some cold reception hall. I don't want to sit and watch you do the same thing. You're endowed, Tally, you served a mission. You know what a temple marriage means."

Tally thought of his baby sister's wedding just two months ago and knew he couldn't dispute his mother's assessment completely. After witnessing temple marriages, and feeling the power of the eternal blessings promised there, a civil ceremony was certainly lacking. But Emma had married a non-member, and she had graduated from high school just a few days before the wedding. He couldn't put his situation in quite the same category as hers. "I'm not Emma," he finally said. "We will be sealed, Mom, that's a promise; just not now."

"I'm not sure she's the one, Tally," she said. "She's so . . . different from the kind of girl I thought you'd want to share your life with."

Tally's face hardened. His mother was direct and stubborn, that was for sure, but she had always been very tender with him too, accepting and open to his thoughts and ideas. He'd never seen her act like this, except when he announced he was moving to Utah. She'd struggled with that, too. He wondered if her reservations had something to do with that. Maybe she felt left out. Then another thought came to him, and he felt like he understood where his mother was coming from after all. "She's not Lacey, if that's what you mean," he said. Ever since Chris and Lacey had married just three years ago, his mother had sung Lacey's praises like a familiar hymn. Lacey was the ideal Mormon girl and everything a mother could want for her son. Tally had never been bothered by his mom's praise of his sister-in-law, until now when he looked at Janet and realized how different the two women were. "Janet doesn't stay home or bake, she doesn't organize neighborhood play groups or do needlepoint. But I love her and she loves me and we want the same thing you and Dad have, the same thing Chris and Lacey have. It's not starting out the way I dreamed it would, but in some ways it's better. I never imagined I'd find a woman like her and—"

"What do you mean 'like her'?" Julie interrupted. "Do you mean beautiful? I can see what you see, Tally," she continued, hitting a nerve in Tally that caused him to clench his teeth. "She's gorgeous, but there is more for you to consider than her measurements—they aren't the foundation of a good marriage."

Tally pushed away from the table and stood up quickly. "Never mind," he said sharply. "I thought you knew me well enough to know that I'm not so shallow as to make this kind of decision based on a dress size. It's much more than that—much more—but it's obvious that you are only seeing what you want to see. I'm sorry that Janet isn't what you want for me, but I'm not going to beg for your blessing. If you haven't noticed, I'm a grown man and I'm perfectly capable of living my own life and making my own decisions." He turned away, still speaking over his shoulder. "We'll head to Jason's tonight so we don't bother you with this anymore." He walked toward the front door as he tried to think of the right way to explain this to Janet. This was definitely not the reaction he'd expected and his heart sank with disappointment. He didn't want it to be this way, but if his mother was going to make him choose between her approval and Janet—it was an easy choice to make. His mother didn't catch up with him until he was on the front porch.

"I'm sorry, Tally," Julie said quickly as she reached out and touched his arm. He stopped and turned, still regarding her with suspicion. Julie managed a small penitent smile. "I'm not very good with surprises, but I had no right to jump to conclusions like that."

Tally said nothing, forcing her to continue.

"We love you so much, Talmage," she said, her eyes filling. "And we want you to be happy."

"I am happy," he said with equal softness and sincerity. "I want you to be happy for me, but if you only measure her against what she isn't, you'll never have the chance to see what she is; what I've fallen in love with. She makes me feel alive, Mom, like there's a reason I'm here. She doesn't care that I'm stuck in the body of an old man, that I'm dependent on some financial price set on all that I lost to survive. And she loves me, Mom. What more can I hope for than all of that?"

Julie nodded when he finished. "Have you guys set a date?"

"No," he said shaking his head, and hoping she wouldn't freak out by the rest of his answer. "But we had talked about stopping at a courthouse on our way back to Salt Lake. We'll save the fanfare for the sealing next year."

Julie's lips pursed together but she had the restraint not to say anything and she looked away, probably to hide her disappointment. After a few seconds she looked at him again. "If you want," she said carefully, as if measuring each word to make sure her tone was right. "I could throw together a simple ceremony for tomorrow night. I'm sure I could get the bishop to do it and we could at least invite the family that lives close by. It wouldn't be fancy, but it would be a better memory than a courthouse."

Tally's initial reaction was to protest, although he wasn't sure why, but he couldn't deny that the idea was also very appealing. This was his wedding day—the most exciting day of his life. "I'll need to talk to Janet," he said, but when she reached out to him he didn't pull away from her embrace. He knew her disappointment was still very strong, but he did understand her feelings. Less than 24 hours ago he didn't think he'd make these kind of concessions, but sometimes changes come quickly and he hoped she could move past her disappointment and try to see in Janet the goodness he saw there. After a few moments Julie pulled back and smiled at him. "I have something for you . . . for Janet."

Tally furrowed his brow but he followed her upstairs. When she opened the velvet box he was speechless and looked at his mother. She placed it in his hand. "You have my blessing, Tally," she said. "And I wish you every happiness."

Tally felt the tears prick his eyes as he hugged his mother once more. She was willing to do whatever it took to convince him of her support and for that he would always be grateful.

When Janet returned, Tally was sitting on the front porch, hands clasped and elbows resting on his knees. Josh immediately noticed the Playskool lawn mower Tally had dug out of the garage and Janet watched him for a moment before joining Tally on the steps. She fanned her face and stuck out her tongue for emphasis. "The humidity is killing me," she said as she pulled at her shirt, hoping to encourage cooler air circulation.

Tally watched her and smiled. "You get used to it."

"You must," Janet said. "How'd it go with your mom?" she asked after a few more seconds.

"Good," Tally said with a nod. Then he opened his hands and twisted a ring off the pinky of his left hand. Janet's eyebrows went up and he indicated for her to put out her hand. She did and he slid the ring onto her finger; it was almost a perfect fit. "This was my grandmother's wedding ring," he explained as Janet held it up to catch the sun. It was white gold, with three diamond chips on either side of the diamond in the center. It was simple but elegant and Tally loved seeing it on her hand. "It became my mother's when Grandmother died and she wanted us—you—to have it."

"Really?" Janet said as she looked at him again, the look on her face was so vulnerable, so hopeful that he instantly decided not to tell her the details of the initial conversation he'd had with his mother.

"She also offered to put together a very simple ceremony tomorrow evening, and watch Josh overnight so that we can have at least one night alone."

Janet's mouth opened and her eyes went wide. "Really?" she said again. She turned to look at the ring again. "I . . . I don't know what to say."

"Just a yes or no," Tally said. "I told her we'd discuss it." Janet continued to stare at the ring on her hand and then she leaned toward him. He put one arm around her shoulder.

"What do you think?" she asked.

Was there anything to think about? he wondered. "I think having some family around and enjoying my mom's famous cheesecake beats the socks off some cold ceremony in a courthouse."

Janet nodded, but he wondered why she wasn't happier with the idea—to him it was a no-brainer. She kinked her neck to look at him and he was comforted by her smile. "You're sure it's not too much work for your mom?"

"She offered," Tally said as he kissed her quickly before she rested her head against him again. "And I think it would be a much better start—for all of us."

"I love you, Tally," she whispered, completely changing his train of thought. He smiled, it was the first time she'd said those words without him saying them first and he just now realized how hungry he'd been for this moment.

"I love you too, Janet," he replied and he felt his heart grow wings.

After running to the local courthouse and obtaining a marriage license, they spent the rest of the day getting acquainted with Tally's new horse, Barrington, at Jason's ranch about 30 miles north of Oklahoma City. After meeting Jason, who Janet found to be very friendly, she met Leslie, his wife. For Janet, Leslie was confirmation of why not all women were meant to be mothers; at least not with so many children. Leslie seemed ready to break down the second they got there and was so busy running this way and that, getting one thing or another that Janet got motion sickness just watching her. Leslie and Jason had five children under the age of eight, the two youngest were twins and Janet hoped they would all be potty-trained by the time their mother had a serious nervous breakdown, but she doubted it. Jason wandered around the property with Tally and Janet, while his wife's shrill voice echoed from the house. "Don't let her fool you," Jason had said when a particularity loud 'what are you doing!' rang from the house, "she thrives on the chaos." Janet wasn't so sure, but she had a very deep belief that all women were in charge of their own destiny and if Leslie didn't like it, she should do something to change it; at the very least have her husband help out. Instead, each time Jason tried to help, she told him to show them something else or to get out of the way.

By the time they left, Janet had decided she'd be very good about taking birth control measures and realized she and Tally hadn't discussed family plans. She wasn't sure how she felt about the possibility of having another child, but she decided not to bring it up—not now at least.

They decided to leave Barrington at Jason's until after their honeymoon and pick him up on their way back to Salt Lake, which meant Janet would have to see Jason and Leslie twice more, at the wedding and when they picked up Barrington for good. She didn't mind being social, but she hated the way their eyes slid back and forth between her and Tally, as if they were trying to figure out an equation of some kind. It embarrassed her, but Tally didn't seem to notice. They didn't get back to Tally's parents' house until almost ten, and Tally's parents were already asleep.

She breathed a sigh of relief when she finally laid down in bed, accompanied only by Josh's soft breathing in the crib next to the bed. Despite her excitement, and how touched she was by the way things had gone with his mother, Janet couldn't seem to put her nerves to rest. Was she doing the right thing? Was she ready for this?

Part of her wanted to be Tally's wife so badly she didn't want to think about the complications, but another part of her was nervous about the changes this choice was going to make in her life. She liked order, she liked routine and Tally was an uncertain variable. Yet she felt guilty for even questioning the circumstances. Tally was a good, kind man. She had no reason for doubts like this. How could she be so ungrateful?

Still, as the hours of darkness continued, the doubts only became stronger and it wasn't until she had taken two Xanax and an Oxycontin that she finally fell asleep in the early hours of morning. She'd been trying to cut down on the pills, bothered by how important they had become, but she didn't hesitate much tonight. She needed something to calm her nerves. She didn't wake up till almost eleven the next morning. Josh was already gone from his crib and she felt embarrassed that someone had had to come in to get him—she hoped it was Tally. She was groggy and her limbs felt heavy, but she took her 'vitamins' and felt better after she took a shower in the old porcelain bathtub. When she went downstairs, Tally was already gone running errands, and Josh was in the backyard helping Tally's dad mow the lawn. She watched him riding on his soon-to-be-grandfather's lap as the riding mower went around and around the yard. Josh's world was about to get so much kinder; full of aunts, uncles, cousins and grandparents. She couldn't help but be lifted by the thought. He would have so much more than she'd ever had and it would no longer be just her and Josh. Tally was so good with him, and his parents treated him as if he had always belonged to them. She was excited about all the good things and forbade the doubts to enter her conscious thoughts. This was her wedding day; it was a day to celebrate.

"We'd be happy to watch Josh if you'd like to go look for a dress."

Janet turned and smiled at Julie, still feeling a bit awkward. Despite their blessing, Janet knew she wasn't the woman Tally's parents would have chosen. But she was content with pretending everything was fine if they were. They all loved Tally, and he deserved all their efforts to get along.

"Are you sure?" Janet asked, although the chance to get away from everyone for a little while was extremely tempting.

"Of course," Julie said as her eyes moved to watch Josh and Phillip on the mower for a moment. "We love having grandchildren around. You can take my car. I'll be cooking all day."

There seemed to be a silent kind of jab in her statement, as if she were really saying 'go, have a good time, I'll do your job for you better than you could ever do it yourself.' But Janet forced a smile and decided to take the comment at face value. "If you're sure you don't mind?"

"Not at all," Julie said as she turned back to the kitchen. "I'll get you the keys and draw you a map to the mall."

After a few hours of slow shopping, Janet eventually found a nice off-white silk skirt and matching top with short sleeves and a high neck. The full-length skirt moved with liquidity and although it wasn't fancy, it was elegant and the fit couldn't have been better. As a fashion major in college she'd learned to sew and the skill had come in handy throughout her life. She typically tailored her own clothes, when she had time, but was glad she didn't need to make alterations today. The other selling factor, other than the perfect fit, was that it was about the only thing she could find even close to a wedding gown that wasn't really a wedding gown at all. She liked the classic lines of this dress, knowing it would be something she'd get to wear again.

When she got back to the house at four o'clock, the house was already full of people, probably the whole Relief Society pulling together to make a wedding on 24-hours notice. Julie must have heard her come in, since she came out of the kitchen to meet her.

Julie took one look at the dress and her face fell. "It's not white," she said flatly.

Janet looked at the dress, she hadn't even thought about the choice in color. She felt her cheeks pink as she reminded herself that she wasn't a virgin, maybe she'd unconsciously chosen the off-white dress for a reason. Julie met her eye with a censoring look and Janet knew she was thinking the same thing. "I don't look very good in stark white," Janet finally said, but the awkwardness didn't go away.

Julie smiled politely, although it was obviously forced, and turned back for the kitchen without saying another word. Janet hurried upstairs and by the time she shut the door to the guest room her stomach was in knots. This wasn't going well and she questioned whether or not she could follow through with it. She suddenly felt the desperate need to see Tally before the ceremony. If she saw him; even for a moment, surely all her doubts would disappear.

When he knocked on the door a few minutes later and asked if he could come in, she said he could and nearly flew into his arms once the door was shut behind him. "Hey, what's the matter?" he asked as he pulled back a few minutes later. His eyes were warm and full of concern; she felt instantly guilty for giving him more reason to worry.

"I don't know," she said quickly as she turned away and stared at the dress she'd already laid out on the bed. "I'm doing everything all wrong."

Tally embraced her from behind and she leaned into him, closing her eyes and wishing they could leave, right now.

"Is this about the dress?" he asked.

"That and everything else," Janet said as she opened her eyes and stared at the dress again, hating that his mother had chosen to discuss it with him; she must be even more upset than Janet had thought. It was supposed to be her wedding gown, a symbol of their new lives together but it seemed soiled now. "I'm not what she wants for you, Tally. We all know that and everything I do just seems to make that more clear."

"My mother loves me, Janet, and she'll learn to love you too. We knew it would be complicated and this is just one more part. I talked to her about the dress—she's an old fashioned woman, she thinks a bride should wear white."

"It is white," Janet argued, trying to get a feel for what Tally thought of it. "A lot of brides wear off-white wedding dresses."

Tally turned her in his arms and smiled his understanding. "That's what I told her. And as far as I'm concerned, you could wear red and black stripes," he said sweetly.

"I'm nervous," she whispered. She wondered where all her maturity had gone; she suddenly seemed to have no confidence at all.

"How nervous?" Tally asked, and although he was trying to sound easygoing, she could see the fear in his eyes and she knew what he was thinking.

She thought of all the bustle going on below them, all the time and money these people were putting on the line for her and she felt horribly guilty for even considering backing out. "What if things don't work out, Tally? What if I ruin everything and you end up hating me? I don't think I could handle it. I really don't."

Tally looked at her for several seconds, and the tenderness in his eyes made her want to cry. "I will never hate you, Janet, and things are going to work out. But if we need to wait, it's okay; we can do that. I don't want to pressure you into this."

She loved the words he was saying, but she could tell that although he didn't want to pressure her, he also knew what kind of price they would pay if they called it off. She could only imagine what his parents would think of her then, after enlisting all their friends and neighbors in the efforts to make this a special day. She forced a smile and accepted that she couldn't back out now, at the same time she knew she really didn't want to; she just hated the insecurity she was feeling. "I'm sure it's just nerves," she said with as much confidence as she could muster. But as soon as she said it, she felt the constriction in her chest, and the next breath she took was a gasp for air. Normally, Janet noticed the smallest signs of an attack coming on and treated it before it ever got this far. It had been so long since she'd had a full attack that the sudden symptoms shocked her and she felt the panic rising fast. She put a hand to her chest and tried for another breath as Tally let her go. *Oh no,* she thought to herself as she felt the panic threatening to consume her, *not now—not in front of Tally.* She started scanning the room with darting glances, trying to remember where she'd put her pills. Tally's eyes were wide with concern as he watched her.

"Janet?" he said as she headed for her suitcase. "Janet, are you okay?"

No, I'm not okay, she wanted to say but it was all she could do to draw a breath. She felt the sweat on her forehead and her heart was racing as she started throwing clothes around in search for her medication. Where had she put the pills? The mental clouds were moving in fast and she couldn't remember—that made her panic even more. Tally knelt down beside her and asked again what was wrong. Her stomach was starting to ache from the sheer act of trying to breathe and she could only imagine what she looked like right now. She managed to say 'pills,' although it took her several breaths and the different sounds came out as horrible grunts and gasps. Good thing she'd told him about the attacks. Thankfully, Tally understood and took over the search. He looked around for a few seconds and then asked her if they were in her planner. Her planner! Of course. She nodded frantically, but lost her balance and fell back against the bed as she tried to stand, her vision was beginning to tunnel and Tally's voice was sounding further and further away. Tally asked her where her planner was but she couldn't remember. He started giving her ideas, and when he mentioned the car, she nodded again. He quickly looked between her and the door but she waved him out and let herself slump to the floor. She laid on her back and tried to slow her thoughts as she closed her eyes and tried to draw deep breaths. She was beginning to think she was going to lose consciousness when Tally and his parents suddenly appeared at her side.

Tally and Julie helped her swallow a pill, but she put up two fingers so they helped her take another one. Julie swept the wedding dress onto the floor as Tally and his dad helped her onto the bed, but Janet didn't watch it crumple to the floor. She couldn't allow herself to think of the dress right now. Julie was saying something about it taking a few minutes for the pills to work, but that Janet's color was better. Janet didn't focus on the words they were saying, in fact she ignored all of them completely. She rolled onto her side, away from Tally and his parents, but she continued to struggle for every breath. She suddenly felt hands on her head and her initial impulse was to shake them off, she didn't want to be touched, but then Julie explained that Tally and his dad were going to give her a blessing. She couldn't remember the last time she'd had a blessing and felt awkward, but it was the last of her worries and so when they spoke, despite her straining attempts to breath, she tried to concentrate on the words. It was pointless to even try and pay attention. Each breath was like a mangled moan and all she could think about was how humiliated she was to have them see her this way. But the pills, and perhaps the blessing too, were working. With every passing moment she could feel her chest muscles relaxing and her mind sharpening, although the pills kept it from coming completely clear. She closed her eyes and felt the tears begin to fall a few moments later as the blessing was completed. Tally kissed her temple and her tears became hot against her face. She knew at that moment she was making a big mistake, even though the blessing had told her to surround herself with people who would love and support her. How could she possibly have thought she was ready for this kind of change in her life? She was making a mess of everything and they weren't even married yet.

When she finally turned back to the room after several minutes, Tally and his dad were gone and the door was shut, but Julie was neatly folding the clothes Janet had thrown out of her suitcase. Janet wished she had never come to Oklahoma; this was her worst nightmare. Julie looked at Janet and smiled, there was something different about it and Janet noticed that the tension they'd shared in their other encounters wasn't as thick as it had been. Janet couldn't meet her eye, but noticed the wedding dress was now hanging on the back of the door. She was so embarrassed and couldn't think of what to say—something that never happened to Janet Stewart.

"I told Tally to go help his father in the yard for a few minutes, he was having a hard time doing nothing. He'll be back in a little while."

Janet nodded, but didn't meet her eye.

"How long have you been having anxiety attacks?" Julie asked, and there was a softness in her voice that Janet hadn't heard before. She wasn't sure whether she liked the sympathy; it made her uneasy and she just shrugged.

"That's okay," Julie continued. "You don't have to tell me if you don't want to. Are you feeling okay now?"

"I'm still a little out of it," Janet said as she slowly sat up. She turned so that her legs were hanging off of the bed and took a deep breath, hoping to clear her head a little more. "I'm sorry, Mrs. Blaire, what you must think of the crazy woman your son is marrying."

Julie didn't say anything as she came and sat on the bed next to Janet. Janet didn't look up and felt reduced to childhood for about the hundredth time since pulling up to their house. "First of all, call me Julie," she paused and Janet wondered if she was considering asking Janet to call her Mom instead. If she was thinking it, she decided against it. Janet couldn't blame her. "Tally didn't tell you I was a nurse?"

Janet shook her head.

"I don't work anymore, but I know what panic attacks are and I know how frightening they can be. That doesn't mean you're crazy."

"I'm not so sure," Janet said, feeling a surge of bravery. Maybe Julie deserved to know what her son was getting into. Janet didn't know what else to say though, so she apologized again.

Julie put a hand on Janet's knee and the thought crossed Janet's mind that perhaps the attack had given Julie permission to take on a more protective role, rather than an adversarial position. "No, I'm sorry," she said. "I haven't been very warm to you and I owe you an apology. I'm afraid I've become very protective of Tally since he got hurt; and it's hard for me to let go. But just now, when I saw him bolt out the front door, unaware of his knee and desperate to help you, I saw something I haven't seen in a long time."

Janet looked up at her then, curious to hear what that was. Julie met her eye and smiled. "Purpose," she said simply. "He's worked hard, but he's done it with the hope of a second-rate future. Today, I realized that you reflect all the things he thought he might never have. You're giving him the opportunity to be a father and a husband and that is a priceless gift for which I'm very thankful." Janet felt tears in her eyes, but she knew Julie would think it was for joy. In truth it was fear that Julie might be wrong, she wondered if perhaps she would only become a burden to him. "He loves you very much, Janet. And I want nothing more than for the two of you to be blissfully happy. So forgive me for my doubts," she said as she smiled again and her eyes traveled to the dress hanging behind the door. "And I'm sorry about the dress; it was very unfair of me to judge you that way. It's lovely; you'll look like Miss America in it." They were silent for a few moments. "Can I get you anything?" Julie finally offered.

Janet shook her head and tried to look confident once more. "Thank you," she said. "You have no idea what it means for us to have your support."

Julie stood and smiled again as she headed for the door. "Why don't you rest for a little while. I'll come let you know when it's time to get ready. We thought we'd push the ceremony back till about nine o'clock so it won't be so hot." Janet nodded her agreement, but as soon as Julie left the room she put her face in her hands and cried.

An hour before the ceremony, Janet met Tally's parents' bishop for the first time. The two of them listened to all he had to say and Janet smiled and answered all the questions as she was expected to but she couldn't help thinking of what he would say if she dared be honest. If she told them she ate pills like M & M's, that one of the biggest motivations for this marriage was that she doubted she could keep her hands to herself, or that she'd never liked the temple and had only been twice in her whole life—what would he say? It wasn't a mystery, she knew what he'd say—that this was a mistake. Yet when she looked into Tally's face she couldn't help but smile. They'd make it work, somehow.

At precisely 9:10, Tally stood in front of the bishop, underneath a weeping willow tree, in the back yard of the home he'd grown up in. Earlier that day he and his father had trimmed the cascading branches away just enough to make an alcove big enough for three people—the bishop, Tally and Janet. Then the sisters in the ward had braided flowers into the willow branches, creating a beautiful arch that faced the rest of the yard and was lit up by the evening sunset behind them. Their guests, no more than 40 or so, sat in chairs borrowed from the ward house. Tally was hot, both with the summer humidity and the anxiety of the moment. Rather than rushing to find a tux, Tally had purchased a new suit that morning and his mother had quickly tailored what she could and duct taped what she didn't have time to sew—but standing in the setting Oklahoma summer sun in a suit didn't help the temperature problems he was experiencing at all.

The button was pushed on the CD player placed in a window and the familiar tune of 'Here comes the bride' began to play. Josh started clapping from where he sat on the front row as Tally, and the rest of the crowd, turned expectantly. Tally's breath caught in his throat when he saw her. Phillip stood at Janet's side and her slender arm rested in the crook of his elbow. Her hair was done up in large loops on her head and accented by some of the same flowers that adorned the tree behind him and the bouquet of flowers she held. She had no veil. The dress was as beautiful as he had known it would be, moving with her as she walked carefully toward him. Her expression was formal, if not a bit guarded, but when she finally looked up and met his eyes, the tiniest of smiles played on her lips. She was breathtaking and Tally was speechless.

Phillip reached Tally and kissed Janet sweetly on the cheek before placing her hand in Tally's and taking his seat on the front row. Tally looked at her and smiled as he gave her hand a squeeze. She squeezed back but didn't meet his eyes this time. The bishop began and they both stood quietly as they listened to the advice and counsel he gave—again—since most of it was exactly what he'd told them an hour ago when he'd met with them privately. He then said the fateful words and Tally and Janet turned toward one another. A moment of hesitation crossed Tally's mind as he noticed how scared she looked. It seemed to be more than nerves, or cold feet—it was actual fear. But then it passed as quickly as it came and she smiled and leaned in for their first kiss as man and wife. He tried to look her in the eye again to see if he could read her thoughts but she wouldn't meet his look and they were soon turned around to face their guests. Tally's concerns were quickly dismissed as reality descended—they were married! Janet was his wife!

The evening sun turned to dusk and dusk faded to night as Janet played the part of the happy bride for the guests, still shocked this had really happened. At nearly 10:30 she excused herself and went to the guest room where she shut the door and leaned against it. She'd taken another Xanax right before the ceremony, three in a four hour time period, and she felt dizzy and a little sick to her stomach. As she took deep breaths she went over the ceremony in her mind. It was a beautiful setting, everything was perfect, except that she'd just gotten married again. For the third time. What was she thinking? Tears threatened but she quickly stood up straight and took one more deep breath. As her chest expanded she thought of all her fears and reservations one last time, but as she exhaled she blew them all out too. She loved Tally, that much was certain—that was enough. They would be happy, everything would be fine. And she was happy, she was glad—she wouldn't allow herself to think of anything negative. She didn't want to ruin this.

A light knock sounded on the door and she put a big smile on her face. He'd seen something in her face just before they kissed—she knew the look had concerned him. That meant it was her job to make sure he had no doubts. Hers would surely pass, but she couldn't allow him to wonder. She centered herself, cracked the door and smiled.

"Are you ready to go, Mrs. Blaire?" Tally asked.

She opened the door all the way and decided not to change out of her wedding dress after all. "Are you ready, Mr. Blaire?" she asked back as she stepped forward and slid one finger down the length of his tie, stopping at the waistband of his pants.

"Oh, I'm ready," Tally said breathlessly.

Janet smiled and was relieved that the arousal she felt, the building excitement, was completely natural. Her doubts were fading already.

CHAPTER SEVEN

Monday night, Kim hung up the phone and nearly ran to her daughters bedroom where Allen was in the process of trying to get Lexie ready for bed. Kim stopped short at the doorway, however, and leaned against the doorjamb for a few moments as she momentarily forgot her haste. Lexie had just turned a year old last month, yet Kim still hadn't lost the fear that it was all too good to be true. Allen continually reminded her that she'd been through the fire already and that now she was just basking in the warmth from the other side, but it was hard to believe sometimes. Allen looked up and saw her standing there as Lexie tried to roll away from him. He quickly turned back to his baby girl and placed his large hand on her stomach firmly enough to keep her from wiggling away. "Stay," he said. Lexie looked at her mother with big blue eyes and stuck her hand in her mouth as if to say, 'fine, just get it over with.'

"Guess who got married Saturday?"

"Your bachelor brother Chris," he said easily.

Kim shook her head. "Try again."

"Uhhhh, Oprah Winfrey."

"No," Kim said with just a hint of a laugh. "Even weirder."

Allen finished putting Lexie's clothes back on and picked her up by her armpits. She immediately wiggled and kicked her feet until he put her down on the floor. It had only been a few weeks since she'd gotten the walking thing down and she was still trying to make up for lost time. As soon as Lexie gained her balance, she ran to her mother and lifted her arms. Allen rolled his eyes at the obvious preference and gathered up the dirty diaper. "Why don't you just tell me," he said. Then he added with sarcasm, "The suspense is killing me."

"Janet."

Allen paused mid-step and Kim watched closely as his face seemed to harden. As soon as he noticed his response, he guarded his expression and continued his task of throwing the diaper in the diaper pail. He said nothing.

"Don't you have a comment?"

"Nope," he said bluntly. He walked past her in the doorway, kissing her quickly on the forehead, and continued toward the kitchen. She followed, anxious about his reaction.

"I'm not happy with that response." She watched him shrug his shoulders and hurried a few steps so she could grab his arm with her free hand and turn him to face her. "Why are you acting like this?" She transferred Lexie to her other hip.

Allen looked down at the ground for a moment before meeting her eye. "How would you like me to act when my ex-wife gets married for the third time?"

"Not mad," Kim said. "Especially not jealous-mad."

"Whoa," he said, finally interpreting her concerns. "I'm not jealous."

Lexie started kicking, apparently not interested in her mother being stationary. Kim put her down and she sped for the living room, wobbling down the hallway. "Then how do you feel?" she asked.

Allen put both hands on her shoulders and ran them down her arms. "I just hope it's good for Josh," he said.

"And?"

"And that's it," Allen said with another shrug. "Josh already suffers enough having to put up with Janet and everything her life entails. I hope she didn't marry some loser who will make it that much harder."

Kim let out a sigh of relief. Since the very beginning of their relationship, Janet had been an issue for them, and when Kim finally met Janet, the issue just got worse. Since they'd been watching Josh, things had been better and Kim had become quite comfortable dealing with Janet and her crazy life, but now and then the fear that she couldn't hold a candle to Janet, in certain areas, continued to haunt her. "She called to say we wouldn't need to watch Josh when she goes out of town next week, he'll be staying with her husband."

"Oh good," Allen said with a disappointed shake of his head. "The bum doesn't even work."

"He does work," Kim quickly corrected. "He flies out of town a few times a month to fix some kind of machinery all over the country, and she asked if we would still watch Josh when their trips overlap. I guess they got married at his parents' house in Oklahoma a few days ago. They're driving back home now."

"You mean she took off work?" Allen put a hand to his chest to add to the drama in his voice. "How unlike her."

"Allen," Kim said in a reprimanding tone. "She's got pretty good taste in men." She then added, "I don't think she'd marry a loser."

"Josh's dad was a loser," Allen reminded her with a smile. "I think I was just a lucky break for her."

Kim laughed and bent down to pick up Lexie who had wandered back. She didn't know what to say, so she dropped it, but she couldn't help wondering about the whole situation herself. Janet was a very complex person. She often expressed how badly she felt that she didn't get more time with Josh, but yet she never did anything to change it. She was beautiful, almost too beautiful, and although she was always very nice, polite and well-spoken, Kim never really felt like she 'knew' Janet very well. She sighed and took Lexie into the living room to play. She wondered what Janet's new husband was like and hoped, like Allen did, that it would be a good situation for Josh. She knew that it could either be very good or very bad.

They arrived in Salt Lake Wednesday afternoon, a week after they'd left. Tally had made reservations at equestrian hotels along the way and Janet had thoroughly enjoyed the time spent with her new husband. It was hard to believe that she was really married, but so far it was exactly what she had hoped it would be and the doubts that played at the back of her mind were all but forgotten. She did feel that wholeness, that completion she felt she'd been missing before. Any concern, for either one of them, that Tally's lack of sexual experience, and her having too much, would be an issue was fully extinguished on their wedding night. Tally's tenderness and enthusiasm were truly intoxicating and any doubts were quickly doused. She hadn't even taken as many pills as she usually did and was sure that was a sign that this marriage was a good thing.

Tally was only able to drop her off in front of her condominium complex since the colt needed to get home and there wasn't room to park the trailer at the condo. He took Josh to Willard with him, and although Janet missed them both, she also liked having the evening to herself. She'd always liked alone time and was grateful to still have some.

Thursday morning she went to the gym, having missed a full week of exercise, and then went to work—it was nice not to have to get Josh ready and drag him around with her; she could get used to this. She was anxious about the meeting she had asked Cathy to schedule with Jay this morning; she knew he wasn't impressed with her impromptu vacation, but what could he say? She'd never taken any vacation time in the two years she'd worked there; she'd even gone back to work after only four weeks of maternity leave, and she *had* gotten married.

As soon as Cathy arrived and realized Janet was in her office, she was all over her with questions about Tally and the wedding, letting Janet know that she'd been the topic of too many conversations during her absence. "I didn't even know you had a boyfriend," Cathy said, and Janet wished she hadn't called and talked to her secretary on Monday. Cathy had been too stunned to say much then, but it was obvious that her shock had passed.

The meeting with Jay went well. He was open to the idea of her moving to the Ogden store, but continued to express his surprise at her decision. She just smiled and kept stating her point of view, but when she left the meeting she felt great; like she'd gotten her power back. After the meeting she was swamped trying to catch up with as much as possible. By the time Cathy was getting ready to leave, her head was killing her again.

"Do you have any of those pills left that I gave you?" Cathy said when Janet mentioned the headache.

"I left them at home, but I've got a long night and they tend to make me tired anyway. You haven't got something that can get rid of the headache but not wipe me out, do you?"

Cathy looked instantly uncomfortable and shifted her weight from one foot to the other.

"What?" Janet prompted, wondering at Cathy's hesitancy. Surely she didn't have sudden qualms about giving Janet some meds, they'd gotten way past that.

"Um," Cathy hesitated again. When she spoke again she spoke quickly, nervously. "I've got something I can give you if you want, it'll get rid of the headache and keep you awake as long as you want."

That sounded perfect! "What is it?"

"My boyfriend calls it Splash," she said evasively.

"Well, what is it?"

Cathy shrugged as if to say she didn't know, but she wouldn't meet Janet's eyes. "All I know is that it works. I'll give you one if you want to try it."

Janet hesitated, not liking Cathy's obvious discomfort. Then she looked at her desk and the piles of paperwork she had to get caught up on as much as possible if she were going to keep her commitment of going to Tally's for the weekend. The possibility of not seeing Tally is what eventually made up her mind. She nodded. "Let me give it a shot."

Cathy nodded, left for a minute or two, and returned with the pill and a bottle of water. "It'll last for about 24 hours, but when it wears off, you'll know it and you'll need to sleep as soon as possible, but I think you'll like it. I'll see you tomorrow," she said.

"Thanks," Janet said. Cathy left and as she placed the pill in her mouth an instant hesitation gripped her. She froze, not used to having second thoughts, and for a moment considered spitting out the new pill, but it was already dissolving on her tongue. She cringed at the acidic taste and quickly took a long drink of water. As she put the bottle down she thought to herself *I hope I'm doing the right thing*, and then shook her head. When it came to taking pills she knew she hadn't been doing the right thing for a long time and she was reminded that with the promotion being over and done with it was time to cut back. And she committed to do it . . . just as soon as she got caught up. With Tally beside her it would be easy to stop now.

She called Tally a few minutes later, caught up on everything that was going on in Willard, said hello to Josh and then explained the amount of work she had to do.

"Well, call me if you need some help staying awake," Tally said as they finished the conversation.

"I will," Janet said, wishing she was spending the night with him, in his house, his bed . . . rather than in her office all alone. "I love you," she said, liking how comfortable she was beginning to feel saying that.

"I love you too," he said. She could tell he was smiling.

Within the hour she noticed three things, and assumed they were the effects of the Splash. First of all, her headache was gone, but she also felt a burst of energy and her focus seemed to be sharpened. It was like nothing existed except the paperwork in front of her—she felt great, like everything was perfect and she hadn't a care or concern in the world. She even giggled once or twice when something in her piles struck her as funny. She made more progress than she ever expected, and she actually finished everything she'd hoped to get done without collapsing from exhaustion. She'd assumed she'd have to come in early tomorrow and stay late to get it caught up. Amazed at the progress she'd made, she looked up at the clock and her mouth dropped open. It was after four o'clock in the morning. She could only stare. In her mind she calculated the hours and discovered she'd been working for twenty hours straight! How was that possible?

She sat back in her chair and considered the situation, it was hard to comprehend and so she checked the clock again, then her watch and then the time on her computer. They all agreed that it was after four. She shook her head and wondered what the rest of her day was going to be like. Was she going to collapse by nine a.m.—in the middle of her meetings? She was afraid that was exactly what would happen, but Cathy had said it would last 24 hours—Janet hoped that would be the case.

Finally, knowing that she would only make herself more anxious if she stayed, Janet decided to go home, shower and change; she didn't want anyone to know she'd spent the whole night at the office. At home, she wondered if she should try and sleep, but it felt like the middle of the afternoon and although she laid down for a few minutes, her mind was anxiously planning her day and she finally gave up getting any rest. All day she waited and waited to fall flat on her face, but she felt fine. The energy surge she'd experienced the night before had worn off, but she wasn't that tired. She couldn't get over how weird it was. At five o'clock that afternoon she straightened her desk and left for the whole weekend, further amazed that she didn't have any work to take home with her. On her way to the car she called Tally and told him that she'd be there around 6:30.

By the time she arrived at Tally's, she could tell that the medication had worn off completely. She had a hard time driving, her eyelids were so heavy, and finally had to blast the radio and crank the air conditioner to keep her senses alert. More than once she drifted into another lane, only to be startled to awareness by the horn of another driver. The last twenty minutes were accomplished with a continuous prayer that she would make it there safely. So it was with great relief that she pulled into Tally's driveway and made her way inside. Josh ran toward her immediately; she almost didn't notice and suddenly started feeling sick to her stomach. Her head was spinning and she had a hard time keeping her balance.

"Are you okay?" Tally asked as he came around the corner and reached out to steady her.

"I don't feel very good," she said slowly. Tally helped her to the couch, where she immediately collapsed.

"What's the matter?" he asked.

"I don't know," she said slowly as she started shivering. Tally rubbed her arms and tried to keep Josh from jumping on her. Suddenly she got off the couch and ran for the bathroom, where she promptly threw up. Close on its heels she felt her breathing begin to strain. *Come on*, she thought to herself, *give me a break*. But within a few seconds she found herself in the middle of a full blown panic attack on the bathroom floor. Tally tried to help her up but she told him she was better where she was and instructed him to get her pills from her purse. By the time he returned, her vision was tunneled and her stomach hurt from trying to draw a breath. She was curled up on the floor, afraid at any moment she was going to throw up again.

"Which one?" Tally asked as he pulled several bottles from her purse, looking at them with concern.

She managed to say Xanax between forced breaths. She tried to take the pill from him, but she was shaking too badly. Finally, she just opened her mouth, humiliated that this was happening, as Tally placed two tablets on her tongue. Meanwhile Josh started to cry from where he stood in the doorway. Tally turned and gathered him up, trying to comfort him while still looking at Janet in total fear.

After a few minutes the attack had subsided enough that Janet was able to lift herself from the floor. What had been exhaustion before the vomiting and the attack was now bordering on loss of consciousness. Tally put Josh down and helped her to her feet. Josh began screaming again. They both ignored the toddler as Tally helped her to the bed, where she collapsed again.

"I'm sorry, Tally," she choked as she started to cry, overwhelmed by what was happening.

"It's okay," he reassured her tenderly. "I think we should take you to the ER."

"No," she said with shake of her head. "I just picked up some kind of flu bug or something . . . and it brought on the attack. I'll be fine." Her head was still spinning—no it was the room that teetered and swirled.

Tally didn't seem convinced, but she could tell he didn't want to force the issue. "Can you help me get undressed?" she asked as she realized she didn't have the strength. He helped remove her clothes, down to her garments and then tucked her in. Josh was still screaming as he tried to climb up on the bed. Tally picked him up and had to wrestle him to be still.

"I'll come check on you once I get Josh settled down."

She nodded as he left the room and immediately fell into a deep sleep.

When Tally went to check on her half an hour later, she hardly responded to him. He retrieved the bottles of pills from the bathroom and took them into the kitchen. Two of the four bottles were real prescriptions, but the other two bottles had no label. He got a sick feeling in his stomach and stared at the bottles as he tried to make sense of it. He knew she took something for the attacks, but he didn't know why she was on all these other medications. Suddenly, he was startled by a chubby little hand flashing up on the table and grabbing the closest bottle. Tally immediately sprang up and chased Josh down, tickling him in order to distract him from the bottle long enough to relieve him of it. Josh's giggles helped relieve Tally's heaviness, and once Josh was completely incapacitated Tally put all the pill bottles in a high cupboard, out of the toddler's reach.

"How about we watch *Monsters, Inc.* again," Tally offered, as Josh pasted himself against Tally's legs. Tally winced slightly; he'd be grateful when Josh was little taller, so that he didn't hit Tally's knees in quite that spot.

"Mikeisowsky," Josh said, and Tally couldn't help but smile, momentarily lifted above his concerns for Janet. He bent down, picked up the black-haired scamp and proceeded to turn on the VCR. Tally sat on the couch and Josh sat next to him, resting his little hand on Tally's thigh. Josh went to bed at nine and Janet didn't wake when Tally slid into bed beside her. He tried to move around in hopes of waking her but she didn't respond at all. It wasn't exactly the way Tally had expected to spend the weekend following his wedding day, but he felt immediately guilty for his disappointment. This week, even with her absence, had been the best week of his life. Josh was a handful, a lot more work than Tally had expected, but he enjoyed having him around and looked forward to the three of them meshing together as a family. Having Janet this close, however, put his body on alert and it was all he could do to keep his hands to himself and respect the fact that she didn't feel well. Finally, he rolled so that his back was to her and took a deep calming breath. He hoped Janet would feel better tomorrow, and, he added almost as an afterthought, that nothing was seriously wrong.

It was nearly eleven o'clock the next morning when Janet woke up. Tally, of course, had been up for hours. He'd taken Josh with him to go feed the horses and do the other morning chores. Then they watched Barrington run in the pasture for awhile. Josh loved it. After they brushed down all three horses, they went for a walk though the patch of trees in front of the house. When they got back, Josh wanted to play in the field and Tally was going to sit on the back patio and watch until he noticed that Janet was up. When he went inside, Janet was sitting at the kitchen table with a glass of water she seemed to be working on. She looked pale and had circles under her eyes, but she looked better than she had last night. Tally kissed her on the forehead.

"How are you feeling?" he asked as he rubbed her shoulders.

"Better," she said with a weak smile, closing her eyes to enjoy the massage. Then she shook her head, "I'm sorry about last night."

"Don't be silly," Tally said as he took a seat next to her, feeling guilty for his lascivious thoughts. "How are you feeling today?"

"Much better."

Tally smiled and wasn't sure what to say next, whether to bring up the pills or not, but he decided to wait. He could tell she was still not feeling well. "Can I get you anything to eat?" he asked. "I made pancakes for breakfast and there's still some batter in the fridge, would you like me to make you some?"

She gave him a humorous look. "You're such a better wife than I am," she said with a shake of her head. "I buy my pancakes frozen."

Tally chuckled. "Would you like some?" he asked again, already heading for the stove.

"Thanks, but I think I'll go lay back down—I'm still exhausted."

"Okay," Tally said, shutting the cupboard that he'd opened. He went with her back to the bedroom, kissed her sweetly, and reluctantly shut the door as he left the bedroom. Now what, he thought to himself as he headed back outside to check on Josh. His desire to spend some time with his wife made everything else seem terribly lacking. But what choice did he have? He went outside and asked if Josh wanted to help him pull weeds. It was mid-August, and very hot, but Josh didn't seem to notice and Tally needed something to take his mind off the disappointing weekend.

By Sunday afternoon Janet was finally feeling better, well enough to go to church and be introduced. Luckily they had the late block, she didn't get up till almost noon. She was very gracious, but mentioned afterwards that she didn't fit in very well.

"What do you mean?" Tally asked in surprise. Several women had come and introduced themselves and the meetings were top notch—it wasn't even a high counsilor Sacrament meeting. He'd thought it had all gone wonderfully.

She shrugged. "All these women are so different from me. They make their own bread for Heaven's sake. They're all housewives."

"Not all of them; some work."

"On farms," she said quietly.

"No," Tally said, trying not to be offended but having a hard time. He loved these people. They were friendly, hard working and family oriented. It was disappointing to hear that Janet didn't share his opinion. "There are some farmers, true, but I've never met people who are so hard working and generous; they're good people."

"I didn't say they weren't," Janet continued. "They just aren't like me."

"No offense, Janet, but you can't expect anyone to be just like you and for someone who hates being judged, you're sure quick to make judgments."

Janet sighed in surrender. "Forget it."

They pulled up at his house a few minutes later and Tally could feel the tension. He whipped up dinner while she finished putting together Josh's room. Tally had gone down to Salt Lake on Friday and brought up most of Josh's furniture and clothes, but hadn't had time to put it all away. They ate dinner and although Tally tried to ignore the earlier exchange they'd had, Janet seemed closed off.

"I didn't mean to be so defensive," he finally said once they were sitting down to eat.

"It's okay," she said as if she didn't care. They lapsed into another silence.

"So what's your schedule this week?" he asked a few minutes later.

Janet swallowed her bite of lasagna, but didn't meet his eyes when she spoke. "I need to head home in about an hour. I've had two weeks without any trips, but they start up again this week. I'll be flying into Boston on Wednesday. I'll be home Saturday morning."

"Oh," he said with disappointment as he realized he wasn't going to see her for almost a week. "I'm going to miss you."

She looked up at him and smiled, putting his heart at rest. "I'm going to miss you too."

About an hour later, while Tally was giving Josh a bath she came into the bathroom holding her purse. "Have you seen my medication?" she asked.

Tally turned, he'd almost forgotten about that. Using the edge of the tub for support he unstopped the drain and pushed himself slowly up to a standing position—Josh loved trying to stop the water from disappearing. "Yeah, I put them in the kitchen," he said. He walked past her and she followed him. "Why so many bottles?" he asked, trying to sound as casual as possible. He was still concerned, no, maybe curious was a better word, about the medications, but he didn't want to start an argument, especially after the tense afternoon they'd shared.

"Oh, I was cleaning out my desk and found all these old prescriptions from forever ago. I've heard you're supposed to dump them down the toilet, but since I was at work I decided to do that at home."

Tally reached into the kitchen cabinet, where he'd put the bottles, and took them off the shelf. He was tempted to check the ones with labels as verification of their expiration dates, but immediately chastised himself. She said they were expired prescriptions, and that was all he needed to know. "I can throw them out for you," he offered as she took them rather quickly and put them back in her purse.

"That's okay," Janet said. "You're busy with Josh, I'll take care of it." She looked up and they smiled at one another. He pulled her into his arms. It felt so good to hold her again and he tried to implant the memory of having her so close. Six days without her felt like an eternity. When he finally pulled back they shared a soft kiss. He had hoped she'd be willing to stay a little longer; they hadn't made love since their nights on the road, but the guilt descended at the same moment the thought came to his mind. She still wasn't feeling well; he needed to be a little more understanding, but it was hard to be patient.

"I'll see you next weekend," she said softly. "And I'll make this one up to you."

Tally nodded and watched her drive away after she said goodbye to Josh. He wondered at the odd feeling he had about everything that had happened this weekend and asked himself for the first time if maybe they *had* moved too fast. He tried to tell himself that it was just the circumstances of the weekend, but it had more to do with her attitude than anything else. Yes, this was the first time he'd seen her since their trip to Oklahoma and she was sick, but she seemed withdrawn, distant from him, and it seemed so easy for her to leave. The mood of the argument continued to gnaw at him—he hated contention.

You're overreacting, he told himself, *it was a very simple disagreement and it's not that big a deal.* But he wasn't sure if he believed it.

A naked and soaking-wet Josh suddenly crashed into the back of Tally's knee's, nearly knocking him off balance and getting the lower half of his pants all wet. Tally turned quickly. "Oh, now you're in for it!" he said sarcastically. Josh screamed and ran for his bedroom, with Tally hot on his trail—limping only slightly. *Surely things will be okay,* Tally continued to tell himself as he caught Janet's son and twirled him in the air. Why would we have felt so strongly about getting married if it wasn't going to work out?

Janet turned up the radio as she drove back to Salt Lake, hoping that the pulsating rhythm would drown out her thoughts. It didn't work and she turned it down a few minutes later, irritated by the banging music. She reviewed the weekend and shook her head in disappointment. *Why am I like this?* she asked herself. It had been their first time together in over a week yet she'd stepped behind this wall and been distant and ungrateful. More than that, she'd flat out lied to Tally about the prescriptions. She sighed in exasperation. She didn't understand why she did these things, and if she didn't, how was he supposed to make sense of her behavior? Was it just that she was working so hard? Was it because of the new pill Cathy had given her? Even as she asked herself the questions she knew none of them were the reason. It was just as it had been in her other marriages, she just couldn't get close. For some reason, getting close was equal to giving up control and the very idea of giving up control, even a little bit, scared her out of her mind.

And the pills aren't helping, she thought as her eyes drifted to her purse on the passenger seat. They made it too easy for her to pretend, to hide, and yet she was so embarrassed that Tally had found them. Did he believe that they were expired? Her pulse quickened as she considered how close she'd come to getting caught. *Caught?* she repeated in her mind, not liking the implication of her own word.

Over the weekend she'd needed four Xanax a day just to keep calm—it scared her how often she'd thought of taking more. The 'O' pill Cathy had given her before the Oklahoma trip turned out to be Oxycontin and she'd taken one every twelve hours or so as well. Even now she had a burning desire to take one more pill, if only to put all these thoughts to rest for a few hours. *What's happening?* she thought as tears came to her eyes. She knew she should have let Tally flush them, maybe she should tell him her concerns with how many she was taking, how badly she wanted them all the time. But that control issue popped into her mind again. He wouldn't trust her again if he knew how desperately she needed and wanted these medications. He would think she was weak, that she wasn't the woman he thought she was. But *was* she woman he thought she was? She knew the answer and it made her feel even more miserable. She didn't want to lie to him, she didn't want to live some façade. More than any time in her life she wanted to be real with someone. More than anyone she'd ever known, Tally made being herself seem okay. But she just couldn't take the step past her barriers. She'd never done it before and what if she was wrong? What if by exposing her secrets, her weaknesses and her fears Tally decided he didn't like who she really was? She let out a ragged breath and shook her head in frustration. There were no answers. She just had to keep doing the best she could and hope that would be enough—it was really the only choice.

Monday morning Janet was back at work bright and early. As soon as Cathy came in, Janet asked her to come into the office.

"That pill made me sick," she said, trying to soften the accusation in her voice. "What was it?"

Cathy didn't answer the question. "Did you lay down as soon as you felt it wearing off?" she asked.

Janet hesitated, just now remembering Cathy's instruction to do so. "I left for Willard, and by the time I got there I was sick and almost delirious. I slept for almost 15 hours straight."

"And it kept you up for 24 hours," Cathy added. "That's what you wanted. I'm sorry it made you sick—it does that if you don't take another one or lay down. I didn't mean for it to ruin your weekend."

Janet felt her irritation melt away under Cathy's penitent look. She shrugged. "I did get a lot of work done," she admitted. It was on the tip of her tongue to add that she wouldn't take it again, but she didn't say it out loud. It had allowed her to catch up with her work overnight. She wouldn't make it a habit by any means; but she wasn't going to discount its value, either. She ignored the pangs of conscience completely. Cathy's phone rang, and Janet waved that she could go answer it. Cathy left gratefully and a few moments later announced that Jay was on the phone. Janet took a breath and answered it. He wanted to meet with her—now. She said she'd be right there and could only hope she wasn't about to be fired.

When she reached Jay's office he indicated for her to sit down. When she did he handed her a stack of papers. She recognized them immediately as the purchase forms used for corporate purchasing. Since she was only a regional purchaser, she'd never filled them out; she'd only seen the receipts on certain purchase orders that crossed her desk. Had she gotten the corporate position it would be her signature at the bottom, but instead it was Sheryl's bubbly scrawl on each form. She couldn't imagine why Jay was giving her these forms. Was he simply trying to rub it in? She looked up with a questioning, and guarded, look.

"Take a look at the forms," he said. "Tell me if anything looks amiss."

Janet returned her gaze to the papers in her hand. Immediately, certain figures jumped out at her. The purchase amounts had been added at the retail level, not the wholesale amounts and the portions ordered of certain things weren't rounded to the nearest case. She flipped through sheet after sheet and each one was as big a mess as the next. Finally she looked up, feeling rather satisfied with herself. She'd told Jay that Sheryl wasn't up to the job, and apparently she was right. But she didn't say anything—she knew she didn't need to.

"Can you fix those?" Jay asked.

"Yes," Janet said confidently, bolstered by his faith in her.

"I know you said you're interested in a store position, but is there any way you'd consider taking the management job instead? It's obvious that we chose the wrong person for this position and I owe you an apology."

Janet's heart soared. She was getting a second chance! Then she froze and remembered the arrangement she and Tally had made. But how could she turn her back on this? It was her dream, a dream she thought was no longer within her reach. And yet here it was again, staring her in the face. Could she turn her back on this second chance? She didn't even hesitate to answer.

"I wanted a store position because my corporate aspirations had been cut off—if it's available to me again, I want it."

"You're sure?"

"I'm positive."

Five minutes later she walked swiftly to her office, a satisfied grin on her face. She was being given another opportunity and she wasn't going to pass it up. In her office she picked up the phone to call Tally, excited to share the triumph—but she hesitated. He would not see this as a good thing, but she simply couldn't turn it down. She hung up the phone and decided to wait for the weekend. By then she'd have come up with the perfect way to tell him. She'd stop at Victoria's Secret and pick up something soft and sexy to help convince him that it would be okay. She felt a twinge of guilt, both for changing their plans single-handedly and manipulating him into accepting the change—but, the same response overwhelmed her inner protests—she could not say no to this. It was everything she wanted. If Tally truly loved her, the way he said he did, he wouldn't want her to give this up. She was married, yes, but that didn't mean that she was going to give up her life, her goals and ambitions. One way or another, Tally would have to understand.

CHAPTER EIGHT

"Are these for a special occasion?"

Tally looked up from the display of cards and smiled at the woman behind the register. Her face was partially hidden by the huge vase of roses she was ringing up—30 long stemmed red roses in fact. "My wife and I are celebrating our one month anniversary," he said proudly as he selected a card from the rack and slid it across the counter.

The florist raised her eyebrows. "One month?" she said in surprise. "Let me give you my number; you'll have expectations to meet after this—oh, and you can have the card for free." She smiled broadly. Tally paid for the roses, thanked her and left with a grin on his face.

Josh was at Chris and Lacey's for the night and he was surprising Janet with roses, dinner and a one night stay at a bed and breakfast. An evening together without Josh demanding their attention and Janet catching up on paperwork seemed like a Caribbean Cruise at this point. He pulled up to her office a little before 5 p.m.—he'd never been there before and took time to admire the elegant décor in the lobby. When the doors of the elevator opened onto the sixth floor he walked up to the reception desk and moved the flowers so that they wouldn't block his face.

"Can you tell me where Janet Blaire's office is?" he asked.

"Janet Blaire?"

"Janet Stewart Blaire," Tally corrected, including her maiden name this time.

"All deliveries are to be left at the front desk," the receptionist informed him as she put her hands on the vase.

She thinks I'm a delivery boy? Tally thought with dismay. "I'm her husband," Tally said as he pulled the vase back. "I'd like to give them to her myself."

"Oh . . . of course," the receptionist minced. "Let me call her office."

"I'd like to take them to her myself," Tally repeated more sternly. He was her husband, for Heaven's sake, surely that gave him some credibility. "Can you point me to her office?"

The receptionist hesitated for another moment and then pointed down the hall on the left side of her desk. "Fourth door on your left, the first office is her secretary, Cathy. She can announce you."

Announce me? Tally thought. *Where am I, Buckingham Palace?*

The shy brunette's eyes went wide when he told her who he was a few moments later. "I'm so glad to meet you, I'm Cathy. Janet didn't mention you were coming," she gushed as she stood up and put out her hand.

Tally shook the proffered hand. "Well, it's a surprise,"

Cathy hesitated. "Oh," she finally said as she sat back down. "Janet's in meetings till about 5:15 or so—you're welcome to wait in the waiting area and I'll tell her you're here."

"Is she in her office?" Tally asked. Though the frosted glass he could see that the room was dark.

"No, she's with the other corporate managers in the conference room."

Tally let the word 'corporate' slide past him without a second thought. "Can I wait in her office then?" he asked, unsure why she hadn't offered that in the first place.

"Uh, well . . . uh."

Tally was getting irritated. Their first month of marriage had been anything but easy. With Janet's travel, Tally's job and increasingly full photography schedule, they hadn't had much quality time together. Josh's continual presence also gave them very little opportunity to be alone. When they were together they were often bickering about their lack of time together. It was a silly cycle, and Tally hoped it was just a normal transitioning experience that would in time fade away. They had known there would be complications, but living with them had been harder than he expected. After hours and hours on his knees he'd resolved to try harder. He hoped this weekend would give them a chance to reconnect; he felt they needed it. After going through all the trouble to arrange this get-away he didn't appreciate being treated like an insignificant visitor. "I'll wait in her office," he said in a tone that told Cathy he wasn't asking for permission. Her mouth moved but she said nothing and he didn't stay to hear her vocalize any more protests. He walked past her desk and entered Janet's office.

After flipping on the light, he looked around the room and whistled under his breath. It was huge, with a dark plum color on the walls and cherry wood furniture. He was surprised, since she'd never mentioned how nice it was—but they didn't have much time to talk about things like that. He placed the vase on the desk and smiled at how well the elaborate bouquet matched the room. Along one wall was a leather sofa. He sat there first, testing it out, but found he couldn't sit still. This was a part of Janet's life he hadn't explored before and he found it exciting to be here. He looked at the books on her shelving. Most of the titles were motivational, like 'Power', 'How to Win Friends and Influence People', 'The courage to be Rich'. Most of the other books were on fashion and design—none of them held much interest for him.

He turned toward her desk and that was when he saw the nameplate he hadn't noticed before. Etched in the gold plate was the name 'Janet Stewart.' Tally furrowed his brow and picked it up, noting that it didn't say 'Janet Blaire.' *They just hadn't gotten around to changing it,* he told himself. Then something else got his attention. Underneath her name it read Corporate Purchase Manager. He repeated the title in his mind twice more—that was the job she didn't get—he was sure of it.

A strange feeling rolled down his back and he glanced at the papers on her desk. After a few minutes of thumbing through piles of paperwork he came across a handwritten note. "Congratulations on the promotion!! You're the woman for the job. Best wishes." It was signed by a woman named Carol and dated almost two weeks ago. He felt a fire start in his belly and was soon making a mess as he looked for more proof that she had lied. Why would she keep this from me? he thought as he continued his searching, but he knew the answer. He and Janet might not know each other well, but he could put the pieces together well enough.

"Tally!"

He looked up to see Janet in the doorway. She had a huge smile on her face as she looked at the roses on her desk. She cocked her head to the side and walked toward him. "You are so sweet."

Tally picked up the nameplate and held it up. She stopped and they stared at each other for several seconds. "When did you plan to tell me?" he asked as calmly and evenly as he could manage.

Janet let out a breath of defeat and he wondered if she would have ever told him had he not stumbled across the information. She took a moment to shut the door to her office before responding to his question. "I'm sorry," she said in what sounded like a sincere tone. "It happened so fast and then I meant to tell you, and the moment was never right and . . ." her voice trailed off and she looked at him with sad eyes. He felt himself wavering already.

"It's been two weeks," Tally reminded her. "You couldn't find time to tell me in two weeks—and why didn't we talk about it? We had an agreement, Janet, I thought we were working together on something."

"I knew you wouldn't be happy, but I just couldn't say no—"

"Couldn't or wouldn't?" Tally interrupted.

As soon as he finished talking, it was as if a wall had come up behind her eyes. She lifted her chin and the sorrow he'd seen just moments ago disappeared. He'd seen the defense before; she used it anytime she was mad, but he hated being shut out on something as important as this and it made him even more angry.

"When we got back from Oklahoma, Sheryl had made a mess of things. Jay asked for my help and he offered me the job. It's what I've always wanted, Tally, you know that."

"You said you didn't want it anymore," he replied, standing up from where he'd been sitting behind her desk and dropping the nameplate onto the desk with a resounding thud. "You said you didn't care, that you wanted a store position as soon as possible."

"That was when I thought this was out of reach."

"And so everything we talked about, all the plans we had, just went out the window? How could you do this without discussing it with me? And then how could you keep it from me?"

"How can you stand there and question my decision at all?" she spat back, her eyes furious. "This isn't about you, Tally, and I don't belong to you. I don't need your permission."

Tally straightened. "I never said you did," he said very slowly. "But we had an agreement that—"

"That changed," she cut in, folding her arms and staring him down. There was no sympathy for his feelings, no admission that she'd done something wrong.

"And I'm just supposed to accept that everything's different now?"

"Not everything," she said. "Just this."

"Just this?" Tally repeated. "This is everything, Janet. It was your job that was keeping us apart in the first place, and now you've taken on more responsibility. That changes the whole plan."

"So it's all because of my job," Janet said. "Not your horses, or your job—mine." She shook her head. "If you want me to say I'm sorry, fine, I'm sorry things didn't work out the way *you* wanted them to. But I would never make you give up your dreams, Tally, and if you really loved me you wouldn't ask me to give up mine."

"If *you* really loved *me* you would have told me about this in the first place, then we could have at least discussed it. But you didn't give me the chance."

"I wonder why," she said angrily. "Look at your reaction."

Tally took a deep breath and headed for the door. She didn't make any move to stop him.

"Happy Anniversary," he said before shutting the door behind him. The secretary was gone and he walked straight for the elevator. He was nearly to his car in the parking garage before Janet caught up to him. Her demeanor had once again changed; she was the humble sympathetic Janet now—he couldn't keep up with her mood swings.

"Tally, I'm sorry," she called to him.

He stopped and turned, but said nothing, allowing her to catch up with him. "I am sorry, Tally," she repeated. "Things have just been so hard this month. I didn't want to make it all worse."

"You should have told me," he said, but the softness in her eyes was having its effect on him. It *had* been a hard month, they'd had issue after issue to deal with and although she was wrong about this, he didn't want to push her further away.

"I know," she agreed, reaching out and placing her hand on his arm. At her touch the anger faded even more. All he thought about when they weren't together was Janet. He wanted her with him all the time and it felt as if they were always apart, always separate. More than anything he wanted them to be a team, working on common goals and being together as much as possible. "Can you forgive me?" she asked, cocking her head to the side again.

Tally sighed. How could he say no to that?

Later that night, long after Tally had started snoring softly, Janet got out of bed. They'd had a nice evening, but there was tension in the air and the situation had never been completely resolved. He'd reserved a beautiful room that looked over the Heber Valley. She stared out across the moonlit landscape and made some decisions about her life and about her future. She loved Tally, she loved the completeness he'd brought into her life, but she had given him the wrong impression during that week in Oklahoma. Things had been so out of whack for her. She was overwhelmed by everything and it had made her much too vulnerable. Despite his differences from Allen and Craig, in some ways she now knew he was just like them. He had a picture of what he wanted her to be, and didn't like it when she didn't fit the mold. But she loved him, she wanted him in her life—they just had to establish boundaries. She knew the process wouldn't be easy, but despite how much she hated disappointing him, she knew that he had to come to terms with who she really was. That meant she couldn't let him think he had control. She'd given in tonight because she knew she should have told him sooner, but from now on she wasn't going to put things off. In the morning, she would bring up the promotion and they would discuss it, but she wouldn't back down. She would make sure he understood that this was where she wanted to be. They would deal with things up front and he would just have to accept her limitations.

She turned and looked at him, wishing that she could be the woman he wanted. He brought something into her life she hadn't had before, but she wasn't sure what it was and she couldn't afford to let that slow her down. If she'd learned anything in her life, it was that she had to be strong, and she had to take care of herself. Other people, like Josh and Tally, could make life sweeter, but she couldn't count on them to know what was best for her. She went to her purse and took an Oxycontin and a Xanax, knowing she needed to get some sleep. She no longer calculated how many she took each day; she'd successfully trained herself not to think about it. With the extra responsibilities of the new position, she didn't have the time or energy to worry about it. Tomorrow morning she and Tally would have their final discussion on the subject of her promotion. Somehow, Tally would have to understand.

CHAPTER NINE

Thanksgiving Day—Two and a Half Months Later

"Hello," Tally called as he opened the front door of his brother's house.

"Hello!" came the reply from the kitchen. Tally took a minute to release Josh from his jacket and then told him he could go play with Chris and Lacey's daughter Sophie. Sophie was a few months younger than Josh, but they played well together, just as cousins should. *Cousins*, Tally repeated in his mind as Josh scampered down the stairs to the basement. Tally straightened, ignoring the additional ache in his knee due to the increasingly cold temperature of late. It was Thanksgiving Day, and Lacey and Chris had invited him to spend the day with them and their children. They were all planning to go to Oklahoma for Christmas, which meant Thanksgiving was spent at home.

Lacey was standing at the counter shaping dough into rolls when he entered the kitchen. She looked up when he entered and smiled. "How are ya?" she asked.

Tally smiled and hoped his expression betrayed none of his inner feelings. "I'm good."

"Is the cold getting to you already?" she asked sympathetically as she watched him limp toward the counter.

"A bit," he said as he sat on a bar stool and lifted his leg so he could stretch it out. "I had a five day job in North Carolina last week, and my knee hasn't forgiven me for it yet."

"Can I get you anything?"

Tally shook his head; he had no desire to be waited on. Lacey looked toward the doorway he'd just entered and just raised her eyebrows; she didn't need to use words to ask the question. "Janet had to extend her trip to San Diego," Tally explained. "She'll get back tomorrow morning."

"Oh, I'm sorry," Lacey said. She then immediately turned her attention back to her baking as an awkward silence descended. It had been three-and-a-half months since he and Janet had gotten married, and Lacey had met her only once, despite the monthly dinners Tally had attended and the fact that Lacey had watched Josh several times when Tally had photo shoots and Janet wasn't around.

He thought back to their wedding day, to how perfect it had seemed and wondered for the thousandth time why he didn't foresee that the complications they tried to remedy would never go away. The overnight get-away on their one-month anniversary was supposed to be a chance for them to reconnect, but it had proven to be just the opposite. In the morning, after a tense but enjoyable evening, Janet had stated in no uncertain terms that this job was her top priority. He tried not to get angry, he tried to discuss things calmly, but she seemed ready for a fight. Over and over again she accused him of trying to make her into something she wasn't. He finally realized he wasn't going to convince her otherwise by harping on the issue, so he quit talking all together. When they picked up Josh from Lacey that afternoon, they weren't speaking and Janet went home right after church the next day. Since then he'd decided to be supportive and they'd tried to ignore the broken promise, but it was hard to do; at least it was for him. Tally had gone to the temple several times since then, seeking peace and inspiration and although it made him feel better the only revelation he'd had was that he didn't know Janet very well and he didn't know what to do to make things better between them.

"Hey, big brother!"

Tally turned to the stairs leading down from the second floor and smiled at his little brother. Chris held Angie, his 6-month-old daughter, in his arms, but shifted her in order to clap Tally on the back as he passed on his way to the other side of the counter. After easing the baby into the infant-swing in the kitchen, he kissed Lacey on the cheek and then began scanning the countertop.

"I've hidden everything," she said over her shoulder.

Chris made an exaggerated moan and slumped his shoulders dramatically. "You're so mean to me." Their easygoing companionship made Tally ache inside.

Lacey just shook her head, her blond curls bouncing as she did so. Lacey reminded Tally so much of his mom; he was sure they were cookie cutters of one another. Like his mom, Lacey was short and on the chubby side. She had big blue eyes and dimples when she smiled; and she seemed to smile all the time. Chris had definitely married a woman just like Mom. In contrast, Chris was tall and thin; too thin in Tally's opinion. He owned his own hair salon in Salt Lake City and did pretty well for himself, although Tally rarely missed an opportunity to tease him about his profession. In many ways, such as occupation and body type, he and Tally couldn't be more different, but in other ways they were definitely brothers. But Chris was more than a brother, he was Tally's best friend.

"I think the game's started," Chris said, already halfway to the TV on the other side of the greatroom.

With joviality he didn't feel, Tally waved toward the TV. "Well, by all means, turn it on. Is it Thanksgiving or not?"

After the football game came Thanksgiving dinner, followed by naps for the kids, bringing blessed silence. Lacey went upstairs to nurse the baby, leaving Chris and Tally to drink their root beer floats, a Blaire family Thanksgiving tradition, by themselves.

"So how are things, Tal?" Chris asked.

Tally didn't know whether he was relieved or annoyed at being asked; he knew exactly what Chris meant. Perhaps yesterday he'd have smiled and said it was fine, but after getting Janet's phone call last night and having the argument that followed concerning her inability to make it home, he was in no mood to keep pretending that everything was fine. "Things are pretty lousy right now," Tally said.

"That bad?"

Tally nodded and stirred his float a few times. "It hasn't turned out the way I thought it would."

"She still hasn't changed her mind about getting a store position?"

Tally shook his head. "It's not a subject we talk about."

"Is she still coming home on the weekends?"

"You mean to my house?" Tally asked, looking up and meeting Chris' eyes for the first time. He shook his head again. "Her home is in Salt Lake and I'm coming to think she has no intention of ever leaving it. But no, she rarely comes to my house on the weekends anymore. This new position is more demanding than the last one. She seems to be having more and more trips that overlap the weekends. She hasn't seen Josh for almost three weeks, and it doesn't seem to bother her a bit." This was all so embarrassing, he sounded like such an idiot—but he didn't care, he felt crushed by everything happening in his marriage and desperately hoped someone could say the magic words that would make everything all right.

Chris was silent for several moments. "Is the adoption still going through?"

Tally nodded. "As far as I know it is. I've done everything she's asked me to do, but I don't know exactly how it's progressing. We hardly seem to talk anymore." He paused, realizing how insane his marriage had become and he began to feel the emotion rise in his throat. "I don't know what to do," he choked, shaking his head in embarrassment. "I've tried everything I can think of to make her want to be with us, to make it easier for her to be around us; but nothing seems to change. I even listed the house last month, deciding that I'd move to Salt Lake, but she told me to take it off the market as soon as I told her about it. She didn't want me to 'give up my dream.' I've gone and stayed at her house a few times during the week, but she's at the office 'til almost ten, sometimes 'til two or three in the morning, so it doesn't make any sense to sit around and hope she'll show up."

"You don't think . . . she's seeing someone, do you?"

"It's crossed my mind," Tally admitted sadly. "But in my heart I don't think so. When we are together, and we're not arguing, everything is still there; it's like a time warp. But she's got this obsession about her work. She's taken on extra projects and volunteers to do extra training. They had a hard time finding a new person for her old position so she did that job, plus this one for awhile, and now every time a purchaser quits she does the work herself until a replacement is found. It's insane how much she's doing. She'll promise me she'll be out for the weekend, and then cancel at the last minute. When she does come, she's either so exhausted she sleeps the whole time, or she brings home so much work she ignores us anyway. I think she's living off of Xanax, Diet Coke and No-Doz pills but she absolutely *won't* talk to me about that. If I ever say anything negative, she turns it into a fight, and I'm tired of fighting."

"Oh, man," Chris said with a shake of his head. "I'm so sorry, Tal. I wish I had some advice for you."

"I went and talked to my bishop last week, and I'm sure you can imagine how hard that was for me," Tally admitted, finding it hard to stop now that he'd gotten warmed up. Chris was well aware of his difficulty with the new bishop after having been released from the Young Men's organization last February, he would know what a big step it was for Tally to go to the same man for counsel. "After we got married we had her records transferred to my ward, since she was going to be there on weekends; but I bet she's only been half a dozen times, if that. I thought maybe he'd have some advice—I was desperate."

"What did he say?"

"That improper preparation rarely yields the results you're looking for in a marriage."

"Ouch," Chris said.

"Yeah, I didn't feel much lifted by that, but I have to admit he's probably right," Tally replied with a shrug. He continued to stare at the frothy brown concoction in his glass. "We were so . . . into each other then, and we barely knew one another. The attraction was so strong that it just made sense to do it right."

"Do it right?" Chris repeated. "I thought you were saying you didn't do it right."

"By 'right,' I mean that we both seriously wondered if we could keep our hands off each other much longer."

"Ohhhh," Chris said with a nod as he finally understood. "That kind of doing it right."

"The irony is that we hardly have the chance for sex now because we're never together, and when we are, we usually end up in an argument. So much for our bright idea; it's such a mess."

"Do you still love her?"

The emotion came back in droves and Tally had to swallow in hopes of avoiding further embarrassment. "I do," he choked, covering his eyes with one hand. "I've prayed about this nonstop and I know that the woman I fell in love with is still there. I just don't understand what's happened and I don't know how to find out. When we got married I knew it wasn't going to be easy, but I did pray about it and I did feel that it was the right thing to do. I didn't marry Janet just because we were so attracted to each other, or just because she was pushing for it—I truly felt it was what the Lord wanted me to do, but believing that makes it harder to make sense of now. Why would He want me to have put myself in this situation?"

"That probably makes it harder to pray about what to do now, doesn't it?"

"Absolutely—not that I haven't prayed about it . . . every day! But I haven't gotten any answers and if I did I don't know that I'd trust them anyway."

"Maybe you guys should try counseling."

"I mentioned that too, but she said she isn't that type of person. Her first husband is a psychiatrist and she has a sort of grudge against the profession because he always tried to 'pry into her business.'"

"Do you have any other ideas?" Chris further probed. "Is there anything you can think of that might be part of this?"

Tally shrugged. "I really don't know," he admitted. "Maybe I'm an idiot, but I don't know. She doesn't talk to me about personal things, and quite frankly I just don't know her well enough to know if this is different than how she used to be, or if it's just the way she is. But she seemed so different in the beginning, I just wish I knew what has changed."

"You said she's taking a lot of pills; do you think that's part of this?"

"I know it is," Tally said. "It's not normal to take the amount she's taking, and ever since I brought it up she won't take them around me and hides her meds—but again, what do I do about that? I've tried talking to her. I've tried not talking to her. I've gone to the bishop. I've asked her to go to the bishop with me. I've suggested counseling. I've prayed and gone to the temple—I've done everything I can think of, yet every time we see each other it's as if she's added another layer to the wall she's building. I really don't know how much longer I can take it. It's driving me crazy."

Their conversation continued to cycle through his mind as he and Josh drove home that night. Once Josh was asleep, Tally sat down with a pad of paper and a pen. He started listing what he wanted out of his marriage, and came up with a list of twenty-seven things, then he put a check mark next to those that he felt he and Janet had accomplished. It was a pathetically small number, and even the ones with a check next to them seemed to be a stretch. The truth was that nothing had turned out the way he'd hoped it would, well, except Josh. Having Josh around all the time had taken some getting used to, but the two of them had formed a deep bond over the last few months and Tally couldn't imagine life without him. Josh was also likely the biggest reason Tally didn't confront Janet more than he did. The thought of losing Josh was frightening, and he didn't want to push Janet into taking such a measure. In trade, however, he felt as if his heart was slowly breaking and he didn't know how much longer he could take it. He felt as if he'd aged five years in the last four months and he wondered what had happened to those two kids who were so crazy about each other. It seemed like someone else's life.

Pushing the pad of paper away, his eye caught a picture on the mantle. It was a snapshot taken on their wedding day. He'd had it changed from color to shades of brown and gold, a Sepia finish, and enlarged it to an eight by ten portrait. In the photo, Janet hung onto his arm, leaning toward him and smiling broadly into the camera. The expression on his own face was one of absolute delight, but as with any picture it only showed the outside. How many photos had he snapped where just moments before people were screaming or arguing, yet when he started the countdown they put on their masks and appeared to have no worries at all. He knew, despite how intensely happy he appeared, that on the inside he was unsettled about the concessions he'd made, he worried about the complexities they would face. As he looked at her brilliant smile he wondered what was going through her mind at that moment. It was impossible for him to believe she felt as happy and content as the camera made her seem. He knew better than that now.

The pit in his stomach made him unable to stare at their blissful image any longer. He turned his head and looked out the back window. It was a full moon and the landscape was illuminated by the white light. He looked at Willard Peak, with all the shadows enhancing its rugged silhouette and then his gaze traveled to the distant lights in the windows of the homes scattered around his own. What went on in those families—in those other 'picture perfect' lives? he wondered. Did they have secrets like he did, humiliating things that ate at them? Did other people struggle with the seemingly good choices they'd made? When they'd married he thought he and Janet were starting a life together, building on a foundation. Though not the start he'd dreamed of, it seemed secure enough. It wasn't perfect, but it was good—wasn't it? But if there had been any base in the beginning, it was falling apart and he wondered if there had ever been much hope at all.

It had been good to talk to Chris today, but he knew that even his brother couldn't really understand this. Maybe no one could; it certainly felt that way. Even talking to his Father in Heaven didn't seem to be helping much. He got up from the table and limped to his room. His knee was bothering him more than usual so he opened the cabinet and retrieved his pain pills. He didn't take them very often, and tried to deal with the pain as long as he could, but he really needed some relief tonight.

To his surprise there were only a few pills left. *That's odd*, he thought to himself. He could swear it was half-full the last time he'd taken one. But he shrugged his shoulders and went to the kitchen to get a glass of water. He probably just didn't remember and he was too tired to think about anything else tonight. Janet would be calling in the morning and he knew he'd spend a long night anticipating the conversation that would take place when she did.

Janet stopped at the office on her way home Friday morning. No one was there, since the entire office staff had been given the weekend off for the Thanksgiving holiday. Cathy had left a package that Janet needed to pick up, though, so the stop was necessary.

Just as Cathy had said it would be, the box was in the bottom drawer of Cathy's desk. Janet took it out and opened it immediately, smiling with relief as she inspected each selection. The Xanax, Oxycontin and Splash were all there, as well as some of a sleeping pill Janet had started taking a few weeks ago. Janet retrieved her wallet and wrote out a check for twelve hundred dollars without thinking twice, put the check in Cathy's desk and entered her own office. There were a few things she needed to check on before she left.

Hours later she looked up at the clock and sighed. She hadn't expected having so much to do. What was supposed to be a quick stop had taken her whole day, and she still wasn't caught up. She picked up the phone and called Tally.

"Hey there," she said with a smile.

"I thought you were landing this morning," Tally said blandly.

"I had to stop by the office and you won't believe how much work I have waiting for me! I think I'll finish it up tonight and come in the morning. Will that be okay?"

Tally was silent. "When you get here, we need to talk."

"Why?" she asked, concerned at the tone in his voice. *Had something happened to Josh,* she wondered. As always, she chose to ignore the problems in their relationship unless confronted. She knew Tally didn't like confrontation and she'd learned to use that to her advantage.

"Do you really need to ask?"

"If this is about Thanksgiving, I'm sorry," she said, although she couldn't keep the annoyance out of her tone. "I told you there was nothing I could do about it." Why was he making this so difficult for her? It was already hard enough to be away from them so much, why couldn't he just be happy about seeing her?

Tally said nothing.

"I've missed you so much," she finally said in a sweet voice, trying another route. "I can't wait to see you guys."

"Really," Tally said sarcastically. "I find that hard to believe."

Instantly the anger she'd been trying to keep at bay exploded. "Well, then maybe I shouldn't come at all! I'm doing the best I can, Tally, a little appreciation would go a long way here!"

"Appreciation for what?" Tally replied with anger. "You would rather do anything than spend time with us and I'm tired of sitting here waiting for you to decide you've got time to work us in. Josh deserves a mother and I deserve a wife who cares about us enough to want to be with us now and then!"

"I do want to be with you," she countered. "That's why I'm staying late to get all this done, so that I can be with you guys. I am busting my hump over here and all you can do is complain."

She heard Tally take a deep breath on the other end of the line. "When you get here tomorrow, we need to talk," he said again.

"Fine," she said before hanging up the phone. Immediately she opened the box Cathy had left for her and took a Splash tablet. Since taking it the first time, she hadn't gotten sick again because she'd learned that, just as Cathy had told her in the beginning, as soon as she felt it wearing off she had to either take another one, or fall asleep right then. But since the effects lasted about 24 hours from the time she took the pill she was able to plan her days accordingly. Because of all those things, she only used it when she really needed the boost. She'd found that a couple Oxycontin helped her relax enough for normal days and a double dose would get rid of a headache. She still took the Xanax when the stress was threatening to overwhelm her but prided herself on how little Xanax she was taking these days. She didn't factor in that she was taking so much of everything else she didn't need it as much, instead she chose to see it as progress. Now that she had the sleeping pills she could remedy almost any problem. Any reservations she'd once had about taking the pills had long since dissipated. They were prescriptions, and they helped her not only keep up, but to far exceed the demands placed upon her. She had to be careful about the times she took the pills, since some of them made it hard for her to focus or keep up with conversation, but she'd almost perfected it so that she seemed to always be at the top of her game.

Tally and Josh came to mind again, and her heart swelled. She hated that Tally was so unhappy and she missed Josh terribly. When faced with the actual choice of the job she'd always wanted, or settling for the arrangement she and Tally had discussed, she found out just how badly she needed the validation of the job. And she knew it wouldn't be forever, just so that she could prove to herself that she was capable of this kind of demand. And she had to admit she loved being in charge. She was over all the purchasing for the entire Western United States. Everyone in every department of every store answered to her. They knew her name and regarded her with respect. It was exhilarating and she wanted to enjoy every minute of it. Next August, when she'd completed a whole year and finished implementing all the new programs she was creating, she'd let it go and move on to something that worked better for them. If only she could make Tally understand. Everything would be perfect if he could understand why this was so vital to her and not take it personally.

She pushed the thoughts away, however, and got to work. By two a.m. she'd be done, then she could drive straight to Willard. A smile played on her lips as she imagined Tally's reaction when she slid into bed beside him. Her fingers began to fly across the keyboard as the motivation to see her two men grew stronger and the Splash kicked in. She'd go home and make it all up to him. Everything would be fine.

Nearly twelve hours later Janet turned the key in the back door and opened it quietly. It was almost four o'clock in the morning, and freezing outside, but she didn't want to wake Tally up just yet so she hadn't opened the garage. She tiptoed into the master bedroom and watched him for a few minutes in the dark. She really had missed him. Quietly she began removing her clothes, then she pulled back the covers. She felt him startle, but immediately silenced any protest with a long kiss she felt sure well communicated her deepest feelings. At first she could feel that he was resisting, so she pulled back and whispered how sorry she was and that it would get better. Then she kissed him again, and this time he was much more receptive.

When he was asleep again, she slipped out of bed and retrieved her jacket from the chair where she'd laid it when she came in. She also grabbed her garments and went into the bathroom to get dressed. In her front jacket pocket was a slim plastic pill case. Tally's concern with her pills had become apparent after the first couple of months, since then she'd chosen to leave the bottles at home and just bring a supply with her. The case easily held twelve pills and she removed one, the new sleeping pill, and then rummaged in the cupboard until she found Tally's pills, Loritab. She took one of those too, not wanting to waste her own and then slid back into bed with her husband, hoping the pills would work even though she'd taken the Splash just 12 hours ago.

"Everything okay?" he asked groggily as she laid her head on his chest.

"I'm with you," she said softly, absorbing the feel of him, the smells, the warmth of being together. "Everything is perfect."

Tally wasn't convinced that weekend whether she was serious about doing better, but they were able to discuss it the next day, after Janet woke up at one in the afternoon. And they didn't argue. Janet promised to come home every weekend. Tally didn't get his hopes up too much but he was willing to give it a shot. He'd told himself all along that any changes had to be her choice and this seemed to fit into his hypothesis. Through the month of December, she did do better. She came up every Saturday morning and they spent the weekends together. She went to church, met some people there and never brought up anything negative, but he sensed she wasn't being very honest with him, like she was putting on a show. Still, it was hard to complain since she was doing everything she said she would do. With things going so well, it was hard to make a big deal about how bad things had been, so Tally simply hoped that the good changes would last and did his best to enjoy his time with Janet to the fullest.

They went to Oklahoma for Christmas, and that was when he began to notice new changes he didn't pick up on in Utah. He wasn't sure why he hadn't made the same observations at home—the seemed so obvious now. Her hands shook much of the time, and she had a hard time with things requiring fine motor skills like tying the ribbon on presents, or putting batteries in Josh's toys. She was much more distant with his family than she'd ever been, not that she'd been around them much, and she seemed constantly irritated or annoyed. His sisters Camilla and Emma had never met her and he hated the impression Janet was giving to them and their husbands.

At Christmas Eve dinner she didn't eat much, complaining that she just wasn't hungry and it prompted him to notice how thin she'd become. She had always been slender, but had easily lost fifteen or twenty pounds since their wedding day. It made her look old and tired. At night when he tried to get close to her, she claimed she was uncomfortable making love at his parent's house. It was impossible not to remember the nights they'd spent there in the summer, the near magnetic pull they'd had toward one another and he felt even more depressed. The memory of that night came back to him, when she'd said she feared he would look back on that night and hate her for it. He didn't hate her, but he wasn't sure exactly how he felt and he did wish that they had waited, made sure they knew one another before they rushed into marriage. All the counsel he'd gotten throughout his life seemed to echo in his mind and he now understood so much more. It had only been five months, but he hardly recognized the woman he'd married.

Seeing her from his family's perspective brought out things he didn't want to acknowledge. He had wanted so much for his family to like her, but, instead, he was embarrassed by the way she spoke to them, often saying things that either didn't make sense or were border-line rude. She often repeated herself over and over in one conversation and she was continually on edge. Even with Josh she was short and explosive, causing Tally to create more and more distance between her and her son. He didn't understand what was happening, but he felt very protective of Josh. It was obvious to everyone that Janet didn't want to be there. She would excuse herself to take naps, five-hour naps, every day. When she wasn't present, the tension would leave and things would get back to normal. But if she was around, conversation became stilted, and people found other things to do. It was heart-breaking for Tally. He felt hopelessly torn and wished they hadn't come at all. He'd never been so embarrassed and felt like he had to justify her every word or action. By the time they left after their three-day stay, his family had completely stopped talking when she was around and none of them had dared say anything to him about it, not even his mother.

In the rental car on the way to the airport, Tally could no longer keep his thoughts to himself.

"Are you feeling okay?" he asked after several minutes of silence.

"I'm fine."

He glanced at her, she was staring out the window and in the morning light looked very pale. "You don't seem like you're fine."

She whipped her head around and glared at him. "What's that supposed to mean?"

Oh, boy, Tally thought to himself, *here we go.* But he didn't feel like avoiding it anymore. "Well, for starters you've been ornery and irritable for this whole trip. You act so put out to have come here at all and I'm wondering if something's wrong, if there is something we should talk about."

"Do you have any idea how much work is waiting for me back at the office?" she returned without any restraint of her irritation. "I should have spent 16-hour days at the office, but I came out here, to be with your family and now you're mad because I didn't act thrilled to death that I'm falling so behind?"

"Or maybe I'm mad because I'm tired of the office running our lives. It dictates when we see each other, for how long and now it's even overtaken Christmas. Something is really messed up if you can't ever do anything but work."

Janet snorted and folded her arms. "You weren't complaining when I paid for the airfare to fly out here."

"You offered!"

"And look what kind of gratitude I get. I spent three miserable days in Oklahoma, and all you can do is complain."

"Miserable?" Tally repeated. "Three days with my family bending over backward to try and make you happy are miserable?" His head began to throb. He couldn't stand this.

"Bending over backward," Janet snorted with a shake of her head.

"Every person there wished I hadn't come."

Tally took a deep breath. "Good point," he said between clenched teeth.

She turned and scowled at him one more time before looking out the window again. Josh started fussing in the back seat and they both ignored him. Tally didn't know if he had ever been more angry in his life. He wished she hadn't come, he wished she'd stayed in her beloved office and listened to Christmas music on the radio while he took Josh alone. Then everyone could have enjoyed the holiday. As it was, it had been miserable for everyone; Janet, himself and his whole family. She hadn't wanted to be there and he knew he'd never make the same mistake again. All she cared about was herself and her job, the rest of them were just inconsequential irritants in her life. *How did I get into this?* he asked himself. And why was he still putting up with it?

They flew home in silence. When they landed and got Tally's truck out of long-term parking she said she needed to go to the office. He was relieved that she wasn't coming to Willard. After dropping her off at her condo, Tally and Josh proceeded home. As he drove he was reminded of all the concerns he'd had at Thanksgiving time and berated himself for not dealing with things back then. He felt used and manipulated and he was tired of feeling this way. He was tired of everything. When he kneeled to say his prayers that night he realized that he was completely empty. He didn't have the strength to utter one more prayer on behalf of Janet or his marriage. He'd been turning to the Lord for months and felt he'd received very little. Deep down he knew this was his fault—he was the one who had disregarded the counsel he'd received all his life, but he still couldn't make sense of what he thought had been an answer to his prayers about marrying Janet in the first place. It was all so confusing and he wondered if what he thought was an answer was simply a projection of what he wanted so badly. With all that, it seemed to make sense that the Lord would hold out on him, make him suffer—and he was suffering. It hurt so much to feel so unwanted and he just didn't know what to do about it.

He got up without even starting his prayer; he didn't have the energy and, in fact, he didn't want the help. If this was some kind of penance then he may as well endure it, get it over with, and look for answers when he knew what he was going to do about the mess he'd made.

Janet didn't call him for four days, and then she only wanted to talk to Josh. When Tally got back on the line, she hung up. For the next two weeks he didn't hear from her at all. But the following Saturday, almost a month following their trip to Oklahoma, she surprised him by showing up at the house, once again contrite and apologetic. He'd made no progress in working out things in his mind and he regarded her with suspicion, wondering why she was there.

"I have to fly out tonight," he told her when they'd gotten over most of their initial awkwardness. Janet was sitting on the floor, turning pages of a book with Josh, while Tally sat on the couch on the opposite side of the room. He watched her hands shake as she turned each page and wondered what was going on with her. He hadn't seen her take pills for a very long time, but he had no doubt that was simply because she hid it better than she used to. He wished he dared bring it up.

"You do?" she whined as she looked up at him. He had taken the month of December off, but now his schedule was picking up again and he'd been unable to avoid a weekend job—he usually tried hard not to work on Sundays but it couldn't always be helped. "Who's watching Josh while you're gone?"

How had it happened that her son was solely his responsibility? "There's a lady in town that does day-care, she's going to start watching him so that I don't have to take him to Salt Lake every time. Her name's Rosy." This was the first time they'd even spoken about the change in child-care and he was curious to see how she would react. He almost hoped she'd get mad about him making such a big decision without her.

"Oh, that's good," she said easily, turning her attention back to the book without concern.

Tally wasn't really surprised. Everything concerning Josh and his care had slowly transferred to him over the last few months. In fact at times he wondered if she hadn't married him simply because the nanny hadn't worked out. It had solved a lot of her problems, that was for sure. "You can just drop him off on your way to Salt Lake Sunday," he continued after a few moments of silence.

She immediately turned to look at him. "Me?" she said in surprise. "Aren't you going to take him over there tonight?"

Tally watched her and had to consciously keep himself from screaming. Didn't she see what she was doing? He took a calming breath before he spoke. "I was, but since you're here it makes sense that he stay with you. He's really missed you and I figured you might want to spend some time with him."

She seemed to be considering further argument, but finally nodded. "Fine," she said evenly.

Tally stood up and went to pack. He was strangely nervous about leaving Josh with her, but he assumed that was just because it had become so rare that she was alone with him. She'd been so volatile at Christmas, but surely that was just the stress of staying with his family and the holiday in general. After a few minutes of thinking about it, he ignored his discomfort and told himself that Josh needed to remember who his mother was and she certainly wasn't taking the initiative.

When he left a couple hours later, he kissed her goodbye, but she wouldn't look at him. The pouting didn't even bother him, he was used to it. She reminded him of their meeting to sign Josh's final adoption papers on Thursday and he assured her he would be there, relieved that the adoption was finally going to be done. Then he gave her Rosy's address and drove away, wondering how much longer he would be expected to put up with this. He was running out of motivation and wondered if his determination to hold on to this marriage would suddenly disappear once the final adoption papers were signed and recorded. It was hard for him to answer the question. He loved Janet, at least part of him still did, but he wasn't sure if it was worth it any more. Maybe he'd bring up counseling again; without some outside help he didn't see how he could take this much longer.

Wednesday, Tally was back in the great state of Utah and drove straight from the airport to Rosy's house. He was excited to see Josh, he'd missed him so much. After knocking he heard footsteps and Rosy opened the door with a confused smile.

"Hello, Mr. Blaire," she said with just a trace of a Spanish accent. He'd been led to her through some members of his ward and he'd only met her a few times; but received glowing references when he called some of the other parents, whose children she watched, and he had a very good feeling about her.

"Hello," he said with a smile. "And you can call me Tally. Is Josh ready?"

"Josh is not here," Rosy said with an odd look on her face as two kids ran circles around her legs before chasing one another into another room.

"What?" Tally asked. The smile disappeared and anxiety crept into his chest. What did she mean, Josh wasn't here?

"Your wife called on Sunday and said he was not coming—she did not tell you?" She continued to look at him oddly and he let out a breath.

"She must have left me a note at home," he explained as he turned toward the car. "I haven't stopped there yet, sorry to bother you."

He got in the car and hurried home as he tried to come up with any possible explanation for the change in plans. Not only had Janet not contacted him, it was totally out of character for her to care about, let alone change, plans concerning Josh. He remembered the look she'd had on her face when he'd informed her she would have a full day in Josh's sole company—he didn't know what to think of this now.

At home there was, in fact, a note. It simply said that Janet had decided to take Josh to Salt Lake with her for a week or so, she'd missed her little boy and would call him later. Something didn't feel right and although he couldn't quite put his finger on it, he was sure there was something more to this. A sick feeling lodged in the pit of his stomach as he considered that perhaps she was having second thoughts about the adoption. He picked up the phone and immediately called her office. No one answered and his fear continued to increase.

He hung up and tried her cell phone—that was how he tracked her down, in order of priority: work, cell phone, then home—it was very backward. She picked up on the second ring.

"Hi, Tally," she said. Her tone sounded flat and . . . planned. Tally's concern over the situation increased.

"What's going on?" he nearly spat into the phone, unable to keep the unease out of his voice.

"Nothing," she said sweetly. "I've just missed Josh and so I decided to bring him home with me rather than take him to some stranger's house. We're having a great time."

Yeah right, Tally thought. "Your note says you're taking him for a week?"

"I'll bring him back up on Sunday, or I might keep him for two weeks—I'll have to see how it works out."

She was bringing him back! That brought some relief, but there were still a thousand questions in his mind. "Where is he when you're working?"

"I've taken a lot of time off, so mostly we're together—it's been fun. I should do it more often."

Tally wasn't sure what to do. He felt badly for being so suspicious, but he couldn't seem to shake it. He thought again about the adoption papers they were signing tomorrow and couldn't fathom what he'd do if she decided not to let him become Josh's legal father. "Well, maybe I should come down and we can all spend some time together," he offered lamely.

"No," Janet said as if it were a silly idea. "Just let me have some time with my boy—I'm sure you could use the break and it's been so long since I've had him all to myself. Oh, someone's calling on the other line. I've got to go—I'll talk to you later."

"Wait," he said quickly, still trying to put all the pieces together. "Why don't . . ." but the line was already dead. He hung up the phone and stared blankly at the wall for a few moments before grabbing his keys off the counter where he'd just put them and deciding to head for Salt Lake. Something wasn't right and he wasn't going to let himself be played the fool this time.

It took nearly an hour to get to Janet's condominium complex. The code for the gate was the same it had been at Christmas and he pulled into her driveway a few moments later. He wasn't sure if she was home or not, but decided to let himself in with his key and find out for himself. As he approached the front door he could hear the TV and for some reason felt like he shouldn't make too much noise.

Quietly, he put his key in the lock and turned it. Then he pushed the door open, slipped inside and took a few steps to look into the living room. He could see Josh playing in front of the TV and felt himself relax, only now admitting he was afraid something had happened to him. He took another step, not bothering to be quiet this time, and apparently Josh was alerted. He looked up and broke into a wide grin as he scrambled to his feet.

Tally froze when Josh turned to face him and his stomach dropped. Almost the entire left side of his face was covered with a mottled black and green bruise. Josh reached him seconds later and had to whine before Tally gathered himself together enough to bend and pick him up. Holding him, and looking at the injury up close made Tally want to throw up. Josh garbled and garbled, unaware of why Tally was so silent.

Tally heard movement and turned toward the stairs, narrowing his eyes as Janet nearly ran down the last few steps. "What happened?" he asked between clenched teeth.

She looked frightened and hesitated two seconds too long. Tally's worst suspicions seemed confirmed by her silence. "What did you do?" he continued.

"I . . . I didn't do anything," she quickly said as she continued forward. She attempted to take Josh from him but he pulled him strongly away and took a step back. "He fell," she said as if Tally should have guessed that.

Tally felt the anger in himself rise and bubble over, but he restrained it only because he was holding Josh and didn't want to frighten him.

"He fell and so you decided to conveniently keep him away from me?"

"No," she countered, her own tone as angry as his. "I'd already called Rosy and decided to keep him with me this week, and he fell off the back deck."

"And landed on his face?" Tally seethed.

"Yes," Janet said simply. She put her hands on her hips and cocked her head as if daring him not to believe her. He didn't need to be dared—he didn't believe her for a second. Something in the depth of his soul knew that whatever happened had not been an accident.

"I'm taking him home," Tally said when he realized that he was about to erupt. He moved toward the door but she stepped in front of him.

"This is his home," she said boldly.

Tally shook his head and tried to push her away. "I'm taking him *home*," he said again, slowly, clearly—to be sure she didn't misunderstand.

She didn't give up, but when she tried to block his way again he pushed her away roughly. "Do you honestly think I don't know you hurt him, Janet?" he pointed to the bruise as Josh cowered against his shoulder, not liking the angry voices. "Do you honestly think I'm that stupid?"

"I didn't hurt him, he fell, and you can't take him away from me, I'm his mother."

"You're a lousy mother, Janet. And you won't hurt him again!"

Her eyes seemed to catch on fire and she took a deep breath as she grabbed onto Josh again. Tally didn't hesitate to push her out of the way again, causing her to crash into the wall behind her as she let out a grunt of surprise. He didn't stop as he headed for the door again, but Janet didn't stop either.

"Give him back to me, Tally!" she called as she grabbed Tally's shoulder.

That was it, he couldn't take it. In one movement he put Josh down and rounded on her, screaming. "Touch me again and you'll regret it, Janet. Do you hear me?! This is over, it's done—I'm not playing this game anymore, not when Josh is the one who suffers." As he spoke he walked toward her, glad that she backed up as he did so, glad that she was afraid. Part of him hoped she would give him an excuse to hit her, show her what it was like to be hurt by someone bigger and stronger than she. "I don't know what's going on with you and I don't know how to fix it—but Josh and I are not going to stand in the line of fire any longer. You've had one day alone with him in six months and this is what happens?" he waved his hand, indicating Josh who was standing by the door, crying and confused.

"It *won't* happen again," she said after a moment of silence. "It was an accident, I was—"

"It won't happen again," he repeated, not sure if he was more relieved or sickened to hear her admit it. "It will never happen again." She backed into the couch and he took two more steps so that their faces were only inches apart. His mind was going a million miles a minute. "You will not do this to us any longer."

She dropped her head and started to cry. Tally didn't stay long enough to feel any sympathy. He turned, scooped a crying Josh into his arms and slammed the door behind him. Luckily he had his own car seat in his truck, so he didn't have to get the one out of Janet's car. It was several blocks before his rage had passed enough for him to consider what his options were now and he wished he could just stay mad. He had no clue what he should do. *You need to go to your bishop,* said a little voice in his head that he hardly recognized. For a moment he considered it but he didn't know what protocol the bishop would have to follow if he knew a crime had been committed and Tally just couldn't trust the process. He wasn't ready, not yet.

Kim looked up at the door when the doorbell rang, as if she could see through it and know who was on the front step. Then she walked toward the door, wiping her hands on the front of her jeans. She was making homemade pizza for dinner and wondering why she bothered, it was so much easier to just call Domino's and she doubted her attempt would taste half as good. She opened the door and smiled.

"Tally!" she said in greeting and then her eyes shifted to Josh and her smile fell. She reached out as she inhaled slightly. "What happened?" When she looked up at Tally again she was struck by the fallen look on his face and the tears in his eyes.

"I need some help," he said flatly. "Allen isn't around, is he?"

Kim called Allen at work and he was home within twenty minutes after successfully rescheduling his two remaining appointments for the next day. When Allen came through the door he smiled sympathetically at Tally and the two of them went into the den while Kim took care of the two babies, hers and Janet's.

They were in the office for over an hour before coming out, both of them still looking as glum and troubled as they had when they went inside. Tally thanked them both, took Josh and left. As soon as the door shut behind him Kim turned her questioning gaze on her husband. "Well?"

Allen let out a breath. "He's a better man than me. I think I'd have beat her unconscious." He reached out and took Kim's hands, looking at her deeply. "I'm so glad I'm married to you."

Kim smiled, but she still felt sick inside. "It's so hard to believe she could do that."

"Talking to Tally, we realized there is a lot more going on than he thought. I think the continual state of denial in which she's lived her life for so long is finally catching up to her." He let out a long arduous breath and stared blankly at the carpet beneath his feet. "She's a mess."

"What's Tally going to do now?" She led Allen to the couch and they both sat down, facing each other. She was glad Lexie was still asleep so that she could focus on this. The homemade pizza was getting cold on the counter, but she didn't care—she had a microwave and this was much more important.

"He actually called her when we were in the den. They have their final meeting with a judge tomorrow to finalize Josh's adoption. He told her he wouldn't turn her in if she promised to follow through on the adoption."

Kim let out a breath and nodded; that was a good idea. "And then what?"

"He's going to meet with the bishop after they meet with the judge and then he's planning to go to his parents' for a week or so, to let things settle. She was really upset, crying and apologizing over and over. She wants to go to marriage counseling, to work things out. He said he'll think about it—he's pretty overwhelmed right now."

"She wants to go to counseling? That's a good sign, isn't it?"

Allen shrugged and looked over her shoulder. She sensed he was replaying his own marriage to Janet in his mind and Kim remembered all the times he'd shared his concerns about the kind of mother she was. "Janet doesn't like to lose," he said simply. "It's hard for me to believe that saving this marriage is anything more than a form of victory for her."

CHAPTER TEN

The next morning Tally dropped Josh off at Kim's and went to the courthouse. He wished he were in a better frame of mind to appreciate all Allen and Kim were doing. They were the first people who came to mind after he'd left Janet and come up with the idea to black-mail her into following through with the adoption. He needed allies and Kim and Allen were the closest thing he had.

It was all he could to do be cordial and play the happy husband role while they sat through the meeting. If it hadn't been so vitally important that he give every impression things were perfect, he was sure he'd have never pulled it off. But if the judge delayed the final-ization, he knew he'd be in an even worse situation. He kissed Janet when he arrived and even forced himself to hold her hand through the proceedings, but he couldn't look her in the eye and he ignored any attempt she made to speak with him. When they finished signing all the documents, he kissed her again and they walked out of the court-house together. When they reached the front steps he dropped her hand and walked away. She called after him, and he heard her start to cry but he didn't care—he couldn't care. She was a stranger to him, a stranger who had hurt his little boy. His heart was broken and any love he'd felt for her had disappeared. He felt just as he had when he'd finally accepted that Tabitha was no longer a part of his life and he couldn't allow himself to think of Janet any differently. All that mattered now was Josh, his son, and he would not fail Josh the way his mother had.

Friday night Janet looked at the clock and sighed. She still had work to do, but she knew she needed to leave for Willard soon. After Tally had left her at the courthouse yesterday she'd gone into a panic. She hadn't really thought he would go through with it, and when he had kissed her and held her hand she felt sure there was a chance. But then he'd left her standing on the courthouse steps and she knew that the situation had turned desperate. He was so angry, and she couldn't blame him. She couldn't believe what she'd done, she still wasn't sure how or why she'd struck out at Josh the way she did—it had been a crazy moment and she regretted it with every fiber of her being. If only she could convince Tally of that. She knew their marriage was slipping away, and she felt powerless about what was happening, but she had to hope that there was some way they could fix it. Tally loved her, she knew he did, and that meant there was still a chance. She'd go to Willard and they would face everything, every bit of it. She'd tell him about the pills that were getting out of control, and anything else he wanted to know. What had happened with Josh was the final evidence that things had to change. She loved her son, and if her problems were now affecting him so drastically she knew things had to get better, fast, before something worse happened and she found herself without any hope at all.

On top of what was happening at home, her work was getting sloppy, she was forgetting appointments and Jay had written her up last week for messing up a major order that resulted in losing an entire line. Janet had never been written up at any job she'd ever worked. She was also losing more weight and her hands shook as soon as anything started to wear off. Because of the money she was spending on her pills, she wasn't making ends meet the way she used to either. The Xanax alone was costing her $300 a week, and the Oxycontin was $30 a pill. Just those two alone, without the Splash or sleeping pills, took a big chunk of her income. In fact, she wasn't sure she'd have enough to make her house payment next month since her savings had been slowly draining away. It was time to do something. She'd known it for weeks, but now she could see that she was losing Tally and Josh both. That couldn't happen. She'd been unfair and they'd been suffering, but she knew, if he'd give her a chance, they could get back to where they'd started. Tally loved her, and that was a powerful thing. And now that Josh's adoption was final they had even more reason to make things right.

Because of the problems she was having at work, however, she knew she had to do her best to catch up before she went home to deal with the personal issues she was facing. So she finished the order she was proofing and then turned off the lights as she left the building. Everyone else had already gone home and her feet echoed as she walked through the empty hallways. She walked faster than usual, anxious to go home, her real home, where Josh and Tally were waiting for her. When she entered the underground parking garage she was surprised to see a car next to hers. She slowed her step, but then sighed with relief when Cathy opened the driver's door of the other car and got out.

"You scared me," Janet said lightly as she increased her pace. "I thought you were a rapist or something."

"I'm in trouble," Cathy said bluntly.

Janet got within a few feet of her secretary and stopped. Cathy had seemed fine at work today. Janet couldn't imagine what had happened and why she thought Janet could do something about it. Janet had enough of her own problems. "What's the matter?" Janet asked casually, her mind still very much on her own troubles.

"I need to get out of here and I don't have anyone else to go to for help."

"What are you talking about?" Janet asked, finally paying attention.

"Kay doesn't have friends that work at a pharmacy," Cathy said, looking at the ground. "He used to, but the guy got fired for stealing the meds. But by then he'd hooked up with some guys who make runs to Mexico to get the pills. He and Kay have been running the meds themselves."

Janet felt her face go cold and she leaned forward. "What?" she hissed. She'd known the prescriptions were illegal but she'd taken comfort in the fact that they were from a pharmacy. Knowing she was taking street drugs was a shock she didn't know how to deal with. "You've been getting my stuff from some junkie?"

Cathy looked up at her and Janet was surprised by the anger in the smaller woman's face. "Kay's not a junkie, he's just a dealer, and you know you can't get this stuff without a prescription, Janet. 'Splash' is the street name for Speed." She was mad and Janet stepped back in surprise; Cathy was always so mild. She didn't like the change and her mind was still spinning.

"You should have told me that," she said lamely as the magnitude of what she'd just learned settled upon her.

"You should have known," Cathy countered strongly. "But the fact is I put my butt on the line to get you your stuff and now I need you to help me."

"You're kidding, right?" Janet said in disbelief as the anger rose in her chest. "You tricked me into getting involved with some illegal drug trade and now I'm supposed to help you get out of it?"

Cathy ignored the statement and continued as if Janet hadn't spoken at all. "One of the guys Kay was trafficking with was arrested this afternoon. Kay and I need to get to Mexico, right now."

"Pay for it yourself." Janet stepped past her, barely glancing at her former secretary. "With how much Kay charges, you two should have more than enough."

Cathy's confidence was slipping, Janet could see it, and the fear she'd been hiding was easier to read. Janet couldn't believe that Cathy had involved her with something like this. She wasn't a junkie, she was an executive. Executives didn't buy illegal drugs from dealers. This was crazy!

Cathy touched Janet's arm, stopping her thoughts. Janet met her eye again and Cathy's expression became even more pleading. "Janet, please," she said softly, her chin starting to quiver. "We'll both go to jail if we get caught . . . and they'll probably find out who we were selling to."

"You're threatening me?" Janet said, still reeling from the shock.

"No," Cathy said quickly with a shake of her head for emphasis. "But Kay keeps good records and if he gets caught I'm sure they'll find whatever information they need. If we get out of here, all that disappears with us."

Janet just stared at Cathy for several seconds, weighing out her options. She felt sick and scared, but she knew she couldn't take a chance of getting caught. Could things get any worse? In the last few days everything had been falling apart; she didn't know how to cope with this. Cathy continued to stare and Janet knew she was trapped—there was no way out of this and she couldn't afford being arrested right now. She wasn't sure how she'd get her hands on much money right now, but she also knew she had to find a way. No doubt the cops wouldn't buy her story of not knowing what was going on. "I can't believe you did this to me," she finally said.

Cathy looked at the ground. "I only wanted to help you."

Janet shook her head with frustration. *Some help*, she thought, but she knew she had little choice. "How much do you need?" she finally said; she just wanted to be done with this.

"About four thousand dollars."

Janet let out a breath. Four thousand dollars!! How was she going to find that much money, especially on a Friday night? Still, did she really have a choice? Suddenly she just wanted to get it over with and maybe it would be a good thing—a clean break from the pills, from Cathy and her drug-dealing boyfriend. She had no doubt that the meds were a major factor in everything going wrong in her life. "If I do this, I never want to see you again; is that understood?"

Cathy nodded and Janet let out a breath of frustration. "It's going to take me a little time to get this kind of cash."

Cathy nodded again. "I could meet you at your house or—"

"No," Janet interrupted, her mind going a mile a minute trying to come up with a plan. "I'll meet you back here at eight o'clock."

Just over an hour later Janet pulled into the parking garage. Cathy was already there and as quickly as possible Janet gave her the envelope with the money and walked away. It had taken several ATM withdrawals from what was left of her savings account and an 'Easy Money' store to cash a post dated check for the remaining amount, but she'd been frantic about getting it all; it was her ticket out of the mess she'd unwittingly gotten involved in. She was almost to her car when Cathy called out to her. She turned and Cathy was running toward her. She held a business card out to Janet. Janet looked at it and read the name Brady Shaw and all the contact information on how to get a hold of him. She looked up at Cathy. "What's this?"

"The name of a new contact for you," Cathy said, and her expression showed that she thought she was doing a great thing.

Janet slapped at her hand and the card fell to the ground. "I'm done with it, Cathy, I thought I made that clear."

"Well, just in case you need anything—"

"I don't," Janet said strongly. "I've just learned a powerful lesson on what happens when I trust in anything, or anyone, other than myself."

Cathy blinked and her chin trembled again. *How pathetic*, Janet thought to herself as she got into her car. But she wasn't sure who she was talking about, Cathy or herself.

She pulled out of the parking garage and felt a kind of numbness fall over her. She would go to Willard, right now, and tell Tally everything. The possible ramifications of this scared her to death. What if the cops somehow found out about her anyway? What if Cathy made contact again? Her stomach was on fire; she was so scared, and her hands were shaking. What if giving Cathy the money just opened her up to being blackmailed again? What if someone came looking for her later? She was almost to the freeway when she had to pull over due to the panic she felt rising in her chest. She'd told Cathy she was done with the pills, and she was; but she had to ward off the attacks. So she quickly took just one Xanax. But after a couple minutes she had to take another one. Only when her breathing had gotten back to normal did she pull back onto the road, more anxious than ever to get to Tally. He would surely know what to do, and even though telling him scared her to death, especially after everything that had happened, he was all she had and she needed him more than ever.

It was almost ten o'clock when she pulled up. The house was dark, but she thought nothing of it; he often went to bed early. She parked in the driveway and went around to the back door. It took her a minute to find her key, and then she opened the door slowly, not wanting to wake either of them. She thought about the time she'd snuck into bed with him; but that wasn't appropriate this time. They needed to talk.

She tiptoed into the bedroom and felt for the switch on the wall.

It had a dimmer on it and she turned it all the way down before clicking the light. There was just enough muted light to allow her to see, but it wouldn't be too bright for Tally. She looked toward the bed, so relieved to finally be here, but her smile fell as she stared at the empty bed. "Tally," she called quietly. Then she walked to the master bathroom and turned on the light, illuminating the room a little more. She called his name again, but heard only silence in return. She continued calling his name as she searched every room in the house, frantically hoping she would find him. Where was he? Where could he have gone?

By the time she made it back to the kitchen, she was trying to think of any possible explanation. Did he have a business trip she didn't remember? Or had he gone somewhere else. Something in the back of her mind seemed to know something, but she couldn't bring it forward—she couldn't remember. Then she saw the note on the counter. It wasn't written to her, it was to Justin, a neighbor kid that often took care of the horses when Tally went out of town. Scanning it quickly, she learned he was planning to be gone for at least a week, and at the bottom was a number at which he could be reached. The number was familiar, but she couldn't place it. Picking up the phone, she dialed quickly.

"Is Tally there?" she said as soon as the phone was answered. She thought it might be his mother's voice.

"Yes, I'll get him." It was definitely his mother; she recognized the disapproval in her mother-in-law's voice.

Janet held her breath until she heard his voice, but her confidence suddenly disappeared. As soon as she opened her mouth she started to cry, totally overwhelmed by everything that had happened during the last two days. She knew she sounded crazy, but she couldn't stop herself from blubbering how sorry she was, that she'd do whatever it took to make things right and that she loved him. Over and over again she told him that she loved him. He said nothing. "Please come back," she pleaded. "You don't know how much I need you right now."

"Janet," he said in frustration. "I told you I would talk to you when

I got back."

"Back?" she whimpered. "You went to your parents'?" she asked, even though she knew he was there. Not having him nearby made her frantic.

"I told you I was coming here when we spoke on the phone Wednesday, don't you remember?" The accusation in his voice was impossible to ignore, but she chose not to focus on it.

Had he told her he was going to Oklahoma? That whole phone conversation Wednesday was a blur. All she remembered was that he wouldn't turn her in if she signed the papers the next day. "That's right," she said, as if she did in fact remember. "I really need to see you, talk to you. I'll come to you, right now I'll—"

"I need some time," Tally said firmly. "I told you that."

"But I need you, Tally," she said, sniffling. "I need you more than I ever have before."

"That's not saying much though, is it," his voice was hard now. "After all the time I've given you, the least you can do is give me some time now."

Janet swallowed and started to cry again. "I'm so sorry, Tally, but please, please don't do this." She worried about Cathy coming back, or Kay; she hated being alone right now but she didn't know how to tell him what had happened. It felt like too much had already been said.

"It's done," Tally said. "And I need to know what you're taking and how much."

She hesitated, how did he know about that? Even though she'd come to Willard with the intention of telling him about the medications, now she didn't want to give him any more reason to pull away. "What are you talking about?"

"I'm an idiot for not doing anything before, but it all makes sense now and I need you to tell me the truth. What are you taking?"

"You know what I'm taking," she said evasively. "Some Xanax for the panic attacks and then something for my headaches now and then."

"Don't lie to me, Janet," Tally said. "I know it's more than that, and I think you have a drug problem. It's why you can work till all hours of the morning and why your hands shake all the time—it's probably why you couldn't handle your son, why you—"

"I do not have a problem, and they aren't drugs; they're medicine," she quickly interjected, suddenly defensive even though she knew full well that there was a problem, medicine or not.

Tally was quiet. "Janet, I need to make something very clear to you. I will not put Josh in a situation where what happened last week might happen again and as long as you're taking these drugs he'll be at risk. I won't even consider trying to fix this marriage if you don't stop using."

"So you want me to go unconscious with panic attacks and stay in bed for days with headaches?"

"I'll say it again," Tally said slowly, like he would to a child. "As long as you are using, we will not be with you."

"He's my son, Tally," she said between clenched teeth. "You can't take him from me. I have legal rights and you have nothing without my consent."

All he said was, "I have Josh." Then he hung up before she could say anything else. She slowly took the phone from her ear and stood there for several seconds before walking to her car as if in a daze. How could he think those things about her? She took too many pills, but she wasn't addicted. She could stop anytime she wanted to and she'd prove it to him. She didn't need anyone to help her, and when he came home she'd be able to tell him that she was clean—then everything would be better.

CHAPTER ELEVEN

Tuesday afternoon, Janet laid in her bed and stared at the ceiling. She was freezing and no matter how high she turned the heat up or how many blankets she piled up, she just couldn't get warm. Next to the bed was a mixing bowl, in case she got sick again and couldn't make it to the toilet; it had happened twice already and the sour smell of vomit permeated the room. She was shivering so badly she could hardly breathe and her whole body was covered in cold sweat. She didn't know how much longer she could hold out.

Friday night, as she headed back home from Willard, she'd been determined to go straight; she wouldn't take another pill. But then she'd gotten sick to her stomach and she'd had to take something. So she told herself she'd just start cutting down for now, by the time Tally got back she really would be clean. She'd take something every four hours the first day, then go to six, then eight and so on. On Saturday she got moving boxes and started packing like a mad woman, hoping it would take her mind off of things. But she was shaking after only two hours and so she had to make a new plan. Then she started having panic attacks one right after another, so she decided she'd just take the Xanax; nothing else. But she had to take something else when the headaches set in. By morning she'd taken the same number of pills she'd been taking before she tried to stop.

Saturday night she started over and didn't take the two Xanax and the sleeping pill she usually took before bed, but she didn't sleep at all and by one o'clock had a severe panic attack that caused her to black out—she didn't know for how long. Once she gained consciousness she took two pills and told herself that was it; no more. But by four a.m. she had to take more; her body wouldn't let her stop.

On Monday she didn't even try, and it was a good thing since she'd had to deal with the absence of Cathy and maintain that she knew nothing about it when she got to work. It was a relief that no one seemed to suspect she was involved, especially after the police came and cleaned out Cathy's desk, removing a few items they seemed to find interesting. They did ask a few questions but she dodged them easily enough. After they left she held her breath, waiting for them to come back, but they didn't. It took more than the usual amount of pills that night to calm her nerves, but she'd determined that tomorrow was the day. She'd go clean tomorrow.

Tomorrow was now today and she thought she was going to die. She called in sick and didn't take anything after her usual morning pills for the day; she had to get a few things done. But she wouldn't take anymore pills. She'd stop cold turkey.

She looked at the clock, still shivering and tried to figure out how long since her morning pills. It had been four hours, yet it felt like days. She tried to think of how many pills she'd taken in the beginning, when she'd first started having the attacks, and remembered that she used to take one Xanax every few days and only when she had an attack. Now it took nearly eight of those same pills to just function on a semi-adequate level. She took nearly the same amount of Oxycontin and she couldn't sleep without the sleeping pill or wake up without the Splash. *How did it get this bad so fast?* she asked herself as she shook uncontrollably. And why couldn't she stop?

The phone was off the hook since she couldn't talk to anyone anyway. Another hour passed and she threw up again, heaving into the bowl next to the bed. She looked around the room, at all the blankets, the spots on the carpet and the mixing bowl in her hands. The tears started to fall and she stumbled downstairs as the last of her fragile willpower deserted her completely. She'd left everything but the Xanax in her car last night after work, and then she'd hidden the Xanax in the freezer. She took them out now, barely able to undo the lid, her hands were shaking so badly. It seemed to take forever and then she took three, sure that she would die if she didn't. Once she swallowed the pills she sank to the floor and laid on her side, hugging her knees to her chest as reality dawned. She couldn't stop. She'd thought she could but she couldn't. Tally would be coming home at the end of the week and she would have to either tell him the truth and know that he would have nothing to do with her, or she'd have to lie to him and experience his heartbreak later when he learned the truth. Either option would never work. She couldn't hurt him anymore, but she couldn't stop taking the pills either.

Wednesday morning she retrieved her stash of pills from the car and spent nearly an hour hiding them all over the house. She needed to know they were close, that she wouldn't be separated from them again. When she was finally convinced that she was safely surrounded, she swallowed an Oxycontin and took a shower to wash away the sour smell. She went to work because she couldn't think of anything else to do. When she pulled into the parking garage she made a slow inspection of the area where she and Cathy had parked Friday. Cathy had tried to give her the card of a contact; she hoped it was still on the ground somewhere. After half an hour she gave up the search; it was gone. That meant she had no supplier. She wouldn't be able to get more pills—the thought was paralyzing.

The phone rang all morning, since all calls to Cathy's line were now automatically forwarded to her own. After the first three calls she turned off the ringer; she didn't want to talk to anyone and her head was killing her, despite the Oxycontin. When the mail came, she sorted through it and stopped when she got to the manila envelope from her attorney. Most of her personal mail came to the office, since it was where she spent most of her time. She knew what it was without opening the envelope and felt a mixture of sadness and relief descend upon her as the decision was instantly made. She'd been searching her mind for a solution all day, and now she had it. Immediately, she set about putting her desk in order, making notes on each of her projects so that whoever took over her job would know what had and hadn't been done. That afternoon Jay called her to his office.

When she got there two other men were waiting for her. She knew they were detectives.

"These men would like to talk to you about Cathy," Jay said with guarded eyes. She nodded and watched the replay of a video of the parking garage on the TV Jay kept in his cabinet. It had been taken the night Cathy disappeared, they said, and she watched her and Cathy talk in grainy black and white, then she handed Cathy something that Cathy immediately stuffed into her pocket. Janet wasn't even scared and when they asked her what had been exchanged on the tape, she said she owed Cathy some money. They kept asking questions, but she sidestepped or flat out lied about every one of them. After nearly an hour Jay asked them to leave. They said they would be contacting her later, that she wasn't to leave Salt Lake.

"What's happening, Janet?" Jay asked as he looked across the desk at her. His face was pinched and she knew that learning all this had been a major blow for him. She felt badly that he was affected too and wished she'd thought of all the other people she'd pulled into this mess before now. "Your work isn't what it used to be and now this. Did you know she was involved in something like this?"

"Yes," Janet suddenly said. Jay's eyebrows shot up, but she was amazed at how good it felt to tell the truth. There was really no reason to lie any longer anyway. She didn't care what people thought of her, she didn't care what kind of judgments came her way. She'd only stalled the detectives because she'd known her plans wouldn't go through if she were sitting in jail. "I'm probably one of her best clients."

"Janet," Jay said after several seconds of shocked silence. "I . . . uh . . . can't . . ."

"You don't have to fire me. I'll quit. I'll finish up the things I'm working on and go home." Her tone was completely even, devoid of any emotion or inflection. Jay didn't seem to know what to do.

"Uh, maybe you should just go home now," Jay finally said when he found his tongue again. "We have a program set up that will cover treatment and you can get your stuff another time; but you'd better go. Call me tomorrow and we'll work out the details."

Janet stood up and nodded. "That's a good idea," she said blandly. "I am sorry, Jay, I never expected things to get so out of hand."

She stopped in her office to get her purse and the manila envelope that she hadn't opened yet. As she headed back toward the elevator she could feel the eyes of her co-workers following her. But she didn't care. It was all over with now; everything was done. She had no family to worry about her, no friends who would miss her in their lives. Josh and Tally had already left and now she had no job to go to every day. There were still a few things she needed to do at home, a few details she needed to put in order; but they wouldn't take long and then she'd be free of everything.

"Are you about ready?" Allen called from the kitchen.

Kim rolled her eyes. Allen had come home with tickets to a Jazz game and she had canceled her plans to go to a Mary Kay party, although she wasn't heartbroken about missing it. She got herself dressed up, arranged for a babysitter, got Lexie ready and was almost done packing the diaper bag in the same amount of time it took Allen to change into jeans and a Utah Jazz sweatshirt. She wondered how he'd survived as a bachelor. "Just about," she said in a tone that she hoped conveyed her irritation.

A few minutes later they were on their way. They always passed Janet's street on the way to Allen's parents' house, Lexie's babysitters tonight, and tonight they both glanced down the road. As they passed the street sign, Kim got a strange feeling in her chest. Maybe it was just remembering all that had happened—was still happening.

"I wonder how she's doing," Allen said half a block later.

"Me too," Kim replied. There were a few more seconds of silence and Allen slowed down to stop at a red light.

"Um . . . do you think we should check in on her?"

Kim wanted to protest since they were already behind schedule, but she couldn't. The feeling of trepidation was getting stronger and she found herself nodding. "I'm sure it will only take a minute," she said, as if trying to emphasize that she didn't believe anything was wrong.

"If that," Allen agreed. He put on his blinker and turned around in the next parking lot.

A minute or so later they pulled up in front of the big iron gates. They both stared at the locked gates that denied them entry, maybe they weren't supposed to check on her—maybe their concern was just that—concern. But Kim could feel an increased urgency, and when another car pulled in front of them and punched in the gate code she nudged Allen to follow the other car in. He did as he was told.

The first thing Kim noticed when they rounded the corner was that the garage door of Janet's condo was open. That was odd, since Janet was usually pretty fastidious about details like that. Allen pulled into the driveway and turned off the car. They stepped out at about the same time. They both looked at the garage and then each other. Kim knew he had noticed the same thing about the garage being open.

"Let's go through the garage door," Kim suggested, the anxiousness growing by the second; something didn't feel right. Allen nodded and after their knock wasn't answered, he looked at Kim and turned the knob. It wasn't locked.

"Janet," Allen called as he opened the door, knocking as he did so. Kim followed him in. "Janet are you . . . ." They both saw her at the same moment and Kim couldn't breathe. Janet was sitting at the table, but her head was flopped over as if she'd passed out. Her hair covered her face and arms as if it had been poured out of a cup. Next to her outstretched hand was an empty glass, knocked over but still rolling slightly from side to side. A small puddle of water had formed on the table where the contents of the glass had spilled out.

For an instant they were both frozen, in the following instant they were on the move. Kim shook Janet's shoulder first hoping to rouse her, but when her arm limply rolled off the table Allen grabbed her hair and gently pulled her head back. As he raised her head, her hair swept pills off the table in every direction, causing a pattering sound that echoed throughout the room. Janet groaned but her eyes were still closed and her face devoid of any color. Only then did Kim realize what was really going on.

"Call 911, Kim," Allen said urgently. Kim ran for the phone while Allen began rummaging through drawers until he found a wooden spoon. The 911 dispatcher answered and Kim started giving them the information while she fumbled through a stack of mail trying to find Janet's address.

Kim found the address and turned toward Allen and Janet in time to watch Allen stick the handle of the spoon into her mouth. Kim had to turn away in order to keep from throwing up herself as Janet's limp body suddenly retched forward, spewing out the contents of her stomach all over the kitchen floor. Vomit splashed onto Allen's pant leg, but he didn't seem to notice. Janet was still leaning forward, draped over Allen's arm so that she wouldn't aspirate the vomit, but as soon as her body went limp again he made her throw up a second time. By now the floor was covered, and much to her disgust, Kim could see that the contents contained pills in various stages of digestion. Allen shoved the spoon down Janet's throat twice more, until he was convinced that there was nothing left. Then he met Kim's eyes for the first time. Tears were streaming down her face as she looked from her husband's scared expression to Janet's limp and pale body sprawled out in his arms. The dispatcher was still on the phone and interrupted her thoughts by saying the ambulance was at the gate and that they needed a code. Kim was explaining that she didn't know the code either when they said someone had let them in.

Ten minutes later Kim watched the doors to the ambulance close before it pulled away, sirens blaring, on its way to the hospital. Allen took her hand and led her to the car where she stared blankly out the window while they followed the paramedics. It was difficult to absorb everything she'd just seen. She'd had no idea how big a problem Janet really had.

"Tally!!"

Tally and Josh both looked up. They were cleaning out the garage; well, Tally was cleaning out the garage, and Josh was ensuring he didn't run out of things to put away. Tally didn't mind Josh slowing his progress since the task was mostly to work out some nervous energy anyway. And it seemed to be working. He hadn't thought about the pit in his stomach for at least two minutes.

"Yeah," Tally called back, going back to his current project of reorganizing the tool box. When she didn't answer him he turned to see why. Julie was standing in the doorway, her face pale and her eyes huge.

Tally quickly walked toward her. "What is it?"

"Um, that was . . . Kim Jackman on the phone," she said in slow halting syllables as if having to find the words as she spoke.

"Kim?" he repeated. Why was Kim calling him at his parents' house? How would she have gotten the number?

"Um, you need to go to Salt Lake; Josh can stay here. I'll call the airline." She turned, as if she was going to leave it at that. Tally took another step and grabbed her arm before she could get away.

"What's wrong?" he demanded. "What happened?"

"Janet's okay," Julie said, but he could tell the calm in her voice was forced. "But they went ahead and took her to the hospital."

"Why?" Tally asked, his mind a whirl of thoughts and questions. He shook her arm to show her what a big deal this was. "What happened?"

"Nothing," Julie said, her voice sounding even calmer. "She's fine, she just took too many pills and they made her sick."

Tally shook his head. He had no desire to go back to Utah and see Janet. "If she's fine, she doesn't need me," he said as he turned back to the garage and let go of his mother's arm. His father's voice made him turn back.

"You need to go to Salt Lake, Tally," his father said strongly. "Your wife needs you."

"Why?" he asked stubbornly.

His parents shared a look. "She overdosed," Phillip said. "They don't know if she's going to make it."

All the thoughts swirled together like a tornado and Tally just stared. "What?" he whispered. They didn't answer him and he looked away. For almost a minute there was silence as Tally tried to sort out one thought from another. "You'll keep Josh?" he finally asked as he watched Josh trying to open a can of paint now that no one was watching him, completely oblivious to what was happening. His parents nodded but he continued to stare at Josh, Janet's son, as the news he just heard repeated itself over and over in his head.

Kim had taken Lexie to Allen's mother's house; that was where she
started the investigation to find Tally's parents' number in Oklahoma.
She'd actually tracked down his brother in Bountiful first and he was
planning to meet them at the hospital soon. When she returned to the
hospital, Janet was still in the emergency room. Kim looked across the
room to the still body and felt a shiver run through her.

"You okay?"

She looked up at her husband and smiled wanly before looking
back at the activity flurrying around Janet's bed. "Not really," she said
as her voice shook. "Are you?"

Allen said nothing. He didn't need to, she knew what he was
thinking. She knew how powerless he felt, how strange it all seemed;
and she knew that his thoughts, like hers, weren't only about Janet. It
was impossible for Kim not to think of all the hospital visits she'd made
when it had been her son, Jackson, in the hospital bed. She would
never forget that fear, that loneliness of not knowing what tomorrow
would bring. She also couldn't help but wonder what Tally was going
to do when he arrived. She hoped she'd be gone by then, and felt
instantly guilty for wanting to skip that part. But she honestly didn't
know if she could stand what she felt sure she would see in his eyes.
Her own pain was still very fresh, and the events of the last few hours
had only intensified the anguish. Yet the supreme tragedy was that the
pain she was remembering was the result of an accident. Janet had
made this decision on purpose.

"Janet Blaire!"

Allen and Kim turned toward the breathless voice at the same
time. The man with his hands on the reception desk was a total
stranger. However, he turned to look at them and seemed to know that
the three of them shared some kind of connection. He took a few steps
toward them.

"I'm Chris Blaire, Tally's brother." His voice was hurried and his
eyes showed the same panic and fear they had been working through.
His eyes then traveled past Allen's shoulder and focused on Janet. The
fall of his expression brought tears to Kim's eyes and she turned to
look again; as if she could ever forget.

Chris let out a long ragged breath as he stared. Then he looked between the two of them. "Is she . . . going to be okay?"

Allen opened his mouth to answer just as a new flurry erupted around Janet's bed. They watched as even more personnel converged around her bed. Someone called for an 'ultrasound' and someone else drew the curtain completely shut. None of them breathed.

"Ultrasound?" Chris whispered. Then he looked at Kim and Allen again. "She's—," he couldn't seem to finish the question and Allen and Kim had no answer anyway, although it was nearly impossible to fathom. There were no more words to say so they simply stared at the curtain around her bed and waited with their hearts in their throats.

After a few more minutes they sat down on the blue plastic chairs in the waiting room. There was nothing to do and nothing to say, at least not out loud. Kim dropped her head, clasped her hands together and started praying fervently for Janet, Tally and Josh; that things would be okay, that they would all get a second chance. When she lifted her head she noticed Chris and Allen were in much the same pose and she began praying again, begging for peace and comfort, healing and strength. It was hard to keep the fear at bay but she tried her best, knowing that faith and fear couldn't exist together.

It seemed that they waited forever. Finally, a doctor stepped outside of Janet's curtain and called out 'Blaire.' Three heads came up and they were instantly on their feet. The doctor saw them, nodded and walked to where they were.

"Are you family of Janet Blaire?" he asked.

Kim and Allen looked at Chris, and he seemed to realize for the first time that he was the only family member present. "I'm her brother-in-law," he said quickly. "Her husband is flying in from Oklahoma, he'll be here around midnight."

The doctor nodded and looked back at the chart. "Well, she's lucky to be here at all," he said gravely, looking up at them. "We pumped her stomach, although there wasn't much left, and gave her something to bind what's left of the medications in her system and keep them from passing through her liver. But she took a lot of pills and she's in a coma. We've decided to send her up to ICU, now that she's stable." He stopped and looked at the three faces. "We only have preliminary blood work and it shows that her toxin level is very high. It will be awhile before we know anything for certain." The doctor said it with as much compassion as they could hope for from a man who faced this kind of trauma on a regular basis. "The medications she's taken will peak in a few hours and then begin to wear off; that will give us a better idea of what we're dealing with. Until then, we're doing everything possible to counteract the long term effects of what she's done to herself."

"Is she going to die?" Chris finally said out loud. The word hung in the air.

"I don't think so," the doctor said and they all let out a sigh of relief. "But, best case scenario she'll have a long recovery; physical and psychological."

"And what's worst case scenario?" Kim asked, wanting to face it now.

"Neurological and liver damage are our biggest concerns, although there's a chance she'll never come out of the coma. What you need to understand is that she didn't take a few too many pills—she didn't accidentally overdose. She made a conscious choice not to survive and she did everything she could to ensure it would happen. Even though she was brought here so quickly, her body had already absorbed enough medication to kill any one of us. Ironically, it's her own tolerance that saved her life. However, like I said, we really won't know for awhile."

"What was the ultrasound for?" Kim asked after another long and strangulating silence.

The doctor looked down at the chart again and Kim prayed that he wouldn't say what she feared he was going to say. "I should really wait for her husband to discuss it."

"You should really tell us first, let us be ready to support him through it."

The doctor looked up at him and let out a breath that seemed to say 'I hate this part.' "Unless requested not to, we run mandatory pregnancy tests on female patients when we do the rest of the blood work.

Her test came back positive."

Kim closed her eyes slowly and felt not only tears in her eyes but bile in her throat. The doctor continued, "The ultrasound showed that the fetus was about eight weeks developed."

"Was?" Kim didn't even know she'd spoken out loud, and then braced herself.

"There was a heartbeat," he confirmed. "But it is utterly impossible that the fetus will survive and there is nothing we can do to save it."

Chris made a sound as if he'd been punched in the stomach and walked away from the group. Kim wiped at her eyes and watched him go. Allen was the only one to thank the doctor who told them Janet would be taken to the ICU within the hour. Then he left.

Allen placed a hand on Kim's shoulder and she turned into him, finally giving into the tears. "How could she do this?" she sobbed against his shoulder, overwhelmed by all the feelings raging within her. Whereas she'd felt sympathy for Janet a few minutes before, she was now disgusted and angry. After losing her son, Jackson, she couldn't fathom the disregard Janet could possibly have had for her own child. *Eight weeks*, she repeated to herself. She finally pulled back. Allen looked at her sorrowfully, but said nothing. "I'm going to pick up my baby and go home," she said as she turned and wiped at her eyes.

Allen opened his mouth, torn between wanting desperately to go with her and feeling obligated to stay. She looked at him. "It's okay," she said evenly. "You can stay."

He didn't know what to say. He well knew what Kim was thinking, how this tore at her, he felt the same way; but he couldn't imagine leaving Chris to face Tally alone, especially with this new development. "I'll come home as soon as I can," he said. She smiled and turned toward the door, but not before he saw the disappointment in her eyes. Kim had always struggled with his relationship with Janet, mild and disconnected as it was. He knew that his staying was painful to her in some way, and could only hope that as she thought it through she wouldn't get sidetracked by her own insecurity. As a psychiatrist he'd been called out on many suicides and knowing what lay ahead he couldn't ethically leave. The resident psychiatrist would be called down soon and he knew that he could fill in some blanks. Beyond that, he had serious concerns about Tally's reaction to this and he couldn't leave Chris to face it alone.

"Allen?" Chris asked some time later. They were in a different area of the hospital now, sitting across the hall from the window that looked into Janet's room of the ICU. Allen had explained to Chris his relationship to Janet, and the discussion he and Tally had about Janet's drug problem. Then they discussed the events of the day and how Kim and Allen had played into them; but they hadn't said anything for several minutes.

"Yeah?"

"Do you think we should give her a blessing?"

"I think we should wait for Tally."

Chris nodded and was silent for another minute or so. "Do we tell him about the baby?"

The baby, Allen repeated in his mind. *Not the pregnancy, not the fetus; the baby. Tally's baby.* "I don't know," he groaned.

"He'll be devastated," Chris continued. "I don't know how he'll deal with any of this, but especially . . . that."

"But not to tell him?" Allen added, playing devil's advocate. "Is that fair? If it were me, I think I'd want to know."

"Would you?" Chris said, turning to look at him. "Would you want to know that the woman you thought had answered all your deepest prayers, and later broke your heart, had also killed your child?"

The words stung and Allen felt the lump rise in his throat. He could only shake his head, unable to find the words to continue. He knew he didn't know how Tally felt; he couldn't know. But he'd felt the sting of Janet's choices in his own marriage to her, and because of that, he knew how torn Tally already felt between his feelings for Janet and his anger at the way she constructed her life, and therefore Tally's life as well. The battle of his own marriage to Janet had been very similar, but they had never faced anything like the events of the last couple weeks. When he'd talked to Tally last Wednesday, Tally was all but determined to file for divorce, and it was hard for Allen to blame him. He had little doubt that this new information would be the straw that broke the camel's back, yet his sympathy for Janet couldn't be ignored. If she lived through this, and if Tally left her, she would be facing all the complications of her life alone—he didn't know if she could do it.

His chest felt tight as he imagined how he would feel in a similar situation. Chris had gone silent too, surely having similar thoughts. After several minutes Allen spoke again. "It's really not up to us, the doctors will tell him."

"Oh," Chris said dismally. "I hadn't thought of that."

CHAPTER TWELVE

It was after midnight, Utah time, before Tally's plane landed. He was in no hurry to get to the hospital and took the time to get his truck out of long-term parking. The closer he'd gotten to Salt Lake the more his trepidation increased. He hadn't made sense of this in his mind yet—he hadn't absorbed it and he wanted to put off whatever was ahead as long as he could. His wife was a drug addict, a child-abuser, and now she'd overdosed. It was a very hard reality to face.

"Janet Stewart Blaire," he said when he reached the reception desk. The steely haired receptionist typed her name into the computer. Then she looked up. "Are you a family member?"

"Yes," he said. "I'm her husband."

"I had to ask because only immediate family is allowed in the ICU, she's in . . ." Tally didn't hear anything more and was immediately reminded of his own experience in the ICU. It seemed further proof of how serious this was. He felt a hand at his arm and looked up. Chris looked at him, but didn't smile. Tally opened his mouth to speak but knew no words came out as the 'absorption' he'd been waiting for seemed to suck the very air from his lungs. Allen was there too and they guided him toward the elevator. As they headed for Janet's room, Tally only picked up a word here and there as they attempted to fill him in. Suicide . . . liver damage . . . just in time . . . coma . . . 24 hours critical. When they reached the room, Tally just stared through the glass. Janet lay prostrate on the bed. Her eyes were closed and a venti-lator tube was taped to her mouth. Tally walked in slowly and sat down, not taking his eyes off of her for a moment as he kept telling himself he wasn't dreaming. This was real! There were IV's in her hands and arm, and various wires disappearing under her hospital gown. He reached for her hand, but hesitated and pulled his hand back. He was afraid to touch her; he didn't *want* to touch her. He still felt dead inside and he didn't want to run the risk of reawakening any part of himself that would make this harder. Instead, he pictured in his mind how she'd looked on their wedding day, how excited he'd been about sharing a life with her. And now she was here, in the ICU—maybe dying. Tears started to fall as he mourned all that could have been, all the expectations that had broken apart. "What happened to us?" he asked quietly as he stared at her. "How did we get here?"

"Mr. Blaire?"

Tally looked up and wondered how long he'd been sitting there; he really had no idea, but he noticed that at some time he had taken her hand in his. It felt so cold. "Yes?" he answered.

"I'm Dr. Henry," the middle-aged woman said by way of introduction. "I've been taking care of your wife since she was moved to the ICU. Are you ready to talk?"

Tally appreciated her sympathetic question, but he wished that by not discussing this, he could make it go away. He simply nodded and stood up, returning Janet's limp hand to the bed where it had been when he entered.

"Would you like to come to my office?"

Again he nodded, and followed the doctor, explaining to Allen and Chris, who were still waiting in the hall, that he'd be back in a few minutes. He noticed a look pass between them, a mixture of guilt and expectation, as if they still knew something he didn't. However, he didn't have the time to dwell on it as he followed Dr. Henry down the hall and took the seat she offered to him once they entered her small office. Once they were sitting he steeled himself to hear the details that everyone else was trying to spare him.

"We just got back her last set of labs, and it's looking better," Dr. Henry said with a hopeful smile. "Her toxin levels have leveled off; that means that they'll soon be heading down and we've already noticed some increased cognition . . . that means she's more responsive then she was."

"I'm familiar with the terms," he said quietly. "You can use the bigger words."

She nodded slowly before continuing. "Coming out of this coma will be slow. It isn't the way you see it happen on TV; it takes time." Tally nodded again; he knew all this already. "We're still watching her liver enzymes, but they are looking a little better. She's basically a healthy person and it's obvious that she hasn't been involved in long-term abuse; if she had, she wouldn't have the strength to break the medications down the way she's able to. Her heart has returned to normal rhythms but it will be a few days until we find out how severe the damage is to her liver." Tally let out a long deep breath and felt just the beginning of anger to burst through the shock and sadness. He'd fought so hard to regain his health, his life, and she had taken hers so lightly. It was only one detail of this entire situation, but it seemed to be the only one he could focus on right this minute. The doctor continued. "We did a CT scan and it showed that there is no physio-logical damage to the brain." Tally knew that meant that the x-ray of her brain didn't show any physical damage caused by any kind of stroke or hemorrhage. "But until she is more alert, we won't know exactly what kind of damage has been done in that way. However, that brings us to a definite concern we have right now. Do you know what and how much medication she's been taking?"

"I have no idea," he said blandly.

"Well, we were able to identify what pills she took based on the sample the paramedics brought in with her. Our tests seem to show she didn't take anything we didn't have a sample of. The medications she used were Xanax, Oxycontin and speed. Xanax is a form of tranquil-izer called Benzodiazepine, which is a class of drugs that should not be stopped all at once. Oxycontin is an opiate, another class of drugs that needs to be slowly decreased. Speed affects an entirely different part of the central nervous system. We need to wean her off of the drugs, so to speak, or the withdrawal symptoms could cause even further damage. Without knowing how much she's been taking we can't be sure where to start. Are you sure you don't have any idea? Even if it's only how many total pills she's been taking, anything?"

"I don't know my wife very well," Tally said, barely curbing the anger that was continuing to build. He was starting to wonder if he knew her at all. The woman he married, the woman she showed to him at that time, wouldn't have done this. How could he have misjudged her so badly?

Dr. Henry leaned forward, looking at him sympathetically. "And there's one more thing," she said quietly. "Have you and your wife been using any birth control measures lately?"

Tally's spine prickled. Why use birth control when you almost never had sex? "She used that patch thing," Tally told her, wondering why it was important.

"Xanax decreases the preventative properties of birth control pills or the patch. The more she took, the less effective the patch would be." She stopped speaking and Tally stared at the desk top, thrown back into the shock he'd been in the process of working through.

"Are you telling me she's pregnant?" he asked in a choking voice and he immediately knew that was what Chris and Allen had been keeping back. He'd known it was something, but he hadn't had time to imagine what was worse than what he had already learned. He was furious with them for not preparing him for this.

"She was," the doctor said with sympathy. "With the amount of medication she took we knew it would only be a matter of time. Her HCG levels, that's the hormone responsible for maintaining a pregnancy, are decreasing with each lab and we couldn't find a heartbeat as of an hour ago . . . I'm very sorry."

He couldn't think of anything to say. Time seemed to have stopped and he was waiting for someone to turn his life back on again. Then again, he wondered if he wanted everything to start again; he wasn't sure he could handle feeling anything right now. *Janet was pregnant*, he repeated in his mind. *Not only had she tried to kill herself, but she had . . .* he couldn't even say the words in his head. He clenched his eyes shut and dropped his head in hopes of regaining his composure. Somewhere in the back of his mind he felt, almost heard, a door slam shut, as if part of him had just stepped out of the situation entirely.

"It's possible she didn't even know she was pregnant," Dr. Henry continued. "It's not unusual for women to have a short period in the first few weeks of pregnancy and depending on how much she was taking, she might not have even been aware of her cycle. Perhaps she forgot to change a patch—there's no reason for us to think that she knowingly—"

"Enough," Tally interrupted as he put up a hand. He didn't want to hear the justifications or the possible explanations. All he could see were the facts, blaring at him, taunting him. The way he saw it, Janet had come up with the cruelest, most vile way to get back at him for taking Josh away and forcing her to go through with the adoption. The last time they spoke, he had ended their conversation with the words 'I have Josh'—and now that was all he had—more than that, Josh was all he wanted from her. He stood up and took a deep breath, holding in the feelings and emotion that he could feel beginning to rage. "I've got to go," he choked as he turned to the door.

"There's a crisis counselor on call, I can—"

"No," Tally said with a shake of his head. "I don't want to talk to anyone."

Dr. Henry nodded, her face showing sympathy. But Tally didn't want it—it wouldn't change anything. "We find that it's often very helpful to . . ." Her voice disappeared as Tally kept walking. He didn't want to talk to anyone who was going to try to convince him to deal with the thoughts and feelings exploding in his mind. He didn't want anyone to speak of 'support' or 'compassion,' especially if those words were directed toward Janet. He wanted to rant and rave, scream and curse, but all he could do was clench his jaw and try to ignore the fire in his mind. Chris and Allen both stood like obedient children as he approached them.

The expectant look on their faces confirmed what he suspected, that they already knew about the pregnancy. It only increased his anger and he walked past them without saying a word. Allen and Chris exchanged a questioning look, then Chris hurried toward him. He touched Tally's arm, causing him to turn.

"What?" Chris asked, searching Tally's face.

Some of the anger Tally had been unable to get in touch with erupted. "I need friends right now," he said loudly, causing Chris to startle and pull back. "Not babysitters." He pointed toward Janet's room and looked back and forth between Chris and Allen, not looking in the direction he was pointing. "I look and feel like a big enough fool without you setting me up. She didn't overdose; she tried to kill herself." He paused and took another breath. When he spoke, the words came out in a hiss. "And she's losing the baby. The least you could have done is prepare me for that."

He turned away and started walking out of the hospital. Chris looked over his shoulder to share a repentant look with Allen before hurrying after his brother.

"Tally, I'm sorry," he said when he caught up with him. Tally didn't look at him and kept walking. Chris continued to follow a step behind. "Where are you going?"

"I'm going to Janet's," Tally said.

"Umm, are you sure—"

Tally looked at him strongly. "I'm going to Janet's." Then he started walking again.

"Do you want me to come with you?"

"I don't care what you do," Tally called back as he reached the elevators and pushed the down button.

Chris hesitated and then ran back to tell Allen they were leaving.

Allen nodded and then called Chris to stop. "Has anyone called Tally's bishop?"

"Uh . . . I don't think so," Chris said distractedly as he looked back down the hall toward Tally, not wanting him to get out of sight.

"I'll try and track him down," Allen said, then he waved Chris off.

Chris hurried to catch the elevator, relieved that Tally hadn't caught one already. Tally didn't say a word and since Chris didn't know what to say, he said nothing.

Chris followed Tally to Janet's house and pulled up next to him in the driveway. Chris stayed in his car for a moment and weighed his options as he watched Tally walk toward the front door, his limp exaggerated by the flight, the cold and the time of night. Chris's wife was at home, awaiting an update. Allen was at the hospital, probably trying to figure out how he was going to get home since Kim had taken his car earlier and trying to get ahold of Tally's bishop, a man Chris doubted Tally had any desire to see. Chris wished he were anywhere but here. But he didn't feel like Tally should be alone, so he turned off the car and hurried to follow. Tally was unlocking the front door, but didn't look at Chris when he caught up.

As Tally opened the door he couldn't help but feel anxious at being at the 'scene of the crime' so to speak. He paused momentarily and then flipped on some lights and walked into the kitchen. Dried vomit still covered much of the kitchen floor and the smell caused him to wrinkle his nose. In his mind's eye he pictured the entire scene; how it had happened, what Kim and Allen had done when they found her. His stomach lurched as his eye was drawn to the pills on the floor and tabletop; the murder weapon. He thought of her sitting at the table, one by one swallowing the pills that she fully believed would end her life. What was she thinking? he wondered, still disconnected from the full reality. How did she think I would react when I found out what she'd done? Did she know she was carrying my baby—that ending her life would end another's?

Then he saw the envelopes, still lined up on the table. The one with his name on it called to him. He picked it up and opened it. Chris watched him from where he stood by the front door, as if he wanted to make sure he was close to an exit should this whole thing get to be too much.

Tally,

I've left you with the best part of me; I know you see him as the gift he is. I'm screwed up, Tally, I always have been. You got sucked into something you couldn't understand and couldn't change. I should never have married you; we were too different. I'm sorry to add one more complication to your life; but in time I'm sure you'll see the wisdom of my choices.

Janet

Tally's stomach felt like lead as the cruelty of her words, the coldness of it, washed over him. He dropped the letter to the floor and looked over the adoption papers she'd included. Had she been waiting for the adoption to become final? He'd already considered that she'd married him to get a full-time-nanny; had that all been part of her exit plan? She didn't even write that she loved him; maybe she didn't. Maybe she never had. All the feelings they'd had, feelings that once seemed to overwhelm them both—everything had been a game. She said he'd been sucked in; that's for sure. He'd never expected she would do something like this—to him, to Josh, and without the least amount of regret or apology. This was Janet? His wife?

The rage and sadness and confusion he'd been holding back suddenly burst through and he was suddenly awash with a burning heat so intense he felt as if his flesh was on fire. How could she do this to him? What had he ever done to deserve this in his life? *Why me, why Janet, why now?*

As the rage overcame him, he grabbed the kitchen chair closest to himself and threw it over the table. It crashed into the back of the couch, the back splintering, throwing shards of wood across the floor. Without pausing for even a second he lifted the edge of the table and threw it over, dumping the large floral centerpiece and everything else left on the table to the floor. He hardly noticed Chris flinch from where he still stood by the front door. If Tally had legs that worked, he'd have run at top speed for as long as his lungs held out to expel the adrenaline and anger. But he didn't have that option, however, he had more upper body strength than most men. He hoisted another chair and threw it toward the TV; it crashed through the screen, sending a shower of blue sparks throughout that area of the room.

"Tally!" Chris exclaimed in shock as he flattened himself against the wall.

"Get out!!" Tally screamed, the veins in his neck bulging as he pointed toward the front door. His face was red and his eyes were wide. He kicked at another chair, sending it skidding across the tile floor. It hit a lamp, causing it to hit the floor and shatter with another spray of sparks.

Chris shook his head, although Tally knew he was tempted to leave.

"Then shut up," Tally screamed just as loudly as he lifted and threw another chair. It struck the wall, punching a hole in the sheetrock and breaking off one of the legs. Chris backed toward the kitchen, hoping to stay out of the range of fire. Tally's heart was pounding and he could hear the blood rushing in his ears as he continued to throw and smash all the trappings Janet had chosen to surround herself with. This was the home she'd chosen over his, these were the things she found more comforting than her husband and child. Had she ever wanted to share his life? he wondered as he continued to vent his anger. Had she ever loved him, even a little bit?

When the kitchen area was empty he moved onto the living room, picking up the chairs from where they had landed and throwing them again. He knocked over the stacks of boxes Janet had apparently been in the process of filling at some point. Then he swept the books off the bookshelves, pulled the curtain rod from above the windows and used it to hit and hammer the walls and other furniture. He wanted more destruction, more pain as he tried to let out what he was feeling in the only way he could.

More than once Chris tried to intervene, tried to get him to stop by telling him the neighbors would hear and call the police, but Tally ignored him, he didn't care. He'd never been so angry, he'd never been more hurt. The onslaught of these feelings overwhelmed him and he couldn't seem to get them out fast enough. Finally, Tally picked up one chair, already beyond repair, and spun around before releasing it with a grunt of exertion.

Chris watched the chair sail into the kitchen and hit the cabinets above the stove before crashing onto the floor. The force broke one of the hinges on the cabinet, leaving it swinging back and forth on the hinge that had survived. When Chris looked back at his brother, trying to keep his fear in control and wondering if he should call the police himself, he was surprised to see Tally leaning against the emptied bookshelves behind him, both hands on his knee. The anger was gone, and his face was contorted with pain.

Chris hurried to his big brother. Tally pushed him away. "Let me help you," he said with frustration as he tried to help Tally stand. Tally pushed him away again. Chris stumbled backward, falling over a box. He fell to the ground but didn't try to get up. Tally didn't even look at him, but Chris watched as his brother's shoulders fell and he dropped his head. The big man, who moments ago had destroyed the house in a fit of rage, crumpled like a little boy. The tears rolled down his cheeks and Chris could no longer keep back his own emotion. Slowly, Tally sunk to the floor, forgetting his knee as he raised his hands to his face and began to sob. Chris came to him and kneeled at his side, wanting to comfort him somehow, but Tally pushed him away again. Chris couldn't swallow the lump in his throat. He knew there were no words of comfort for him to give—and it was obvious Tally didn't want his petty attempts. There was nothing he could say and very little he could do to even scratch the surface of the hell Tally had been thrust into. Tally covered his head with his arms as if to try and protect himself as the whole room seemed to shake with his sobbing.

"Hey, Dad," Chris said when his father answered the phone the next morning. It was only seven o'clock in the morning, but he'd gotten very little sleep and had no reason to put off the phone call any longer.

"Chris," his father said with relief. "We've been waiting to hear from you. What happened?"

Chris took a breath and proceeded to fill his father in on the events of the last eight hours. His father expressed his own shock and grief. "How's Tally?" their father finally asked.

"I had to call Allen, Janet's ex-husband; he's a psychiatrist. He was able to convince Tally to take a tranquilizer and then we gave him a blessing. He finally fell asleep around four this morning. I wish he could sleep for the next month." He paused, remembering the harrowing night. "But he's a mess, Dad," Chris finally continued. "I've never seen anyone act like this. I don't know what to do for him, and then he did something to his knee last night. It's all swollen and he can't bear any weight, yet he insists he's fine. Is there any way you and Mom can come out? I know it's hard for you to leave, but I can't do this myself; there's just too much."

When he hung up a few minutes later he dropped his head into

his hands again. They would come as soon as they could; thank goodness. Allen had managed to track down Tally's bishop and Chris had
spoken to him that morning. Bishop Baker was planning to come see
Tally at his house that night, but Chris hadn't told Tally that and wasn't
sure he dared. Tally's feelings toward his bishop weren't necessarily
positive, but he *was* Tally's bishop, Tally's steward and Tally needed
counsel.

It was after two o'clock when Chris pulled up to Janet's house
with his parents and Josh. Tally had still been asleep when he left to
pick them up at the airport so he'd just left a note. He'd already warned
his parents about the state of the living room but reminded them again
before he opened the door.

"Oh my," Julie said when she entered. Phillip opened his mouth
and looked around while letting out a long breath. Then Josh, who had
been in Julie's arms, wiggled to be put down. Julie hesitated, afraid of
him somehow hurting himself, until she heard Tally's voice.

"There's my little man!"

Josh had apparently already seen him and ran to where Tally was
laying on the couch; one of the few items in the room that wasn't
damaged beyond use. He was leaning against one of the arms of the
couch, with his legs stretched out and she wondered how long it had
taken him to get downstairs by himself—but then she wondered if he'd
slept on the couch. He was still wearing his jeans from the day before
and Julie could see where his swollen knee was pressing against the
fabric. She winced internally, knowing that the injury was more
serious than she had feared. Josh reached Tally and jumped, causing
Tally to quickly catch him mid-jump and lift him over his injured leg.
Gingerly he placed Josh on his lap and tried to soften his pained
expression. "How's my buddy," he asked haltingly. Julie felt her heart
break just a little more. He loved this boy so much. How would he ever
forgive Janet for what she'd tried to do to him?

"How are you doin', Tal?" his mother asked as she came and bent
down to kiss his forehead.

"I've definitely been better," Tally said without meeting her eyes.
Then he smiled as Josh scampered over the back of the couch and

plopped to the floor with a thump. "But it helps to have my guy back," he said with forced brightness. Josh laughed and Julie relaxed a little. She'd worried that bringing Josh back so soon would make things even harder on Tally; but now she knew she'd done the best thing she could. Her eyes traveled to his knee.

"That doesn't look good," she said.

"It'll be okay," Tally said nonchalantly, "I just need to stay off it for a while. Make sure Josh doesn't go in the kitchen; it's a mess."

"You should go see the doctor," Julie said as Phillip picked up Josh and scowled at the mess on the kitchen floor. Julie looked at her son strongly.

"I really don't feel like it."

"Tally, you need to get it looked at; it's awfully swollen."

"Fine," Tally said, sounding like a teenage boy agreeing to clean his room. "I'll call for an appointment."

When he hung up the cordless phone and handed it back to Julie a few minutes later he told them that his doctor had worked him in at 4:30 that afternoon. But the doctor was in Ogden, 30 minutes away.

Chris exchanged a look with his dad. "If we hurry, we'll have time to stop at the hospital on the way."

Phillip removed the small vial of oil from his pocket and looked toward Tally. "Who would you like to do the anointing?"

Tally took a breath and continued to stare into Janet's face, searching himself to find out how he felt right now. He didn't know; everything was still a big ball of anger and grief woven around itself. "It doesn't matter," he said as he looked away from her face and focused on the digital display that recorded her heart rate and breathing. The machine made little blipping noises and he tried to fight the memories of his own experience of lying in the hospital bed. The difference was that when he'd been there, he'd been fighting *for* his life, not against it. Phillip and Chris exchanged a look and Chris decided to do the anointing. He placed one drop of oil on the crown of her head and placed his hands on top of it. Phillip and Tally placed their hands on top of Chris'. Then Chris took a breath and said the few sentences proclaiming the oil to be set aside for the healing of the sick by those with the Melchizedek Priesthood. He sealed the anointing and removed his hands. He looked at Tally and nodded that he could give the blessing now.

Tally limped closer to the head of the bed while Phillip stayed at his side, holding him up since he couldn't put any weight on his leg. Tally leaned against the metal rail that went around the bed for support. Then he placed his hands on Janet's head and was silent for several seconds. He closed his eyes and tried to center himself, get himself in tune with the Spirit. He opened his mouth to begin, but no words came out. Instead, Janet's letter flashed into his mind. He took another breath and tried to push the image away as he attempted to put himself in the right frame of mind. He tried very hard to ignore the anger and fear, just for a few minutes. He tried to latch onto the feelings of love and concern he thought were still there somewhere.

Again, he opened his mouth to speak, but again his tongue was silenced. In his mind he heard the words of Dr. Henry last night: 'she may not have even known she was pregnant.' His heart skipped a beat and he felt tears come to his eyes. He'd given many priesthood blessings since being given the power to do so; he was usually very good at centering himself. But he felt as if he were grasping at clouds, not the force he knew was there. He tried to utter a prayer for assistance in his heart, but the attempt was feeble and the only thing he could hold onto was the increasing anger and despair. The love he tried to find escaped him and he wondered if he *did* love her, if he *could* forgive her for what she'd done. Everything he'd ever wanted was gone and it was absolutely impossible for him not to blame Janet for the destruction of those expectations. Finally, he opened his eyes and removed his hands.

"I can't do it," he whispered. Chris and Phillip looked up at him. "I'm too angry," he continued as a single tear escaped and trailed down his cheek. "How can I ask for God's power when I feel so dark inside?" Tally shook his head in frustration and disappointment and hobbled away from the bed with Phillip assisting him.

"How can you not?" Chris responded. "The darkness won't go

away on its own."

Tally didn't answer as he wiped at his face and shook his head. His custom-made crutches, left over from his recovery, were in Willard, but Chris had bought him a cheap wooden pair at a drugstore not far from Janet's house. Tally picked up the crutches from where he'd rested them against the wall. He tucked them under his arms, looked at her once more and clenched his eyes shut. "I just can't do it," he said again and headed for the door as the humiliation overcame him. He wasn't sure how he'd become so disconnected with the Spirit, but now, when he needed it the most he found himself totally and completely helpless, abandoned and alone.

Phillip started to follow him but then stopped. Tally continued without him, moving down the hall with practiced movements. A member of the hospital staff stopped Tally not far from the room and Chris and Phillip watched as Tally turned and followed.

Phillip looked at Chris, his eyes heavy with sorrow and his heart in this throat. "I guess I better do it then," he said. Slowly he turned and walked to where Tally had been standing a few moments before. He placed his hands on her head, took a deep breath and after a few seconds of silence began the blessing. "Janet Stewart Blaire, by the authority of the Holy . . . ."

The voices had been fading in and out for awhile, Janet didn't know how long. In her mind she could see each voice as if it were a color, and they mixed together like the rainbow effect of gasoline in a puddle of water; moving in and out of the other swirls of translucent color. Trying to separate one voice from another was impossible, and each time she tried too hard, she'd fade away from everything and the world would go black again. When she came back up to the surface this time she heard a voice she felt was familiar. It seemed to echo in her head, but she couldn't remember who it belonged to.

" . . . we bless your body with the strength to heal itself, that your recovery will be whole, and remind you, Janet, that your Father in Heaven loves you."

Who's talking, she wondered, wishing she could identify the voice. She tried to speak, to ask who this voice belonged to, but the only sound she heard come was a kind of groaning gasp as she strained against some kind of force that wouldn't allow her to talk. The room went silent, and she wondered if she had in fact spoken after all. But then the voice continued, faster and louder, as if excited about something. "We bless your mind that it will be strengthened too, and that through the recovery ahead of you, you might find peace and love; knowing that you are a precious soul, a loved daughter of God."

What were they talking about? she wondered, thoroughly confused by what was happening. Her nose itched and she tried to raise her hand, but couldn't seem to lift it; she felt as if it weighed a thousand pounds. *What was going on?* she asked herself again and then tried desperately to remember how she'd gotten here, wherever 'here' was. The words continued, but she could feel herself fade away again. It was just as well, considering that she couldn't speak or move. What point was there in being aware of what was going on around her if she couldn't respond to it? But this time, even though she lost contact with what was going on outside of her, she felt a warmth, like falling onto a huge down comforter. She mentally wrapped herself up in the billowing whiteness and took a deep breath. *Everything will be okay,* a voice called out to her. She searched to find the source, but just like the other voices it was impossible to distinguish, but it too sounded familiar—as if she'd heard it before. *Everything will be okay,* she repeated to herself. She didn't know what would be okay, or what the voice meant, but it made her feel better somehow. So she relaxed into the comfort, feeling it caress her face, and pulled it tightly around her shoulders. *No need to wake up right now,* she told herself. Just enjoy the peace a little longer.

Phillip finished the blessing and slowly removed his hands. The room was silent, and they all stared at Janet for several seconds. Then Phillip looked up at Chris, the other set of hands for the blessing. "Did you hear that?"

Chris nodded, "It sounded like she was trying to breathe on her own."

"She moved her hand," Julie added, still staring at the hand in case she tried again. She had arrived in time for the last few sentences of the blessing after Tally had returned to the car and taken over the care of Josh. She'd hurried up to Janet's room to find out what had happened since Tally was silent on the subject; all he'd done was shake his head when she asked.

"It could have been an involuntary twitch," Chris said.

"I know the difference between a twitch and a voluntary movement," Julie said. "She tried to move her hand."

Just then Janet's chest shuddered again, just like it had the first time. "I'm getting the nurse," Julie said. "Tally did the same thing when he started regaining consciousness." She left the room, leaving just Chris and Phillip behind.

As Julie and the nurse entered the room Janet attempted to breathe again. "That's great," the nurse said as she hurried to the machinery and started checking gauges and wires. After a few seconds she stood back up. "I've set it to allow her to take her own breaths if she wants to, the vent will only kick in if she goes too long without breathing on her own."

"Oh, thank heavens she's progressing so quickly," Julie said, staring at her daughter-in-law again. "How is everything else going?"

"Pretty well," the nurse said with a nod. "She had a mild seizure last night; we think it was due to withdrawal from the medication, and so we upped her Xanax. The seizure doesn't seem to have been severe enough to cause any damage. Her liver enzymes are not where we would like them; that's why her skin is beginning to look yellow. The toxins usually broken down by the liver cause the discoloration in her skin. Hopefully, her liver will kick in soon and it will start repairing itself, but we're watching it very closely."

They all nodded soberly, afraid to ask any more questions for fear of what the answers might be.

With the current state of Tally's knee he couldn't get in and out of the truck; it was too high off the ground. So Chris traded Tally his Acura for the truck for as long as Tally needed it. Driving to the doctor's office in the back seat of Chris's car was likely the longest drive of Tally's life. He knew they were all brimming with counsel and advice, but were afraid to say anything. They thought he was fragile, that he couldn't handle their opinions, but that wasn't the case. He didn't feel as if he were about to shatter into a million pieces; he was past that. Now he felt very well put together, in fact, in some ways, he'd stepped out of the equation entirely. This was Janet's decision, not his. She had problems, BIG ones, but she hadn't turned to him for help. His response to her choice was that he would focus his energy on himself and his son. There was nothing he could do for Janet anyway. She'd made that very clear.

"I'm afraid I don't have good news," the doctor said to Phillip and Tally after returning with the x-rays. Julie and Chris were entertaining Josh at a nearby McDonald's. He slid the new x-ray onto the light box and flipped the switch, illuminating the internal picture of Tally's knee. It was all Chinese to Phillip, but Tally seemed to see whatever problem the doctor was talking about.

"I slipped the pin," Tally said.

The doctor nodded and pointed to one of the long dark spots on the X-ray. "It's pretty bad," he said; Tally just nodded and continued to look. "And it's causing some ligament problems as well. We'll have to go in to fix it."

"When?" Tally said with calm acceptance.

"Soon."

Phillip looked between the two of them as they continued to stare. "How soon?" he finally asked, thinking of Janet in a coma in Salt Lake. This was a turn they didn't need, yet; Tally was amazingly calm about the extra complication.

The doctor let out a long breath as he thought about it. "How about Monday? I mean we could wait as long as a week, but you'll need to stay off it—completely off it, until we go in to prevent further damage. The sooner the better."

"Monday's fine," Tally said.

The doctor nodded and started making notes on Tally's chart. "I'll send you to the lab to get your blood work right now and call you tomorrow with a time. You'll need to plan on a few days in the hospital; it's not going to be an outpatient procedure. And then you'll need another two full weeks flat at home; after that you'll have some physical therapy and you'll have to be very careful. I don't want you working for at least three months; do you understand?"

Tally nodded.

Phillip let out a breath. "That's not going to work, his wife—"

"It'll be fine," Tally said, giving his dad a pointed look. He turned back to the doctor. "It'll be fine."

It took several minutes for Tally to get his pants back on and move to the waiting room. The doctor had given him a prescription for some anti-inflammatory medication and some other pain pills. When he handed Tally the prescription he said, "Be careful with these; if you take too many you'll find your body wanting more."

"I'll keep that in mind," he said dryly and put the paper in the back pocket of his jeans.

In the hallway Phillip finally spoke up. "When would you like to see Janet again?"

"You heard the doctor. I need to go home and stay off my feet."

Phillip stopped and waited for Tally to look at him. "She's your wife, Tally. She needs you."

"She never needed me, Dad," Tally said sadly, not meeting his father's eyes. "And she doesn't need or want me now. I've accepted that. It's time you guys do the same." He started forward on his crutches again, but Phillip grabbed his arm and stopped him again.

"She's had a drug dependency, Tally. She hasn't been herself, and you're giving up on her without even trying. Don't you want to fight for her, just a little?"

"I have been fighting for her and with her since the day we married, and this is where it got us. The battle she needs to fight is of her own making. I can't help her find what she needs."

"I think you can," Phillip continued. "I think it's your responsibility to be there for her when she comes out of this, to help her through what lies ahead. You know better than anyone what it takes to get your life back."

"You're right. I do know what it takes to fight for life, but that's not what Janet's doing. She gave up—and I don't understand that one bit." He moved away and didn't stop this time. Phillip started walking too, sick at heart and unsure what, if anything, they could do to help him see another option. However, he felt Tally's determination, heard the resolution in his voice and knew that if Tally set his mind to it, he could follow through with his decision. He'd seen the same trait work when Tabitha left and through the months and years of recovery. However, this time he didn't think it was such a good thing that Tally could turn off his emotions and move on. This time, he thought it might be the biggest mistake Tally had ever made.

That night the bishop came to the house. Tally had not been overly excited about the impending visit but he knew he'd put it off too long already—it was time to face the music. As soon as the bishop arrived, Julie and Phillip took Josh with them to take Chris back to Salt Lake. The bishop took a seat opposite the couch where Tally had his leg propped out and asked if they could start with a word of prayer. Tally was actually tempted to say no for reasons he didn't understand but he simply nodded. Knowing Tally couldn't kneel the bishop got on his knees alone, bowing his head in reverence before beginning his prayer. As the bishop began to pray Tally felt the peace of the Spirit he had missed so much and he opened his eyes to look at the man who had the power to invoke its presence. Seeing the bishop, the father of his ward, kneeling in humble supplication was a shocking contrast to the bitterness Tally had felt toward him for so long. *Whether through mine own voice or the voice of my servants, it is the same.* Tears pricked his eyes as he realized how unfair his judgments had been, not only toward the bishop, but to himself and Janet too. The grudge he'd hung on to had kept him from seeking counsel and he wondered if things would be different if he'd not let their differences taint his heart so much.

When the bishop was seated again he met Tally's eyes and Tally knew that this man was called of God. Just accepting that knowledge, lifted his heart and he found that for the first time he could talk about all that had happened without restraint.

The bishop left nearly an hour later without cramming his thoughts and ideas down Tally's throat as Tally had always feared would be the case. Tally had shared his frustrations, his anger and resentment and the bishop hadn't told him it was evil and horrible. Instead his only counsel was that Tally begin praying again. Honest and humble prayer, he said, was the precursor to every miracle. Tally wasn't sure what the miracle would be, but he was willing to exercise some faith in the bishop's counsel and he'd always known it was what he should be doing, even when he couldn't seem to force himself to follow through. That night he prayed for the first time in too long and despite the whirlwind of life swirling around him he felt a calm, a peace he had desperately missed. He wondered at how he had let it slip away in the first place and hoped he could ensure its continued presence.

But as the hours of night slipped by he wondered if feeling the Spirit was enough. He knew the Lord wasn't going to force him to make a specific decision about his life and about Janet and it frustrated him. He knew the Lord's answer would be the right one and yet he didn't know if he was entitled to know the Lord's will on this at all. Despite a lifetime of lessons and counsel it was hard to see himself as worthy of the Lord's help when he reviewed all the mistakes he'd made in the last several months. He felt as if he'd made a mockery of all he'd been taught and he wasn't sure how to ask for forgiveness. As he drifted off to sleep he was reminded of counsel he'd given many times to new members when he was serving his mission. 'Being a member of God's church does not mean life will be easy, that trials will not arise, but it does mean that you and God are on the same team.' He wanted desperately to believe that. He only hoped he could.

CHAPTER THIRTEEN

Tally didn't look anyone in the eyes as he was wheeled toward the front door of McKay Dee Hospital in Ogden, Utah, the following Thursday. The surgery had gone well, and after three days in the hospital, mostly to observe that everything was as it should be, Tally was able to go home. Tally watched the floor tiles disappear in front of him as he rolled along and wished he weren't so helpless, in every way. The bishop had come to see him last night and they'd spoken again. This time the bishop had left Tally with information about an LDS 12-step program just recently introduced to members of the church. Although it was designed for addicts, the bishop felt Tally might like to understand the steps himself, to prepare him for all that Janet was learning. Tally wasn't sure how it would benefit him, seeing as how he hadn't come to any conclusions about his role in Janet's life, but he'd glanced through the information anyway and couldn't help but admit that the steps, or principles, made a lot of sense.

The bishop was taking things slowly, careful not to push Tally too far and Tally was grateful. But at the same time he wanted answers and although he was praying again and feeling peace once more, he still didn't know what to do. The impotence to make a decision was incredibly frustrating. And there was no indication that Janet wanted him to be a part of her recovery. The note she'd left made that very clear and the last thing he was going to do was force himself to be a part of her life—again.

"Are you sure you'll be okay at home by yourself?" Julie asked after Phillip helped get Tally situated in the back seat.

"I'll be fine," Tally told them for the eighteenth time. His dad was flying home today; after they dropped Tally off in Willard, Julie was driving Phillip to the airport in Salt Lake. She was staying for another couple of weeks to help him recover; he felt like such a child.

"It'll be a couple of hours," Julie said, as if she thought he'd forgotten.

"I will be fine," Tally said again, looking forward to some soli-tude—he was tired of being surrounded by people all the time. "Are you going to pick Josh up from Lacey on the way back?"

"I'd thought it might be best to leave him there for a few more days; let you get your strength back."

Tally wanted to protest, aching to have Josh with him again, but he knew that it wouldn't be fair for his mom to take care of two chil-dren. He nodded and stared out the far window, watching the homes and pastures fly by. He couldn't help but wonder what Janet was doing today. His mom had told him that she was fully conscious now and doing well. He'd acted as if he didn't care, but inside, a small part of himself relaxed, knowing she was okay. He was still so confused and hurt, and he didn't know if he could ever forgive her. In fact he wondered if he wanted to. It seemed much easier to just sever her from his life than to battle her forever. He didn't know how he could ever trust her again, yet he felt guilty for not wanting to try. He sighed deeply and ignored the worried look his mother gave him. How had life gotten so screwed up? Was there any hope it would ever get better?

"Okay, Janet," the nurse said. "We're going to pull out the IV now, it'll be just a few more seconds . . . okay, we got it."

Janet just stared at the ceiling, as she had for the last two days since she'd come out of the coma and been moved to a regular hospital room. Her thoughts were slow, she felt nauseated and her coordination was clumsy. Several times a day people would come in and ask her questions like what day it was, what year it was and who was president. The last few times they'd done it she'd been able to answer all the questions correctly. They smiled and acted thrilled with her progress; she'd closed her eyes and wondered how they could get so excited about something so stupid. With every passing hour her thoughts were clearing and her faculties were coming back but she still didn't know what was going on.

"My . . . husband," she asked in a raspy voice. The ventilator had left her throat raw and scratchy. "Has he . . . come?" Tally seemed to be the one thing she could think about, focus on. She wondered why he wasn't here.

"He had surgery, honey; remember?" the nurse said in a motherly voice, even though she wasn't much older than Janet was. "It will be awhile before he'll be up and about." Janet tried to nod. She'd forgotten about the surgery, but she remembered now. They told her that he'd come to see her the first night and when he went back home, he'd hurt his knee somehow. She wished she'd been able to see him that night; she wished he was here now so she could ask him what had happened. She was pretty sure she'd been in a car accident, it would explain everything; but even when she asked someone, they never told her if she was right or not.

"How are you feeling today, Janet?"

Janet looked at the woman who'd spoken to her and wondered where the nurse was who had just been here; but maybe some time had passed since then. She couldn't seem to keep track. Janet didn't know if this woman had been here before; if she had, Janet couldn't remember her name and she didn't bother to answer the stupid question. She didn't know how she was feeling.

"I'm Dr. Paulson," she said. "Do you remember me?"

Janet nodded and looked back at the wall. If she was supposed to remember this woman she'd say that she did. "It's Tuesday . . . Bush is the president. My . . . name is Janet and I'm at . . . .a hospital in Salt Lake." Her words were coming out slow and halted and it frustrated her. They were clear in her head, but when she tried to get them out, they seemed to get nervous or something.

Dr. Paulson smiled, "Very good, except that it's Thursday. Now that you've become familiar with the basics, are you ready to move onto the harder questions?"

"I . . . don't know."

"You're being released in a few more days," Dr. Paulson continued. "And you'll be moved to an inpatient drug rehabilitation facility."

Janet opened her mouth to speak but Dr. Paulson hurried to continue before she could get the words out. "Your husband already signed the forms and you'll be able to finish your recovery there while you learn to live without the drugs."

Janet looked at the woman quickly. "He was . . . here?" she asked.

"When you were still in a coma," Dr. Paulson answered.

Then she remembered the other things Dr. Paulson had told her. "Drug rehab?" she asked.

"Do you remember how you got here?"

She shook her head and realized that she didn't really want to know. She wondered why.

"You tried to kill yourself, Janet," Dr. Paulson said bluntly.

Janet opened her mouth to protest, but as she did the memories started to flow back into her mind. She remembered Tally yelling at her, Cathy asking for money and the weekend she'd spent trying to stop taking the pills. Her stomach sank and she closed her eyes against the onslaught of memories of that day; of getting the adoption papers, of being questioned by the police and realizing she had no supplier for the pills. Instantly she was doused with the emotion of those few days, the reality of the decision she'd made. Then her eyes flew open and she sought Dr. Paulson's face again. "But it didn't work," she said slowly. Dr. Paulson shook her head, watching Janet closely as she spoke. "Kim and Allen Jackman found you; probably within minutes of you losing consciousness. You were in a coma for five days, and you've been slowly recovering."

Janet was taken back to just before she started taking the pills that day, to the realization that everyone would soon know of the things she'd done, the choices she'd made; but at that time she'd expected they would find those things out without her having to face their knowledge. "Everyone knows," she whispered.

"Knows about what?"

"The pills."

"Yes."

Janet felt tears prick her eyes and although she tried to hold them back, she couldn't. She turned her face away from Dr. Paulson, wishing she would leave her alone to digest all of this, but Dr. Paulson made no efforts to leave.

"Janet," the doctor finally said to get her attention back. "Were you aware that you were pregnant?"

Janet's eyes flew open and she turned her head to look at Dr. Paulson in absolute shock. "N–No," she finally stammered as the emotion rose in her chest. She closed her eyes against it and shook her head. "I'm not . . . I can't . . ."

"You had a miscarriage," Dr. Paulson said as gently as she could. "And the hospital performed a D & C; that's a procedure that clears out the uterus to make sure there are no further complications."

Janet kept her eyes closed, but she couldn't hold back the emotion and she began to cry openly. How could she have been pregnant and not known? But she knew the answer to that question, the last two months of her life were a complete blur. She'd been having blackouts and complete periods of time had somehow disappeared from her memory. She hadn't even thought about her cycle; hadn't noticed if she missed a period. "Was it the pills?" she finally whispered when the emotion passed enough for her to speak again.

"Probably."

Her face contorted. "Does Tally know?"

"Yes."

She immediately started crying again and turned onto her side, away from Dr. Paulson again. She hadn't necessarily wanted another child, certainly not so soon, but to know that she had been pregnant . . . with Tally's baby . . . and . . . *Oh God,* she cried out in her mind. *How could I let this happen?*

"You and I will have the opportunity to face that, and other issues, once you are admitted to the rehab facility. Until then, I want you to keep one thing in mind. You decided at some point that your life wasn't worth living. Now you are faced with three choices. The first is to attempt suicide again; many people in your situation do that, and although we will do everything we can to keep you from that end, if you're determined; you will find a way. The second option is to choose life, but continue to keep all the thoughts, feelings, and truths you were trying to run away from to yourself like you always have. Basically you will do the same things you've always done and hope for a better result; Albert Einstein, and the founders of Alcoholics Anonymous, call that the definition of insanity.

"The third option is to realize that you've been given a second chance to make sense of things that you couldn't make sense of before, a second chance to repair what has been broken and start a new life, as if the old Janet and all her troubles truly died that day. You're the only one who can make that choice."

Dr. Paulson then left the room. As soon as she was gone Janet raised her hands to her face and began to cry again; harder than she could ever remember crying in her whole life. She couldn't even kill herself right and now she had to find some way to try and find a future again. She thought of Tally and she wished she could just disappear, melt into this hospital bed and be gone forever. How would she ever face him again? Did she even want too? Why couldn't she have died? Surely it would have been less painful than this.

Janet arrived at the inpatient rehab Saturday afternoon. Dr. Paulson was waiting for her and showed her to her room. It was roughly the size of Janet's walk-in closet at home and it held two beds, one desk and one small closet. This was basically a mental institution for druggies, and she was one of them? The thought gave her butterflies and she asked herself for the millionth time how things had gotten to this point. Her roommate was named Shandy, and she was in a session right now. Janet would meet her later.

As soon as she put her things away, Dr. Paulson took her on a tour. The building was nice, in an industrial sort of way, and Janet took note of the different rooms and their purposes: group therapy room, arts and crafts and the common area where the 'residents' would eat, visit and watch select TV shows. When they finished the tour, Dr. Paulson showed her into a small office. It was nearly the same size as the room where Janet would be staying, but it was nicely decorated.

"Did you think about those three options I told you about on Thursday?" Dr. Paulson asked when they were seated.

Janet nodded but she didn't speak. She didn't like this place and she didn't like Dr. Paulson. This was not where she wanted to be and she wanted nothing to do with any of it. But she had no choice—and she really didn't care all that much.

"And?"

It had been extremely hard to wade through everything in order to make a decision. In the end she didn't feel like she really had a choice; surely no one would accept that she still wished for oblivion and knowing what she knew now she knew that she wouldn't make such a horrible decision twice. "I guess I choose life."

"You guess?"

Janet turned to face her. She didn't care what this woman thought, she didn't care what anyone thought, so she may as well be honest. "I didn't want a second chance."

"But you got one. What do you want to do with it?"

"Nothing," Janet said as she looked at a family picture behind Dr. Paulson's desk. Dr. Paulson was apparently a grandmother. Janet wouldn't have guessed that; she held her age well.

"Nothing?" Dr. Paulson asked. "You don't want to do anything with another opportunity to fix whatever went wrong?"

When Janet spoke again, her voice was heavy with bitterness. "My choice wasn't to be here. Why you expect that five days in a coma and the knowledge that everyone knows I'm a junkie should give me the motivation to make some heroic rescue of something I didn't want in the first place, is a mystery to me."

Dr. Paulson was silent for a few moments, then she put her pen on the desk and leaned back in the chair. "Well, if that's the case then I'm just wasting my time," Dr. Paulson said, instantly losing the kindness she'd shown up to this point. "If you aren't willing to work for your life, then I'm not going to waste my time on you."

"Then what am I doing here?" Janet asked with a little shake of her head.

"Whether you wanted a second chance or not, you got one. We're here to make sure it's a real chance. The only way to do that is to get you off the drugs and remind you what reality really is. Then you'll leave, and you'll do whatever you want."

Janet snorted and looked away, oddly upset by this woman's lack of compassion. Some therapy.

"I only take patients who are serious about living a new life, who look at having survived as a rebirth. If you can't look at it that way, then I'll assign you to one of the other staff members. They'll try and get you in touch with what brought you to this, but they won't work half as hard as I would have."

Janet looked back at this woman and just stared. "You obviously don't care either way, so why should I?"

Dr. Paulson took a deep breath. "Do you know why you came here?"

"You made me!" Janet nearly spat back at her. She'd have been just as satisfied being dumped on the street.

"I've worked with your ex-husband," Dr. Paulson said evenly.

Janet's eyes narrowed. "Allen?" she asked, although it was a stupid question. She sat up a little straighter, feeling strangely surrounded. "I don't need him running my life."

"Oh, of course not," Dr. Paulson said sarcastically. "You've done such a good job yourself." They both stared at each other for a few moments and Janet cursed Allen for sending her to this woman; she didn't need this right now. "He asked me to bring you here because I'm very good at preparing my patients for life again—but if you don't do your part, my methods will just be painful, without any benefit."

"Well, I don't need any more pain. I'd be happy to have a staff therapist for as long as I have to stay here or you could just let me go home."

"If you went home right now you'd be dead in a day. You're a sick addict and you can't take care of yourself."

Janet clenched her jaw, furious that anyone could say that about her. "I am not a sick addict and I have taken care of myself all my life."

"Fine," Dr. Paulson said as she started making notes on the papers Janet assumed consisted of her 'chart.' When she finished she looked up, not bothering to smile. "I've assigned you to a therapist and after detox you'll get a daily schedule. If you change your mind and decide you want to face this head on, you know where to find me."

Two days later Janet lay on the narrow bed, staring at the ceiling that swirled above her while she took long laborious breaths. Sweat dripped off her forehead and now and then she could feel her eyes rolling back into her head. "Please," she whispered loudly for what had to be the thousandth time. "Just give me another pill."

"All I can give you is another aspirin and I can't give you that for another 22 minutes," the nurse said from her bedside as she mopped more sweat off Janet's forehead and instructed her again on how to take long deep breaths. "We have to stick to the schedule in order to wean your body off the medication."

"I'm going to die," Janet continued. "If I don't get those pills I'm going to die."

"If you keep taking those pills," the nurse said calmly, "they'll kill you." Did she think that was some kind of dissuasion for Janet? She'd failed at solving her problems on her own, and now she was forced to do the one thing she couldn't do herself. At this moment she'd give anything to go back and make sure she'd never survived in the first place.

Janet closed her eyes and tugged again on the restraints tied to her wrists and ankles. In the hospital, she'd been given enough medication that the withdrawal symptoms had been minor. But once she reached the rehab, Dr. Paulson had designed a more intense withdrawal program for Janet to start immediately. Things had gone from bad to worse since then. It was now Monday afternoon, and she'd been tied down for nearly an hour after taking a swing at the nurse. Her stomach was in knots, her chest throbbed and her head felt like lead. Her throat was dry, she was sweating like a pig and yet they continued to tell her that this was normal. All she wanted was one more pill, one little pill. Was that so much to ask? But instead of relief she was forced to lay here like some psychopath.

"It's going to get better," the nurse said sympathetically as tears leaked out of Janet's eyes. Janet just shook her head. She'd given up on hoping for anything to get better. She'd come to the rehab with at least some hope that things would start looking up, but now she wanted oblivion more than anything. She wanted to return to the mind-numbing comatose state from which she'd never wake up again.

"By tomorrow things will be brighter," the nurse continued, interrupting Janet's thoughts. Janet just closed her eyes and let the tears come. She didn't believe anything would get better; not for a moment. The road to recovery and overcoming all she'd done seemed much too long to walk alone. And she knew she was alone; totally and completely alone. Worse yet, her loneliness was her own fault. There was no one to blame but herself. Tally hadn't contacted her, not that she was allowed phone calls or visitors yet, but even when she could have those things she wondered if he would, if he should. Look what she'd done to his life. Who cared whether she lived or died at this point? She didn't, and she had a very hard time believing that anyone else did either.

By Monday Tally was feeling better, physically at least. He was able to get up and go to the bathroom with only minimal assistance and Josh was back home, which brightened the entire mood of the house. Julie did most of the care taking, but Tally read and napped with Josh as often as possible. The ward had brought meals in ever since Tally had gotten home and Julie appreciated the help since she was overwhelmed by just how much was needed by these two boys of hers, not to mention the horses and house necessities.

Monday night the bishop came for a visit, and Julie excused herself from the conversation, taking Josh with her downstairs while she folded some laundry. As soon as they were gone the bishop again opened their meeting with prayer, another powerful reminder to Tally of who this man worked for.

When he'd taken his seat again, they discussed how Tally was feeling and how Tally's follow-up appointment with his doctor that morning had gone. Then the bishop turned his powerful gaze onto Tally and smiled. "I'd like to talk about something different tonight, if that's okay," he began.

Tally wondered what else there was to discuss other than his failing marriage that loomed like a black hole in the center of everything. "Okay," he said, his confusion obvious.

The bishop nodded. "It's about your release from Young Men's last year."

Tally instinctively stiffened; he wasn't sure he wanted to get into it. It seemed easier just to move on—and he definitely didn't want to bring those thoughts and feelings to the forefront again. He had no doubt they were better left in the shadows.

The bishop nodded again, as if correctly interpreting Tally's response, before launching into the story he'd apparently come to tell. "When I was called as bishop, one of the first things I was instructed to do was review the auxiliaries and see if any changes were necessary. Well, I had followed an excellent bishop and each organization seemed very well intact. The Young Men's was especially effective—the four of you had been called just a few months previous, you were all enthusiastic and I knew that you all worked very well together. With all that said it was very odd when, after meeting with you as I did with everyone in the different auxiliaries, I felt very strongly that you should be released.

"But the feeling made no sense to me. We'd had a nice visit, I was so impressed with you and your dedication to your calling. It was obvious to me when we met that you loved being involved that way, and I saw no reason to make a change. But the feelings persisted, and every time I saw you for the next couple of weeks I was reminded of this feeling. But I remained stubborn and finally spent a great deal of time praying about it, wanting to be sure. After fasting over the issue I felt a nearly overpowering feeling that it was time for you to settle down and start a family and part of that required that you be released from your calling. So I did it, but I took it a step further and believed, totally of my own accord, that I should also encourage you to attend the singles ward." He paused and smiled apologetically. "I knew when you left that meeting that I had offended you, and yet due to my own pride and determination to be 'right' I didn't do much to remedy that. I got caught up in the feeling that I was the bishop and you sustained me, therefore you needed to accept my counsel and advice." He let out a deep breath and shook his head.

"When you came in to discuss your marriage with me in

November I gave you the counsel I felt you needed, but I could see that you weren't very open to it and I knew it was because of the way I handled your release." He quickly put up a hand to stop Tally from speaking. "Now don't get me wrong, I'm not saying that releasing you was wrong, only that I didn't follow it up correctly. And I'm sorry for that, Tally. Especially after all that's happened. I kick myself for making myself so unapproachable."

Tally nodded, feeling foolish and arrogant for ever doubting this man's motives. "You are my bishop and I did sustain you. It was my own pride that made me so arrogant and unreceptive. I had thought the reason you released me was because of my knee, that you thought I couldn't keep up."

The bishop raised his eyebrows. "Oh, absolutely not," he said in surprise. "In fact I thought that, physically, the calling couldn't be more perfect. It kept you moving and the boys had an excellent example in overcoming adversity. Not to mention you'd already committed to go to every scout camp all summer—as it was they had to scramble for people willing to rearrange their schedules. I can promise you it had nothing to do with that."

Tally managed a small smile, more relieved than he felt was warranted to know that he hadn't been discriminated against. But the bishop's explanation still didn't make a lot of sense. "I'm not trying to doubt the Lord, or your ability to follow through on His guidance, but I can't help but wonder, if I'd still had the calling and not been offended by having been released, if I wouldn't have made better decisions."

The bishop leaned forward. "What decisions?"

"Well," Tally said slowly. "Marrying Janet for starters. Maybe if I hadn't let my own anger block out so much of the Spirit I would have heard the Lord's wishes a little more clearly."

"You feel you made a mistake in getting married?" the bishop asked, and again he looked surprised at Tally's response.

Tally nodded, curious as to the bishop's surprise. "I went back on my goal to marry in the temple, I didn't act on the little hesitations I felt and look where that got me."

"When we met in November you said you had prayed about it and you felt good about the decision."

"Well, lately, after all that's happened, I wonder if I just wanted it so badly that I made up my own answer—maybe I only thought the Lord wanted me to marry Janet."

The bishop nodded. "I see your train of thought, but if I may, let me ask you to look at the alternative. Do you feel that your marriage to Janet caused her drug problem?"

"No, she was taking pills long before I met her."

"Do you feel her drug problem got worse because of you?"

Tally paused, he'd never thought of that, but he immediately shook his head. "No, I don't think we spent enough time together for me to influence her on anything."

"So, if you hadn't married Janet she would still likely be in the same place she's in right now."

Tally paused, he wasn't sure about that. "Maybe if she'd spent more time with Josh she wouldn't have lashed out on him that day. And if I hadn't left maybe she wouldn't have crashed and burned like she did."

"Do you really believe that?" the bishop questioned. "I've dealt with a lot of addicts, Tally, I've watched their lives spiral out of control over and over again. I've also listened to spouses and parents lament the things they did or didn't do that they feel contributed to their loved one's addiction. Through that I've learned that none of us have more power than the drug. No matter how much Janet loved you, and I do believe that she loved you very much, the drugs overpowered every-thing. It is my opinion that your marrying Janet saved Josh from unspeakable things. If you hadn't taken Josh and left, I don't believe she would have found the motivation to try and go clean."

Tally found it impossible to keep the tears at bay and he wiped quickly at his eyes with the corner of the blanket. "That motivation you talk about is what drove Janet to try and end her life, Bishop, and caused the miscarriage. I can't find peace with those extremes."

"You are a good man with a good heart. I don't believe for a second that you would have married her if you didn't feel it was the right thing to do and I think you know the difference between an answer to a prayer and your own projections. The reason for your doubts are due to the things that have happened since, things you interpret as proof you made a mistake, right?"

Tally nodded but said nothing. "It doesn't work that way, Tally. Bad things happen no matter what. You didn't cause these things to happen. Beyond that, had you not gone to her ex-husband for advice that day, the seeds the Spirit needed to act on would likely not have been there. I don't believe your marriage to Janet was a mistake, Tally. I believe it saved her life and possibly Josh's too."

Tally felt an internal struggle against all the bishop had said. Hearing himself described as a hero for going against all he'd ever been taught seemed wrong and arrogant. "I've been considering filing for a legal separation," Tally said, trying to change the subject a bit. Again the bishop's eyebrows went up in surprise. "I feel like I have given Janet so much control and so much power that I need to make a stand, to show that I'm not a doormat. Even . . . if . . . we make another attempt at this marriage—and I really can't fathom that we will—I feel the need to put my foot down, to draw a line and make sure it's clear that I'm not her lap dog, that I'm not waiting to see what she wants."

"I think that's a big step," the bishop said carefully. "And although I can see your point, I worry that it might give her the opposite impression, that you don't see anything worth saving."

"I don't know that I do," Tally whispered.

"Then you need to spend more time on your knees," the bishop said, he glanced quickly at Tally's legs and looked back up with a slight smile. "Figuratively speaking, of course, and find out for sure. You're battling some mighty powerful demons, Tally, ones that don't lay down and die without a fight; but make sure you're using the right weapons."

Julie entered the room after hearing the bishop leave and she asked Tally how the meeting had gone. He shrugged his shoulders and adjusted the blankets across his lap where he was sitting up in bed. She could see that he had been given a lot to think about and she once again hated the pain and torment she saw in his eyes. Tally had always been such a cheerful person, such a light, and he'd lost so much of that. It tugged at her heart to see him so hopeless.

"What would you think if I decided to file for a legal separation?"

Julie froze and looked up at him. "You're kidding?" she breathed. "Now?"

Tally nodded but didn't meet her eye. "I've thought a lot about it," he said quietly.

Julie sat on the edge of the bed and looked at him sadly. "Tally," she said as she searched for words to communicate how horrible his idea was. "Did you ask the bishop what he thought?"

Tally nodded. "He felt it was too soon to make such a drastic decision, that I need to wait a little longer, but it just feels . . . right."

"Does it really?" she pushed.

Tally sighed. "I feel like I'm being pulled apart, Mom, like I have each foot in a separate boat and they're slowly drifting away from one another. I feel like I have to make a decision or drown. At this point I can't even imagine seeing her again, let alone talking to her, so it seems logical that a separation is the right boat to put both feet into. At the very least it would show her that I'm not waiting to take her back, that I'm not allowing myself to be pushed around."

Julie didn't know what to say. Even though he had shared these thoughts at the beginning, she was stunned that he still felt this way. "Don't make a decision like this just to make a decision. You made promises to God, Tally; even if it wasn't in the temple you promised to love and honor her."

"She made those same promises to me, Mom," Tally said with a hint of anger. "And look where we are now?"

He had a point, but she still felt he was wrong. "At least talk to her, Tally. At least wait until she's released, so that the two of you can discuss it. Give her a chance to explain herself. And take some time to pray about this, to be sure."

Tally didn't respond—she hoped that was a sign that he was listening. She moved closer and wondered if she dared tell him the depth of her experience with depression, even suicide, but she decided against it. She'd never told anyone and she wasn't ready to do so right now. Besides, she didn't feel that he was ready to hear it. He seemed too overwhelmed as it was. "This is a big decision, one that you can't afford to regret later on. Will you please wait until Janet's well again and then talk to her? Will you . . . give it one more try?"

Tally looked up at her and she saw just the hint of hope in his eyes. "I don't know if I can, Mom," he whispered as the tears rose in his eyes. "I don't know if I have it in me. The bishop told me to pray about it and I don't know that I even want to. I can't live like this, constantly wondering what she's doing, if she's okay, whether to believe what she tells me. I was such an idiot for so long and the fear of being played the fool again . . ."

"Tally," she whispered when he didn't continue. "Only the Lord can anchor those boats. He can keep them from drifting long enough for you to make a decision you can live with. But you have to let Him." Tally looked down at the blankets again but not before she saw the moisture in his eyes. She felt her own tears well up and she moved closer to pull him into her arms. "I love you, Talmage," she whispered as his strong arms wrapped around her, relieved that he was finally willing to talk about this. "You're much stronger than you think you are. Pull on every last resource, do whatever it takes, but don't cheat yourself out of at least hearing what she has to say. If nothing else, perhaps her explanations can give you some closure, answer some questions."

He said nothing, but he let her hold him and after a few moments she whispered. "Pray about it, seek for the right answer, the Lord's answer—don't take legal action without finding His will first."

"You have so much more confidence in me receiving an answer than I do. I prayed about my marriage for months and it brought me here, why would the Lord give me direction now, when everything's such a mess?"

"Because He's your father, and He loves you. We do not always understand His methods, but that's what we call faith and I know you're a man of faith, no matter how lost you might feel right now."

"I'll think about it," he agreed a few moments later as he pulled out of her embrace. "But I'm not making any promises."

She nodded, grateful for any crumb of hope he would throw her.

Now, she would pray harder than ever that he would do the right thing—that he would receive the guidance he sought and that his decision wouldn't haunt him for the rest of his life.

CHAPTER FOURTEEN

"So how are you feeling today?" Dr. Marmot asked Friday morning. Janet met with Dr. Marmot every morning and with each passing day she was coming to hate him more and more. He asked insipid questions and then gave her milk toast advice about how to live her life. Today Janet couldn't sit still. She got up and walked to the narrow window. There wasn't anything to look at since the glass was frosted for privacy purposes, but she didn't want a view. As promised by the staff, Tuesday had gotten better, as far as the withdrawal was concerned, and each day since had been better than the last, in some ways. But she was now forced to look at her life without any chemical assistance. It was ugly and she wished she could block it all out again.

All day, every day was spent with therapists who tried to dig into her deepest thoughts and nutritionists who helped her learn what foods her body could handle, what she had to avoid, and what to expect as her liver continued to heal. She also attended an inpatient Narcotics Anonymous group and listened to people whine and moan about their lives. Beyond those 'uplifting' activities, she got to attend behavior management discussions and now and then sat with groups of junkies and alcoholics and listened to all the horribly degrading things they'd done to feed their addictions. She knew deep down that she was one of them . . . but she felt different. She had never resorted to prostitution or burglary, she'd never written an illegal prescription or had unnecessary surgery to secure pain medications. It very hard to relate to these people, despite the constant advice to look for similarities, not differences. And the constant mental energy it required was exhausting.

She was not in the mood to rehash all of this with Dr. Marmot today, but she had to say something or he'd just stare at her in that way that made her want to scream. "I feel like a walking zombie," she finally said as she picked at some chipped paint on the windowpane.

"Why do you feel like a walking zombie?"

"Because I'm not dead and I'm not really alive. I'm stuck in some psuedo-life that I can't get out of."

"What do you mean by psuedo-life?"

She sighed loudly. This was such a waste of time. She would rather bang her head against the wall than try and talk to this guy.

"I can't sleep," Janet continued, trying to change the subject. "I feel sick all day and I still shake all the time."

"That will pass in time," Dr. Marmot said as he continued to scribble in his notebook. She felt sure he was making a grocery list. He didn't seem to even listen to her and she wondered why the facility bothered paying people like him. This was such a waste of time.

She'd spent one full day arranging for Dillard's to pay the 80 percent of her treatment cost as outlined in their program, and in the process found out that this place cost almost $11,000 a month. $11,000 for her to recite bland thoughts and feelings to people who didn't care for her a bit. At least she didn't have to pay all of it herself although she hadn't a clue how she'd come up with the remaining 20 percent. She knew she was flat broke and she doubted she'd have a job when she came back.

Janet leaned her forehead against the cool glass of the window. Dr. Marmot's words of support meant nothing. She'd seen half a dozen different therapists over the last week, and they all said the same thing; that she needed to cope with what had happened and find out why it happened in the first place. Cope—what did that mean anyway? That she ignore it? That hadn't worked before. Maybe 'to cope' meant she should just accept it and move on. That seemed impossible. Through her Narcotics Anonymous meetings that she was becoming familiar with the 12 steps of sobriety. The steps made sense but they dealt so much with God that she felt guilty working toward them. All she'd done flashed through her mind every moment of every day and knowing all that she'd turned her back on Him made it hard for her to reach out to the higher power the 12 steps emphasized. And beyond her guilt was the reminder that just one month ago she was a professional woman who, despite a few panic attacks and an unstable marriage, was doing really well for herself. Now she was a forced to look at herself for what she was—a manipulative self-centered woman with an abusive childhood who had nothing to show for all the work she'd done in her life. She was a nut in a nut house, talking about things she could do nothing about because nothing could change what had happened, what it had done to her and to everyone else.

"I feel dead inside," she finally whispered as the tears began to fall. It was likely the most honest thing she'd said the whole session.

"What used to make you feel alive?" Dr. Marmot asked, the most thought provoking question he'd *ever* asked her.

It took a long time for Janet to answer. "The pills," she finally said, pulling her knees to her chest once more and resting her forehead on them. "They kept me going, they helped me sleep—they allowed me to live a normal life." She missed those little pills as if they were her very best friend. She felt lost without their support.

"What else made you feel alive?" he asked, as if the pills didn't count.

"I don't know," she said softly. "I can't remember."

When she returned to her room, Shandy, her roommate, looked up from the book she was reading. "How was Dr. Milk Toast?" she asked.

Janet plopped onto her bed and threw an arm over her eyes. "As soggy as usual." Shandy smiled and nodded her agreement. Janet was used to other women being put off by her, she seemed to evoke instant jealousy from the feminine gender and it had been years since she'd bothered to notice at all. On their third day as roommates, and after very few conversations, Shandy had broken the ice. They had been getting ready for bed and Shandy said, "You've got to tell me what brand of sunless tanner you use."

"Sunless tanner?" Janet had said as she turned to look at her. "What are you talking about? I don't use sunless tanner."

"Then why do you look like a pumpkin? You've got to tell me so I make sure never to buy that brand."

That was the moment Janet realized that it wasn't her beauty that had put Shandy off, it was something else. The realization was a powerful breakthrough. She'd looked down at her arms that were nearly orange, thanks to the continual build-up of toxins in her skin due to the liver damage. She did look like a pumpkin—no, she looked like an Oompa Loompa from the movie Charlie and the Chocolate Factory. How was it that she hadn't noticed? Janet had then looked at Shandy differently too. In time she found Shandy's nonjudgmental acceptance refreshing. Not once had Shandy criticized Janet or told her what to do; she simply provided the listening ear of a woman totally different and yet strangely the same as herself.

Shandy was also here because of drugs, but she preferred the illegal ones. This was the third time she'd been here; she told off Dr. Paulson on her first visit and had never gone back to her. Janet found a strangely comfortable camaraderie with her odd roommate and especially liked that Shandy didn't mind her complaints of all the time she was wasting here.

"Dr. Milk Toast wants me to write a 'Dear John' to my drug of choice," Janet said with a shake of her head. "Can you believe that? I think he needs treatment more than I do."

"Actually that's a pretty helpful thing," Shandy said with a nod. "They'll make you read it to the group—it's a powerful exercise."

Janet made a face and shook her head, she didn't buy it at all.

"What are you reading?" Janet asked after a few more minutes as she rolled onto her stomach. Lunch would be served in twenty minutes and then they had more group sessions throughout the afternoon.

"I'm not reading," Shandy said as she put the book down with a sigh as she looked off into space. "Tomorrow's visiting day," she said as she tucked a lock of curly over-colored red hair behind her ear. "I'm afraid my ex isn't going to bring the kids."

"Oh," Janet said. She hadn't even considered getting a visitor although she'd be officially allowed to have them now. The bishop in Tally's ward had requested a clerical visit last weekend but the facility hadn't allowed it and she hoped he wouldn't come back. She didn't know Bishop Baker very well, having only met him once, but she knew that Tally didn't trust him a whole lot and that was enough for her. The only person she wanted to see was Josh, but surely no one would bring him all the way down here. She refused to think about it. "How many kids do you have again?"

"Three," she said with a sigh. "I got a photo from my mom today in the mail." She got up and went to the desk. A moment later she handed Janet a snapshot taken at Christmas time. Three scraggily haired kids smiled back at her. Despite their worn and mismatched clothes their smiles were sincere and Janet smiled back at them. She wondered what it was like to be Shandy's child and actually thought she had a pretty good idea. Shandy wasn't all that different from Janet's own mother, something Janet had realized right away and thought would cause friction. Instead Janet found herself finding a lot of comfort in trying to understand this woman in a way she'd never understood her own mom. It was hard to think about the kids, though, knowing how crazy their lives were and she wished them luck. She knew Shandy's problems would trickle downhill just assuredly as Janet's mother's problems had. Then she was reminded that it hadn't been a treat for Josh to be her son either—again she pushed the thought away. She didn't want to think about Josh; it hurt too much.

Janet handed back the photo. "They're cute," she said as Shandy stared into the picture again.

"I swear if he doesn't bring them I'll kill him."

Janet laughed, but stopped when she realized Shandy wasn't laughing. "He's always working against me," she said bitterly as she continued to stare at the photo in her hands.

"He brought them last week, didn't he?"

"Yes, but he hinted he might not make it this week."

"Maybe he's busy," Janet said flippantly as she rolled onto her back once more. When Shandy didn't answer, she turned her head and was startled to find Shandy staring at her.

"Those are my babies," Shandy said darkly, making Janet's skin prickle. "They are a part of me. If he even tries to turn them against me I'll kill him."

Janet felt chilled but immediately shrugged it off. Shandy was nice, but she was a little weird sometimes. She'd get obsessed about certain things and didn't stop until she got her way. Yesterday she'd thrown a tantrum about being forced to eat peanut butter sandwiches with grape jelly, not strawberry jam. Janet had been embarrassed, since they were sitting at the same table, but she also found it kind of funny. There wasn't much to smile about in this place; she liked that Shandy provided a little relief to the monotony. It got even better when someone brought her a new sandwich—with strawberry jam. Shandy had winked at Janet and smiled victoriously. Shandy had issues, but who didn't?

The next morning, Janet went to the arts and crafts room. It was Saturday, visiting day, and all sessions and activities were suspended until three o'clock that afternoon to allow residents to have personal visits. She'd chosen to keep herself busy, away from every one else, in order to avoid the reminder that she had no one coming to see her. Allen had written her; he asked how she was, told her he hoped things would get better, but it was awkward and she hadn't written him back. She'd attempted to write Tally, but couldn't find the words and the stress always gave her a headache which she could only take Aspirin to remedy.

The arts and crafts room reminded her of summer camp, although she'd never gone. The room was full of every artistic medium imaginable; clay, paint, pencils, plaster, crepe paper, markers, even paper mache. A few people were in there and she just looked around, rolling her eyes at how juvenile this all seemed.

Eventually she found the watercolors and paper, deciding that painting would probably be pretty soothing, although she hadn't painted since her high school art class. She sat down at a small table and stared at the blank paper. This is so dumb, she thought. But then she shrugged her shoulders and started spreading the colors across the paper. She didn't know what she was painting, but eventually realized it was similar to the view from Tally's house. It made her smile, but also tugged at her heart a little. She'd already accepted his silence, and she didn't fault him for it; but she wished there was some way. She'd been using a glass of water to rinse her brush and when she finished and had stared at the picture for awhile, she dumped the glass over her picture. The gray water covered the landscape she'd painted and ruined all her hard work—it was almost poetic. Then, before the emotion could overcome her again, she got up and left as the water dripped onto the floor.

That afternoon she received a phone call from Tally's bishop. She didn't know what to say and the conversation didn't last long. He asked if he could come give her a blessing but she said no. The last thing she needed was an ecclesiastical guilt trip for what she'd done, and right now anything associated with God just seemed to make her mad. The bishop asked if he could call again and she said he could, but when she hung up she hoped he would forget all about her. She hoped everyone would.

Through the next week she continued her meetings with Dr. Marmot, but they weren't very helpful. She didn't feel any 'empowerment,' but she had no choice but to meet with him, so she simply did what she was supposed to do. Now and then she would see Dr. Paulson in the hallways and she wondered if anything would be different if she had chosen to use her as her main therapist. But then she would remember that Allen had recommended her, and how abrupt and harsh she'd been. Those reminders were all Janet needed to keep her satisfied with Dr. Marmot. She'd also come to embrace the 12 step program of Narcotics Anonymous a little better. It was still hard but she was making progress. She was still focusing on the first step which was to accept that she was powerless over her compulsive and addictive behavior. It was hard for her to admit that, to admit she couldn't fix it alone, but she could feel the truth of it and so she was trying to work toward it, almost feeling guilty about what a relief it would be to not take the blame any longer. At least it was something to look forward to.

But where her days were getting slowly better, at least taking on a routine quality she could appreciate, Shandy seemed to be slipping into a very dark place. Shandy didn't want to talk like she used to and she'd often look around with darting glances, as if watching for something. As Saturday had gotten closer she'd started mumbling about her husband not bringing the kids again; in fact it was all she would talk about. Her ex-husband had brought them last week and Janet had thought that would be the end of Shandy's obsession, but it had only given her a few days of relief. This time it was worse than ever. In a group session on Thursday Shandy totally lost it. She started screaming at the top of her lungs about the conspiracy against her when the moderator suggested that perhaps it was better for her kids not to see her here. The orderlies had to drag her away. Janet had been scared to death, and even though Shandy was much calmer when Janet saw her next, Janet found herself keeping her distance. Shandy's similarities to Janet's mom had crossed a line that Janet didn't feel comfortable with and it made her own childhood even clearer, something she didn't want to relive.

On Saturday morning, after Shandy had left to wait for her visitors, Janet sat down to write Tally. But she didn't know what to say—as usual. She couldn't find the words to adequately explain and she didn't think he wanted to hear a feeble attempt. Finally, she put the pen down and rested her elbows on the small desk. She'd been here two weeks and she didn't feel much different than the day she'd arrived. She had no idea where her job stood, financially things were a mess and Josh and Tally were gone. She didn't feel any great hope for her future, any motivation to create something out of what was left. The only thing that had changed was that her head was clearer; she could think things through, but it didn't give her any great comfort. Being able to see and comprehend all that she had done, only made her wish that Kim and Allen hadn't come and rushed her to the hospital at all. She still felt that everyone would have been better off if she'd died.

"Janet, you have a visitor in room six."

Janet looked up at the staff member poking his head in the door, unable to hide her surprise. After a slight hesitation she stood and made her way toward the visiting rooms reserved for private meetings. She hoped it was Tally and yet talked herself out of it at the same time. She opened the door to room six and tears immediately filled her eyes as Josh wiggled out of Julie's arms and ran toward her. She'd just been lamenting her life all together, but those thoughts disappeared at the sight of her son. She scooped him up and held on tightly as tears fell down her cheeks. He evoked something within her that had not died that day. It was a strangely painful feeling to hold him again, especially since she was now well aware of what she'd done to him now that the meds weren't clouding her mind. He only put up with the embrace for a few seconds before pulling back. "How's my baby boy?" she choked, not bothering to wipe at the tears.

"I s' go'da da Ma'ma."

Janet laughed. "Da Ma'ma," she repeated. She kissed his forehead and adjusted him onto her hip. Then she looked at Julie, her husband's mother, and felt her embarrassment keenly. "I don't know what to say," she finally said through her tears as Josh wiggled out of her arms and headed for what Janet assumed was a bag of his toys on the other side of the room. "Thank you for bringing him."

Julie smiled and in a surprising gesture stepped forward and pulled Janet into a hug. At first Janet was stiff, Julie had never hugged her before. But then she heard her mother-in-law start to cry. More tears welled in her eyes and she returned the embrace, realizing that she had never hugged another woman in her whole life. It was at least a minute before Julie pulled back and looked at her with soft eyes filled with love and compassion that Janet found frankly surprising. "I'm so glad you're all right," she said with a teary smile.

"Really?" Janet asked without meaning to, but once it was out she was glad to have said it.

"Is it that surprising?"

"After everything I've done to you and your family, yes."

"How are you?" Julie asked, changing the subject.

"I'm okay," Janet answered, almost believing it for the first time.

"Good." Julie squeezed her arm and looked at Josh who was approaching them with an armful of books. Janet immediately sat on the floor and he sat on her lap. For the next twenty minutes she read the books over and over again, letting him turn the pages when he wanted to and not feeling any of the frustration that had accompanied her interactions with him in the past. When a staff member poked his head in to tell them time was up, she was hesitant to let him go.

"How long will you be here?" Julie asked.

"Two more weeks, I think," Janet said as she helped Josh put the things back in the bag.

"Are you worried about starting up when you get out?" Now this was the Julie Janet remembered, but the harshness she'd perceived before wasn't there.

"It scares me," Janet admitted, looking away to hide her embarrassment at her own honest answer. "But I've gotten involved in NA here, Narcotics Anonymous, and I'll stay involved after I'm released. There are behavior therapists who have helped me learn how to manage an attack without the medication—it's helping." She didn't say that the future still looked very gray and daunting to her.

"It's going to be a very different life for you when you get out."

"I know," Janet agreed. She paused for a few more seconds before continuing, unable not to ask the question on her mind. "Ummm, how's Tally?"

"I assume you want the honest answer?"

Janet nodded, not liking the preface.

"He's thinking about filing for a legal separation."

Janet wasn't as shocked as Julie probably expected her to be, but the sadness was nearly overwhelming. She nodded and looked away.

"I'm sorry," Julie said quickly. "I shouldn't have said anything."

"No, it's okay," Janet said, meeting her eyes again. "I can't blame him too much. He doesn't deserve this."

"If it makes you feel better I think I convinced him to wait until you're done here to make any firm decisions. He said he'll wait to meet with an attorney until after your release."

Janet's eyes went wide and just a hint of hope blossomed in her heart. "He agreed to that?"

"Yes," Julie said with a small smile of triumph. Then her smile faded. "But Tally is a stubborn man and I'm not sure if anything, or anyone, can really get through to him. The bishop has talked him into attending an LDS 12-step program next week, when he can get around better—I'm hopeful that will help."

The silence was uncomfortable for a few more seconds as Janet absorbed that information—but the hope hadn't died; there was still a chance. Knowing he was learning about the 12-step program also gave her a lift, it was something that, although apart, they were doing together and she felt her motivation to apply herself increase.

Josh came back, having given up on getting the books back in the bag. She picked him up and hugged him tightly. When she pulled back, she smiled sadly. "Your mama loves you, Joshy," she whispered, touching his curls and trying to implant his face into her memory. It was impossible not to remember that the last time she'd seen him half of his face was black and blue because of her. She wanted to tell him how sorry she was for being such a lousy mother but instead she just said, "She loves you very much."

A few minutes later, Janet said goodbye and then went in her room and cried for nearly an hour. Seeing Josh made her feel even more confused. There was so much joy in him, and he made her feel good—but was it enough? It hadn't been enough before, yet it was the only thing she had now. She thought of Tally wanting a separation that would eventually lead to divorce and she cried even harder. She didn't know how he could ever forgive her, but she couldn't imagine a life without him.

When visiting hours were over, Shandy came into the room. Her face was pinched but her eyes were wild. Janet felt instantly concerned and asked her what was wrong.

"He didn't bring my babies," Shandy muttered, then she launched into a long litany of profane description of her ex-husband. When the tirade reduced to mumbling she climbed up on her bed, hugged her knees to her chest and started rocking back and forth. Janet was concerned and wondered what had happened to the woman she had laughed with only a couple weeks before. It was as if she were a different person. After a few more moments the discomfort in the room became stifling and Janet excused herself. She went to the nurse's station and when they saw her standing there, one of the nurses came over to the microphone that allowed the sounds of their voices to travel through the glass.

"I'm concerned about Shandy," Janet said.

The nurse nodded, but she had a look that seemed to say 'what do you know.' Janet ignored it and continued. "She's been acting really strange the last few days and her kids didn't come today."

"We've got it covered," the nurse's voice crackled over the speaker before she turned away. Janet let out a breath and walked away. There was nothing else she could do.

CHAPTER FIFTEEN

The next morning Janet woke up and stretched her arms above her head, noting a definite difference in how she felt today. She'd slept better and did a quick inventory of what was different. Then she smiled and remembered Josh, the way he'd lifted her spirits. She was grateful for the change and she hoped it was a step in the right direction. She looked over at Shandy's bed and lifted herself up on her elbows when she realized that, although disheveled, the bed was now empty. That's odd, she thought to herself as she pulled back the covers and pivoted on the bed so that her feet touched the cold floor. Shandy was never the first roommate up in the morning, and this being Sunday she had an extra hour. Not thinking it overly strange, considering Shandy's behavior this last week, Janet made her bed and got dressed as usual.

When ten minutes had passed, and Shandy hadn't come back, Janet decided to go to breakfast without her—she actually had an appetite for the first time in weeks. Throughout her solitary breakfast Janet kept an eye out for her roommate, but Shandy never showed. When she finished she checked the room and then took nearly twenty minutes to walk the whole facility, coming back to their room when she finished. The room was still empty. Janet had a funny feeling and she thought back to the look on Shandy's face yesterday when her children hadn't come. After a few more minutes and another walk around the facility she went to the front nurses' station. She had to bang on the glass to get their attention.

"Do you know where Shandy is?" she asked the nurse that approached her.

"Isn't she in her room?" the nurse asked.

"I've been looking for her for nearly half an hour; she wasn't in our room when I got up." The nurse took Janet's concerns seriously this time and called over her shoulder for someone to order a facility check. Immediately everyone was ordered to the main common area, then the entire building was searched. Within another half an hour it was obvious that Shandy wasn't here. Janet was immediately taken into a room and questioned about what she knew. After what seemed like forever they let her go, content with the fact that she really didn't know anything. When she exited the room Dr. Paulson was leaning against the wall as if she'd been waiting for Janet to finish. Janet read the grave expression on her face and asked, "What's wrong?" not even caring about the tension that remained between them.

"Come with me," Dr. Paulson said as she took Janet's arm gently. She led Janet to her office and instructed her to sit down as she shut the door.

"What's wrong?" Janet asked again. Instead of going around the desk Dr. Paulson sat in the chair next to Janet and turned it so that they were facing one another. Janet looked at the doctor with concern as her stomach started to burn. "Did you find her?"

Dr. Paulson cleared her throat. "Do you know much about why Shandy's here?"

"Drugs," Janet answered.

"That's part of it," Dr. Paulson confirmed. "But the rest of it is that Shandy has a mental illness called Bipolar or manic depression; have you heard of that?"

Janet shook her head.

"Someone without manic depression experiences slight ups and downs as a normal part of life." She moved her hand up and down in a gentle motion, as if imitating waves. "A manic depressant experiences both ups and downs to the extreme." She moved her hand as if imitating waves again but this time it was much more dramatic, pitching even higher and falling much lower. She finished her visual example and put her hand back in her lap. "Shandy is classified as a clinical or severe manic depressant. When she's up, she feels better about herself and life than you or I ever do. When she's down she can hardly function. She's been taking medication to even out her moods for several years. But sometimes, she goes off of her medication when she's feeling up because she feels so good she's sure she doesn't need it. That creates a big problem. Beyond her mental illness she has had an ongoing problem with illegal substances. When she goes on a binge, which usually coincides with an 'upswing,' she throws her brain chemistries into sheer chaos. She was brought here because she was found running through the streets naked. She thought she was invisible." Janet furrowed her brow. People really did that? "She does something like this about once a year or so and she's ended up here for the last three episodes. Her mother pays for it. We keep her 'til she's straightened out and then she goes back into the real world again. She'd been here about a week when you showed up, and she had just started descending from the 'high.' I'm sure you noticed the changes."

Janet nodded, remembering it well.

Dr. Paulson continued. "When she's up, and doesn't have the right build up of meds to level her off, she feels invincible, almost immortal. When she goes down she has equally intense feelings of despondency and paranoia. Because it takes a few weeks for her meds to equalize, she wasn't spared from that drop the way she would have been had she remained on her medication. The higher the high, the lower the low. I don't know how she managed to get away from here. As you know, our security is very tight."

"What happened?" Janet asked anxiously. She appreciated the background, but her concern for Shandy was growing.

"She went to see her children, but her ex-husband wouldn't let her in—it was about three o'clock this morning." Dr. Paulson paused and she looked Janet in the eye, her expression sad and full of compassion for what she was about to say. "They got into a heated argument and the police were called. Before the police arrived on the scene Shandy produced a gun, another variable we don't understand yet. She shot her ex-husband . . . and then she turned the gun on herself."

Janet just stared and pulled back. "What?" she breathed.

"She's made choices that make her very volatile—apparently things were worse than we thought. If we'd known she was this low, we'd have had her confined—but she's been here enough to know what to say and what not to say. Even in her 'low,' she seemed to know what games to play."

Janet closed her eyes and took a deep breath, forcing herself to calm down. "What . . . about her children?" she asked, seeing it for a moment through the eyes of the scared child she had once been.

Dr. Paulson was silent for several seconds. "They're okay," she said softly. "I mean, they weren't physically harmed, but they saw the whole the thing. They called the police."

Janet stared at the floor, slowly absorbing the facts. "Is her ex-husband dead?"

"Yes."

Janet let out a strangled cry and wrapped her arms around her stomach, sick and overwhelmed by what she'd heard.

"Shandy was a very sick woman," Dr. Paulson continued as she placed a hand on Janet's knee. "I'm sorry. I know you were close."

Janet felt her chin tremble and then she began to cry. She dropped her head and sobbed for what seemed to be a very long time. She'd only known Shandy for a few weeks, and yet the blow was devastating. She imagined the three faces from the photo Shandy had showed her and imagined them watching their mother shoot their father and then kill herself. How could Shandy do that to them? "I feel so . . . betrayed," Janet finally said, answering a question Dr. Paulson hadn't even asked yet.

"And yet you barely knew her," Dr. Paulson pointed out.

Janet looked up and felt as if all her insides were suddenly on fire. The implication was not lost. She'd put the people she'd cared about the most through these same feelings. Even as she made the comparison, a hundred what-ifs began cycling through her head. What if she'd tried to talk to Shandy more? What if she hadn't gone to bed early last night? What if she'd reported the seemingly casual threats Shandy had made against her husband? What if she'd forced the nurse to take action yesterday when she reported that something was wrong? What if . . . what if . . . what if? She felt numb but it was impossible to not move to the next line of thoughts; the thoughts Tally must have had. What if he hadn't gone to Oklahoma? What if he hadn't taken Josh with him? What if he'd been home that night she drove to Willard? What if he'd forced her to admit to her problems? What if he hadn't let her get away with so much?

She pulled her knees to her chest and wrapped her arms around them as she began to cry in gut-wrenching sobs. She'd known she'd hurt him, she'd known that she caused him to suffer; but until this moment she didn't know what that felt like. She felt sickened by herself, amazed that she could hurt someone that she loved so much. The next thought that crossed her mind was the same one she'd thought a hundred times a day for the last two weeks, 'I wish I were dead,' but this time she stopped it before it had a chance to register. She didn't want to die, she didn't want to leave things the way they were. She didn't want to leave Tally and Josh with the devastating pain Shandy had just left behind. Dr. Paulson's words echoed back from that first day. Janet had been given a second chance, and so far she'd taken little advantage of the opportunity.

She lifted her head and looked at Dr. Paulson through swollen eyes, unaware of how long she'd been lost in her grief. "I want life," she said in a strangled voice. "I at least want the chance to try and make this right."

"Are you sure?" Dr. Paulson asked. "It's not an easy choice."

Janet nodded.

"If you're serious we'll start by doing a complete autopsy of your life; pulling it apart and looking at every part of it piece by piece. You'll be forced to face things I guarantee you've never faced before. Are you sure you're ready to do that?"

"I'm sure," Janet said, her tone only a little stronger. "I'll do whatever it takes."

Dr. Paulson smiled. "We'll get started tomorrow."

Strangely, Janet knew exactly what would happen when she met with Dr. Paulson the next morning. In the last two weeks she'd analyzed her childhood, her mother, her marriage and her career. She'd talked about Josh and her ex-husbands, everything—but she knew this would be different. Dr. Paulson wasn't here just to listen. Janet knew that through that door lay something much more painful than anything she'd done before. Something totally and completely against her nature. But along with the fear and trepidation was the knowledge that this just might be the key to her future. If she could truly work through the grime she'd chosen to hide from all her life, maybe, just maybe, she could find that life was worth living, that joy could be found and that there really was hope after all—even without the pills.

Once they got started, Dr. Paulson didn't hold back. When Janet felt overwhelmed and started to cry, she was given exactly two minutes to compose herself. They spent the whole day dissecting her childhood, delving into more painful situations, all the while trying to understand how those things influenced her future—which was now her present. When they finished for the day Janet decided to skip dinner. She was physically and emotionally exhausted and fell immediately to sleep, haunted by memories she'd spent 30 years trying to forget.

When she woke up the next morning, she put the pillow over her face and wished she could somehow get out of this. But there was also a strange kind of curiosity of what lay ahead. Although it was incredibly hard, and in total opposition to the way she'd lived her life to this point, there was a sense of relief, like a misty substance she couldn't grab on to. But it was there nonetheless and it excited her, just a little bit—just enough to get her out of bed. As she got ready she noticed that the color of her skin was nearly back to normal. That was a good sign. It meant that her liver was still making progress.

That night, after another exhausting day of finding all the character flaws that contributed to her being here, she went to her NA meeting and focused on the first step again, but with new understanding. With the change in her perspective she understood what it meant not to beat herself up for all that had happened. It wasn't about not taking accountability for what she had done and somehow blaming God, it was admitting she'd been wrong but that she had a compulsive disorder she couldn't overcome if she continued to try and do it alone. She left that meeting with a new ambition to find the strength to conquer this. She'd allowed it to control her life by trying to deal with it by herself and she couldn't do that anymore.

Julie rolled the wheelchair into the small room and handed Tally the papers they'd been given at the door as she placed him at the end of a row of chairs. "Are you sure you don't want me to stay with you?"

Tally shook his head and smiled. "I'll be okay. I'll call if I need anything."

Julie nodded and left the room after agreeing to pick him up at 8:30. Tally's smile faded and he wished he were going with her. But he'd promised the bishop he would be here tonight, and here he was.

He'd made sure to get there plenty early so as not to draw so much attention, but it didn't seem to matter. There were only five people in the room but each of them smiled at him as if they were old friends. One woman, in her twenties Tally guessed, and several pounds overweight came and sat in a chair beside him before putting out her hand. "I'm Carly," she said by way of greeting. A dimple showed on her cheek when she smiled and Tally smiled back but tried not to meet her eyes.

"Tally," he returned, shaking her hand and dropping it quickly.

"I haven't seen you here before," she said, still smiling.

"I've never been here before," Tally answered.

"Well, that would explain it then wouldn't it," she laughed at her own joke and then her face grew more serious. "May I ask who referred you here?"

"My bishop," Tally said, then suddenly he understood the implication of his own words and hurried to clarify. "But I'm not, you know, an alcoholic or anything."

"Oh," she said easily. "Me neither, but take me to Chuck-a-rama and I may as well be."

Tally furrowed his brow, thoroughly confused. She seemed to understand the question.

"The 12-step program, although established by and for alcoholics, is actually helpful for anyone with any kind of addiction; drugs, alcohol, sex, pornography, even food—my drug of choice. It's not the substance we choose so much as what it is about us that makes us compulsively seek it out to dull the pain of other things."

Tally was silent and finally he smiled. "Oh," he said dumbly, unsure of what else to say. A few people wandered in and she waved at someone and started to stand.

"After group I'd be happy to answer any questions you have, okay?"

Tally nodded and watched her approach and hug another person. For the next hour and half Tally listened to a lot of things he didn't understand. Different people stood and talked about some success or struggle they'd had during the past week. The group applauded and gave feedback each time. Some people had achieved different milestones in their recovery and received tokens or plaques and the group repeated different mottos that, although somewhat familiar from TV and movies he'd seen, were new to him. He'd heard of sponsors in Alcoholics Anonymous programs and apparently the same thing applied here. The bishop had told Tally to come tonight to become familiar with what Janet was learning and Tally felt just the flicker of a connection to his wife once more.

Later that night, after kissing Josh goodnight and thanking his mom for all her efforts on their behalf, he read over the papers he'd brought home, specifically the sheet that listed the 12 steps or principles of the program. With each step was included a few scriptures and he opened his Book of Mormon to look up one reference listed under the first step of admitting no control over compulsive addictive behavior.

Alma 26:12: "Yea, I know that I am nothing as to my strength I am weak; therefore I will not boast of myself, but I will boast of my God, for in his strength I can do all things . . ."

Tally put the book down as the message of the scripture pierced his heart. But it wasn't Janet's recovery that he brought to mind; it was his own. His heart had become hardened over the last several months, yet he believed what he'd just read with all his soul. He dropped his head and offered a simple prayer of forgiveness, asking the Lord to strengthen his weaknesses and give him the insight to do that which was right by his family. When he lifted his head he hardly noticed the tears on his cheeks as he looked up the next reference and focused on the flicker of hope he could feel inside himself. The bishop had been telling him in every meeting that he was too hard on himself, that he needed to find hope; until now he hadn't been able to find it. But tonight had given him the motivation he needed and as he continued to read and ponder he couldn't help but hope Janet had found some peace this way too.

By Friday, Janet was exhausted. All the emotions of the last four days had drained her of energy. When she entered Claire Paulson's office that morning she was told they would be addressing the subject of forgiveness. Janet was actually intrigued by that, she'd love to know how to obtain forgiveness for all she'd done. But when Claire explained that the forgiveness they were going to talk about was directed toward her mother, Janet stiffened. They had their first real argument and Janet got up to leave. She was furious and felt completely betrayed. Had Claire not heard a word of the horrible things Colleen had done to her all her life? Had she forgotten the beatings, the drinking, the continual put downs and insults? The mere idea of forgiving—that was impossible. With her hand on the door-knob, Claire's voice stopped her.

"Does your anger hurt your mother?"

Janet took a deep breath, almost too angry to talk—almost. "My mother is dead."

"Exactly, so does your anger and bitterness hurt her?"

Janet said nothing.

"But it eats you up," Claire continued. "It always has, even when you ignored it. Your anger and hurt only hurts you; it doesn't affect her in the least."

"It never did," Janet said softly. "Even when she was alive, she didn't care what I thought of her."

"So what's the point of giving your power to her now? You only have so much energy—or power as I like to call it. Hating and hurting takes a lot of that energy, a lot of work—why waste it on her?"

It was too simplistic, too easy. Janet shook her head and stared at her hand on the doorknob.

"If you leave now," Claire said, "you don't get to come back. I'm not forcing you to agree with me, and I can't make you forgive the woman who hurt you so badly—but don't think you can walk in and out of here whenever you don't like what I bring up. You said you wanted life. I'm here to help you find it."

Janet gritted her teeth, but her hand slipped away from the doorknob. She came and sat down, pulling her knees to her chest and nodding. She would listen, then she would make her own choices on what she did. The rest of the day they went over all the people she felt had wronged her. Besides her mother, she found she was bitter toward Travis for being such a doormat and then dying, leaving her alone. She was angry with Theresa for taking her mother's love, what little there was of it. There was still anger at Allen for not giving her a second chance when Josh was born, at Craig for getting her pregnant in the first place, and then leaving her. And, beyond all those things she found she was even angry with Tally, although she felt guilty for it. It angered her that he let her use him the way she did, that he allowed her manipulation with so little complaint. Claire didn't tell her that was horrible or cruel, but she instructed Janet to really think about her true feelings toward Tally over the weekend.

Janet couldn't think about anything else for the rest of the evening and the more she thought about him the harder she cried. How could she be angry with him when all he'd done was love her, help her and try to do what he thought was best? In her heart she knew he was forgiven before she'd even met with Claire today. She loved him, she missed him and she'd hurt him so much. She wondered if Claire could go talk to him about forgiveness, for she was the one in need of his mercy.

At two o'clock in the morning she got up and turned on the light, her eyes drawn to Shandy's empty bed. She stared for several seconds before getting a paper and pen from her drawer. In all the time she'd been here she'd thought of a thousand things to say to Tally, but tonight the words were clearer than they'd ever been and she knew it was time to write them down. When she finished she felt as if a huge weight had been lifted and she hoped that when Tally read it he would feel the same way.

Saturday morning she stayed in her room, still overwhelmed by the issues she'd faced during the week and grateful for a day to try and make sense of everything. So much had happened, and yet there was still so much to do. She opened the drawer over and over to look at the letter she'd written but was strangely reluctant to mail it. His silence was hard to ignore and she couldn't help thinking that any efforts on her part would be interpreted as more manipulation. The prospect of something so personal being taken wrong frightened her, so she decided to wait until she had fewer doubts. As she shut the drawer for probably the eighteenth time that day, a staff member informed her that she had a visitor.

When she walked out of her room, she was further surprised to find Julie waiting for her in the hall. She immediately looked around for Josh.

"I didn't bring him this time," Julie said. "But I got permission to take you out to lunch."

"Out?" Janet said, surprised. She looked to the staff member at the front desk and he nodded.

"We already cleared it with Dr. Paulson," he said. "You have two hours."

Julie watched her for a moment. "If you don't want to go—"

"No," Janet cut in as she looked down at her T-shirt and sweat pants. "Just let me change."

Ten minutes later she signed her name in the register, promising to be back at one o'clock, and followed Julie out to her car. Julie drove them to TGIFridays, near the Cottonwood Mall, and they ordered their meals.

The damage done to her liver caused digestion problems she might have for the rest of her life. If she ate too much fat, or not enough, she would get nauseated, or have stomach cramps. It didn't help that the food at the facility was horrible. TGIFriday's was a welcome change and she chose a chicken dinner on the 'light' menu. They chatted for a few minutes about Josh and the horses, purposely avoiding Tally, until they reached a lull in the conversation.

"I've geared up for weeks to tell you something, Janet," Julie finally said. "But please be patient with me—it isn't easy to share such well kept secrets." She paused and took a deep breath. Janet's curiosity was instantly piqued, wondering what could possibly be so difficult for Julie to tell her, yet part of her was uncomfortable to have a deep conversation. Heart-to-hearts had never been her strong point.

"After Tally was born," Julie began. "I had a really hard time getting back on my feet. Back then they called it the 'baby blues' but I wondered if what I experienced was more than that. I was tired all the time—I mean *all* the time. And I couldn't seem to do the bare minimum I needed to take care of my house and this new baby. It was nearly six months before I felt like I was myself again. Until then I just wanted to sleep all day long. I would cry for no reason at all and I knew that had Tally not been such a wonderful baby I never would have been able to make it through those first months. Back then, we didn't talk about things like that with our girlfriends. I was a new mother, and I was supposed to be happy, thrilled with this baby and strong enough to deal with this change in my life. There were no magazine articles or commercials advertising what to do when life overwhelmed you. Being a member of the Church I had an adamant belief that having the true gospel in my life was enough to conquer anything and I dared not tell a soul how bad it really was. I was sure that meant I didn't have a strong enough testimony.

"In time it passed and I let out a sigh of relief. Then I had Chris, just 16 months after having Tally, and it was worse, but I still managed to hold it together on my own; although there were many days when I just didn't know how I would make it until Phillip came home. After Camilla two years later I was a wreck and I couldn't function. The simplest of tasks were like climbing Mt. Everest. I knew something was wrong with me, that it was more than a lack of faith, and I called the only person I thought might know what it was—my mom. She came and stayed with me for over a month, but we never talked about why she was there. She pretended she was on vacation while I laid in bed all day. I knew she was embarrassed by my weakness and was glad when she could go back home.

"Phillip and I decided not to have more children after that, but when Camilla was almost four we found out birth control isn't fool-proof. I was pregnant, again. By then I knew that something about having babies didn't agree with me, but I just geared up for what I knew was going to happen. I made Phillip buy me a freezer to put in the garage and I filled it with meals, anticipating the baby's arrival and my inability to function. Tally and Chris were in school all day, and I was sure that would help too, lighten the load a little bit. I even arranged with a neighbor to take Camilla during the day for the first few weeks after the baby was born. I thought I had all the troops lined up. But when Emma came, I hit the wall harder and faster than I ever had before." She stared at the table top and paused for a moment as if reliving the time. She looked up and met Janet's eyes. "Emma was a horrible baby. She had colic and didn't sleep very well. By the time she was three months old, I'd had it. I lived hour to hour, not day to day. I was afraid of what would happen when I really hit my limit and I constantly felt it hanging over me, as if waiting for the moment it would engulf me.

"One day it was so bad that I knew one of us had to go." She stopped, her face showing how hard it was to say that. "I stared at my beautiful daughter and imagined myself covering her nose and mouth until she couldn't breathe. If she couldn't breathe she couldn't cry. If she didn't cry, I could hope for sanity again." Julie closed her eyes and winced slightly. "But I knew those thoughts were evil and they scared me so badly. I ran into the garage, shut the door and started to cry, yet I still couldn't drown out Emma's screams in the other room. I didn't know what to do, who to talk to. I was literally trapped by this ten pound baby and I felt utterly hopeless. Phillip knew I struggled, but he had just opened the store, and at that time women were just expected to deal with it. But I couldn't anymore. Phillip was an avid hunter at that time, and he kept his guns in the garage. The next thing I knew I was holding his shotgun in my hands. I even loaded it. I stared down the barrel for what felt like forever, still crying and knowing that I couldn't survive even one more day. Life had become so dark that I didn't know where the light was anymore, so how could I follow it?" She paused and Janet felt a lump in her throat as she imagined the scene. She could relate so well to those feelings and she knew that it took a lot of courage for Julie to share this with her.

"What stopped you?" Janet finally asked.

"Tally came home from school," Julie said as she wiped her eyes. "I heard the front door slam shut and he called out to find me. I then realized what I was doing. I saw at that moment that if I followed through with this, I would be taking away Tally's mother, and Chris's and Camilla's and darling Emma's. My life was not my own, it had been bought at a high price on a hill called Golgotha, and it wasn't something that could ever be replaced. I put the gun down and called a neighbor to come and get my kids. When Phillip came home I showed him the gun and he finally realized how much bigger this was than we had thought. My mother came again, but this time I went into a place kind of like the place you are now. They didn't do as much counseling as they do for you, I'm sure, but I learned that I wasn't crazy. I suffered from post-partum depression; today I think they call it post-partum psychosis. After I realized what it was I had my tubes tied, to make sure I never had another baby. Phillip was very supportive and as Emma got older I could handle life better. I went to school to become a nurse when Emma started first grade, and I worked in the maternity ward, with new mothers. I made sure that none of them went home without knowing what post-partum depression was. Now and then I still struggle with the blues but I've learned how to handle it well enough that it's never threatened to overcome me like it nearly did that day."

"That's why you were so understanding when I had that attack on my wedding day," Janet said as realization dawned. She'd always wondered why Julie's attitude had changed so suddenly.

Julie nodded. "I never had panic attacks, but I saw the same kind of vulnerability in you that day; a kind of kinship, I guess." Their waitress returned just then and placed their plates in front of them. They thanked her, but didn't eat right away.

Janet looked at the napkin she'd been twisting in her lap and felt as if a huge breath was sucked from her chest. She wasn't alone; it was a monumental discovery. "When all this happened with you," Julie continued. "I thought that if I'd had access to anything that could ease what I was feeling back then, I'd have gone to great lengths to find that relief—I can see how a little pill could become your sole support. I know what it's like to come to the end of your rope and not have the strength to hold on anymore. Yet, I've never told anyone about my struggles, not even all those new moms I counseled. I hate knowing I can't 'do it all' and part of me still wonders if I had just a little more faith, could I have pulled it off? Was there some prayer I forgot to say, some element of the gospel I didn't understand? Over the last week or so I've come to realize that I've done myself and my family a great disservice in not being open about my own problems. I shouldn't have let my pride stop me from teaching my children about weaknesses and now Tally can't seem to make sense of what's happened."

"Don't take responsibility in things that are not yours, Julie," Janet said quickly. "I made my choices and Tally did the right thing, he saved Josh's life the day he took him from me." Her voice cracked and she took a breath, knowing she needed to change the subject before she completely lost control of her emotions.

"The neighbor I called to take my kids that day is the only person other than Phillip and my mother who knows what happened; to this day she remains one of my dearest friends. When I was in the facility, she would send me little cards and letters, just to make sure I knew she cared. There were days when they were the only light I could grasp. I mean, I was surrounded by the pictures of my husband and children, I had my scriptures with me all the time; and yet sometimes all those things just felt like more of the problem, not the solution they should have been. However, to know I had a friend who loved me despite my problems and was willing to share such personal things with me was just what I needed. It allowed me to believe that I was an important part of my life; it wasn't just about everybody else."

"I think my problem is just the opposite; my life has always been just about me."

"I didn't say our problems were perfect reflections," Julie said with a smile. "Just that we have some very painful things in common. I've been trying to find some way I could help you through this but I've been trying to do it without having to cross the line of secrecy I've worked so hard to protect. I finally realized that perhaps that was the only thing I could do, the one thing you needed."

"I've always been a solitary person, Julie, but I've never felt so alone as I have the last few weeks," Janet whispered, getting emotional again. "You have no idea how much your trust and support means to me."

Julie smiled and reached out to place her hand over Janet's. "I have a very good idea, actually. A very good idea indeed. Now let's eat; there's one more place I need to take you before recess is over."

They finished their meals and then got back in the car. When they pulled up to the gate at her condominium complex Julie looked over at her. "What's the code?" she asked.

"83 . . . 4 . . . 5," Janet said, hoping she was right. Her memory wasn't as sharp as it had once been. "Why are we here?"

"You'll see."

They pulled into the driveway and walked to the front door. Julie had already gotten Tally's key to the condo. She unlocked the door and then hesitated. Julie looked at Janet, her hand still on the doorknob. "Have you ever heard that anger is a secondary emotion, a symptom of the actual feeling?"

"Yes," Janet said slowly, concerned at what Julie was so nervous about. "They talk about that in group all the time."

"Well, keep that in mind," Julie said as she opened the door.

Janet nodded and walked past the older woman. When she crossed the threshold she froze and her eyes slowly traveled from one end of the room to the other. She could hardly believe what she was seeing. Everything was ruined, destroyed. Parts of broken chairs were strewn all over the place, dishes were broken, boxes toppled and the smell . . . it was horrible. She had to cover her nose and breathe through her mouth to keep from throwing up as she continued to survey the room. The curtains were torn off of the window, allowing enough light to illuminate the mess. Janet could only stare. Julie came to stand beside her and surveyed the room as if she hadn't seen it before either.

"After Tally saw you that night, he came back here and erupted.

Chris almost called the police and it's miraculous your neighbors didn't. That's how he blew out his knee. Chris finally called your ex-husband to bring him a tranquilizer and help give him a blessing."

Janet walked slowly into the room, taking it all in and unsure of how she felt. To know he had been this angry frightened her. But if he cared enough to show this kind of reaction, there had to be hope that she could resurrect his feelings. She felt even greater motivation to try—and to try hard.

They left a few minutes later and before Julie returned to Willard Janet retrieved the letter from her desk drawer, glad she hadn't mailed it. As she passed it through the window of Julie's car, Julie handed her a small package the size of a book. It was wrapped in leftover Christmas paper and Janet took it with some hesitation.

"It's my favorite book of scripture," Julie said, seeming to be a little embarrassed.

"Thank you," Janet said with a sincere smile. It had to be a Book of Mormon, it was the right size, and she wondered why Julie was giving it to her. She had her own set of scriptures in her room, although they'd been virtually untouched. Assuming Julie was just being a good member missionary by trying to remind Janet of what she believed in, she said goodbye and watched Julie drive away before turning and going inside, relieving the nervous orderly that had been assigned to watch her while she was outside.

When she got back to her room she opened the package and was surprised to find a hymnbook instead of the Book of Mormon she'd expected. *My favorite book of scripture,* Julie's words echoed in her head. Janet had never thought of hymns like that before. She laid back on her bed and opened the book, its new binding protesting her intrusion. The first song in the book was 'The Morning Breaks'—she'd never heard of it and turned the page. The next song was 'The Spirit of God' and she read through the first two verses, remembering the words she'd sung many times. As she went to turn the page again she noticed that some of the pages were marked with little blue post it notes.

The first marked song was on page 86, 'How Great Thou Art.' The reverent power struck her as she read the words and tears came to her eyes as she wondered if she believed God to be as omnipotent and merciful as the song portrayed. She wasn't sure and so she turned to the next marked song, page 219, 'Because I Have Been Given Much.'

She couldn't even read this one, it felt like a brand burning on her chest to even think of all she'd been given and thrown away. So she turned to the next song, the last one Julie had marked, page 241, 'Count Your Blessings.'

She nearly shut the book, irritated at Julie's selections. Was this some kind of penalty? A reminder of how little she had in her life right now? But as she contemplated closing the pages her mind began rehearsing the well-known song in her head. It was a catchy tune and of their own accord her eyes began to follow the words as the mental music played on. *'When upon life's billows you are tempest tossed, When you are discouraged thinking all is lost, Count your many blessings name them one by one, And it will surprise you what the Lord has done.'*

She didn't read the chorus, instead her eyes traveled back to the first line and she read it again. *Tempest tossed,* she repeated when she'd finished the first line. If those two words didn't describe her life right now she didn't know what did. She read the second verse which talked about burdens and it reminded her of Tally and all she'd laid at his feet. With tears blurring the words on the page she read the last verse of the song.

'So amid the conflict, whether great or small,
do not be discouraged; God is over all.
Count your many blessings angels will attend,
Help and comfort give you to your journey's end.'

She laid the book on her chest and let hot tears course down her cheeks as she wondered if this were really true. Were her struggles and conflicts within His power, despite how huge they were? She honestly didn't know but she desperately wanted it to be true and that was a new level for her in and of itself. What she did know, was that her choices had released a tempest into Tally's life as well as her own and she hadn't been fighting very hard to try and make it better.

At that moment she wanted Tally so badly her stomach hurt and yet she tried to contemplate what she would do if he were not a part of her future. With so much baggage now unpacked, thanks to Claire, she was ready to think about her future—to calm the tempest as best she could. She said a silent prayer in her heart that Tally would let her try, that he would give her one more chance. If only she knew where to start.

CHAPTER SIXTEEN

Chris and Lacey came to dinner in Willard, and stayed 'til late. Julie didn't bring up her visit with Janet, in fact they ignored the subject of Tally's wife all together, all of them knowing it was still a tender thing. After Chris' family left and Josh had been put to bed, Julie entered the living room and watched her son for a few minutes. He was reading through the packet of information about the 12 step program again and although she didn't want to interrupt such a noble activity, she knew she had to get this over with or lose her nerve all together.

"Can we talk for a minute?" Julie asked. He looked up, seemingly surprised at the ceremony of her request and nodded as he put the pamphlet down.

As she sat she saw the suspicion in his eyes and berated herself for making him distrustful of her motives. She'd been pushing him about easing up on Janet for weeks, but without telling him why it was so important. That suspicion would be over soon, however, and a chill ran down her spine at the realization of what she was about to do.

It took nearly twenty minutes for her to tell the same story she'd told Janet earlier that day, and when she finished she was too emotional to discuss it. Telling Janet had been one thing, but to admit to her own son that she'd once contemplated unthinkable things was very humbling indeed. Finally, she handed Tally Janet's letter and excused herself, promising to discuss it with him in the morning. Then she fled to the room she was staying in downstairs and called the only person she knew could understand.

"Phillip," she said when his sleepy voice answered the phone. "Julie?" he asked. "What's wrong?"

"I told him," she cried as fresh tears fell from his eyes. "I had no idea it would be so hard."

Tally sat in the living room for several minutes digesting what his mother had just told him and looking at the letter in his hand. To say he'd been shocked and surprised was a complete understatement, to say the least. He'd always seen his mother as powerful and able to do anything . . . and in fact she had, he just hadn't realized how much she'd really conquered. It was hard to take, though, and he was unsure how he felt about her not telling him before now.

He looked down at the envelope in his hand and couldn't help but remember the last letter of Janet's that he'd read. The letter was now somewhere amid the wreckage of Janet's home, which to the best of his knowledge hadn't been touched, and he found himself reluctant to open this one. But Julie had said Janet was doing better, that she'd asked about Tally each time Julie had visited and he couldn't deny how much he longed to feel some kind of connection to the woman who ruled his thoughts every moment of every day. Most of those thoughts were angry and resentful, but she ruled them all the same.

He opened the envelope, and said a little prayer in his heart before he started reading.

Tally,

It's two o'clock in the morning and I can't sleep for thoughts of you and all I've done. I've lifted my pen a hundred times and tried to find the words, but I've finally accepted there are no words that could possibly convey understanding or beg your forgiveness. But I've realized that to say nothing helps nothing either.

Tally, I am so very sorry for all I've done. I'm sorry for taking so many pills, hiding the problem from you and keeping you at too far a distance to do anything about it. I'm sorry for all I've done to Josh, physically and emotionally. I'm so sorry about the baby—although I didn't know I was pregnant, I should have, and my ignorance doesn't change what I destroyed. I'm sorry that my actions have taken the light from your eyes and that you are now forced to try and make sense of insensible things. I'm sorry for all the dreams I have ruined for you and for my impotence to make everything all better.

I don't know where we will be in one month, one year or ten years, but I need to know that you know how very much I love you, how grateful I am to have married you and what a blessing you were to me and to Josh. I'm learning so much here, things I've ignored and avoided for too long, and because of that it's hard to imagine trading all that had to happen to bring me to this point, but I ache to know that you suffered so much, and that you continue to do so.

I didn't write this to beg for forgiveness, or to try and talk you into giving us another chance—it was simply time that I broke the silence I've been hiding behind. I love you, Tally, more than I can say. I owe everything I have to you—my son, my life, and all that I'm learning here. Thank you for all you've done and for not letting me get away with it any more.

> *Love Always,*
> *Janet*

Tally read it three times before he looked out the window again. Sighing out loud, he felt some of the darkness lift. There was no doubt but that Janet's words were sincere and they soothed some wounds, even if he found some of it hard to believe. The flicker of hope increased just a little. Just enough for him to think maybe they had a chance after all. He'd already promised his mother and his bishop that he would at the very least hear her out, but not until now did he want to see her for himself, not just to fulfill a promise. With his crutches as support he got off the couch and made his way to his bedroom wondering exactly how the future was going to play out.

"Your mandatory four-week inpatient stay is over on Saturday," Claire said Monday evening after a brutal, but eye-opening discussion about Janet's feelings toward Tally. She was glad she'd pondered on it so long over the weekend so that she knew how she felt because Claire didn't mince words and she pulled out all the stops. Janet was glad to be able to share her feelings so openly, since it made them that much more real to her but she was also grateful they were changing the subject.

"You can stay as an inpatient for up to 45 days, but if you want to switch to outpatient, just coming during the day while you transition back into life, you can do that instead."

Janet looked down at her hands and said nothing. She'd been made aware of this from the beginning and at first she'd been counting the days, but now she wasn't sure she was ready. Leaving here meant she would leave her only real support unit behind her. The thought was a frightening one.

"Just think about it," Claire said. "You don't have to decide right now.

Late that night, Janet continued to rethink the discussion of the day. Claire wasn't Mormon, but she was 'a woman of prayer' as she put it. She'd challenged Janet to pray tonight, in whatever way she was most comfortable. Janet thought comfortable wasn't quite possible; but she had accepted the challenge. The thing that kept her committed to that promise was that she knew it would take a miracle for Tally to give her another chance.

She slid off of the bed and knelt down. As soon as she started her prayer, the tears began to fall and she couldn't seem to stop them. The 'old' Janet had been against emotion of any kind; it was dangerous and it weakened her defenses. But the new Janet found an odd satisfaction in letting it out, like finally realizing she'd been holding her breath. She'd made a lot of progress in dissecting her life, and she felt free of many burdens she'd been carrying. But when she thought of Tally, the sadness and despair confronted her. There was no peace with what she'd done to him. Through her sobs she pleaded with the Lord to give her the strength to face him again. She knew she could never make things right, but she hoped that he could forgive her and give her one more chance to be the woman he thought she was in the beginning.

When she finally finished her prayer, her nose was stuffed and her blankets were wet, but she kept her head down and waited, as she'd been taught to do as a young woman and rarely done. Two minutes passed, then three, four—she wondered if perhaps she wasn't going to get an answer. Perhaps the chasm she'd created between herself and the Lord was too great. Tears came to her eyes again, but she didn't give into them. Instead she prayed again. She'd been taught that if she offered a broken heart and contrite spirit, the windows of heaven would be opened to her. Only now, after so many bad choices, did she know what a broken heart truly was, and just how contrite a spirit could be. If those teachings were true, she would get what she'd come for. When she finished this second prayer, she again remained on her knees and waited for an answer. Again nothing came, and she wondered if the 'nothingness' was the answer after all.

Her heart dropped as the nothingness continued. Perhaps what the Lord was trying to tell her was that she wasn't supposed to pursue Tally any longer. Maybe she was supposed to let him move on without her. As the enormity of that decision settled in her stomach like a knife, she realized that she had to put her faith in God's will, not her own—this was a problem she could not solve herself. If she was destined to a future without Tally, she would have to have the Lord's help. It was an oddly comforting feeling to let someone else decide, much like the peace she'd felt when she admitted that alone she could never overcome her addictions. But she felt as if her chest were made of stone as she realized that Tally might not be within her reach. She hung her head and offered one more prayer, one of thanks for Tally, for all he'd given her and Josh and then she said the fateful words she had never in her life uttered. 'Not my will but thine be done, I will follow your lead in this because I know you will be beside me, and Tally, through whatever our futures may be.' She ended her prayer and felt the tears fall as she imagined a future without Tally; it was overwhelming, but if that was the Lord's will, she would trust in it.

Suddenly, just as she was rising from her knees she felt a tingling sensation go down her back. It seemed to radiate around her ribs and settle in her chest. She took a deep breath and as she inhaled it was as if a breeze washed through her; clearing her mind and easing the tension from her body. She allowed herself to relax, allowed the feeling to engulf her and she was taken back to the time in the hospital, when she'd been unable to make contact with anyone. That same down comforter wrapped around her and she remembered the words she'd been told when she'd been in the coma; *everything will be all right.* She wondered if this was in fact confirmation that she was not supposed to share a life with Tally. Then she pictured Tally the first time they had met. His tenderness and goodness had been obvious to her then. He was so full of joy and strength; she'd envied those traits. He was everything she wasn't. Perhaps she had pursued him in hopes of learning from him; however, as had always been the case, when that pursuit brought him too close, her guard had come up and she'd had to do whatever she could not to allow him to have any power over her. After a childhood of being at the mercy of her mother's temper and tantrums, Janet had learned how to protect herself. When Travis died, she had found herself in a world where there was no one to trust. Rather than risk trusting the wrong person, she trusted no one but herself, and then she'd ended up giving what control she had to her little orange pills.

But she was past that now. She'd been given a second chance, a new life. *What kind of life do you want this time around?* A voice asked her in her head. It was a simple question to answer. She wanted Tally, and she wanted a family with him. The same tingling feeling descended once more and she smiled as she realized that the Lord hadn't withheld an answer because Tally wasn't meant for her, he'd withheld it because she hadn't turned her will over to him. She knew that it was still entirely possible that she had caused more damage then she could repair, but she was willing to take that risk and what's more she knew that God was on her side this time—there was no more powerful combination than a humble heart and the force of her Father in Heaven.

The next morning she started the questions with Claire. What do I do now? How do I start? Of course, Claire didn't put up with that and Janet was soon the one answering, rather than asking, the questions.

"You seem really excited about the chance to see him again," Claire said.

"I'm scared to death," Janet admitted. "But I am excited—I'm finally ready to at least try."

"Really?" Claire prodded.

"Really," Janet agreed.

Claire then picked up the cordless phone on her desk and held it out to Janet. "Call him."

Janet froze. Call him? Just like that?

"You said you were ready to try," Claire said tauntingly. "Either you are or you aren't."

Janet stared at the phone as if it were a snake ready to strike. She swallowed and slowly took the phone. After a few more moments of hesitation she dialed the number, not allowing herself to back out. The phone rang twice before Julie picked it up. Janet sighed in relief, she didn't know what she'd have said if Tally had been the one to answer.

"Julie?"

"Janet!" Julie exclaimed in a happy voice that relaxed Janet just a little. "Uh . . . is everything okay?"

"Yes, yes," Janet replied. Her heart was pounding in her chest and she could feel the sweat gathering on her forehead. Amazingly, since cutting down on the Xanax and getting the continual counseling, her panic attacks had all but disappeared—she almost wished for one right now, though; it would get her out of this. "I was wondering if Tally was around."

"Um, yes," Julie said, not hiding her surprise very well. "I'll go get him."

It was the longest ten seconds of her life and when Tally said a cautious hello she felt as if she might melt through the chair and become a puddle on the floor. "Tally?" she asked, as if she didn't recognize his voice. *Does he know it's me?* She wondered. He didn't answer and she knew that even if Julie hadn't told him it was her on the phone, he knew now. She took a breath. "I . . . I don't know where to start," she said lamely, searching her mind for some magical words to make everything okay—there were none. "But . . . I . . ." again she searched for the words. Did she say she was sorry? It sounded so trite, but was it right not to say she was sorry? She let out another breath and looked away from Claire's probing gaze. "I get out on Saturday," she finally said—apparently she'd made up her mind to switch to the outpatient program. Although in truth she knew that she just couldn't stand not to see Tally when she knew she could. "I would like to come up and talk to you." It wasn't genius and it wasn't eloquent, but the phone didn't seem to be the right medium through which to discuss their lives. A face-to-face discussion would be much more effective and the thought of seeing him again made her whole body tingle just a little. Tally didn't answer. "Please, Tally," she said softly, willing the tears to keep at bay but unable to keep the emotion out of her voice. "I promise to leave when you want me to go."

The silence that followed her final plea seemed to stretch on for miles and she said a silent prayer in her heart. "I'll be at home Saturday. You can come up if you want to," he finally said. No grand promises, but he'd agreed to see her. She smiled widely and gripped the phone tighter.

"I'll be released around two, I can come up right after that."

Tally said okay and hung up the phone. Janet hung up her phone as well and handed it across the desk to Claire. "He agreed," she said with amazement. Then her eyes went wide. "Now what?"

"What do you mean?" Claire asked with a little laugh.

"What do I say to him?"

"The truth," Claire said simply.

"The truth?" Janet repeated.

Claire leaned forward and struck the pose of the teacher, as she often did when she had a point to make. "If you were to break down the word 'honesty' to its Latin roots you would have two words—hone and est. The meaning of the word hone is to be one. Est means what is. So the literal meaning is 'to be one with what is'. When you talk to Tally, you need to be one with what is. No excuses, no justification— just what is, and what was. With a little luck, he'll feel the difference and you'll have a chance. If he still can't get past all that's happened, at least you will know that you were honest with him."

"It might be the very first time I've ever been completely honest," Janet said distractedly as she tried to imagine what the encounter would be like.

"Then it's about time, don't you think?"

Thursday morning Tally took Julie to the airport. Julie had been in Utah for almost a month and Tally was pretty much self-sufficient.

He'd even started driving again on Monday. Since it was his left knee that had been operated on, it wasn't too difficult a task. Since their heart-to-heart Saturday night and Janet's phone call on Tuesday, there had been a different feeling around the house, more openness. Julie had considered staying for one more week, but Phillip needed her home and she had things she'd put off for too long. After Tally's countless reassurances that he was okay she gave in and made her flight reservations.

After Tally dropped his mom off and headed back to Willard, he began to think of what would happen on Saturday. What would Janet say to him? How would she try to make up for what had happened? Part of him would like very much to watch the hurt in her eyes if he told her he wanted nothing to do with her. But he was determined to keep an open mind, to give her a real chance. He'd started praying for the strength to be fair and he hoped it would help. Saturday would be a big event, one they would both remember for the rest of their lives. Regardless of what the outcome was, he knew he would never forget the day.

Saturday morning Janet woke up early and packed her bags. She went to breakfast but decided to just have some orange juice. Since talking to Tally she felt twice as much energy, twice as much motivation and twice as much clarity as she looked at the things Claire helped her delve into. To know there was a chance, even a slim one, seemed to give her purpose again. And yet she was still so nervous about seeing him. She and Claire had spent a great deal of time discussing the many ways Janet had learned to manipulate people—it was sick how good she had become. But she wanted to be different. She didn't want to trick anyone, especially Tally. She wanted to be absolutely sincere, but after so much insincerity she worried if she knew how. Claire was convinced that Janet could be whatever she wanted; she said over and over again that this was a rebirth—a true second chance, but it was up to Janet to make sure it was a second chance worth taking. With all the counsel and advice, Janet found herself analyzing everything she said, everything she did and everything she thought about. Was this really how she felt? Was that an honest response? It made her dizzy at times but it also assured her that behaviors could be changed. She desperately wanted things to be different this time.

Amid all the growth and progress, her release had loomed bigger and bigger in her mind, and now it was here! The prospect of returning to normal life was invigorating and petrifying all at once. She knew that in here, she was in a safe place, her own private bubble with people who understood the problems she was having. It was their job to help her overcome the obstacles in her way. She thought of Shandy, of her pattern of coming to this place over and over and felt the familiar ache. Remembering what she now knew of Shandy's life, and the traumatic way in which it came to an end, strengthened Janet's resolve not to fall victim to her weaknesses again.

She had started reading her scriptures this week and her prayers, although still hard to say, had become part of her daily routine. Her spiritual development wasn't something she and Claire discussed beyond trusting in God's strength rather than her own, but the intricacies of the Mormon church were something Janet spent a lot of time pondering. It had become easy for her to base her level of activity, even her testimony of the gospel, on the people at church—making her involvement about them, not coming unto Christ the way it should be. That was a factor she knew had to change. In hindsight she could well see the pattern of her life, the way her life had always been better during the times she was active in the church. She'd survived adolescence, gone to college and married Allen when she'd been active. Then as her activity in the church deteriorated, so did her marriage to Allen. She refused callings, didn't participate in her ward and slowly fell away during her marriage to Craig. It was during her return to activity that she'd met Tally, and it was after she had her records transferred and stopped going again that the meds got out of control.

She hadn't been perfect just because she was active, but she had been better—she could see that now. She was determined to strengthen those spiritual muscles she had allowed to atrophy over the years and she knew that they would be her strongest defense. It was scary to realize how ignorantly vulnerable she had been, and how real a possibility of repetition she faced, but she felt anxious to get started.

At nine o'clock she left her bags in her room and went to Dr. Paulson's office. They would meet for a few hours, then she would sign the papers and she would be free—at least until 9:00 Monday morning when she was ordered to report back to the outpatient program she would attend for another two weeks.

"Are you ready for this?" Claire asked once Janet was seated.

"I am," Janet said, fidgeting nervously as she spoke. "I'm scared and overwhelmed, but I'm ready."

"Good," Dr. Paulson said with a nod. "I have only a few things to go over with you, and then you can go."

Janet's whole body tingled in anticipation and she took a deep breath.

"When you go out those doors today," Dr. Paulson began in a serious tone of voice, "You will be leaving the only support unit you've known during your recovery. There will be no one to tell you what to do. You'll also be returning home to a whole slew of problems. Besides the circumstances of your husband and son, you have bills that have gone unpaid, your job is questionable, and from what you've told me of your house, there is a lot of work to be done. You have relationships to reestablish and a lot of things to work out. It will be overwhelming and you will find the addiction you created screaming for relief. I want you to remember a phrase...ready?"

Janet nodded.

"A pickle can never be a cucumber again."

Janet furrowed her brow, then realization dawned. Claire must have seen her understanding. She nodded and continued. "You are an addict, Janet—a pickle. You will never not be an addict again, no matter what you do you can never be a cucumber, no matter what. You need to continue your involvement in the 12 step program, either Narcotics Anonymous like you have been here, or with an LDS group in your area. You'll need to go to as many meetings as you possibly can, at least 5 times a week and twice that if you can, so that you create a support community for yourself. You will get a sponsor who will act as your guide, your mentor—a fellow addict who is clean and can support you in staying that way. I know this type of thing goes against your very nature, but I can not impress strongly enough how vital it will be to your recovery." Janet nodded and swallowed again. Her new life would be completely different than the one she had been living. It was a very intimidating prospect. "You have very few people capable of supporting you through this and I guarantee if you try this alone you will fail.

"You are recovering, but you are still an addict and you always will be. When you go to a new doctor, I want the first thing you say to him to be that you are a recovering addict. Make sure this gets put on your chart and that the doctor understands how serious it is. You can never own another narcotic prescription. I guarantee that if you do, it will destroy you.

"You mentioned that you stole pills from Tally. If you work things out he needs to keep those pills under lock and key, seriously. You cannot have any access to them. If you have surgery, even another root canal, make sure they do not prescribe you narcotics. If they do, rip up the prescription in front of them—even doctors don't always understand the full spectrum of addiction. An analgesic is a form of pain pill that does not lend itself toward addiction. You will have to be proactive about this. You can take analgesic painkillers, like Tylenol, Naproxin and Ibuprofen, but you can never take another narcotic. You can't take diet pills, No Doz tablets or most cough medicines. In your 'take home packet' you'll find a list of what you can take but you will have to learn to deal with certain levels of pain and discomfort. You can never take Xanax, Valium or any other form of tranquilizer. I can refer you to some good books and programs to continue the behavioral control we have taught you—but you can never take another pill for the attacks. You need to fully understand that your addiction is as much a part of you as your husband's knee is a part of him. There are certain things he will never be able to do; he has accepted that and restructured his life. You will have to do the same thing, and you will need to be conscious of it every day for the rest of your life."

Janet stared at the floor, overwhelmed as she started looking at her life, which was already so insecure. She imagined how far-reaching these other changes would be and it scared her. Claire kept speaking.

"When you abused the medications, you turned on a switch that told your body it needed those things. You convinced your physical systems that Xanax was more important then food and water and that you should never have to feel pain. We've weaned you off of the pills, but that hunger is still there, like a parasite. It's waiting for any invitation to roar back to life—it is up to you to make sure that never happens." She paused for a few seconds until Janet raised her eyes. "The good news is that you are an incredibly strong woman. You have overcome a lot of adversity in your life, and you can do this too. You have a bright future ahead of you, despite the struggles that will be there. If you can keep your focus, surround yourself with supportive people, and not forget how close you came to not having this second chance, you will find more joy than you have ever known because you are freer than you have ever been."

Janet wiped at the tears in her eyes and nodded. "Thank you," she whispered. "I couldn't have done it without you."

"You chose life," Dr. Paulson said strongly. "That was the biggest step."

A cab met Janet at the front doors a short time later—several hours earlier than Janet had expected. Janet gave the driver her address. When he dropped her off she took a deep breath. There were unfamiliar cars in the driveway and she wondered with trepidation who would possibly be here. When she opened the front door the first thing she noticed was that the smells that had assaulted her last week were gone and in there place was the stinging smell of bleach and Lysol. The broken furniture had been removed, and the shelves and boxes had been restored, although the damage done to the walls and such was still apparent.

"Janet?" Lacey and Kim stood at the top of the stairs and hurried down to greet her. Janet was shocked to see them. "You're home early," Lacey said.

"Yeah, we finished sooner than expected. You guys did this?" Janet asked as she looked around her home again.

"Actually," Lacey said as she wiped some sweat from her forehead. "Julie started it before she left. I told her I'd finish up for her today, but Kim beat me to it."

Janet looked from one face to the other and felt the blasted tears come to her eyes again. "I . . . don't know what to say," she finally admitted.

"We're about done," Kim said with a smile. "How are you?"

"I'm fine," Janet said, still stunned and unsure of how to act, surprised that after a month in drug rehab she could say she was fine and really mean it. "I was going to head up to Willard."

They exchanged a look that told her they already knew she was going. She tried to read their expressions but she couldn't be sure if they looked anxious or excited about the pending meeting between Tally and herself. Lacey continued into the kitchen where she began rummaging through cleaning products stored under the sink. "I found some pills," Kim said as she took a step closer to Janet. "I flushed them."

Janet blinked and suddenly remembered hiding the pills all over the house, so that there would always be some close by. It seemed totally demented now, but at the time it had given her a great deal of security knowing that no one could ever find them all. Now the idea that she was surrounded was frightening. "Thank you," she said. "Did you find the ones in the freezer?"

"The freezer?" Kim said with a furrowed brow as she headed toward the kitchen. "I didn't even think of looking there."

"How about the nightstands?" Janet asked eagerly as she followed. She suddenly imagined herself sitting at home one night and finding an old bottle. The thought scared her to death and she wrapped her arms around her waist as if to keep from touching anything at all.

"Those are the ones I found," Kim said as she opened the freezer and started rummaging. She found the bottle within a few seconds and immediately took it to the sink where she turned on the disposal and emptied the bottle. Watching the colored tablets bounce along the bottom of the sink sparked a near compulsion in Janet to rescue them. Almost two hundred dollars worth of pills were being ground to dust;

was she really going to let that happen? She thought of the analogy Claire had given that morning about the addiction being like a parasite, waiting to be fed so it could roar back to life, but her mouth was still dry. *I'm a pickle, I'm a pickle*, she chanted in her mind, *I'll never be a cucumber again*. She forced herself not to watch and continued thinking of hiding places—she couldn't afford to miss any of them.

"There are some in my overnight bag in the master closet," she said quickly. "And in that cupboard," she pointed to the cabinet above the stove with the broken hinge. "There's a bottle of 'Vitamin C' but it's really Oxycontin."

Kim and Lacey exchanged a look and Lacey got the vitamins out. "I think there's a little pill box in my study drawer."

Kim was already half way up the stairs and Janet nearly winced as she heard the pills Lacey had retrieved go down the sink. In her mind she started adding up the money she'd spent—$300, $200, $500, it made her sick to her stomach.

"Anywhere else?" Lacey asked when she shut off the disposal.

"There's a pair of old sneakers in my closet. I put a bottle in there."

Lacey looked at her strangely and Janet looked away. She knew they understood she had a problem, but they didn't know what a twisted thing it had become near the end. "There's a few inside one of the coffee mugs in the cabinet…" her voice trailed off and she realized that she couldn't stay here. Even as she spoke, part of her was hoping they wouldn't find them all. In fact a few hiding spots had come to mind that she hadn't mentioned.

Kim came back down the stairs and stopped when she saw the look on Janet's face. "Are you okay?"

"I can't stay here," Janet said almost breathlessly. "I hid pills everywhere so that no matter what happened I would always have some on hand. I'll never remember all the places I put them."

Kim was nodding her understanding. "Okay, why don't you go; we'll scour the place before you come back."

Janet knew they didn't fully understand, but that didn't matter. She understood and she knew it was time to go. As it was, she remembered that just a few steps away, hidden along the grooves of a white picture frame sat a very innocent looking white pill that no one would notice unless they knew right where to look. She looked at both of them sincerely. "I'm so sorry," she said in a shaky voice. "I'm sorry you're spending your Saturday doing something I can't do for myself."

"Hey," Lacey quickly interrupted. She stepped forward and put a hand on Janet's arm. "We came because we wanted to do something for you. Go see Tally—but call us later, okay?"

"Okay," Janet said with a nod. "Thank you."

She went into the garage and found the destroyed furniture they had put there. Walking carefully around it she reached her car and climbed in. Her purse was still on the front seat and as soon as she saw it she nearly ran back into the house. This was getting ridiculous!

"Can I take one of your cars?" she asked as she burst through the door that connected the garage to the house, as if someone was chasing her with a knife—she wasn't sure she would feel much different if there were an actual person. "Mine is . . . well . . . I . . ."

"You can take mine," Lacey said as she dug her keys from her pocket. She gave Janet a look that communicated that she understood there were pills in the car. Janet thanked her again and hurried out the front door. But when she sat behind the wheel she dropped her head. *I'm insane to think I can ever live a normal life,* she said to herself. *How can I function this way?* Then she closed her eyes and offered a prayer of strength to her Father in Heaven. She could do this, but not alone. God was on her side, so were Claire, Julie, Allen, Kim, Chris and Lacey. She lifted her head, started the car and pulled into the street. Now all that was left was trying to make things right with Tally. It was by far the hardest thing she'd have to do.

CHAPTER SEVENTEEN

The phone rang four times Saturday morning before Tally was able to pick it up, and as soon as Josh wasn't restrained he ran outside with only one shoe on. Tally sighed with exasperation and put the phone to his ear.

"Hello," he said distractedly as Josh disappeared from sight outside the kitchen window. Sometimes that kid had more energy than Tally knew what to do with.

"Hey, Tally, it's Derrick."

"How ya doin'?" Tally said. Derrick Fisher only lived a few houses down the road and came over nearly every day to see how Tally was doing. He'd even helped Tally build a ramp that made it possible for Tally to get on and off a horse again. Tally hated to be a burden, but he had to admit it was nice to have friends, and getting back in the saddle again had been very good therapy. While they worked they had also discussed Janet at some length. Derrick was easier to talk to about Janet than his mother had been.

"I'm good. Yourself?"

"Good," Tally said simply. He wasn't much in the mood to talk right now.

"I was wondering if I could borrow your four wheeler later. The boys and I wanted to go up to the bat cave but we're short a vehicle— I'll trade you a Sunday dinner for the loan."

"That's fine," Tally said with a smile, although after his meeting with Janet today he didn't know that he'd be good company at dinner tomorrow. "I'm about to go riding, so I won't be here, but I'll leave the barn open."

"You're sure you don't mind?"

"Not a bit."

"What time is Janet coming up?"

Janet, Tally repeated in his mind as butterflies erupted. He was going to see her today for the first time in over a month—he was so nervous. He didn't know what he was going to say, he didn't even know how he felt about seeing her. It still felt like his feelings were all bottled up, available, but hard to get to, and he was afraid to unleash them—afraid of history repeating itself. Even with all he had learned it was scary and he was anxious about the results of this meeting. "Around 4 o'clock I think."

"So you've got time for a couple hours of riding; that'll be nice."

"Yeah, it's good to be on a horse again—I'm hoping to make it to the glen, but we'll see. Come get the four wheeler whenever you want."

Derrick thanked him and hung up. Tally found Josh's other shoe, grabbed their jackets in case it got cold, adjusted his arm brace crutches and went outside. The weatherman had forecasted a storm front moving in that evening, but the calm before the storm was beautiful and he knew he'd have a few hours of nice weather—he was glad to be able to get out of the house and hoped the ride would clear his head and help him work out the thoughts and feelings still muddled together in his mind.

It wasn't quite 1:30 when Janet pulled into Tally's driveway and shut off the car. She was early and hoped he wouldn't mind—she was so nervous. It didn't seem right to walk in as if she had any ownership, so she went to the front door and rang the doorbell—her stomach was in knots. What if he slammed the door in her face? What if he yelled and screamed and told her he didn't want to see her again? The thought made her wince but she took another breath and rang the bell again. Good or bad she had to get it over with—but she hoped and prayed the result would be one that wouldn't haunt her for the rest of her life.

No one came to the door and so she tried the knob. Had he seen her pull up and was hoping she'd go away? The door opened and she stepped inside calling his name. The house was silent, but she did a full walk through anyway, calling for Tally and Josh as she looked around the home as if she'd never been here before. The clock on the wall told her she was more than two hours earlier than she'd said she would be. She wondered where they had gone and hated how normal their lives were without her. After a few more minutes she went outside and headed for the barn, thinking perhaps they were out with the horses.

They weren't in the barn, but Branson, Tally's stallion, wasn't in his stall. Janet hadn't thought Tally was up to riding yet, but apparently she was wrong. She took a deep breath and sat down on a bale of hay to wait for their return.

After ten minutes she couldn't take it anymore. She'd watched Tally saddle the horses more than once and she figured it couldn't be too hard. She opened Ginger's corral and realized she wasn't even bridled. *Hmmm, this ought to be interesting*, she thought to herself. But she didn't have anything better to do so she got the bridle off the tack wall and tried to remember how Tally had done this.

It took nearly half an hour to get the horse ready to go, then she stood back and realized she'd put the saddle on backward. *What does Tally see in this?* she wondered as she bent down to undo the strap she'd just finished tightening around the horse's belly.

"Janet?"

She looked up quickly, thinking Tally was back; but instead there was a man who was vaguely familiar. "Uh, hello," she said as she searched her mind for his name.

"I'm Derrick Fisher," he said to remind her. "I'm Tally's home teacher, I live down the road."

She noticed that he said he was Tally's home teacher, not her and Tally's home teacher. "That's right," she said with a smile. "I . . . uh . . . well, I was saddling the horse."

Derrick continued to stare at her and she knew that he knew a lot more about what had happened than she had hoped he would. She wondered if Tally had told everyone, but then she chided herself—he had every right to tell anyone. In fact she was glad he had someone to talk to. "Tally said I could borrow his four wheeler," Derrick explained. "He's out riding; he didn't expect you until 4:00."

"I know," Janet said, embarrassed by how much this man knew.

"I'm a little early—I figured he was out on Branson and I thought maybe I'd ride out to meet him." The idea sounded kind of dumb now that she'd said it out loud.

Derrick was silent again and Janet looked away from his probing gaze. "The saddle's on backwards."

"I'm not much of a cowgirl."

Derrick smiled too and came over to help turn the saddle around. He also fixed the bridle she'd managed to put on incorrectly and adjusted the stirrups to the right length. "Tally's gone riding every day this week," he explained as he did the final details. Janet had stepped back and was content to watch. "He and I built that ramp," he pointed over his shoulder and she looked in that direction. The 'ramp' looked more like a small staircase. It had handrails and a four-foot platform at the top. It was about four feet tall and from the beams of the barn hung a bar, like a trapeze bar, she assumed Tally used that to lift himself on and off—she was impressed by the ingenuity. Derrick continued, "By using the ramp he can get on and off the horse without help. With this warm spell we've been having, he hasn't missed a day."

"He loves to ride," Janet mused. "Do you know where he went today?"

"The same place he always goes; that glen, but I know he was planning to be home in time for your visit so I doubt he made it all the way there." He finished making the adjustments to the saddle and stood up straight.

"It probably makes more sense for me to wait here," she said. "But I was hoping to make an impression with my efforts."

Derrick smiled. "I think that's a great idea." He turned and led the horse out of the barn. "I talked to him almost two hours ago, so you should come face to face with him pretty soon." He squinted up at the sky. "But there's a storm coming in, so just make sure you both beat it home."

Janet looked up too and saw the clouds he was looking at; they looked to be a long ways away, although she'd noticed that the air had chilled a little. It was still in the sixties, she'd guess—warm for March. She grabbed a heavier coat from the house just in case, an old one of

Tally's that she would fit in reasonably well if she rolled up the sleeves several times. When she put it on she could smell him and she pulled the collar to her face as she inhaled deeply. Her motivation to see him again kicked into overdrive and she hurried outside to where Derrick was still holding the horse. He helped her into the saddle and pointed toward the cemetery road. "You know the way he usually goes?" Derrick asked. She nodded, "Through the cemetery, to the north and never along the highway."

Derrick laughed and nodded his agreement. There were several ways of exiting the property, the most obvious were going through the front gate, but she and Tally had always gone through the back since the back led toward the mountains.

She got the horse going and thanked Derrick once more before she headed toward the field, glad to have some space to get reoriented to guiding the horse. Luckily, Ginger was an easy ride. By the time she reached the highway she felt pretty comfortable. They crossed the road during a break in traffic and began the slow ascent through the cemetery that would take her to the dirt trail. With any luck she'd meet up with Tally soon. The prospect gave her butterflies. She leaned back in the saddle a little bit and started going over what she would say when she saw him.

The ache in Tally's knee caused him to turn around earlier than he'd expected to and reminded him he hadn't taken a pain pill before he'd left. It was likely the coming storm that was causing the increased aggravation to the joint but he was in no mood to push it. The dirt road that led to the glen was butted up by several orchards. Normally, he didn't like to cut through people's private property and he hated riding along the noisy highway, but the uneven trail was causing him a great deal of discomfort so he began scanning the orchards for a road that would take him down to the highway, hoping the smoother surface would be easier on his knee. After a few more yards he found a road in good condition and turned the horse.

Within a few minutes the trail was blocked from view and Tally had almost reached the highway. He told Josh that they had another mile to get home and Josh continued to chatter about every thing he saw—cars, cows, birds—oblivious to Tally's discomfort. Tally hugged Josh with the one arm he had wrapped around the little boy, but then clenched his teeth and took a deep breath as Branson stumbled. *One mile*, he muttered, trying to focus on Josh's babble to take his mind off his knee. *I can make it for one mile.*

By the time the housetop came into view over the scattered trees the wind had picked up a great deal. The weatherman had forecasted rain in the evening but the storm had proven him wrong. Branson knew his way from where they were so Tally gave him his head to find the barn himself while he attempted to protect Josh from the increasing wind. Josh huddled against Tally's chest and Tally did his best to comfort him and keep him warm. Branson made it to the barn just as the rain began to fall and Tally guided him to the platform. Tally's knee was killing him and it took all his concentration to lift Josh off his lap and then dismount, using the trapeze bar to support his weight as he transferred himself to the platform. His crutches were waiting and he quickly slid his arms into the circular braces and limped down the stairs. He'd left his knee brace in the house, since he couldn't ride with it, and he quickly wrapped the reins of Branson's bridle around the center post in the barn to avoid having him run off. Then he turned toward the house, moving as quickly as his knee would allow as Josh ran ahead.

Josh seemed extra tired today and complied easily to go down for his nap once Tally promised him some chocolate milk when he woke up. He really was a good little boy. Tally shut the door to the room and went to the kitchen where he found his pain pills and took one. The clock told him it was nearly 4 p.m.; that meant Janet would be here any minute. Until then, he needed to rest his leg. He went to the couch and gingerly lowered himself down. Branson needed his saddle taken off as well as a good rub down, but that was going to need to wait for a little while. Tally knew he'd pushed it too far today and considered calling Derrick to come and take care of the horse for him. But he hated relying on other people all the time. He'd just rest for a few minutes, wait for the painkiller to kick in, then he'd go out and take care of the horse. If Janet came during that time he'd just make a new plan. His stomach was still in knots and he wondered how the meeting would go. It would be awkward and he wondered how two people so uncomfortable with each other could possibly resurrect a marriage that had been almost non-existent in the first place.

"What have you done, Janet?" she said to herself. She looked around at the brush and dry grass surrounding her and cursed herself for leaving the main road. After riding for what seemed to be forever, and heading up the little canyon area she remembered, she'd come to a three-way fork in the road. She wasn't sure which one was right, and so she stayed on the same trail she was on. The path looped and turned as it grew thinner and thinner, just like the path to the glen did, but the brush had become thicker and the trees she remembered were not coming into view. She finally admitted to herself that nothing looked familiar—she'd taken the wrong road. She managed to turn the horse around, but somehow they'd ended up on a new road she didn't recognize at all. She tried to remember where she'd made the wrong turn and scanned the area to see if she could find where it joined the path she'd been on. Several yards away she thought she saw a better trail and decided to turn the horse again. In the process of turning she looked up at the sky.

The storm that had looked a long ways off when she started was getting much closer, and the clouds were looking much darker than she'd thought they were when she and Derrick had stared up at them. The temperature had dropped and the wind was whipping her hair in all directions. She'd been riding for well over an hour, but she'd kept telling herself she'd meet up with Tally just past the next rise. She knew he was likely home by now. Somehow she'd missed him. She jabbed Ginger in the ribs and decided they'd better do their return trip at a quicker pace if they hoped to outrun the storm. She headed for the new trail and began to follow it, but it twisted around until she realized she was going north again, not south like she should be. She wandered some more, hoping to find the main road, hoping to get out of the mess she'd put herself in, but she seemed to be making no progress at all. The wind picked up another notch and she pulled the jacket close as she scanned the area again in hopes of some kind of landmark. Her nose and fingers were starting to go numb from the cold and the wind.

Ginger seemed skittish; at least Janet thought that was the right word, and she wasn't obeying Janet like she had before. Janet assumed it was likely the approaching storm, but the horse's uneasiness intensified her own.

"I know this is all my fault," Janet said as she prodded the horse forward again. "I'm sorry, girl—just get us home and I promise never to do anything like this again."

Just then the distant clouds rumbled with thunder. Ginger whinnied and began moving backwards. "Wrong way," Janet said as she turned the horse around to face south once again. Then she gently kicked the horse in the ribs again. "Go forward." She clicked her tongue the way Tally often did, but just then a flash of lightening lit up the sky. Ginger immediately went up on her hind legs, turning as she did so. Janet screamed and although she tried to hold on, she felt the reins slide from her frozen fingers. She didn't have a chance to catch herself as she slammed into the ground, but a ghastly crushing noise resounded in her ears as her whole right leg exploded with pain. Following an instruction Tally had given her, she immediately rolled as far from the horse as she could to avoid being trampled. She crashed through some brush before stopping and then the pain shot up her leg again. She was breathing hard, with her face in the dirt, and took several moments before slowly moving her head to look at her leg, It felt as if it had been sliced off, but nothing seemed out of place. It took her a few minutes to get herself sitting upright and then she winced as she tried to untie her shoe. Every touch was like fire in her ankle. She felt tears in her eyes just as the first drops of rain hit her face.

She looked up to see the clouds directly overhead, and looked around for Ginger. The sky had darkened in just the last few minutes, but it was light enough to show her that the horse wasn't there. Janet called out for the horse a few times, her voice edged with panic, but all she could hear was the wind and rain. Finally, she dropped her head and told herself that crying would do no good. But she cried anyway. All she'd wanted to do was meet Tally, and now she was stuck in the mountains with no way out in the middle of a thunderstorm. She was not the kind of girl who knew what to do in this situation. She hadn't even gone to Girl's Camp. The rain started coming harder and she noticed just how cold it was. She let the long arms of Tally's coat cover her hands, and then she used her palms to drag herself backwards until she was against the small trunk of a very pathetic-looking tree. It didn't shield her from much, but it seemed better than no cover at all; as it was, she was nearly soaked already. She felt like such an idiot! But her next though was even more depressing. She'd taken the wrong road and it was raining hard; would anyone be able to find her?

One month ago she'd been convinced she had nothing to live for. Now, the prospect of freezing to death was absolutely terrifying. She bowed her head. "Please help someone find me," she prayed out loud. Her voice sounded very small compared to the tempest raging around her. "Please give me the chance to tell Tally how I really feel." When she lifted her head she knew she had to get back to a road. She was in the middle of brush and trees and if there was any chance that she was going to be found she had to do whatever she could to get herself to a main road. She started to move and clenched her teeth at the incredible pain the movement created. She didn't know how far away the main road was and yet she didn't think she could make it ten feet. But she had to. Looking ahead of her, to the south she hoped, she focused on a rock about five feet away. I'll scoot that far and rest, she told herself as she carefully turned around so that her back faced her goal. Using her hands and her uninjured leg she started pushing herself backwards as her wet hair began to stick to her face. *Keep moving*, a voice said in her head, *don't stop*. She nodded as if letting it know that she'd heard and hoped she would encounter a road soon.

CHAPTER EIGHTEEN

Pelting drops of rain beating against the window awakened Tally but it took him a few minutes to realize that he'd fallen asleep. His first thought was that Branson was still saddled in the barn. Luckily his knee was feeling much better. He listened for Josh but didn't hear him talking to himself so he picked up his crutches and lifted himself off the couch. He took another few minutes to strap the ugly brace onto his leg. It didn't allow him to bend his knee, but it kept him from injuring the still tender joint and he was supposed to wear it most of the time. He looked at the clock and felt his heart drop. It was almost 6 p.m. and Janet hadn't come. He looked at the floor and let out a long breath. Maybe there wasn't a second chance for them; maybe she'd already made that decision. He didn't wallow for long, though; as was his nature he focused on something else and headed out to take care of Branson.

He took broad 'steps' with one leg and two crutches through the rain to the barn. Branson was still waiting patiently. Tally apologized and quickly removed the saddle. When he went to put it on the bench he noticed his other saddle was missing. Immediately he turned his head toward the horse stalls. Barrington, the colt, whinnied a greeting and stared at Tally with his soft chocolate eyes but Ginger wasn't in her stall. His heart sank and he cursed under his breath. Where was his horse? He was not in the mood for this.

"Derrick," Tally said when his home teacher, friend and neighbor got on the phone a few minutes later. "It's Tally, I need some help."

"All right, what can I do for you?"

"Ginger's not in the barn or the pasture and I'm missing a saddle. Did you take her?" It was the only solution Tally could think of—that Derrick had taken Ginger for the trek up to the bat cave with his kids, but he knew it was a frail hope.

Derrick was silent for a second. "Isn't Janet with you?"

Tally paused. "She didn't come—you did borrow Ginger, didn't you?"

Now Derrick was silent. "Oh, no," Derrick said. Then he hurried to explain his encounter with Janet that afternoon.

Tally closed his eyes. She had come! And she'd gone out to meet him. He couldn't deny that he was touched by that, but his thoughts were rolling too fast to focus on it as he tried to come up with a solution. Within moments he knew he'd have to go look for her, and his anxiety increased as the rain began coming down even harder. She didn't know the mountains—she could be anywhere. "Can I bring Josh over there?" Tally asked after a few moments. He'd go out and look around, Maybe she was close by, on her way home when the storm hit. As if on cue he heard Josh talking to himself in the bedroom.

"What are you going to do?" Derrick asked.

"Go look for her," Tally said.

"By yourself?"

"You're welcome to come along, but we need to go now. The storm is really picking up—I'll get the four wheeler when I drop off Josh."

Derrick paused. "Give me ten minutes. I'll bring the four wheeler to you and Sheri will come get Josh."

"No, I'll just come…" the line went dead. "Derrick?" he asked. There was a clicking on the line and the dial tone returned.

Twenty minutes later a posse of four wheelers and pick-up trucks were parked in the large gravel area around Tally's house. At least ten men crowded in Tally's living room as they waited for Derrick to get off the phone. Derrick had organized a whole search team in a matter of minutes—one of the perks of living in a small town. He and Sheri had also called all the homeowners whose property butted against the road Janet had to have taken. From his window Tally had watched as flashlight beams bounced in the dark as each of these homeowners searched the area of road behind their homes. Other people had driven the road as far up as trucks could go; they had found nothing. Derrick was on the phone, but he soon finished the call and hung up. "They found Ginger."

The room went silent. "Where?" someone asked.

"Clint Hunsaker's," Derrick confirmed. Clint Hunsaker owned a large dairy farm near the valley where Tally's glen was located. Without a doubt Tally knew she was up there somewhere—but it didn't give him much comfort. There were a dozen trails up there, some led over the mountains. Janet could have taken any one of them. "They're looking around for Janet, but so far . . . ."

"Give me the phone," Tally said. He put out his hand and Derrick handed it to him. "What's Bishop Baker's number?"

Someone in the room knew it, like he knew they would; he punched it in and turned around, trying to ignore the fact that everyone was listening. The rest of the room was likely perplexed on what benefit their 66-year-old bishop would be at a time like this, but Tally was calling because Bishop Baker was also Doctor Baker and it was the latter expertise that Tally was in need of now. "Bishop Baker? This is Tally Blaire . . . yeah, well I need a favor . . . I need a Lydocaine shot. Could you help me with that?" The other men in the room exchanged glances. Lydocaine, what was Lydocaine?

A few minutes later the front door opened to admit Bishop Baker. He looked around and asked why he hadn't been included in the search party. Several eyes went to the ground and he made a comment about judging him on his age. Tally was on the couch, waiting. He'd already removed his brace and pulled up his pant leg.

"This will numb it but you're still risking damage being done. Pain is a warning sign, not an inconvenience."

Tally nodded and pulled his pant leg a little higher. Then he just looked at the Bishop-doctor. "Please," he finally said. "You know I'm worthless without it."

Dr. Baker took a breath and shook his head as he pulled the small vial of clear liquid and a small syringe from his pocket. "Your surgeon is going to kill me," he muttered as he removed the cap from the syringe and plunged the needle through the rubber lid of the medicine bottle. Tally took a breath and then forced himself to relax, knowing that being tense would only make it more painful.

A few moments later the bishop led the group in prayer, for Tally it was a humbling moment to once again sit on the couch and watch the bishop kneel on his living room floor. But this time he was surrounded by other men, many of whom Tally didn't even know. Yet, they had gathered together in his time of need. The gospel was a truly beautiful thing. When the prayer was done the men filed out of the house, hunkering down against the raging storm.

"Tally," Derrick screamed above the deafening sound of the storm. "I think we need to go back. We can't see a thing."

The men who had come to the house had split into several groups and as the search had deepened each group had broken into smaller teams. The rain was coming down harder than ever, the temperature continued to drop and the dry ground was sucking up the water and creating a virtual mud bog. They had been out for over an hour and several people had called Tally's cell phone to report that they were stuck or had to turn back. Derrick and Tally were on four wheelers, slowly driving along the route Janet would have taken to the glen. Tally was in front and he'd heard Derrick's comment but chose to ignore it. He couldn't go back, not until he knew Janet was okay.

They reached the three-way fork in the trail and Tally paused. Another team had already checked all three routes, but Tally had a feeling. He turned his four wheeler in the direction opposite the one he would have taken to get to the glen.

"They already checked this way," Derrick yelled from behind him.

Tally ignored the comment and continued to scan the sides of the road for any sign of . . . anything.

Janet was nearly delirious. She didn't know how much ground she'd covered but she sincerely doubted she could go even one more foot. Her hands, although still covered with the sleeves of Tally's coat, were numb and caked with mud, as were her bottom and legs. She was soaking wet and felt sure she was going to pass out. Her ankle was grossly swollen and she feared that her shoe was cutting off the circulation in her foot. Every movement brought on droves of pain so strong she could hardly draw a breath. Her head was pounding and she had no idea how much further it would be until she reached the road. It was pitch black and she knew that even if people were looking for her, they wouldn't keep at it much longer. She had to get to the road. Moving her hands a few inches behind her, she used them to lift her bottom and move it back at the same time her uninjured leg pushed her body in the same direction. She doubted she'd moved even six inches. How was she ever supposed to reach that road moving six inches at a time? *I am so not made for this!*

Just keep moving, that voice in her head said.

"I am," she yelled loudly as tears came to her eyes again. "I'm moving as fast as I can."

"Did you hear that?" Tally asked loudly, stopping his four wheeler and leaning into the wind.

"Hear what?" Derrick yelled back.

Tally paused for a minute, then he stood up on the footboards of his four wheeler. "Janet!!" he screamed. Then he went silent and listened. When he didn't hear anything else, he cupped his hands around his mouth and called her name again. The words seemed to disappear into the wind and rain. But he scanned the area and said another prayer in his heart.

Janet froze at hearing her name carry past her in the wind. She was shocked for a moment and then she turned her head and yelled. "Over here!" she began moving backwards again, faster this time—ignoring the painful protests of her leg.

"Janet!" the voice called again and she felt her heart quicken. She knew that voice.

"Tally," she called back, still moving. "I'm right here!"

Seconds later two four-wheelers crashed through the brush around her. One nearly ran her over before she screamed and it came to a stop just inches away. She had lifted her arms to form an X in front of her face, sure the vehicle was going to hit her. When she realized that no impact had occurred, she looked up, but the headlights kept her from being able to see anything. She shielded her eyes and turned her head away from the blinding light just as a wet, but strong pair of arms reached down to help her up.

Janet fought hard to stay awake, but knew she was lapsing in and out of consciousness. She wasn't sure how she'd gotten to the hospital but being moved from the truck to the hospital gurney had roused her.

"She's in shock," someone said.

"She's freezing," someone else added.

"That ankle looks bad," another voice cut in. "We'd better give her something before she comes around."

"No," she said, it came out as more of a feeble gasp. She tried to wet her mouth with her tongue and try again. "Don't give me anything."

"What did she say?"

"I'm . . . a pickle."

"She's delirious," someone said.

"No narc . . . c . . . cotics," she clarified although she felt she'd give just about anything for a double shot of Percocet right now.

"Have we got some Demerol?" one of the voices asked.

"No Demerol."

Janet tried to open her eyes at the sound of Tally's voice, but she couldn't focus and she shut them again, her head was swimming, she felt like she was going to throw up. Tally continued. "She's a recovering addict," he said, and she noticed his voice was full of fear and compassion, not bitterness. "She can't have narcotics."

"Okay, then get me some Toridol and . . . ."

Tally sat in a chair in the hall outside the room Janet had been put in and stared at his dirty hands, turning them over and over as if fascinated by the pattern of mud. Bishop Baker came out of Janet's room and Tally looked up but didn't try to stand. The Lydocain was wearing off and his knee was on fire, but he wasn't thinking about that.

"How are you?" Bishop Baker asked as he took a seat next to Tally.

"Relieved," Tally said as he let out a breath. "And confused."

"About what?"

Tally sighed loudly. "Everything," he finally said. Bishop Baker nodded but didn't speak. "I know we've spent a lot of time talking about this, but it wasn't until I realized she was out there that it all came back, all the things I'd forgotten, all the feelings I'd worked so hard to ignore."

"The good times?" the bishop asked.

"Yeah," Tally said with a nod. "For that moment nothing mattered but that I find her, that I see her again. And yet now . . . I'm afraid to go in that room. I don't know how to make sense of it."

"We've talked about this with me as your bishop, Tally," he said after another pause. "I've given you counsel I hope has helped you to trust God again, to pray and invite the Spirit back into your life—as your bishop that is my job. But now, let me tell you something as a friend."

Tally didn't look at the older man, but he nodded—hungry to hear whatever it was the bishop had to say.

"When my son was fifteen years old, his best friend in the whole world killed himself. They hadn't been getting along so well for a few months, his friend had started hanging out with some weird kids, but when we got the call from this kid's parents, it was devastating. I can't tell you how painful it was to watch my child suffer through something as senseless and overwhelming as that; and it changed who he was, how he lived the rest of his life. It happened almost 25 years ago, and yet if you ask my son about it, he'll still get tears in his eyes. He's convinced that if he'd had a chance to talk to his friend that night it wouldn't have happened, that there was some magical thing he could have done to prevent it. He was just a kid, but that experience was a defining moment in his life and the regrets he feels are very real. My point in telling you this is that my son would give about anything for one more opportunity to make a difference to someone important to him, but he didn't get one and that's what haunts him. His friend didn't get a second chance, and neither did my son. Not everyone does."

Tally felt the counsel to the depths of his soul and the tips of his toes, but he knew why the bishop hadn't told him this before. Until right this moment he hadn't been ready, he hadn't been sufficiently humbled until he'd faced the prospect of losing Janet all over again—and losing her for good. Tally nodded, wrapped in thought, as Bishop Baker stood without another word. For several minutes Tally stared at the gray tile at his feet and listened to the rain as it continued to pummel the windows behind him. He focused on the possibilities he hadn't dared think of before now.

When Janet opened her eyes again, she heard only muted voices coming from another room. She was lying in a hospital bed and the room was dark. She was freezing but she took a deep breath and said a little prayer of gratitude that she was here at all. There was no doubt in her mind that the Lord had protected her, that it was only by the grace of God that she was here at all. It wasn't lost on her that if God could orchestrate such a miraculous rescue, physically, it couldn't be beyond him to repair her spirit too. After several deep breaths and pondering on this new realization, she turned her head and wondered if she was dreaming. Tally was sitting in a chair next to her bed, watching her.

"Tally?"

He simply nodded in response.

She moved her hand toward him and then stopped; perhaps that was a little too forward. He saw the movement and to her great relief he placed his hand on top of hers. She closed her eyes and felt her chin begin to quiver as the warmth radiating from his touch warmed her entire body. She stopped shivering and for several seconds she was silent, then she opened her eyes again. "I'm so sorry," she breathed as her chin began to tremble. It sounded so pathetically inadequate that she searched for more words, but couldn't find anything. "I am so, so

Tally said nothing, he just stared at her; but she felt his resistance, his fear of believing her. She took his hand in both of hers and wrapped her fingers around his large, but dirty hand. Lifting it to her lips she began to cry, pressing his hand against her face, oblivious to the new layer of mud her tears were creating against her cheek. She thought of everything she'd done, every promise she'd broken, every hope she'd destroyed and she wondered how he could ever forgive her for that. She even wondered if he should. But he was here—and that gave her hope. She tried again to find the words to communicate all she'd learned, everything she felt right now, but nothing came. All she could do was cry, overwhelmed that he was here at all and hoping he could sense what she felt, for she was unable to find the words.

Tally stared at her as her tears fell over his rough and calloused hand and he felt his heart soften. Her emotion was so raw, so sincere, it was impossible not to be touched by it. He could also feel the magnetic pull she had on him and he felt tears come to his eyes as he watched her honest reaction to his presence. It was impossible to doubt that she really did love him, that she really wanted him in her life.

"I love you," she said as she kissed the center of his palm and a burning sensation traveled from his hand to the rest of his body. "You don't deserve all the horrible things I've done, but I'm begging you to give me another chance." Her words sent a shiver down his spine and he couldn't doubt how deeply she meant every word. She looked up at him then, pressing his palm against her dirty face as if afraid to let him go. Her eyes were different than he remembered; open and vulnerable, pleading with him to believe her. She continued to cry as she held his eyes, allowing her tears to leave cleansing streaks upon her cheeks. "I'm so sorry," she said again. "Please forgive me, please give me another chance to be the woman you deserve me to be."

Tally felt a lump rise in his throat. "Are you sure it's what you want?" he whispered.

"More than anything in the world. Please give me the opportunity to prove it to you."

The doubts didn't disappear, his guard wasn't instantly let down, but he felt something within him soften even more. "It can't be like it was," he said softly. "I won't do that again."

"Neither will I," she agreed softly, the first rays of hope filling her eyes. "I haven't given you any reason to trust me in the past, I realize that, and I can't make what happened go away. But I love you so much, Tally, and I am free for the first time in my life to truly act on that. I'll spend the rest of my life making sure you never doubt it again. And I need you, more than I can say—I need you."

Just then the curtain around Janet's bed was pulled back and Bishop Baker walked in, not seeming to realize what he'd just interrupted as he consulted some information in her chart. Tally sat back a little bit and Janet lowered her hand to the side of the her bed, although she held on tightly to his hand. "We'll need to wait a day or two for the swelling to go down before we cast that foot, young lady," he said, looking over the rim of his spectacles. "You're lucky that you don't need surgery to fix it."

"Do I have to stay here?" she asked. She hated the idea. She'd just got out of the hospital for Heaven's sake!

"No," the bishop said. "But you need to stay completely off that foot." She nodded and his eyes moved to Tally. "And I'm giving you the same prescription—get someone to watch Josh and stay in bed for a few days. Then go see your surgeon and hope and pray you didn't just undo what he did with that knee of yours." He turned to look at Janet again. "What follow-up care were you supposed to be involved in?"

It didn't seem at all strange that he was asking, she'd lived the life of constant counselors and therapists for a month, asking about her treatment was normal conversation to her. "I was supposed to start an outpatient program on Monday."

"Hmmm," he said, making another note. "With your permission I'll call the facility and see if we can arrange something local." Then he paused and looked between them both. "That is . . . if you're staying in Willard."

Janet didn't dare look at Tally as she considered this change. "She'll be staying," Tally said and she closed her eyes as she let out a breath of relief. What would she have done if he hadn't let her stay?

Someone called for Dr. Baker in the hall and he excused himself for a moment. The silence descended again.

"I already talked to Kim, she told me about the pills—I don't think you can go back to the condo."

"I can't," she said, but was that the only reason he wanted her to stay? The complexity of what they now faced was nearly over-whelming, but then he squeezed her hand and smiled when their eyes met. "I'll call Lacey. I'm sure she'll take Josh for the weekend," Tally said. "We've got things to talk about anyway. A few days forcing us to sit around might be a good thing." He paused for a moment. "If we're going to make this work, we can't live apart any longer."

Janet smiled for the first time and felt her chest relax. He was giving her a chance—she wouldn't take it for granted this time. "It won't be the way it was, Tally," she said. "I promise."

Tally looked at her again, really looked at her and she wondered if she looked as different as she felt. There were no walls left to keep him out, and although it made her uneasy it was also a relief. She hadn't realized just how hard it was to keep up pretenses and she was excited to start over, grateful beyond words that he was willing to take another chance on her. "As strange as it seems, after all that's happened," Tally whispered as he rubbed the back of her hand with his thumb, "I believe you."

Janet's heart soared and she smiled through her tears, still holding his hand as she said a prayer of thanks in her heart. It felt like a rebirth, a new life altogether. The possibilities that lay ahead now were endless. She would not let them slip away this time. Her whole life was before her, and she had Tally and Josh in it again. At that moment life was sweeter than it had ever been and she understood just how amazing the power to choose really was. Claire's words echoed back to her "Not everyone gets a second chance." But Janet had. Janet had been given a second chance and she chose life. She chose life.

EPILOGUE

December 4th—Nine Months Later

Janet finished ringing up the customer and handed her the bag of purchases she had just charged to her credit card. Christmas shopping was in full swing at the Dillard's store in Ogden, Utah, and the tune of Jingle-Bells was barely decipherable over the sound of the rampaging shoppers. As the customer walked away and the next one took her place in front of the register, Janet's eyes caught a familiar face in the crowds of people and her eyebrows lifted.

"Claire," she called out, while at the same time motioning another sales associate to take over. Claire was several feet away, inspecting a rack of ties, but she looked up at the sound of her name and her face showed surprise. Janet briefly explained to the other salesperson that she needed a quick break, but that she'd be right back. The other salesperson nodded and took over the register as Janet pushed through the crowd toward the woman who had started the amazing changes in her life.

"How are you?" Claire asked when Janet reached her, reaching out and taking Janet's hand in greeting.

"I'm good," Janet replied. There was so much she wanted to say. "Um, I have a lunch break in another half an hour, is there any way you could wait for me? I have so much I want to tell you."

"Um, sure," Claire responded. "I've got shopping to do anyway."

Forty minutes later they sat across from one another at the food court of the Newgate mall with an order of French Fries in between them. "What brought you all the way up here?" Janet asked.

"I came up to see my daughter. She lives in Logan. I thought I'd get some Christmas shopping done on the way home. You work here?"

Janet nodded. "I'm an assistant manager, and I only work about 25 hours a week but it's enough to get health insurance and to give me some responsibility outside of my own home. I was going crazy not having a job while my ankle healed." She'd talked to Claire on the phone the day after her adventure in the mountains and she'd sent a few letters, but Claire was no longer her therapist and since Janet was transferred to an outpatient program in Ogden they hadn't kept in touch.

"And how are things at home?"

"Well, Josh is three and a half now," she said with a smile. "We're working on getting him potty trained and he's doing well. He talks a lot and it's fun to actually have conversations with him. I've found that there are actually parts of motherhood I really like, and lucky for me Tally's always there to support me in the other stuff. I don't know how I ever did it without him."

"And how is Tally?"

"He's opening up his own photography studio up in Brigham City at the first of the year," Janet said with a smile. "His knee just hasn't been the same. They've talked about doing a replacement but he's hoping to hold them off. He can't do repair jobs anymore and having a studio has been a dream for a long time—it's exciting to have it actually happening for him." She paused. "We were going to marriage counseling up until last month. They finally graduated us."

"And the counseling helped?"

"A ton," Janet said strongly. "We had a lot of things to face, and we found a really good therapist to help us work through everything."

"Are you still going to NA?"

"I go to an LDS group three times a week," Janet said proudly. "I got my 9 months sobriety token a few weeks ago and I've had a wonderful sponsor who checks in with me constantly. In fact, her husband has become a kind of sponsor for Tally; it's been a really good relationship for all of us to have."

"No backsliding?" Claire prodded as only a woman well rehearsed in the recovery of addicts could.

Janet paused and considered not being totally honest, but knew she couldn't do it. Honesty was always the best policy, she knew that now. "I still wake up most mornings and find myself wanting something to help me get the day going, and then whenever anything stressful happens I want them worse than ever. The 12 steps and my sponsor are helping but I still battle the craving. One day, a dark one when Tally opted to take Josh with him to a photo shoot rather than leave him with me, I ripped the house apart until I found the key to Tally's lockbox. I felt very powerful for about thirteen seconds until I realized what an explosion I held in my hand. I called my sponsor and she stayed with me until Tally came home. Then I had to tell him what I'd done."

Claire raised her eyebrows. "What did he think about that?"

"It wasn't pretty—he was mad and I was so humiliated. But it made us both realize how big this is. He got a combination lock instead of a key after that. Other than that incident, I've done quite well. I don't even take Tylenol as often as I want to. I'm sleeping at night for the first time in years and . . . I'm pregnant."

Claire raised her eyebrows. "You are?" she couldn't hide her surprise and Janet smiled again.

"About eleven weeks."

"Wow, that was quick," Claire said and Janet wasn't sure if she heard censure in her voice or not.

"I'm 36 years old, so I don't have all that long to think about it," Janet said. "Ironically, we'd never talked much about having children together, but it became a big topic in counseling. We decided to have one and then reevaluate our family plans, but I'm glad I decided to do it—you can't believe how happy Tally is about the baby."

"Are you happy about it?" Claire prodded, her tone still suspicious.

"I am," Janet answered honestly. "I'm nervous, but my world has come alive over the last several months. I'm a different person than I was and I feel like I have something to give for the first time in my life. It's a big accomplishment for me to look at Tally and Josh and know their lives are *better* for having me in it. I've never felt that in any relationship before. I've been seeing a therapist on my own and I'm finally grasping what motherhood and families are all about." She paused and leaned forward before continuing. "You want to know what amazing discovery I made just a month or so ago?"

Claire nodded, with an odd look of expectation on her face.

"Well, you know how when I was little I had to do all the house-hold stuff, and how badly I hated it?"

Claire nodded, "That's why you still hated cooking and cleaning as an adult."

"Right," Janet agreed. "What I've realized is that other women don't always like it either."

Claire couldn't help but chuckle. Janet smiled back and continued. "I really thought all those other women liked it, all the time, and they don't. But they want a clean house and healthy meals so they make their peace with all those mundane tasks I couldn't stand."

"Have you made peace with those mundane tasks?"

"I'm working on it," Janet admitted. "But it's getting better all the time and I couldn't have chosen a better partner for things like that—Tally helps me in more ways than I can count. I've made some good friends in my ward and I feel more spiritually centered than I ever have before."

"I'm glad things are going so well," Claire said with a smile. "You look very happy."

Janet nodded and they continued discussing the details of Janet's long, and so far successful, recovery.

As Janet drove home from work that night she reflected on all the changes in her life that she *hadn't* talked to Claire about. She'd never gone back to the condo and they had sold it, along with her car. The profits she'd made from the house, once her debts were resolved, were used to help fund Tally's new studio. It was a gift well deserved and she loved to see his excitement as he pursued a new dream. She was active in their ward in Willard and had come to love the area, the people and their values just as Tally did. She still wasn't passionate about Tally's horses, or the goats and chickens he'd added to his little farm, but it was something he loved and she could appreciate it on those merits alone.

For the first few months Janet stayed in the downstairs bedroom Julie had occupied during her stay. There was a lot to work out before they could share a bed again. The stairs had been an interesting struggle, what with the cast on her leg, but she found a certain level of empathy for Tally in the challenge and she knew that the readjustment period was necessary. And she would never forget the feeling she'd had when he slipped into the bed beside her for the first time. It was nearly three months into her recovery and watching his face in the darkness, feeling his touch again were almost too fantastic to be real because she had missed it and wanted it for so long. Without the wait she wasn't sure she'd have been able to fully appreciate the experience.

In the months that followed, they had both come to realize that there were issues they would likely never resolve. Tally's trust was easily withdrawn when he sensed she wasn't being honest, but it spurred her to live with integrity. There would also always be the fear of relapse, that's why she still attended the 12 step program, why she always would, and why Tally remained vigilant about locking up his own meds. But they were a team and they were working toward a common goal. Some days it amazed her that she dared love him so much and every day she thanked God that he could return that love after all she'd done.

Next spring, a year after her first of many meetings with the bishop, she and Tally were taking their son to the temple, where they would be sealed. A smile lingered on her lips as she thought about that, of how far she'd come—how hard all of them had had to work to get here. And this new baby, Tally's and hers, would be born in the covenant a couple of months later. That was the crowning achievement to all that they'd overcome and it kept her focused, kept her plodding ahead when things got hard.

Being a wife and mother, although still difficult and overwhelming at times, was getting easier. She'd learned to find the sunshine in both roles and wondered how she could have wanted a life without those things. She was part of something great, something timeless and that knowledge was a great comfort, and compass, in her life.

"Everything okay?" Tally asked when she walked into the house a few minutes later. She assumed she was still wearing that silly grin and she smiled wider. He was working on dinner and it smelled wonderful.

She put down her purse and came up behind him, wrapping her arms around his waist and resting her chin on his shoulder. She could hear Josh making car noises in the basement but put off going to see him for just a minute, in order to have this conversation with Tally first.

"I saw Claire today," she said.

Tally craned his neck to look at her. "You did?"

She nodded and picked a piece of broccoli out of the pan on the stove. "She came in to do some shopping and we shared some French fries. She said I look happy." She popped the broccoli in her mouth and gave him the thumbs up sign that she approved.

"You do look happy," Tally agreed, returning to his dinner preparation.

"It got me to thinking," she said. "And I remembered a quote I heard once. I think John Lennon said it, 'Life is what happens when you're making other plans.'"

Could they be where they were, feeling as they did without all the things that happened in between? Since being released from the hospital and with Tally's help, Narcotics Anonymous, good therapists and a renewed investment in her spiritual health her perceptions about life had changed remarkably. She had learned to look for the bright side and to recognize God's hand in everything, especially the trials she still faced and knew she would continue to face throughout the rest of her life. Success was determined by a completely different measuring stick than it used to be.

Tally turned away from the dinner in order to wrap his arms around her and kiss her sweetly. "And life is good?" he asked.

Janet took a step closer and placed a gentle kiss on his lips. She looked into his face, and smiled at her husband. "Life is very good," she said softly. "I love you, Talmage Blaire."

He kissed her again, lightly this time and winked as he turned back to dinner. Little feet could suddenly be heard coming up the stairs and Janet moved away in anticipation of being attacked by her precious little monster. Tally gave her hand one last squeeze as she moved too far away to retain contact. She looked up at him and he winked just as Josh burst around the corner and flew into his mother's arms. *Yes, life is good,* she thought as Josh's curls tickled her cheek. *Life is very good.*

AUTHOR'S NOTES

Prescription drug abuse is not a new problem; however, it continues to be a major social issue. According to the 1999 National Household Survey an estimated 1.6 million Americans age 12 and older used prescription pain medications for the first time in 1998. In the 1980s there were fewer than 500,000 first-time users per year meaning that there are more people simply taking prescribed drugs than there used to be. In the 1960s Valium was called 'Mothers little helper.' In the 1990s Xanax took on that title and more people take Xanax now than ever took Valium then. According to the research of The National Institute on Drug Abuse (NIDA) women are twice as likely to develop a dependency to anti-anxiety and sedative drugs than men. To further overwhelm you with facts, in 1999 almost 2 percent of the population, an estimated 4 million people aged 12 and older, were currently (use in the past month) using certain prescription drugs non-medically, meaning not for the purpose or person prescribed. It is estimated that 7 percent of the total population of the United States has a drug addiction—illicit or prescription.

Utah leads the nation in prescription drug addiction and prescription fraud, a fact that shows Mormons are not immune and sometimes are even more at risk of prescription addiction. Being LDS does not make life easier or give us automatic coping skills, it doesn't mean we don't crave escape and relief from every day or life-long problems. A Mormon who professes to live the Word of Wisdom is less likely to seek out alcohol or illicit drugs; however, if the doctor says it's okay then it seems to become a completely different animal—until it runs your life just like heroin or vodka tonics.

Addiction has recently been recognized as 'Addictive Disease'—meaning that it is more than a simple weakness of character or immoral conduct. The need to find relief, to hide from stressors in our lives is something we all deal with, but someone with 'Addictive

Disease' will take steps that the rest of us will not for reasons related to brain chemistries and past experiences that make them more susceptible. A common side effect of addiction is the loss of hope for recovery and this loss of hope often leads to not taking action. However, addiction in all forms, like other chronic diseases, can be treated.

Alcoholics Anonymous was started in 1932 by Dr. Robert Smith and Bill Wilson—both alcoholics who had struggled for years to overcome their driving need to drink. The program they developed is based on the belief that they could not conquer their addiction without the intervention of a higher power. Their program has grown and expanded with amazing success. All over the world, several times a day, every day of the week, recovering addicts support one another in the process of reclaiming their power and living free of the substance or behavior that has had crippling effects on their lives. Alcoholics Anonymous is based on 12 faith affirming, life changing steps, or principles, and those steps have helped develop sub-groups for all kinds of addiction—Overeaters Anonymous, Sexaholics Anonymous, Codependents Anonymous, etc. In recent years LDS-based groups have combined the 12 steps with doctrine and scriptures. This has been an amazing key to recovery for many members of the church and is now supported by LDS Family Services and individual stakes across the country.

We must never forget that Satan knows our weaknesses and if he can't march in our front door he'll slide through a window. It matters not to him what causes us to turn away from the truth we've been taught. It only matters to him that we leave it behind. But we know that with the Lord all things are possible if we are willing to do what it takes. In 2 Nephi 32:3 it reads " . . . feast upon the words of Christ; for behold, the words of Christ will tell you all things that ye should do." We all have voids that are in need of filling, wounds in need of care, but when we 'trust in the arm of flesh' rather than in the Lord our God it is like fighting a forest fire with a garden hose. In all things, our success or failure comes down to our faith and humility and it is true in overcoming addiction as much as in anything else we may face. God knows us, He knows what demons rage against us and He knows how to succor us if we will but ask in 'faith, nothing wavering' and believe that He has the power to make us more than we are without Him. For further information on the issues discussed in this book please consult the following:

LDS 12 Step organization—Heart to Heart
www.heart-t-heart.org

Prescription Drug Addiction
www.nida.nih.gov/ResearchReports/Prescription/Prescription.html

Suicide
http://www.save.org/basics/facts.html

ABOUT THE AUTHOR

Josi Kilpack was born and raised in Salt Lake City, graduated from Olympus High School in 1992 and currently resides in Willard, Utah, with her husband, Lee, and their four beautiful children. In addition to writing, Josi assists in the management of two assisted living facilities that she and her husband own in northern Utah and enjoys reading, baking and traveling. *Tempest Tossed* is her third LDS women's novel. Her other titles are *Earning Eternity* and *Surrounded By Strangers*. Josi enjoys hearing from her readers. You may email her at kilpack@favorites.com or contact her via her website at www.JosiKilpack.com.